SECTOR 36

VLAD RISCUTIA

CONTENTS

PART EIGHT
EXTINCTION EVENT

EPILOGUE

To the memory of my grandmother, Elena Rișcuția
I miss you Lili

SECTOR 36 MAP

● ECHO POINT

★ VENTURE

DERELICT AIX-VD2 ▬

● EUREKA BASE

★ NS-36-A

◎ GATEWAY RING

● VERDANT   ◉ JUMP GATE   ● FORGE

★ DEMETER   ★ VULCAN

● NOVA PRIME

★ NOVA SOL

● HORIZON STATION

★ M-36-E

LEGEND

★ STAR
● COLONY
◎ RING STRUCTURE
◉ JUMP GATE
▬ ALIEN SHIPWRECK

Viridian Shroud Nebula
Sector 36
Soon after the Tauran War

PROLOGUE

00: CODE WORDS

D octor Linton plots an interstellar course on the tiny skimmer, muttering, "Oh my God" over and over again. He knows a secret. A terrible secret. And now he must flee.

Most scientists are not secretive by nature. Doctor Linton would know—he is one. The more military vessels amassed around Eureka Base, the more boots clacked on the tiles and echoed down the lab's hallways, the more nervous the scientists got. The more nervous they got, the sloppier their data handling became. He snooped. He did it slowly, quietly. He wasn't greedy—he played the long game. Strange things were happening in Sector 36; he wanted to get to the bottom of it all. And then he did. *Oh my God*, he did.

His day job, like that of all the other scientists at the research lab, was understanding the cause of the gravitational anomalies around the dim NS-36-A neutron star. The unimaginative designation stands for "neutron star—Sector 36—first one we care about." From their vantage point on a remote moon, orbiting a small planet about half an AU away from the dead star, the scientists gathered data, analyzed it, and came up with theories. Theories explaining the cause of the FTL, communications, and quantum compute disruptions. Linton was sure they were on the verge of some kind of breakthrough when the Taurans attacked, promptly redirecting everyone's focus.

The skimmer is almost ready to go, its onboard computer running through the pre-flight checklist. Linton is working fast, sweating in the cushioned pilot seat as he plots a course to his getaway destination and another, much shorter flight path to fool the systems keeping watch around Eureka Base. He pauses, wipes his brow, sighs, says another, "Oh my God," and dives right back into the digital. *Almost there.* He needs to get out of here—needs to let the world know.

As humanity spread throughout the Milky Way without encountering any other intelligent life, the consensus veered towards being all alone, Fermi paradox or not. Linton himself had plenty of conversations on the subject with his fellow physicists. His long-held belief was that if the galaxy harbored any intelligent life, we would've run into it by now. He was convinced of this. That was, until the Taurans showed up.

They came into Sector 36 with guns blazing, ready to fight rather than talk. The doctor and his colleagues spent a few tense weeks watching the alien armada heading imminently towards their lab, in their strange stuttering flight pattern of FTL jumps mixed with stretches of subluminal flight. The human military repelled them with equal force and more determination. Eureka Base was ultimately untouched as the Taurans retreated. Unlike Echo Point—a settlement obliterated by a strange Tauran weapon.

As the aliens left the sector, the lab personnel started to relax. But their fears came back as they realized they'd ended up under some form of martial law, the panic of imminent attack replaced by an uneasy tension and menacing secrecy.

The war was allegedly over, but more and more heavily armed ships arrived in the system. Some of the civilians were able to make their way rimward, to the Gateway Ring, to translate out of the sector. Some of the top scientists were asked politely to stick around. By heavily armed marines. He was one of the latter.

As time went by, rumors started spreading throughout the lab. Some were saying Tauran bodies were being autopsied in the lowest underground levels. Others were saying live prisoners were being questioned there. Or subjected to experiments. Some were saying Tauran tech was being reverse-engineered. Doctor Linton heard it all.

He poked around, he asked questions, he read studies. He read some studies he was pretty sure he wasn't supposed to read. He learned code words. He discreetly searched for them, kept pulling on the strings. Some led to dead ends—access restricted, locked down knowledge bases. Some shed a tiny bit of light. He kept at it.

He kept busy. Talked to colleagues, found passwords on desk notes, tried them out. And then, finally, revelation. World-turned-upside-down, everything-makes-sense-now revelation. Not what he was looking for, not what he was expecting, but *oh my God*, what a revelation! An explanation for everything! Changing everything! The world must know! But he can't speak.

He's on a research outpost, effectively under martial law, surrounded by military personnel, overseen by an Omega class AI who is most certainly "in" on it. If he yells what he learned into the ether, it will go nowhere. They would know. They have the capabilities to intercept and filter him out.

He has a plan though. This plan was worked out months in advance. When you can't trust your encryption, when hyperintelligence helps develop your algorithms and promises you it's uncrackable but you don't take its word for it, when you can't out-math it, you need to go back to basics. Primitive cryptography. Your signal can't contain valuable data; it will be intercepted, read, used against you. You need the human connection. Your signal is just a code word. It means only, *I have something to tell you, let's meet up*. All pre-arranged.

Yesterday he sent a message to his friend, complaining about his shoulder. He injured it playing sports a couple of decades ago, and it tends to flare up from time to time. All on medical record. Nothing to see here.

The message means, *Pick me up from Verdant, I have vital information.* His friend is a Spark contact; he won't be the one picking him up. He will just relay the message, get help, get him out of the sector. No decryption could tease that meaning from the payload. The doctor will deliver the secret, in person, to someone who can make best use of it. If he survives. If they don't nab him before he leaves the system.

His exit strategy hits a snag. When all this was worked out—his hideaway spot on Verdant, the codes, the plan—there was no Tauran threat. Travel through the sector was easy. Now it's not. No ships are leaving Eureka Base for the foreseeable future. More military coming in every day. The unexpected war, the aftermath, the display of force, all of these made the scientists sloppy, aided his snooping, but it also makes his departure next to impossible.

He needs to get to Verdant—fast. He will risk it all. He has world-shaking knowledge. Not what Spark was expecting. Not what he was expecting. But more vital than either imagined.

{Control, this is Sunhopper. Requesting permission to take off. Transmitting flight plan,} he sends. The moment of truth. Will his plan work? Will all his secrecy help get him out of here? Or are they going to drag him out of the skimmer, throw him in a cell? He sits frozen, waiting for a reply. The small cockpit of the skimmer seems to shrink around him.

{Sunhopper, repeat your authorization.}

He swallows hard. His throat tightens. *This was a mistake,* he thinks. *They're on to me.*

He spends days restless, feeling the burden of the information he managed to steal. Trying to figure out his next step. Should he wait? Make a run for it? He's no spy, no cloak-and-dagger type, just a PhD in physics who believes in a cause. He lacks the tradecraft to vanish, but he can't sit on what he knows. He doubts anyone on Eureka Base would make it out alive if he waits any longer. So, reluctantly, he decides to flee.

. . .

{Replaying authorization, Control,} he sends, then holds his breath. The moment of truth. Seconds pass. He doesn't dare breathe. Then, after what seems like forever ...

{You are clear, Sunhopper. Stick to your flight path, we have frigates incoming.}

The doctor allows himself an exhale. He wipes his brow again, whispers another, "Oh my God," then takes off, clearing the small landing pad and rising fast through the moon's thin nitrogen-rich atmosphere.

Space is big. Centuries of darkness between stars. FTL makes the distance bearable—but never short. Skimmers are capable of superluminal flight but are still slow compared to larger vessels. It will take him multiple weeks to reach Verdant at full burn. That's if he makes it through all the security that is now surrounding the system. But there's no other way. He has to try.

The barren moon's orbit is chock-full of military vessels of all shapes and sizes. Some as small as the Sunhopper, some way larger than what Eureka Base's modest landing pad could accommodate. Some seem as large as the compound itself. Frigates? Cruisers? Destroyers? He can't tell.

He is watching the small aboveground part of the lab recede as he gains altitude. The many blinking lights, graviton detectors, and rotating antennae converge into a small dot, then disappear. The huge ships grow even larger as the Sunhopper glides closer to them, closer to their glinting weapons.

He maintains a respectful distance, sticks to the flight path he submitted—for now. A joyride—just a change of scenery for a scientist cooped up in a lab. Nothing that would raise suspicions.

He burns a bit farther out than the planned flight path. He waits for admonishment, but none comes. He burns a bit farther out still. The sky is dotted with military ships, bristling with digital eyes—but they're watching for Tauran warships.

By the time a system flags his deviation and reaches out, Doctor Linton punches it to full throttle. He is a speck of dust on a black-and-green backdrop, moving at relativistic speed. The incoming message doesn't reach him. He's out of comms range, alone and afraid, carrying with him the answers to everything.

PART ONE
FIRST MOVER
ADVANTAGE

01: INGRESS

T he heavy cruiser *Dauntless* blinks into shape. Tens of thousands of tons of armor, sensors, and doomsday devices, all assembled at a reasonable price by VoidTech. Its escort of smaller vessels follow, a procession of killing machines covered in sensors and weapon systems, materializing one by one into the eternal night of deep space.

Her stomach churns. She feels her breakfast rising and barely makes it to the toilet as the ship announces, {Translation complete, welcome to Sector 36.} Jump gate travel is instantaneous and allegedly seamless. For most people. Her NeuroSync Rejection Syndrome, a fault in her brain wiring, manifests as intense vertigo during translation. Every single fucking time. Earned her the nickname "Tilt" back in the day. She wishes she weren't the odd one out, but it did save her life, so it's hard to complain.

She flushes, stumbles back to her feet holding onto the sink, catches her reflection in the mirror—a tinge of red streaking her slate gray eyes, brown graying hair tied back in a ponytail, silver graft implants on her temples. She splashes water on her face once she regains her balance, meets her reflection again. *Better.* She looks, but doesn't quite feel, like she can pull this off.

Back out into her tiny cabin, she gazes out the porthole at the putrid green backdrop of the Viridian Shroud Nebula. *I never thought I'd be back here.* So many memories, so few of them good. Mostly the stuff of nightmares. She's brought back to the present by the ship messaging her:

{Travel time to the Gateway Ring: one hour. Please prepare to disembark.} The ship is talking to her, but it doesn't expect a reply, so she doesn't offer one.

She grabs her backpack. She likes to travel light, and she won't be here for long. She checks to make sure her fake ID is handy. The quantum encrypted and signed ID chip lists her as Elena Drake, Vice President of Acquisitions, Obsidian Holdings. The name is real enough, the job less so. It's a great excuse to travel within Sector 36 without raising too many questions. Credentials that should be good enough not to trip any advanced pattern-matching bullshit detectors the sector's AI is running. Credentials that give her a reason to be here and travel where she needs to. She's going to pull a fast one on an Omega class AI. *Time to play chess with a god,* she thinks. Her versus Ingram. She heads out to the main deck.

The main deck is pristine, all white surfaces at ninety-degree angles and a wall-to-wall, synthetic sapphire window to the outside. There's a tinge of ozone in the air, a remnant of the recent jump. Some time ago, Elena used to be accustomed to the low background hum characteristic of military vessels. She was able to tune it out. Proper insulation isn't cost-effective, so military ships tend to be noisier. She's been off duty for long enough that it now bothers her.

Lieutenant Wade and an ensign she hasn't seen before are there, taking in the view. She goes to them.

The ensign is staring through the sapphire glass pane, mouth agape. She looks young, inexperienced, if not innocent. With blue eyes and brown hair, she is a bit shorter than Elena, with a smooth complexion and a sprinkle of freckles. She looks very tense, most definitely on her first deployment.

Elena follows her gaze, is stunned. Dozens, no, hundreds of ships cluster around the jump gate. More than she ever saw at the busiest spaceports. More than she saw during her whole deployment. The *Dauntless* and its escort are just a few drops in an ocean of ships. *Wow,* she thinks.

Wade turns around to face her. "Captain!" Official as always, wearing a spotless uniform, square jaw clean-shaven—the navy ideal personified. His short-cropped black hair is showing only a hint of gray. Lieutenant Marcus Wade, military operator, is level-headed as always, unfazed by the sight.

"Retired, Lieutenant." She hasn't been on active duty for some years now. "The skies are ... busy."

"I've never seen anything like this before," answers the lieutenant. Then, after a short pause, adds, "Go figure, the first non-human intelligence we find, we end up exchanging greetings through gun ports."

Go figure.

"At least things are quiet now," he adds.

"Was it less busy when you were here last time?" she asks. She likes Wade, they spent some time talking during their voyage. Always good to meet a fellow Vanguard. They talked about their respective deployments to Sector 36. He was here just a few months back, during the Tauran War. Coming back for a second tour. She was here long before that, hoping never to return. Yet here she is.

"Aye," he says. "Less busy."

Less busy, even in the midst of the war. Why is Ingram bringing in so many troops now? Now that it, allegedly, negotiated a truce with the Taurans? Now that they are, allegedly, gone from the sector?

"We're going to kick some Tauran ass!" The ensign is green enough to be excited about the prospect of combat.

"I'm sure you will." Elena nods.

"We have to." She turns pensive. "I heard they eat people!"

"Where in the world did you hear that?" the lieutenant asks.

"People are talking, sir."

Elena doubts there's been any official reports on this. As far as she knows, the Taurans entered the sector on some mysterious errand, picked a fight, realized it was tougher than they expected, ended up agreeing to a truce, packing it up, and leaving.

Still, they managed to reduce Echo Point to a wasteland and create enough chaos for years to come.

Plenty of mysteries remain though. What were the terms of the truce? Ingram is fuzzy about it. Will there be more fighting? Ingram says "no" while amassing more military assets. What do the Taurans look like? What is their culture like? Their biology? Their physics? How much do we know? Ingram says "classified for security reasons." She is here to get to the bottom of things, and she doesn't fucking trust Ingram.

The *Dauntless* glides towards the Gateway Ring, a massive ring structure built around a small moon, in close proximity to the jump gate, as the main port city and logistics hub of the sector. The traffic doesn't get thinner. More military ships dot the green gas background of the nebula, more civilian ships waiting for outbound travel approval.

"Is it how you remember it?" Lieutenant Wade asks.

Elena deployed here a few years ago, her first (and thankfully last) time seeing direct action. No Taurans that time, good old human-on-human, machine-assisted killing.

"No. No it isn't." Her mind serves up a montage from the past, teammates screaming, blood, stuff she'd rather not remember. She shakes it off. "I've never seen so many ships in my life either, Lieutenant."

"You think this means more war?" he asks, even-toned.

"Above my pay grade."

She wishes she had an answer for him.

The silhouette of the Gateway Ring is quickly taking shape in the distance. Ships are everywhere. Thousands of them cluster around the megastructure and extend into the void.

"You're heading coreward after dropping me off?" She asks the question mainly to pass time. Where else would they go? All military ships are headed towards what used to be the front line of the war.

"Aye. NS-36-A System. Eureka Base defense."

Through some powerful connections, her organization was able to arrange inbound travel to the Gateway Ring on a military ship. Her not-made-up, ex-military background helped. Once on the ring, she is on her own. She needs to make her way to Verdant, connect with the asset, and bring him back.

"What's your name?" She turns towards the ensign.

"Lila Navarro, sir! Ma'am!"

"You keep those people safe, ensign!" She exchanges a brief, sour smile with Wade.

"Aye aye!"

The Gateway Ring is now taking up most of the view. The megastructure has always been the heart of Sector 36, pumping people and freight coreward to what used to be Echo Point and the now heavily guarded Eureka Base; trailing to Verdant, the agricultural world; spinward to Forge, the mining and industrial hub; and rimward to Nova Prime, the capital; and farther out to the frontier Horizon Station. Its slow-spinning black outer shell is pockmarked by blinking lights. Behind its rim, the ring's interior radiates with the glow of a million streetlamps.

Rings are miracles of engineering. Like jump gates, they're impossibly expensive to build and operate. OmniCore Solutions and Dominion Nexus have the megastructure duopoly. She learned this factoid while putting together her Obsidian Holdings cover. A VP of Acquisitions should know this after all.

There are only a few dozen across the galaxy, and seeing one is always awe-inspiring, even if she was on it before. But the miracle of engineering pales in comparison to the volume of vessels making it look like the galaxy's largest beehive.

She spots a few other heavy hitters like the *Dauntless*: large, heavy cruisers with immense firepower. Around them, frigates and corvettes, slightly less deadly but nimbler. And an assortment of other special-purpose ships. Some of them she recognizes: transports, tugboats. Others she's never seen before. Countless ships.

Mixed between the clusters of military ships are civilian ones. Cargos, ferries, skimmers, all shapes and sizes. Some have likely been waiting to dock for days if not weeks, but the *Dauntless* is military and has priority. They take an ingress vector through the swarm. Smaller ships move out of the way, clearing a path wide enough for the heavy cruiser. It decelerates as it approaches the megastructure, slows down, stops.

{Docking complete,} announces the ship.

She says her goodbyes to the ensign, then to Wade.

"Godspeed, Lieutenant!"

He nods, meets her eyes briefly.

"Safe travels, Captain!"

"Retired," she adds, smiles.

She shoulders her backpack and heads out. The gangway is starting to get crowded. Crew members are disembarking for the short port call, last stop before whatever may happen. She joins the crowd, doesn't recognize anyone as she makes her way off ship.

She wonders how long it will take her to find transport to Verdant. She expected some amount of chaos, given the recent war, but this is beyond imagination. With the sheer number of ships she saw, she wonders what's the impact on in-sector travel.

She wishes she had better intel. The jump gate bandwidth is almost exclusively used for translating military ships into the sector. Outbound traffic is reduced to a trickle. The few civilian ships that manage to translate out bring conflicting information and strange rumors. The broad strokes don't form a clear picture. She is sure someone must be receiving detailed briefs, though these don't make it to the general public. Didn't make it to Spark. Didn't make it to her. The lack of intel is a big risk for her mission. Her instincts tell her so and she trusts her instincts.

She steps out of the dock, into the street, and is shocked anew.

02: QUAGMIRE

So many people! People are camping in the streets, as far as her eyes can see. The air is dusty and stale. Smells of overworked life support systems. Overhead, she can see the ring's surface curving across the sky, between the cacophony of ships. Curving all the way behind a pale moon reflecting streetlights back at her. The perspective makes her dizzy.

It's nighttime but that doesn't mean much on a ring spinning around a moon orbiting a planet rotating around a star. The day/night cycle is erratic at best. Dominion Nexus handled this by adjusting the intensity of street lighting, ensuring some set sinusoidal change in perceived lumens. It doesn't quite do the trick.

She exits the docks and walks down a crowded avenue lined with nanocrete buildings. Tents are pitched next to the buildings, with families inside them. Some are sitting on blankets or chairs on the sidewalk. Around them, other people are walking at a brisk pace. Plenty of vehicle traffic on the road too.

She locks eyes with a young girl for a second. No older than six, blonde hair, green eyes, dirty blue dress. She's sitting on a blanket, next to her mom, under a graffitied wall. Her eyes slide to the graffiti: a human shape being swallowed by what seems to be a small dinosaur. Elena guesses it's the artist's rendition of a Tauran.

She keeps walking. People turn to look at her. Her tidy business attire stands out, something she didn't anticipate.

The street looks familiar, but at the same time very different than she remembers it. It's eerie, like sliding into a parallel universe. Way too many people, more trash, flickering streetlights. Walls are covered in illegible writing and crude drawings. Broken glass. She steps around an orange bag emanating an awful stench, either rotten food or something dead inside. She could use a drink.

She enters the Cosmic Drift, one of the many bars that sprouted around the docks. The overhead display is cracked, so the sign reads "The Co mic Drift." Whether an accident or intentional vandalism, she finds the new name ironically fitting.

She was here during her deployment. The very same bar. She's surprised, she didn't intend to return to this place, but some part of her subconscious seems to have led her here nevertheless.

She enters to find the same small booths, same mock-wood tables and chairs, same black bar top. But the place is packed and looks dodgier than she remembers. A table is broken from what must have been a fight. An almost dried puddle of what looks suspiciously like blood stains the floor. The background noise is a few decibels higher than it should be and it stinks of spilled booze. She is carrying enough tacticals not to worry too much about her own safety. Still, this didn't use to be a dive. She briefly considers finding a different spot, but there's nostalgia here.

Last time they sat in the corner booth. All ghosts now, except her. Last time she was here was right before Forge. With her team, with Darius. She feels a gray sadness deep in her chest. They had no idea what they were heading into, spent a night drinking and having fun. Chief Petty Officer Cooper got so drunk that night, they started calling him "Hammer." Back when the Cosmic Drift had no blood on the floor and no broken tables. Back when the sidewalks were clean and were not filled with despair. She sighs.

She walks up to the bar, takes a seat, orders a Solar Flare. The black bar top is sticky. The bartender is efficient despite the crowd, hands her the drink in no time. She takes a sip, tastes the familiar citrus and subtle spice undertone, but the flavor is somehow off.

She strikes up a conversation with a grizzled man sitting next to her. She notices he has temple grafts like hers. NeuroSync Rejection Syndrome? Puritan? Either way, it's quite a sighting. She could count on one hand the number of people she's met in person with her condition.

"What's going on around here? I just translated in."

He looks her up and down, making her feel slightly uncomfortable. He looks very tired. Unshaven, with deep bags under his eyes.

"Translated *in*?"

She is about to use her fake identity for the first time, try it on for size (*here on business, you see*), but decides to keep quiet instead. He continues:

"You work for Abyssal by any chance?"

He looks disgusted. It's her damn attire; she does look corporate in it.

"Oh, no." She tries a fake laugh, is surprised when he finds it convincing. Thinking on her feet now: "I'm a digital expert."

"Why in the world would you want to be here? Everyone is trying to leave!"

She realizes he's had a few drinks. Not slurring his words yet, but not completely sober either. She wants to keep him talking, maybe learn something.

"Afraid the Taurans might come back?"

"Taurans ... who knows," he says, becoming confidential. He leans in close enough that she can smell booze—"You ask me, there's no Taurans. I think they were made up by one of the mega-corps to take over." He lowers his voice even further. "Or Ingram for that matter. Either way, best not be here."

Her first thought is the guy has been drinking way more than she initially thought. But then again, is what he's saying really impossible?

Not impossible, just highly improbable. She has very limited intel, but even so, this doesn't sound very reasonable to her. The Taurans were here alright, left a trail of destruction behind them.

"I'm Elena," she says. "Where are you from?"

"Jake," he replies. "Verdant. Trying to leave. Abandoned my farm and came here with the family. We've been stuck for days. Almost no civilian ships are moving and we're about to run out of credits." He grimaces.

She thinks of the people camping in the streets. "Family?"

"Yes. Wife, daughter, two sons. This is them."

He sends her a family picture. A smiling Jake, looking much less tired than the present version. Beautiful redhead wife next to him, kids on both sides. The youngest one, the daughter, is a toddler. The other two are teenagers or close to it. The golden fields behind them make it clear the picture was taken on Verdant, probably at their farm.

She looks at him, trying to determine how old the picture is, how far gone are those good times. The Jake in front of her looks somewhat older, but not by much.

"Beautiful," she says.

"Fucking landlord hiked up the price again today. I won't be able to make rent unless I find a buyer for the farm." The implication is clear —Jake and his beautiful family will end up street-side, like the rest of the stranded escapees. And most likely, nobody's buying his farm. Or they're offering peanuts. She feels embarrassed by this, buying distressed property is her fucking cover story!

"I'm sure you'll find a way out," she says, doesn't believe it. He doesn't buy it either.

"Doubt it. I don't have connections. Too many people trying to leave."

"All from Verdant?"

"From all over the sector. Except Forge. Those fucking mega-corps won't let 'em. What about you? Why come here when everyone's trying to leave?"

He's definitely not a big corporate fan, good thing she didn't introduce herself as VP of Acquisitions. She continues the improv act.

"I'm here to find my cousin. He's on Verdant too. We haven't heard from him in a while."

He softens up to this.

"I hope he's OK. Maybe he's here, check the ring before you travel. Most likely he's here. Lots of Verdant folk here now." He gestures towards the outside.

She nods, thanks him for the tip. She is truly sorry for him, but she is on a mission. She needs fresh intel, needs to catch up on the local news. She picks up her drink, stands up, wishes Jake good luck, and manages against all odds to find a small unoccupied booth. She gets online, accesses the local network, soaks in the situation. Her grafts (VoidTech v18 Tactical Edition) offer her a very decent bandwidth for immersion-surfing. Not quite the same experience as regular people, who can use their implants to fully embed in the digital, but top of the line for her condition.

She zooms in on the ring. The Sector 36 Gateway Ring is built to support a permanent population of around twenty million, with a few other million transitory: colonists, tourists, ship crews. Most ships coming or going through the jump gate stop here on the way to their destination. So do most ships traveling within the sector, due to the ring's central location. She puts the overview aside. She knows this already, been here before. She requests a summary of recent events and skims over the data.

At the moment, there are more than a hundred million people here. Four to five times more than Dominion Nexus ever anticipated. Way beyond what the infrastructure can support. Crime is on the rise. People are leaving settlements in droves, trying to book transport out of the sector. They end up here, stuck. As military ships pour in, very little outbound traffic is allowed through. Queues are measured in months.

Her intel definitely didn't cover this. But she is not trying to translate out yet. She needs to get to Verdant. She looks up schedules, transit plans.

For the foreseeable future, there is no civilian transit headed out trailing, towards her destination. Plenty of military vessels headed coreward, to Eureka Base and what used to be the theater of war. There is daily spinward transport to Forge. Corporate paramilitary vessels are also heading to Forge by the dozen—looks like the Abyssal Mining Consortium doesn't trust the military to protect their interests. Or maybe they're just making sure people stay put.

She can afford to pay quite a lot, if someone is willing to get her to her destination. She arrived with enough credits to see her through some major hardships. She would prefer mass transit, stay inconspicuous, fade in the crowd. That doesn't seem to be a viable option though. She gives up and puts out a bid for transport to Verdant and waits for takers.

She gets offline, inhales, thinks. *What if the asset is here?* Jake was pretty tipsy and had some far-out theories. That said, the truth on the ground is a hundred million people are crammed on the ring. Spark got no other signal from Doctor Linton. If he is smart, he'll stay put, waiting for pick-up. And as far as she knows, he *is* smart. *Stick to the plan, Captain.* Retired. Different ball game, same rules.

She'll need a place to sleep—she hopes it won't be on the street.

Back online, searching for lodging. To her surprise, there are plenty of options. Tiny box rooms (the military term is *coffins*) at eye-watering prices. Somehow, someone is profiting from the desperation. She books a room nearby.

Nothing to do but wait for someone to take her bid now. Jake might be right, the asset might be here, but she doubts it. She can't think of a good way to check either way. Any search for "Doctor Linton" would ring an alarm for whoever is tapping the wire. They had a plan worked out long in advance, not much to do now but stick by it.

She needs to rest. She exits the Cosmic Drift and heads towards her rented room. It's on the same ring segment, a few dozen blocks away. She could walk there, wouldn't mind the exercise, but it wouldn't be a pleasant walk. The streets are dirty and way too crowded. She hops on the hover rail instead.

The rail car is spray-painted all over in red and green, in an indecipherable pattern that is meaningless to her. She can't find a seat. She feels a draft once the rail starts moving, counts three broken windows.

The rail goes by what seems to be a street brawl. Onlookers giving a wide berth to a handful of people shoving each other, then throwing punches. She sees one of them go down, catches a glimpse of guns being drawn before the scene slides out of sight. The hover rail continues its glide. People are everywhere, walking, sitting, sleeping, fighting. She never imagined this was what she would find here. Sector 36 never ceases to surprise.

It's a short ride; her room is not far. Once the rail pulls into her station, she hops off and walks half a block to the hotel. She doesn't realize she is being followed.

03: NATURAL SELECTION

Elena grew up on Aurelia, Sector 12. A Gaia world she always misses when away for too long. She misses the unique shades of lapis blue the sky takes on stormy days and the endless rolling emerald hills. She was born in a happy family, with a couple of siblings and a pet cat. She has an older brother and a younger sister. The tabby they adopted is old now, but still hanging in there.

Otherwise a healthy infant, she was diagnosed with NeuroSync Rejection Syndrome at the age of three. A rare condition making her body reject any deep neural implants, which the vast majority of people get before school age to embed in the digital. The digital—the intangible world of algorithms and data flows.

She had to get external grafts, with limited bandwidth—old-school non-intrusive augments. In a society deeply enmeshed with the digital, being completely locked out is not an option. Better to read braille than be illiterate, even if you can't enjoy the colors of the sunset. Her grafts gave her a way to peek inside the digital, never mind the size of the keyhole.

Growing up, she felt isolated and weird—her schoolmates were able to *embed*, while it took her concentration and effort to commune with data. Even worse during her teenage years, when all her peers started *merging*. This was a world of qualia beyond her grasp. She doubled down on proving she didn't need any deep implants. The physical plane might just be good enough still. She got good grades and practiced sports. Not virtual sports, rather ancient, classic sports.

She wasn't alone—NSRS affected some fraction of a percentage of the population. Others declined deep implants for religious reasons, even if their bodies would've accepted them. Yet others did it on principle. Neurals are best done at a very young age. Was it fair for parents to limit their children by withholding implants from them in the name of religion? Or as an act of counterculture? She was only tangentially aware of the raging debate. In her case, it wasn't an option. Her brain stem would simply not accept them. Grafts were the only way to go. She heard of a certain sect of an old religion who made do without grafts, completely cut off from the realm of information. They lived in isolated monasteries, using centuries-old compute to accomplish the most mundane tasks. Not something parents of children with NSRS would consider as an alternative to grafts. Even the biggest rebels drew the line there—virtually everyone without deep implants ended up having grafts.

In school she wasn't alone, but she was lonely. All her classmates had neurals. She felt one step behind, not in on the joke. She compensated by studying hard, working hard. She got good grades despite her disadvantages and excelled at sports. Got deep into martial arts, found this to be a great outlet for blowing off steam after days of struggling to keep up with the faster-moving pace of the digital.

She enlisted, mostly for the structure and her want to make a difference. Feeling at a disadvantage due to her condition and making up for it with grit. Her good grades and physical fitness went a long way. She got into officer candidate school, graduated. Not top of her class but not near the bottom either. On a whim, she applied to the Vanguard program, the elite recon and direct action unit. She was surprised to get selected, despite her obvious limitations. She promised herself to seize the opportunity, poured all of herself into the grueling training. She completed the Specialized Training for Advanced Recon and Survival course, STARS, in a little under two years, emerged as a highly skilled Vanguard. She made it to sub-lieutenant before seeing action.

Then, she deployed—Sector 36, where a new jump gate opened in a new region of the Milky Way, strategically placed between two key worlds. Verdant, trailing—a lush world with rich enough soil to feed a whole sector; and Forge, spinward—an incredibly mineral-rich world.

Corporate interests threatened the safety of the sector. Titanforge Industries laid claim to the astrium deposits on Forge, while the Abyssal Mining Consortium disputed the claim. The two industry giants started bringing in paramilitary groups into the sector and around the planet, causing chaos. Military was deployed to maintain peace.

Sub-Lieutenant Elena "Tilt" Drake arrived in the Verdant Shroud Nebula aboard the heavy cruiser *Ironclad*. She spent exactly one day on the Gateway Ring, hitting the bars with the rest of the crew, including several rounds of drinks at the Cosmic Drift. Then the *Ironclad* recalled its sailors and marines aboard, fired up its faster-than-light engines, and headed spinward towards Forge.

Forge was a powder keg of corporate-speak negotiations and rising tensions. Their first on-site realization was that they were obviously outgunned by the corporate-funded paramilitary factions. Military budgets, while astronomical in their own right, couldn't compete with corporate sponsorship. Their opponents had better technology, faster compute, deadlier weaponry.

They asked for reinforcements. While the AI Council pondered through next steps, violence erupted. Titanforge thugs nuked a hive full of innocent Abyssal miners. Their planet-side headquarters were leveled in return. The military tried to intervene and limit the hostilities, and that was when Elena's NSRS instantly turned from a hand-icap to an asset. Corporate paramilitary deployed advanced hacking technology and started mounting basilisk attacks – remote brain-frying exploits. The digital around Forge was crawling with virtual snakes that would burrow deep inside neurals, bypass defenses, cause the hardware to malfunction. She saw her teammates die screaming while clawing their eyes out.

She was immune, her implants didn't go that deep, didn't interface the same way with her wetware. While their digital experts were busy developing countermeasures, she was field promoted to lieutenant. Their previous lieutenant died bleeding from his ears in front of her. They hit the paramilitary back hard. Both on the ground and in the digital.

Reinforcements eventually arrived. By that time, she was one of the most experienced personnel on site. She showed them the ropes, tactics that worked, shit they got taught during STARS they might as well forget. After a couple more months of senseless fighting and another field promotion, she rotated out as a captain.

The conflict ended soon after with a merger—Titanforge Industries and the Abyssal Mining Consortium became one company and settled their differences at the C-suite level. Troops got pulled back. Recon-struction plans were drafted. The merger generated a few trillion credits worth of shareholder value. Wasted a few thousand lives. The market reacted positively. The AI Council dismissed the peacekeeping troops. Peace was achieved.

Elena went home. She spent some quality time with her parents and aging tabby on Aurelia, punctuated by some vivid nightmares. She had time to think, but couldn't puzzle it out: Omega AIs, orders of magnitude smarter than the smartest carbon-based hardware evolu-tion could develop, steer the world in their inscrutable ways. The AI Council represents the interests of humanity as a whole. Other Omegas sit on corporate boards. Could it be that, in their infinite wisdom, the best path to resolve a dispute between corporations was what she witnessed on Forge? Was carnage the optimal negotiation strategy? Was the stock uptick worth its price in blood?

She decided she was done. Her service obligations fulfilled, she opted not to extend her contract. She was honorably discharged, stuck home for a while longer to figure out what was next. She was losing faith in the system, spoke about it here and there. She was approached by an agent of Spark. By then, the pitch sounded very appealing to her: the AIs are not to be trusted. Hyperintelligence is only one piece of the puzzle. They lack the *spark*—that elusive quality that makes us human. They are too utilitarian and, despite what they want us to believe, they are by no means benevolent.

Spark was an organization dedicated to humanity, with modest funds but well connected. Spark was building a case for change and could use Elena's help. The second time in her life when her NSRS was an asset. Her secrets were harder for an Omega to extract, protected by her lack of deep neural access. Her Vanguard training was an additional bonus. Elena joined. This was another opportunity to make a difference. She had no clear objective at first—just a promise to provide services when called upon. She was onboard with this, embraced the Spark ethos.

Soon after, news broke of the Tauran incursion. Then a brief all-out war. She watched this from the sidelines, kept up to date by watching the news, by talking to other Vanguards she knew from back in the day, by getting Spark briefs.

Then, with no explanations and no human ever talking to a Tauran, a truce. A colony with twenty million people reduced to a pile of rubble. Ingram, the Omega AI in charge of Sector 36, continuously bringing reinforcements while at the same time insisting peace had been achieved. This deeply concerned Spark leadership. The lives lost, the lack of transparency, the looming menace of further conflict.

Spark had people inside Sector 36. One of their assets made contact. Some vital information available, too precious to broadcast in the digital, too many prying eyes there. The agent was fleeing to a safer haven, bringing the secret with him. He needed a way out of the sector, a way to share the compromising knowledge.

They called on Elena. She had the right background and mix of skills for the job. Her NSRS made her brain inscrutable, a big advantage in the worst-case scenario of being compromised.

She agreed to return to Sector 36 and make sense of things. Honestly, she missed the action. After the horrors she witnessed, the intensity of direct action, civilian life felt empty. Her objective was clear enough: contact the asset, get him out, bring the secret to Spark. Understand what really happened and what Ingram was up to. In a best-case scenario, the whole situation might make for an indisputable argument against the AI Council and pave a path towards something better. A brighter future for humanity. Spark had been quietly preparing for this moment for years. If they had the evidence, they would come out. Loudly. Bring the whole thing down. Enough influential people interested to make a difference.

She said goodbye to her family, promised to be back in a few weeks. She hugged the cat, who meowed knowingly, then boarded a transit ship to Sector 7. From there, she was going to get on board the heavy cruiser *Dauntless*. Unusual for a retired captain, now civilian, to board a military ship on deployment, but Spark knew the right people in the right places to make it happen. She would board as a consultant. A Vanguard veteran would have plenty to teach the personnel. Not that she would actually have to do any teaching, it was just the paperwork needed to clear her and get her inbound to Sector 36.

While making her way to Sector 7 and the *Dauntless*, she worked on her identity for the mission. Vice President of Acquisitions, Obsidian Holdings. They gave her a fake ID, a lot of reading material, and a contact at the company's branch office on Nova Prime, the Sector 36 capital. She spent the trip studying, memorizing, rehearsing.

Before boarding the *Dauntless*, she briefly met with another agent. In a dark corner of the crowded port, a corner overlooked by surveillance, she traded the digicard containing her mission brief and cover details for a bag of tacticals. She kept the ID chip. She stuck the gear in her backpack and continued on.

As the *Dauntless* spun up its engines, she reflected on how she never thought she would return to Sector 36. But she was doing it for a good cause. If she played this right, there would be no direct action. A quick extraction, neat and clean. She was cautiously optimistic.

04: APEX PREDATOR

The hotel looks surprisingly nice from the outside. No broken windows. Clean white walls, minus a sloppy "They are among us" scrawled in red paint. The inside is ridiculously cramped, but the filtered air is much cleaner than on the street. She checks in at the kiosk, takes the short elevator ride upstairs, enters her room. *Coffin* is an overstatement. She's seen wider brigs than this. A single bed with light-purple bedding, a narrow desk with a swivel chair, a bathroom with a tiny shower cabin. Barely enough room to walk around the bed. She suddenly feels trapped. She pulls aside the curtains of the only window and gets a third-story-level view of the chaos below. She looks up. Above her, the sky is dotted with ships. She spots a particularly large one on the horizon, which can only be the *Dauntless*.

She inhales deeply, exhales. There's a hint of lavender in the room, a nice, overpriced detail. The room is small but spotless. A welcome change from the overcrowded streets and bars. She sets her backpack down on the bed and sits next to it. She is stuck here until someone picks up her bid. Could be a few hours, could be a few days. She hopes it won't be too many days. She has enough credits to make the trip happen one way or another but would rather not linger here for too long.

It's dinnertime and she is getting hungry. She will shower, change into more casual clothes, and find something to eat nearby before calling it a night. But she has time, decides to get online first.

No new messages sent to her corporate identity, but she sends one out to her contact at the branch office on Nova Prime. Just checking in. *I translated in, trying to find transport to Verdant. Will stop by the office after business is concluded.*

Time to do some recon. For starters, poor drunk Jake might be right. What if the asset is here? How can she tell? How can she probe without arousing the suspicion of whoever is listening in? She knows exactly where on Verdant the doctor is supposed to be: BioFields farm. But she can't straight up go poking her nose there. Careful, she needs to be very careful.

She gets online. Pretends to do some research. After all, she is here on business. She pulls up a map of Verdant. A miniature planet materializes in her mind's eye, rotating slowly. She selects a few random regions, making sure one of them includes the farm she is interested in. The planet is now overlaid with orange patches. Farm names float above its surface.

She asks a few innocent questions: businesses opening and closing (mostly closing these days), people coming and going (mostly going these days). She gets back long lists of names, quickly scans them. No Linton it seems. Is he using a fake name? That wasn't in her brief. She gets nowhere.

She considers looking up passenger manifests but the number of ships leaving Verdant is astounding. Given the situation, bookkeeping is an afterthought. Plus, why would a VP of Acquisition be interested in passenger manifests? That would stand out. She lets the map spin for a few more seconds, then dismisses it.

There's no way to get bearings on Doctor Linton. Since they haven't heard from him, she must assume he's still where he's supposed to be. Otherwise, there would've been a message waiting for her, an update on the situation. Only option is to head there and hope for the best. Jake got inside her head, that's all. The doctor wouldn't just leave his pickup spot, would he?

She gets offline, chews her lip for a while. Time to reach out to Ingram. Say "hi," act natural. As VP of Acquisitions for Obsidian Holdings, not saying "hi" would be out of character, especially given the situation. She's on official business, trying to make her way to Verdant.

Ingram manages Sector 36. Its substrate is a quantum-entangled distributed system with physical nodes across all the settlements in the sector. Its compute capacity is measured in unimaginable orders of zettaflops. Most times, it's willing to spare a tiny sliver of its infinite attention and engage in casual conversation. Because of some ancient customs and proper etiquette, AIs never proactively reach out, *you* have to contact *them*. Etiquette or another subtle way to show us who needs who? She wonders.

She's not looking forward to this conversation. She stands up and tries to pace the room, but it's physically impossible to pace in such a confined space. She sits back down. *Come on, Vanguard,* she tells herself. She gets online. She sends a message to Ingram, asks for a chat. From her experience, Omegas are talkative but obtuse. They enjoy talking in riddles, something she can't stand.

Ingram responds right away, and Elena establishes the connection. Ingram's avatar is a disembodied head, a featureless face, edges dissolving into a lime green wireframe, on the backdrop of the Viridian Shroud Nebula.

She briefly wonders whether it's tailoring its appearance to the interlocutor and, if so, why she finds this avatar so unsettling. She's grateful once again for her grafts and the limited bandwidth they provide. She wouldn't want to get any more intimate with the thing, can only imagine what regular people, with deep implants, experience when they embed for a conversation with an Omega.

"Hello, Captain!" It sounds positively delighted to talk to her.

"Retired," she responds reflexively. "I run acquisitions for Obsidian Holdings now."

"So I heard. How can I help you?"

"I need to get to Verdant. Looks pretty difficult to hitch a ride nowadays."

"Indeed, things are pretty bogged down these days unfortunately. I'm doing my best to move things along but there are … difficulties."

"Can you help me?" A shot in the dark.

"I suggest you put out a bid. I'm positive someone will eventually pick it up."

She already put out a bid. Does it not know? Is it pretending not to know, letting the puny humans keep some sense of privacy? Ingram interrupts her train of thought with a non-sequitur:

"Do you like to play chess, Elena?"

A chill goes down her spine. *Time to play chess with a god.* She remembers telling herself that when she translated in. Just how much can an Omega simulate? How much can it know?

"Want to play a game?" She tries to play it cool.

"I don't like chess," it answers. "Chess is a game of perfect information. I very much prefer poker."

There's a deeper meaning here, but she can't quite grasp it. She lets it go.

"Tell me what happened with the Taurans. What are the terms of the truce?"

"I'm sorry, Elena, I'm afraid I can't do that." A short pause. It's toying with her. "That information is classified."

"Why? For how long?"

She doesn't really expect a clear answer from it. It doesn't disappoint; it avoids her question.

"Why do you want to go to Verdant? I thought Obsidian Holdings acquisitions would be on Forge."

She has her cover story ready.

"We're looking to expand. Farming. Sounds like premium property is cheap on Verdant now. We want to buy the dip. As long as the Taurans don't make a comeback, we see a big opportunity."

"Wisdom of the ages, Elena, don't try to time the market."

"Do you know something I don't?"

"Is that why you're interested in the truce details, Vice President?"

Emphasis on "vice president." She's feeling more and more like a mouse with a cat.

"Yes. And the people have the right to know." Was that last part a slip-up? Will it notice?

"They will. In due time."

"Can you help me or not?"

"Not directly, I'm sorry. But I'm sure you'll make your way to Verdant. And, Captain?"

"Yes?"

"Watch your six." Ominous. Very ominous. "I hear the Taurans eat people." And with that final bit of wisdom, Ingram disconnects.

She goes offline. She is shaking. Feels like puking again. The absurdity of her mission is sinking in. She's not outsmarting an AI. Ingram fucking amused itself during their brief chat. She is angry. Every sentence was a hint that it knows more, more than she can imagine. She is deeply disturbed. She is a mere human, the Omega is an apex predator. Echoes of *homo erectus* on the savanna, coming face-to-face with a saber-toothed tiger. There's no fight or flight. You freeze.

What the fuck am I doing here? This whole thing might've been a big mistake. She might as well have stayed home.

She closes the curtains, undresses, throws her business casual disguise in a disdainful pile, and takes a long shower. The water is hot, and the body wash has a pleasant, fruity smell. She makes an effort to be present, enjoy the warmth and cleanliness, but one-liners keep replaying in her mind. "Do you like to play chess, Elena?" *How the fuck did it know?* Or was this just a horrible coincidence? "Wisdom of the ages, Elena," giving her sage advice. "And, Captain? Watch your six." A very thinly veiled threat.

The way it switched between calling her vice president, captain, and simply by name. That was no accident, Omegas don't make mistakes. What was the meaning of it? To show her it knows, to show her she doesn't have any cover. She's exposed.

She rinses and towels off. She's not hungry anymore, the short conversation killed her appetite. Too wired to sleep too. She considers taking a graycap but decides against it. She's not on a tight schedule after all, and she always wakes up woozy after taking one.

She dims the lights, opens the curtains again, and gets into bed. She tries to steady herself by looking out the window. On the horizon, ships are docking and leaving in a slow-motion hypnotic dance. She tries to make them out by their silhouettes. Most are military, some are freight, some she can't identify.

She hears someone yelling down the street. It's nearby but she can't make the words and it's outside her field of vision. Not curious enough to get out of bed, she continues watching the ships. A while later she hears what can only be a gunshot. This doesn't sound close by. Then another gunshot. Not long after, sirens. She thinks about all the people stranded here, civilians without corporate sponsorship, too poor to afford a coffin. Will they make it out of here? What happens when the food runs out? How long will it take her to get out of here?

She eventually falls asleep out of sheer exhaustion. It's a shallow sleep. She dreams a lot but can't remember any of it. She wakes up after a few hours, just as tired. A tad more optimistic though. She's here on a mission and she'll see it through. And Ingram can go fuck itself. She stared death in the face enough times that the thing's babbling won't throw her off her game. Thinking this makes her feel better. She skipped dinner and realizes she's famished.

She puts on clean clothes, something a lot more casual this time around: a plain cream shirt, navy blue pants. She didn't bring a large wardrobe but is glad she packed a few options. Business smart is not the right attire for the squalor on the ring.

Before leaving the room, she quickly gets online and is pleasantly surprised to find a message waiting for her. Her bid got picked up. She skims the details.

Captain Barabe of the *Charon*. At dock 142. Happy to take her trailing, to Verdant. Leaving in three hours. Company is listed as "Independent Logistics," which sounds a lot like smugglers. A good thing in these circumstances: it's probably her best bet to make it out of here in reasonable time. She acknowledges, drops a message to Captain Barabe that she'll be there.

No need to return to the room, she grabs her backpack, double-checks she didn't leave anything behind, and walks out. Down the elevator and to the kiosk, she checks out, and exits the hotel. The artificial light is brighter, a simulacrum of morning, but the moon is in the planet's shadow now, so there's no real sunlight to speak of. This, combined with her lack of sleep, makes Elena feel painfully jet-lagged.

05: TRAILING

As a major port and the nexus of the sector, the Gateway Ring is famous for its food scene. Establishments known for serving food and drinks around the clock to comers and goers. Based on her experience at the Cosmic Drift, quality might have gone down a notch, but she's sure she can find a good breakfast. For now. Once the supplies run out, the situation will be very different, but she doesn't plan to stick around for that long. It's breakfast, then off to the docks—meet Barabe, board the *Charon*, continue on her mission.

She walks down the street, looking for a place that piques her interest. She's not picky, and especially now is hungry enough not to bother getting online for an informed decision. There's a ramen place across the road, with animated noodle neons dancing up and down, a bar and grill next to it. On her side of the street, there's a Hydroponic Fresh, and a block away an all-day-breakfast restaurant called Star's End, with an exploding nova as its logo. More diners pepper the street but they're too far away for her to make out their names. She sees a spinning orange bell pepper, then farther down the unmistakable purple comet logo of the Stellar Grub ("Serving the galaxy since 2499"). She picks the breakfast place, Star's End. Eggs sound good. And caffeine in whatever form they serve it. After last night she needs a booster.

She's making her way there when she feels a prickle at the back of her neck. She is positive she's being watched. Before second-guessing herself, before coming up with a rational explanation (*maybe I'm paranoid after the conversation with Ingram*), she slings her backpack around, reaches in the pocket, and picks up one of the tiny drones, part of her tacticals package. She pulls it out of the backpack safely hidden in the palm of her hand, though there isn't much to hide. The state-of-the-art VoidTech Autonomous Navigation and Tracking (ANT) is less than an inch long, wispy thin, and by design looks like your common flying insect, a galaxy-spanning nuisance.

She pretends to dig some more in her backpack, while at the same time giving instructions to the tiny spy through her graft.

{Play dead for thirty seconds, then follow me at a distance, relay video.}

She pulls out a tissue, pretends to blow her nose, then crumples it around the drone. She throws the balled-up tissue in a recycling pod and keeps walking through thick pedestrian traffic.

The drone comes to life after exactly half a minute has passed, rises out of the recycling pod shaking off the tissue it's been wrapped in. It's quiet and close to invisible, its tiny black body absorbing the artificial light simulating early morning on the ring. It hovers about twenty feet above the sidewalk and starts following Elena from a distance.

{Establishing video feed,} it sends her.

She connects, can see through the drone's eyes. The bird's-eye view of the street unfolds in Elena's mind's eye. She sees the camping people she just walked by ten seconds ago, she sees people walking behind her. She sees her backpack, herself walking briskly, hopping over a suspicious-looking dark red puddle.

Her first thought is another drone. Standard operating procedure. She runs a segmentation algorithm on the feed but finds no other drones between the ANT and herself. She asks the drone to pan around, look behind, up in the sky. Nothing.

She's either being watched from farther away or she's being old-school followed. Or she's just paranoid. She's not paranoid. She's been in combat—she learned to trust her instincts, and they saved her hide more than once. It's not magic, it's lizard brain hardwiring. Struggling to tell the neocortex, unable to articulate the threat, signaling through feelings instead. Certainty. Dread.

If she's being followed, she needs to figure out by whom. Drones are easier, she has field experience working with drones, working against drones. The spy versus spy shit—that she knows less well. They covered this during Vanguard training, but that was long ago. She's rusty.

In front of the Star's End now, she goes inside, walks up to the bar. Her attention is on the video feed. The ANT shows her two people who were walking just a few feet behind her slow down, stop. They look inside the Star's End. Same back-of-the-neck prickle as before, more intense this time around. *Gotcha.* They take a few more steps forward so they can't be seen from inside the restaurant and stop again.

{Warning: low battery.}

The drone is tiny, agile, and packs a spectacular amount of compute for its chassis. This comes at the cost of lifespan. ANTs are very short-lived. This one did its job though. She sends it final instructions. The drone acknowledges, arcs over the Star's End, and zooms in on the two figures. It takes a burst of pictures, sends Elena a final data dump, and self-immolates before touching the ground.

Adrenaline has reduced her appetite, but objectively she needs fuel. And she needs time to think. She orders a protein-rich breakfast, coffee to go with it.

"We're out of brew, sorry. Would you care for caffeine drops instead?" the server asks her.

"Sure," she answers without really processing the question. She is distracted now, sifting through the drone's data.

She's most definitely being followed. They were walking behind her, far enough to be inconspicuous in the crowd, close enough not to lose her, matching her stride. *Watch your six.* She fast-forwards to the end of the transmission, combines the pictures the drone took into a couple of 3D portraits, rotates them to face her.

While she is sitting at the bar, receiving a plate of fried eggs and synthetic protein strips, in the digital she is staring at two utterly unfamiliar faces. A clean-shaven, middle-aged, tall and muscular guy with graying black hair. A younger, shorter blond guy, making up for his smaller frame with a lush beard. Who the fuck are these guys? And why are they after her?

A couple of caffeine drops sit next to the eggs on her plate. She eats them first, bitter taste barely registering.

She could use some help from Spark to untangle this, but for all intents and purposes, they're unreachable. The network backbone is leaky; she can't message her contact at the Obsidian Holdings branch office with this latest development. The same quantum substrate that enables instant interstellar comms inside the sector is used by Ingram for distributed compute. She doesn't trust the AI not snooping.

Their common vocabulary is severely limited, a handful of code words, none of which corresponds to this situation. Unplanned for. Nobody thought she would get her cover blown within hours of arriving here. On the other hand, maybe her cover isn't blown. Maybe it's just a pair of common thieves taking her for an easy mark.

She ponders next steps. She's taking off for Verdant in two hours. Should she divert to Nova Prime instead? Is she in danger? Was Ingram threatening her or trying to warn her? In a different situation, she would find the breakfast delicious. The eggs are cooked over easy, just the way she likes them. The synthetic protein strips are engineered to taste and smell heavenly. But her mind is racing, she pecks at the food without enjoying it.

How much of a danger is she in right now? The Gateway Ring is severely overcrowded. Murder rates are climbing, and desperation will only make things worse. They could stab or shoot her, drag her to an alley, lose her body among the crime stats. But she now knows they're coming, and she won't go down without a fight. Though she'd much rather avoid causing a ruckus.

Are these some run-of-the-mill criminals, or has she really been compromised? She can easily lose a pair of common muggers, but if they know her identity, that's far more concerning.

Next set of questions: Is *Charon* safe? Can she trust Barabe? Or is she walking into a trap? No certainties in the real world, just probabili-

ties, but she believes *Charon* is safe. For one, her bid was anonymous—
"Independent Logistics" had no idea who, out of the hundred million
people currently packed on the ring, was asking for a ride. Second, if
she was going to walk into a trap, they wouldn't have had to trail her.
Third, any ship she gets on has a tiny but non-zero probability of being
a trap. If she wants zero risk, she is stuck here. Hell, if she'd wanted
zero risk, she would've stayed home. She needs to finish her mission.

She forces herself to eat more while thinking through her options.
She formulates a plan. Lose the tail, get to *Charon*, stay alert. Best-case
scenario, it's a pair of muggers who'll lose interest and find another
victim. Worst case, her mission just got exponentially more
complicated.

She pays for her meal, leaving an egg and a protein strip untouched,
glancing outside to see if the goons trailing her are still there. She gets
a glimpse of someone quickly ducking away from the window as she
turns. They're still there.

She pretends to go use the restroom. It's conveniently located in the
back, around the counter and out of sight. She walks straight past the
door, through the fire exit, into a quiet back alley.

The alley is narrow, made even narrower by an overflowing
garbage pod. A couple of vagrants are sleeping next to it on blankets,
seemingly unperturbed by the stench. She sprints past them, picking
another ANT out of her backpack without breaking stride. She doesn't
have an unlimited supply, but she needs eyes on the alley. She drops it
before turning the corner, positioning it to watch the fire exit she just
came out of. The drone is stationary, which gives it a longer lifespan.
Something to watch her back as she makes her escape.

She pulls up a map of the ring segment, making sure she is headed
in the general direction of dock 142. She continues jogging, sticks to
back alleys for a while, taking left and right turns as she goes. She's
also keeping an eye on the drone's video feed. The alley is quiet,
vagrants sleeping unperturbed. Nothing moves.

After a few minutes of jogging, Elena slows down, decides she can
safely get back to a main street and make her way straight to the docks.

The ANT is at thirty percent power when the back door of the Star's End slams open. The two goons stomp out and look at each other. She watches them through the video feed, smiles, savoring the small victory. *Fuck you!*

One of them turns to the other, appears to say something. The other one spits. They walk to the two vagrants, prod one of them with a boot. A short conversation follows, which Elena can't make out, as her drone doesn't provide an audio feed. There's some gesticulation from her followers, shrugs from the rudely awoken alley dwellers.

By now she's made it to the docks. She is in front of another heavy cruiser, the *Excalibur*, anchored at dock 127. Her eyes are drawn to its massive twin railguns and bow-mounted battery of energy weapons. She nods approvingly and keeps walking.

In the digital, she sees the two walk down the alley, out of frame. They've passed her ANT. A few seconds later a foot comes back into the frame. The perspective swings as one of them picks up the drone. She sees a close-up view of a wall, the dark sky above, then static.

{Connection lost.}

The drone is flimsy, unarmored, made of light synthetics. Easy to crush between thumb and index finger. It did its job though. She knows she lost her tail, is in the clear. They also know she knows, which suits her just fine. *Better luck next time, fuckers!* Hopefully, there is no next time. She is out of here.

She keeps moving. Here, the crowds are even thicker than on the streets, but she joins the flow of people and makes good progress. Dock 128, dock 129. Most docks have ships connected to them; most ships are military.

She is on alert now, keeps looking around, glancing back. It's hard to tell if anyone else is after her, too many people around. But her gut says "no," which is promising.

She's by dock 135, in front of an Abyssal Mining transport named *Hope Eternal*, when she first glimpses the *Charon*. The silhouette looks unfamiliar, even as she gets closer and its chassis takes shape. *Beggars can't be choosers*, she thinks, and presses on towards 142.

06: CHARON

Elena gets a good look at the *Charon* once she reaches dock 142. The ship is small and looks like an older model. In fact, it looks like parts of at least two older models welded together. The fore part is triangular, large synthetic sapphire windowpanes offering a one-hundred-eighty-degree view from the bridge, typical of yachts. But the rounded edges, beige color, and the way the surfaces come together went out of fashion a few decades ago.

The aft of the ship is all business. A bulky cargo hold flanked by two large FTL engines. The paint job is a few shades off from the fore part too, more sand than beige. She notices a thick black streak crossing the top of the cargo hold at an angle, undoubtedly a hit from an energy weapon.

There's no name marking on the hull as far as she can tell, no "Charon" stenciled on its side. This reinforces her belief she's dealing with smugglers. Which is perfect for her—she has the credits to buy their services, and they have the experience and discretion she needs for her mission.

She walks up the ramp to the airlock and presses the "open" button. In a pressurized environment, the airlock acts as a simple door. It slides open and she freezes in place, speechless. Darius greets her with a big smile. She does a double take, stunned by the impossibility. Lieutenant Darius "Easy" Eze—KIA, Forge peacekeeping mission. Disbelief hits her like a physical blow.

"Hi," he says. "I'm Captain Barabe. Call me Jaxon."

She regains her composure, hoping she didn't let her surprise show. Not Darius, but the resemblance is striking. A brother if not a twin. Same intense eyes, same jawline, same height and athletic build.

Jaxon Barabe is wearing olive overalls with a white hexagonal logo embroidered on the chest. She hasn't seen the logo before.

"Elena," she says. They shake hands.

"Welcome aboard!" He smiles again, a big grin. "Mi casa es su casa." He steps out of the way with an exaggerated after-you gesture. She wonders if he's always so cordial or just glad he found a sucker willing to pay the exorbitant fee for a short trip trailing.

"Thanks!" She smiles back. "Hey, pardon me asking, did you know a Darius Eze? Lieutenant? You look a lot like someone I knew."

"No," he says. Thinks about it for a moment. "You're using past tense. I'm sorry for your loss."

"Thanks," she replies. Then, eager to change the subject, "Interesting name for a ship."

He doesn't comment on her remark.

She steps out of the airlock, into a small passageway connecting the bridge to the cargo hold. The opposite wall is uncovered, air ducts and fiber optics on display. Very unlike a passenger ship.

"Let me introduce you to the crew! We're a small operation, but we have big hearts."

They enter the bridge. The large windows offer a broad view of the crowded docks. Three people are there. A man, sitting in a chair up front, at the helm; a woman sitting at a console on the side; and an older man, standing.

"This is Rynn, our pilot. We call him Ghost."

Ghost—a lanky man with brown eyes and long slick hair—rises from his chair and extends his hand. She shakes it. He smiles a thin smile, which doesn't quite reach his eyes. Elena notices he is wearing the same type of overalls as Jaxon. Is that their uniform? He has a tattoo on his neck, the tip of what looks like a wing or a tail disappearing underneath his collar.

"Terek Nassar here is our medic."

Terek, the one standing, is in his late fifties, with salt-and-pepper hair and a full beard. He nods in greeting. He wears a white, wrinkled shirt and comfortable black pants. When he holds out his hand, she notices a few very faint pink stains on his sleeve.

"Call me Doc," he says.

"And Kaela there is our digital specialist."

By *digital specialist* he means hacker. No doubt in her mind now that the Charon isn't on the up and up. Kaela is a petite woman with spiky blue hair and a wiry frame. She swivels her chair to face Elena, doesn't bother standing up.

"Nice to meet you!"

Kaela is wearing a vest with embedded circuitry. Extra wearable compute. Elena remembers this being in fashion about the time she was in the Vanguard program. Some of their digital specialists in training wore these as an affectation. They went out of fashion fast, enough compute around to make them just expensive toys. Kaela must have been a toddler around that time, Elena guesses this is a retro look now.

"I'm Elena Drake," she introduces herself to the group. "Thanks for giving me a ride!"

"Of course," replies Jaxon. "Let me show you to your quarters. It's not luxurious but should be cozy. Unfortunately, most of the volume is for cargo."

Meeting the crew makes her feel at ease. They're genuine, not trying to impress their customer. The mongrel ship, their casual attire and attitudes, none of this looks like a trap she just walked into. Just a bunch of honest smugglers charging her an arm and a leg for a ride to Verdant. She could do worse.

Jaxon walks with her back into the passageway and into the cargo hold half of the ship. The space is large. A flight of stairs descends to its floor, which is lower than the bridge. There's a faint smell of spices in the air. It reminds Elena of exotic flavors, fancy dining.

"What are you carrying?" She doesn't really care to know, just wants to see his reaction.

"Oh, this and that, you know."

A section of the hold is repurposed for crew quarters. White flexi-walls define six small rooms, three on each side. Farther down she sees stacked crates, large barrels, and a couple of large cargo lift drones. The drones are offline, docked and charging. She sees "Abyssal Mining Consortium" on several of the crates. Another one has an unfamiliar, colorful flower-and-leaf logo. Yet another one is covered in graffiti, a drawing of what seems to be a large insect chasing after a group of people. The artwork looks good. Underneath the scene, spray-painted lettering reads, "Remember Echo Point."

Jaxon shows her to a tiny cabin, last small room on the left. Still bigger than the coffin she spent her previous night in, which is perfectly fine for her.

"Here you are. We take off in an hour."

After the initial shock, she realizes Jaxon doesn't look as much alike as Darius as she initially thought. Memory is strange—details fade for better compression, fuzzy pattern-matching. Yes, there's some resemblance, but the overall topology has subtle differences. Details too. Darius had a birthmark on his cheek. Jaxon has some old scars on his chin. Jaxon breaks into a big smile again and she realizes she is staring at him.

"Sorry," she mumbles, "you really remind me of Darius."

"Were you close?" he asks.

"Very."

He leaves her to it, closes the door.

She's only carrying a backpack, so unpacking doesn't take much time. She does it mechanically, routine drilled into her. She thinks. She's glad to leave the ring, get to the asset. She's worried. She translated in thinking she had the upper hand. A fake ID to help her be inconspicuous. But Sector 36 is in a much worse shape than she thought. She didn't even really get to use her fake identity. Except in the short conversation with Ingram, which thoroughly unsettled her. She was being followed, which could mean her cover is blown from the get-go. What did she walk into? How is she going to get out?

One step at a time, she tells herself. *Focus on the mission. Get to Verdant. Retrieve the asset.*

They won't be able to translate out of the sector anytime soon, at least not without help. Once the asset is secured, they need to get to Nova Prime. Her contact at the Obsidian Holdings branch office will provide them with a way out. She gets online, sends him another quick status update. *En route to Verdant to evaluate some acquisitions, see you soon.*

Primitive cryptography, carrying little information in the noise, but that's the best they can do.

In a better situation, she would've picked up the doctor, returned to the ring with him, then translated out on a civilian transport. No way to do that at present, not without help. The mission brief assured her the Spark contact at the branch office could arrange travel. She must rely on him for that. But after witnessing the congestion, she is beginning to have some doubts. How much pull does Spark really have in the sector? There's not much she can do about it now. It's Verdant, then Nova Prime.

She has the next two moves planned out. But there are too many unknowns, too many things that can go wrong to feel comfortable. *Chess is a game of perfect information. I very much prefer poker.* Ingram knows, Ingram knew everything since the moment she translated in. Hell, before that. Who is she trying to fool? She shudders. Not much she can do about it now. Roll with it and see what happens. What a clusterfuck.

She goes back on the bridge at take-off time. The crew is all there, as before. Rynn at the helm, Kaela at her console. The doctor is seated next to Rynn this time, and Jaxon is standing behind them. He turns as she arrives, and she is again struck by the resemblance to Darius. Ghosts. It will take her a while to get used to this.

"... check" she hears from Rynn. She didn't catch the first part. "Warp drive—check." He's going through the pre-flight checklist.

"Pull anchor," says Jaxon.

The *Charon* comes to life, steering engines humming. The ship pushes away slowly, sliding between the anchored ships around it. Once it is clear of its neighbors, it spins one hundred eighty degrees on its axis, so the view of the docks turns upside down, then blasts straight away from the ring's center, accelerating through a clear corridor between the many other vessels milling about.

"Wow." Elena is impressed. "How did you get clearance and a flight path so fast?"

"We have our ways," says Jaxon and winks. "It's even busier than when we arrived a few days ago."

Doc whistles.

The *Charon* zooms by a huge military ship. Its hull is covered with sensor arrays and energy weapon batteries. Elena wonders if it's the *Dauntless*—or has it already left for Eureka Base? Her question is answered once they fly by the heavy cruiser's name marking: *Ares*. Not the *Dauntless* after all. Just how much firepower is Ingram amassing in the sector? To what end?

"See the guns on that ship?" asks Kaela.

"You think the Taurans are coming back?" This from Terek, but they all think it. "What else would you need all this firepower for?"

"I heard Taurans aren't real," says Rynn. "Just a made-up excuse to enact martial law."

Jaxon laughs at that. "Who've you been drinking with on the ring, man?"

"They're absolutely real." Kaela is not amused at all. "Don't even joke about it."

"Sorry," says Rynn.

They fall quiet. Elena is confused by the strange exchange but lets it go.

The *Charon* keeps moving, spins once more as it adjusts bearings towards Verdant. They get one last view of the Gateway Ring, fading into the green tapestry of the Viridian Shroud, a noodle-thin circle from their current vantage point, orbiting a now coin-sized satellite. The ships are too far away to see with the naked eye. Even the imposing *Ares* is no more than a dot. They move out from behind the shadow of the planet around which the ring's moon orbits, into sunlight.

"Going warp," announces Rynn.

"Aye, Ghost," acknowledges Jaxon.

The FTL engines come online. The ship accelerates to relativistic speed, their vista freezing in place.

07: OUSTED

Doctor Linton makes it to Verdant. The trip is long and boring, until he finally arrives. His skimmer slows down as it enters the Demeter System, heads towards the giant green planet.

He looks out the window, takes in the sight. Verdant is a Gaia world, the breadbasket of the sector. It's huge and lush and beautiful. Puffy, artificially seeded clouds ensure the hundreds of thousands of farms covering the surface get enough rain to thrive. The view is a welcome change from the rocky moon of Eureka Base and the dim glow of NS-36-A. He savors every second of it as his skimmer descends through the atmosphere, towards the large port of the capital city. Sylvan Prime is a sprawling metropolis, glass buildings reaching out into the sky. Outside the city, as far as the eye can see, the ground is a patchwork of farms, fields, and orchards in different shades of green and gold. He wonders which one is his destination.

He lands, more than ready to start the next part of his adventure. A part with solid ground under his feet, a real atmosphere, and space to move. Heck, space to run if he wants to. Being cooped up in a skimmer for such a long time really does a number on you.

First order of business: do some minimum covering of tracks. He scuttles the ship, removes the onboard CPU and memory banks, and incinerates them. Erases all ship identifiers. Satisfied that the skimmer can't be traced back to Eureka Base, he steps out of the docks into a sunny morning.

It's eerily quiet, very few people around. Unexpected. Shouldn't this be rush hour? He embeds to catch up on the news, learns that large swathes of the population are leaving the planet and the sector. The brief Tauran War scared them bad. Many left already, many are preparing to leave.

He takes a hover rail, mass transit to maintain anonymity, but doesn't manage to get lost in the crowd—there is no crowd. The car he is in is almost empty, two other people inside. By the time they reach the suburbs, one of them gets off. The rail goes on, past the suburbs, through a satellite town, then out into farmland. He looks out the window, enjoying the scenery, soaking up the sunlight. He notices some farms are abuzz with activity, robot harvesters, farming drones, and people working the fields. Other farms look abandoned, crops wilting, machines offline.

He gets off at Amberfield, a tiny town in the middle of nowhere. The town is a few miles away from his destination, the BioFields farm, property of the Ardens. They are expecting him.

He sends them a brief message, another code word—puts in an order for wheat flour and starplums. This lets the Ardens know he made it to town; they can come and pick him up.

Doctor Linton is looking forward to a hot meal and a comfortable bed. Some company wouldn't hurt either, he only had his grim thoughts for company for far too long. He walks up and down main street, impatient. Like Sylvan Prime, Amberfield is nearly a ghost town. Most stores are closed; most window blinds are shut.

Fortunately, he doesn't have to wait long. A dusty Ridge Rover drives up Main Street, stops in front of him, and a smiling, sunburnt man waves him inside. Doctor Linton gets in. He has never met the Ardens. They're a Spark-arranged connection. He shakes hands with the man.

"Elias Linton," the doctor introduces himself.

"Caleb Arden," the man replies.

Caleb turns the Ridge Rover around and heads back the way he came. On the short drive to his farm, BioFields, Caleb lets the doctor know that they were waiting for him, but they are getting ready to leave the planet soon.

"I have two young ones, you know."

The situation is too scary for their comfort. Rather than risking life and limb, they'll be translating out of the sector.

"You know what happened to Echo Point," Caleb reminds him.

The doctor is about to ask what this means for him, since this was supposed to be his hideout.

Caleb has already thought of this. "You're free to use the house, make yourself comfortable. I'll introduce you to our neighbors, the Blackwoods. They're still around and can keep you company, help out if needed. You won't be staying here too long yourself, right?"

"Right," he replies, though he's not sure when he will be picked up.

BioFields is a medium-sized farm, they grow crops, sell grain, flour, fresh fruit, and wine. The house is big, he notices, as the car pulls into the Ardens's yard. A large dog runs to greet them, wagging its tail.

"This is Rusty," says Caleb, tussling with the dog.

He meets Maren, Caleb's wife, and their two children, Ethan and Lily. He has a late lunch with them. The conversation is awkward, they keep apologizing, keep talking about their travel plans, keep reassuring him.

"How soon are you leaving?" he asks them.

"Tomorrow morning," replies Caleb. "We were just waiting for you to arrive."

He is touched—it seems like he was the reason they're still here. He thanks them profusely, tells them there is no need to apologize, they should do what's best for their family.

After lunch, Caleb walks with him across a field to the nearest house. He introduces him to the Blackwoods. Jake Blackwood is a tall, strong-looking man. Streaks of gray in his black hair. He has temple grafts, something you don't see very often. Probably NSRS, Linton doesn't ask. He meets his wife Emma, their twin sons Logan and Ryan, and their grumpy toddler, Ivy.

"You're always welcome here, Mister Linton," Jake assures him. "In fact, come have dinner with us tomorrow."

Back at BioFields, the Ardens are busy packing, shutting down the operation. He isn't too happy to be left alone in their big house, especially after the lonely skimmer trip he just took, but he is grateful considering the circumstances. That night, he sleeps in a large bed with clean sheets and wakes up refreshed, early enough to catch a beautiful sunrise. He watches raptly as Demeter climbs its way slowly up in the sky, shining over the endless plain.

The Ardens say their goodbyes, take the Ridge Rover, and drive away. Rusty is watching him from the pickup bed. Caleb waves at him through the open window.

The doctor is waiting. All alone now, in the big empty house. He is looking forward to dinner, looking forward to some companionship. After a slow day, he makes his way across the field, towards the Blackwoods.

Dinner is delicious. Afterwards, he and Jake sit on the porch. It's a warm evening, the fields give out a rich aroma, and fireflies are starting their twilight rounds. They make small talk. He learns Jake has some strange theories about a staged alien invasion. Linton could tell him a few facts that would shatter his worldview, but he must stay tight-lipped. He nods, fakes interest, lets Jake talk. Jake hates mega-corps, starts on a tirade against the Abyssal Mining Consortium. Doctor Linton lets him go on, mostly because he craves social interaction. Any social interaction. The skimmer trip took its toll on him. He is too afraid to embed, spend time in the digital, because of the secrets he now carries. He indulges Jake. The man has some very outlandish theories, but outside of that, he is a very nice person. He welcomed him, a stranger, into his home. As long as he doesn't go down some conspiracy rabbit hole, Jake is good company. The doctor tries to gently steer the conversation away from corporate politics.

He walks back to the Ardens's place in the dark, listening to crickets chirping around him. A big bright moon lights his path.

The days pass and Linton is starting to become restless. Waiting makes him feel powerless. He stole a skimmer, ran away from a lab surrounded by the military. He's very likely wanted by now. The longer he stays here, the likelier he's going to be found. Where is his contact? He realizes he doesn't have a Plan B. They were supposed to meet, leave.

Jake announces one evening, during their now customary porch chat, that he'll be taking his family to the Gateway Ring. They'll try to translate out of the sector. They're up to date on the news and the rumors. There are traffic jams, the jump gate is monopolized by the military and corporate paramilitary (*fucking mega-corps!*), people get stranded on the ring. Still, Jake wants to risk it. For a moment, Doctor Linton considers going with them, trying to make his own way out. But that's insane. Rural Verdant is a great place to lie low, unlike the Gateway Ring, where everything is tracked, recorded, analyzed. How can he even book travel out of the sector if he's wanted? He doesn't have a fake ID. He doesn't have contacts there. He needs to stay put, wait for extraction.

A few days later, Jake makes a final run to town while the family finishes packing. Doctor Linton offers to help with anything—he cherishes these last few hours of human company he's likely to have until who knows when. He's observing a couple of hover luggage bags navigate the front porch stairs when he sees Jake coming back in a big hurry, large dust cloud behind his pickup.

"Doctor," he says as soon as he steps out of his vehicle, "there's some people asking around about you."

Doctor Linton feels a void in his stomach. He can't make up his mind whether he should be happy (they're finally coming to pick him up!) or afraid (what if it's not Spark?).

"Who?"

"A bunch of mercenary types. I think they call themselves Eclipse Corps. They're going around town, asking about you. Anyone seen you? Where do you live? Stuff like that. Are you in some kind of trouble, doctor?"

Shit, thinks Doctor Linton, and the uncertainty solidifies into pure dread. Spark doesn't use mercs, they're subtle. That means this isn't his way out, it's way worse. At least if it was the police looking for him, even if caught, he would stand trial, pay for his crimes. But mercs? They would probably disappear him, torture his secrets out of him, and dump him in an acid vat—maybe while still alive. He shakes the thought away.

"What did you tell them?"

"Nothing, of course. Fuck them mercs and their employers! But, doctor, please be careful."

Doctor Linton has no answer to this.

"Those are some very bad people." Jake sighs. "I really wish I could help you somehow. Maybe …" He trails off.

Jake is a good guy; it pains Doctor Linton to see him torn like this. After all, Jake doesn't owe him anything. Still, he is terrified and soon to be alone.

"What?" he asks. "What?"

"There's absolutely no way you can get to the Gateway Ring any time soon. With so many people leaving, it took weeks of waiting in line for us to secure transit."

Doctor Linton knows. He curses himself for scuttling the skimmer —he thought he was smart, covering tracks, but he pretty much scrapped his only ticket out of here.

"I don't think you can go anywhere except …"

"Except what?"

"Forge! Hear me out, doctor. Abyssal Mining …" he spits, as if the name tastes bad. "Abyssal Mining is always looking for workers. Corporate citizenship. If you enlist with them, they'll take you to Forge. They don't give a shit who you are, where you're from, what you did. Sign up for a year-long rotation and you'll be safe." He pauses, then adds, "I can't believe I'm fucking telling you this," and spits again.

Doctor Linton never considered this, but it is an interesting idea. Corporate citizenship means handing his life to Abyssal Mining and a year of hard labor, which he doesn't feel fit for. But it beats torture and an acid vat. If he can somehow leave a message for his contact, pointing them to Forge, they will find him, help him, buy out his contract. It's a bad solution to his problem, but it is a solution.

Doctor Linton says goodbye to the Blackwoods, sees them off, thinks hard about what message to leave. How to tell someone he never met about his new destination while making sure the mercs can't also learn it. He ponders, periodically looking across the fields to see if anyone is coming. After a while, he has an idea.

By the time the black vertibird dives low and the mercs jump out, with tacticals ready, he is off planet.

PART TWO
EXHAUSTIVE SEARCH

08: DESOLATION

Travel to Verdant is uneventful. Elena spends some time with the crew, spends most of her time alone in her quarters. With the crew, she volunteers her cover story—looking for businesses to acquire for Obsidian Holdings.

She learns that Jaxon Barabe is ex-military, like her, though she doesn't tell him about her past serving. He was honorably discharged a while back, before bootstrapping his independent logistics business. In her mind, she puts air-quotes around "independent logistics."

Doctor Terek Nassar used to work big corporate, hated it, is glad to be out of it. The older man has a haunted look about him; she can't begin to guess what he has seen during his corporate days.

Rynn, "Ghost," doesn't volunteer a last name. Doesn't volunteer much at all, preferring to spend his time at the helm, watching the monitors, even though FTL requires no steering.

Kaela—last name Tama, she learns—is the opposite. Excited to have a passenger ("we usually just do cargo"), she is always up for a chat. Elena learns from her that Rynn used to run with some very bad people, until things went south for some unspecified reason.

Kaela explains the strange exchange she and Rynn had when

leaving the Gateway Ring. She used to have a cousin who was living on Echo Point when the Taurans hit it with their strange weapon.

"Joking about Taurans not being real, after what happened, is simply offensive," she tells Elena.

Kaela also elucidates the mystery of their expedite departure.

"The reason we got clearance so fast is that we have an Abyssal Mining C-suite shuttle transponder. I installed it myself!"

What a motormouth, thinks Elena, but she can't help feeling affection for the young woman wearing her heart on her sleeve.

"Shit!" Kaela adds, "don't tell Jaxon I told you that!"

"I won't." Elena smiles.

Kaela continues, embarrassed: "I told you, we usually just do cargo …"

Not very good opsec for a hacker, Elena observes. *She must be better around machines than around people.*

Elena is careful not to divulge anything compromising. She sticks to her cover story. She tells them about her tabby cat, about her favorite foods, about what she saw on the ring. They all comment on the strangeness of the Tauran War and latest developments in the sector. Unlike her, they've been here during the whole thing.

"Since you've all been in-sector during the thick of it," Elena asks them one time when they're all together sharing a meal, "what do you know about Taurans?"

"Not much," replies Terek, "haven't seen one. I think nobody has."

This tracks—pretty much what her brief said and what the popular consensus seems to be. Humanity fought them but never laid eyes on one.

"I heard they're among us, wearing human skins," adds Kaela in a low voice.

"That's nonsense," says Terek.

"Maybe you're a Tauran, Doc," jokes Jaxon, accusing Terek. The older man doesn't appreciate the joke. Jaxon turns his gaze towards Elena.

She smiles. "I'm not a Tauran. But I guess that's exactly what a Tauran wearing my skin would say."

"Kidding aside," says Jaxon, "all I can say is they've been great for business. A lot more things need transport nowadays."

Seeing Jaxon around *Charon*, looking so much like Darius, still stirs memories and feelings inside her. Alone in her quarters, she thinks about the implications of the two following her, and what that means for her mission. There isn't much she can do on the *Charon* while in transit, but she'll most definitely be watching her six once they make planetfall.

The trip is a lot of waiting around, but she's accustomed to it. Being in the military is mostly waiting around. Even at superluminal speeds, it takes a few days to get from the center of the sector to Verdant. Jump gates use different physics—instantaneous point-to-point travel, translating through higher dimensions. But the technology is still too expensive to commoditize, so jump gates are limited to connecting the small network of sectors. Elena suspects the massive construction projects are also earning so much money for OmniCore Solutions and Dominion Nexus that they'd rather not have a cheaper alternative available.

The monotony finally comes to an end as the *Charon* decelerates next to a large, gorgeous green planet. The ship slows down further as it approaches the Gaia world and adjusts course for landing. Elena is on the bridge with the rest of the crew. She watches Verdant, its immense size, its streaks of clouds. It looks somewhat like Aurelia, her home world, but the color tones are off and Verdant is larger.

"I might need a ride to Nova Prime today or tomorrow. Can you stick around?" Elena doesn't want to spend more time in Sector 36 than strictly needed. Pick up the asset, get to Nova Prime, get out.

"Very sorry but we can't." Jaxon sounds genuinely regretful. He might be sorry to disappoint or, more likely, to miss on some extra credits from her seemingly deep pockets. "That cargo we're carrying needs to get to its destination ASAP. We're on a contract and already went out of the way with this stop. If you want, we can swing back in a couple of weeks."

She understands. And she suspects she'll have trouble finding transport, but she needs to try. If nothing is available, she'll have to wait for them.

They work out a deal as *Charon* enters the atmosphere, dives into the clouds. She pays an advance for them to come back and pick her and the asset up if needed. She'll let them know if she finds an alternative way out. They say their goodbyes.

"Take care," says Jaxon as she steps through the airlock, into a breezy evening.

"You too," she answers, raising a hand as she walks away.

By the time she makes her way out of the docks, it's almost nighttime. An inky sky covers Sylvan Prime. The capital city's tall buildings stand dark and quiet. Traffic is minimal, at most a lonely car speeding by on the deserted streets every once in a while. Almost no pedestrians to speak of. Mass transit doesn't run at night, and she missed the last ride of the day. She gets online, tries to find transport outside the city, but comes up empty-handed. Cabs are offline, rental businesses are closed until further notice. Verdant is just as empty and quiet in the digital. Little news, little activity. She gets offline, sighs. *Just when I feel I'm finally making some progress.*

It's getting chilly and she realizes she needs to find lodging for the night, catch a hover rail in the morning. She gets back online to look for a room. Unlike the ring, the options are limitless here. She takes her pick—a roomy suite with a view, very reasonably priced and nearby. She'll spend the night, head out into farmland tomorrow. She walks the silent streets at a brisk pace, mostly to keep herself warm. She could swear she can smell fresh cut grass, but that's impossible from the middle of the city. Farmland is miles away. Must be wishful thinking. She misses home.

She reaches her hotel in no time. It's an imposing fifty-story glass building. The lobby is empty, lights turning on automatically only after she steps through the door. She checks in at a kiosk, nobody to greet her. She takes the elevator up to the forty-seventh floor. The spacious suite looks luxurious: a bedroom with a king size bed, a living room with a couch, an arm chair, and a large table, a bathroom with a tub.

The furniture is, for once, more than utilitarian. Someone put some serious thought into designing the interior, she notices. Everything is color-matched, in shades of pine green, sage, and orange. There's a classic 2D painting hung on one of the walls, a Verdant landscape. She realizes this suite must've gone for some crazy-high rates back in the day. She got it for peanuts, dynamic pricing algorithms defeated by the mass exodus.

She pulls aside the curtains and walks in front of one of the floor-to-ceiling windows, takes a look at the cityscape. The view outside is of mostly blackness, peppered by a handful of lit windows across the street and farther away, and the underglow of the streetlamps. *It's like everyone left*, she thinks. She remembers the people camping out in the streets on the ring. What if Jake, the guy she shared a drink with at the Cosmic Drift, was right? What if the asset is on the ring? This city is not fully deserted, not quite yet, but is dangerously close to it.

It's too quiet and it's making her anxious. She needs to do a little digging, maybe get some reassurance. It will help her sleep better. She gets online, spends a few minutes checking out several random farms. In case someone is snooping on her network traffic, she doesn't want to give any leads. And she is almost certain someone is. She feels anticipation building but knows she needs to be patient. As VP of Acquisitions, she is preparing for a long day of conducting business tomorrow.

She pretends to read through several property records, sometimes following "for sale" details and second opinions from third parties. She's not really paying too much attention, but is nevertheless shocked by the low price tags. She's not a real estate expert, but even she can see how good of a cover story Spark put together for her. If a company was really going to swoop in and buy all this property, they would indeed make a killing. Unless the Taurans return. *Wisdom of the ages, Elena, don't try to time the market.* She shudders.

She takes a deep breath. It's time. She zeroes in on BioFields. The asset should be there. BioFields is not up for sale, but it is temporarily closed. That's strange, though it doesn't necessarily mean anything.

She asks for details, like she did for the other properties. The data stream splits into topics—topography, ecology, stats, history, public business records, customer reviews. This time, she pays attention, tries to sift out some useful intel.

She can't spend disproportionately more time on BioFields than she did on the rest of the farms. If she's being watched, this will stand out to any simple anomaly detection algorithm, never mind an Omega AI.

The farm was operating in the black. She knows just as much about the farming business as she does about real estate, but knows farming is low-margin so being in the black even a little means business is good. Overwhelmingly positive customer reviews, except the latest, which is a low score from someone with the alias "Spark." *What a funny coincidence*, she thinks. Historical records show single ownership by the Ardens, ever since the colony was established. Family business. The farm hasn't been closed for long, they were open just a few weeks ago.

She pauses. That was after they heard from the asset. *How long did it take him to get from Eureka Base to Verdant?* Another, darker thought: *What if he didn't?* The situation on the ground is orders of magnitude worse than anyone back at HQ expected. People are crammed on the ring, stuck. Verdant is desolate. Eureka Base is heavily guarded by military. In-sector travel is next to impossible on some routes. A plausible scenario has Doctor Linton stuck at the research base, with the Ardens waiting for him at BioFields until they decide it's not worth the risk and pack it in. They're probably on the ring, leaving the farm empty. *Shit.*

It's time to move on from BioFields. She switches to a different farm, thinks about what it would take her to get to Eureka Base. Her cover won't work as well there. She would have to come up with a different story as to why Obsidian Holdings is interested in the lab. The security is tighter there too, so her cover might not hold at all. At the very best, it will mean walking a tightrope to retrieve the asset.

After pretending to read through a couple more data streams, she gets offline.

This little bit of research did nothing to ease her mind, quite the opposite. That said, Doctor Linton might yet be hiding at BioFields. She'll go check out the place in person tomorrow.

She should really reach out to Ingram again at some point too. Her briefing was adamant about this, part of staying in character. But she dreads it. *Not tonight,* she tells herself.

It takes her a while to fall asleep. The new possibility of the asset never having left Eureka Base bothers her. The other alternative, more plausible in light of the farm being closed, is he followed the Ardens to the ring. Needle, haystacks. *I really hope you're here, doctor.*

She sleeps, wakes up to the first rays of a golden sunrise. A real day-night cycle for a change, with real, fusion-produced light. She was dreaming. Darius was there. The plot of the dream is already lost, but for once, she knows it wasn't a nightmare. She feels a pang of loss. She showers, takes one final look out the window of her forty-seventh floor room at the meager trickle of morning commute, and heads out.

09: SHOCK FACTOR

She gets online for directions as she steps through the door of the hotel. The hover rail station is a dozen blocks away. The rail will take her all the way to the countryside. She finds a stop just a few miles away from BioFields, in what seems to be a tiny town. Amberfield. She can be there by noon if she leaves the capital fast.

She skipped dinner last night and could use a good breakfast, but she doesn't want to waste any time. She grabs a prepackaged breakfast from a vending machine and eats it while moving. It's a NeoHarvest tasteless wrap allegedly containing all the nutrients one would need. The bright yellow packaging stands in stark contrast with the grayish meal inside. She could do much better on the sector's breadbasket, but she wants to get to BioFields as soon as possible. Too many ways things could go wrong, have already gone wrong: maybe the asset never made it to Verdant; maybe he did, but left for the ring; maybe she is compromised and walking into a trap. She doesn't like the uncertainty. The sooner she gets to the farm and sees the situation on the ground, the better. She thinks about the importance of balanced nutrition as she walks and chews the tasteless breakfast.

It's early morning, the sun is shining as it's starting its trek across a clear sky. There's a warm breeze blowing through the avenue. It's a wide street, with broad sidewalks and multiple lanes, but it's mostly empty. Even at this early hour, when cities usually wake up with swarms of traffic, pedestrians, and drones, she barely sees anyone around. A red car zooms past her as she is finishing her breakfast, too fast for her to catch the make and model. Then nothing for a good minute. Then a blue hovercar, a luxury Lumea by Hoverworks, comes her way from the opposite side. She doesn't care much about cars, but she recognizes the golden crown logo over its shiny grill. The new model does look good.

She turns to watch it go by and notices, out of the corner of her eye, she is being followed again. Same two as on the ring as far as she can tell at a glance. A glimpse of the short blond's beard, the tall one with graying hair. It's them. They're a couple of blocks behind, but hard to miss on the empty sidewalk. She turns back, pretending she didn't see anything. This is really bad. *How did they get here so fast?* Definitely not a couple of muggers. They're after her. With what must be some powerful sponsors backing them, since they tracked her to Verdant so fast and were able to get here as soon as she did.

Old training kicks in. Time to take the initiative. She turns left into a side street, walking slowly, making sure her followers can catch up. The side street is narrow, a one-way, one-lane road and small sidewalks. Windowless nanocrete walls of high-rises on both sides. She keeps going for a block, then takes a right, into an alley. Nobody around, which is exactly what she wants. The alley is empty except for a couple of large garbage pods.

As soon as she clears the corner, she breaks into a sprint. She runs past the pods, takes another right into a side street as she slings her backpack around to pull out her combat gloves. It's been a while since her last direct action, but the adrenaline rush she feels is familiar. She welcomes it as one would an old friend.

Time dilates. She notices detail—the light reflecting off a signpost, the graffiti on the wall ("They are among us"), a puddle on the ground. Back on the avenue now, she turns right again, circling all the way around the block, getting behind her followers. Combat gloves fastened, she activates them.

They come alive, buzzing on her sweating hands. Part of her tacticals package, which she is now very glad she received. She's back on the side street by the time they turn the corner into the alley. She goes full speed now, cushioned shoes making no sound on the sidewalk.

She was physical growing up—wrestling and such—but street fights are dirty. There are no rules, no ref to stop the fight. She knows two against one is not good odds, but the combat gloves and element of surprise give her a comfortable edge. She turns into the alley to see them standing, back to her, likely pondering her disappearance.

They start walking towards the garbage pods. She doesn't hesitate, runs forward, slaps the back of the tall goon's head. Remote deep implant hacking is hard, software fighting software, peeling layers of protection. The gloves do a hardware attack. Nanobots burrow in, bypass security at the physical layer, overload processing units, all in a matter of milliseconds. The guy goes down, eyes rolling, brain shorted, mouth foaming. He'll be out for a good few hours.

The blond one manages to turn around. She uppercuts him in the groin, delivering three hundred volts. He falls to the ground screaming. She slaps his face another three hundred volts then reaches for his holstered gun. She picks it up, shoves it in his mouth, feeling teeth crack.

"Who the fuck are you?"

She can sense the goon soiling himself. She raises the hand not holding the gun, makes a fist. The glove sparkles.

"You better fucking start talking!"

The gun she is holding is unfamiliar—no idea if it's for big game or a bug zapper. Medium-sized frame, comfortable grip, black paint. It has an aim-assist slot, but nothing mounted on it.

He mumbles something incoherent, spits out blood, then suddenly reaches for her graft. Big mistake. She is all instinct at this point. She weaves her head out of the way and in the same instant pulls the trigger, all before her conscious mind even registers any of it. The gun goes off with a loud report. The back of his head explodes, splattering skull, brains, and blond locks of hair all over the pavement. The remaining half of his head bounces up, deepthroating the gun, then falls back with a squelch. The bang echoes in the narrow alley.

She blinks in disgust at the expanding pool of blood and chunks of brain tissue. *Fuck.* The remaining half of his head is staring at her with empty green eyes, red quickly filling the corneas. *Why did you do that, you motherfucker?* There goes being inconspicuous.

She picks his pockets. He's wearing a black shirt, tactical pants, boots. Same as his colleague. She finds nothing but a digicard in his many pockets. She sticks it in her back pocket as she stands up to look around. The alley is empty. Nobody saw what just transpired. But she can't stick around, someone must have heard that gun go off. As empty as the streets are, that blast reverberated for blocks. She looks at the knocked-out goon, then at the gun she is holding. She could probably buy herself some time, but she won't just execute an unconscious person.

She picks a random direction and runs for a block. Stops to dry heave. *Right after breakfast. Fuck.* She continues running for another block. She sticks the gun in her waistband, covers the handle with her shirt. She feels the tip of the barrel moist against her thigh, tries not to think about it. She turns left, slows down to a jog. She checks behind her from time to time but nobody is following. She navigates the alley maze out to a main street, starts walking at her usual pace, catching her breath.

What a mess. She was hoping to get a few answers, knock the guy out. Instead, she blew his brains out. Adrenaline rush is dying down, and she realizes she's heading the wrong direction. Turns back around towards the hover rail, sticking to big streets now, taking a wide path around the back alleys she came out of.

She wonders how soon the police will be after her. Or is the police force also mostly on the Gateway Ring by now? Even if operating with limited personnel, the mess she left in the alley will surely put this on top of their case pile. No witnesses as far as she can tell, but when the older goon wakes up, he can give them an accurate description. That is, if whoever is after her wants to hand this over to the police. Most likely, he'll report back that they've been discovered. Next time, there won't be just two amateurs after her.

What next? Too close to bail now. You know what's next, Vanguard. No way out but through.

She reaches the rail stop half an hour later than planned. Her back-alley stunt and the roundabout path she followed afterwards delayed her quite a bit, but luckily (for a change) she didn't miss the rail. It's running every two hours, and she's there just on time to hurry in before the doors close.

She takes a window seat. Easy to do, since she's alone in the car. At most a dozen people on the whole rail. The rail starts moving, slowly at first, then picking up speed. Empty or almost-empty streets zoom by. She takes a deep breath, slumps into her chair. *Fuck.*

Her mind is racing with implications. Why were they following her? To get to Doctor Linton? Does that mean they don't know where he is and she is leading them to him? That would be bad. Were they just waiting for an opportunity to jump her, meaning they know where the doctor is? That would be worse.

She reaches into her back pocket and takes out the digicard for a closer look. She flicks it around to see both sides. All black, with a red circle on the front. She knows the logo. Eclipse Corps. That makes her feel slightly better. She has killed before. Plenty. But she is not a murderer, this went bad. She will never forget the scene she just enacted, brains exploding onto the pavement at her pull of the trigger. But Eclipse were there during her deployment on Forge. Working for Abyssal Mining. Killing corporate citizens, civilians. She has little sympathy for mercenaries.

She rummages through her backpack, pulls out an interface, connects the digicard, gets online.

Her NSRS makes this type of interaction awkward. Hardware like her digicard-reading interface is developed for embedded interaction. Her lower-bandwidth grafts require custom protocols. Some manufacturers don't implement them at all, some do it as an afterthought. It's usually a struggle to get the data flowing. Not this time. Her interface has decent graft support, but there's no meaningful data to flow through. The content is encrypted beyond her portable compute capabilities. The interface clearly tells her that and, to drive the point home, shows her several columns of indecipherable hieroglyphs.

What about metadata? If she can't get to the content, maybe she can glean some information from there. A name, a location, a timestamp. She instructs the interface to shift focus. No luck. The metadata has been scrubbed clean. As far as the digicard knows, the information has been there since the beginning of time. She gets offline, sighs, puts the digicard back into her pocket.

The only piece of info she got out of it was the logo. Eclipse Corps. It will have to do. She sticks the interface back inside her backpack and stares blankly through the window at the city rolling by.

Sylvan Prime is a large city, tall glass buildings reaching for the sky at its center, with boulevards crisscrossing the downtown area. Sylvan Prime is a ghost town. A ghost metropolis. A car drives by from time to time, the rail passes a lone pedestrian or the rare couple once in a while, but the roads are mostly empty.

The buildings grow shorter as the rail travels through the outskirts of the city. Fewer people around, if that's even possible. Elena feels she is finally starting to grasp just how bad things are in the sector. The Tauran War wasn't just a minor disruption to normal operations. By the looks of it, the world is hanging by a thread. She wonders what it would take for things to return back to normal.

By the time they're in farmland, the rail seems to be the only moving thing on the planet.

10: DOOR KNOCKERS

Elena was leading Task Force Bravo, "Door Knockers." Vanguard. Lieutenant Darius Eze was leading Task Force Charlie, "Brainiacs"—field digital specialists. Task Force Charlie wasn't Vanguard, they were a different elite unit trained in digital warfare. When the deployed military troops started getting brain hacked, they had to react or risk getting decimated. They were well prepared for direct action on the ground but weren't expecting such vicious attacks in the digital. Task Force Charlie got called in.

Forensics found a signature to the brain hacks, attributed them to an enemy digital specialist they nicknamed Joker. The innovative attack used a small flaw in the deep implants to bypass fail-safes and deliver a fatal electric shock to the brain via a poisoned signal. They had to find Joker fast. Rumor spread that Joker wasn't really a person, it was an Omega AI. Corporate. But these were just rumors, Omega AIs had a code of ethics, there were laws against direct use of digital force against humans.

The two task forces ignored the rumors and worked in tandem, drafting plans. They would descend on suspected enemy positions, have Door Knockers secure the perimeter, and Brainiacs secure the digital realm. They were going to take Joker down by any means necessary.

Ground operations on Forge were a delicate business. The population consisted almost exclusively of corporate citizens. Several ongoing legal battles were being fought to determine the bounds within which the military could intervene in such situations. Both Titanforge and Abyssal Mining argued that their contracts gave them sole rights over their citizens. Elena thought they weren't that far from the truth. Mining was a dangerous endeavor, with risks of maiming and death ranging from cave-ins, equipment malfunctions at low depths or too high gravity, to radiation exposure, exotic cancers, and an array of other lifelong illnesses. Struggling with high turnover, unions, and other business-impeding nonsense, the corporate legal departments came up with a novel system inspired by none other than the military. Employees would sign up for a tour of duty, which could be anywhere between a year and a couple of decades, effectively giving up most of their rights to their employer. Guaranteed pay, housing, food, healthcare. Free cancer repair if provably contracted on the job. Generous reenlistment bonuses. Enough people found this acceptable.

To sweeten the deal, mega-corporations had a no-questions-asked policy. Candidates could apply with a criminal record, a fake name, a dark past. One of the advertised perks was legal council to help employees out of their troubles once their tour ended and they resumed their previous lives.

The AI Council argued it was their responsibility to protect the most basic human right to life. The Omega AIs steering Titanforge and Abyssal Mining disagreed. The boards of the two companies, while literally at war, provided a detailed joint breakdown of their employee agreements, arguing it wasn't their problem and pointing to the fine print in their contracts.

The same way employees couldn't be prosecuted for past misdeeds while on site, they couldn't be "rescued" (emphasis on the intentional exaggeration, for the record) from the "evil" (emphasis on the sarcasm, for the record) corporations. The employees volunteered out of regular life to become corporate citizens, and corporate would take care of them (emphasis on the empathic *care*, for the record).

While the court cases dragged on, Elena's job was to hunt Joker. They were waiting for intel to pinpoint their target. The wait was torturous. No matter how many defenses they put up in the digital, every once in a while one of them would fall victim to a brain hack, have their frontal lobe fried remotely. Nothing they could do about it. Elena was safe due to her NSRS, but nobody else was. Morale was low. They were already short-staffed, before even putting boots on the ground.

Finally, word arrived. They had a hive, they had a handful of possible locations. Intel guaranteed they would find Joker in one of them, likely with heavy backup. It was go time.

She jumped off her chair as soon as she got word.

"Let's go get the fucker!"

They were all itching for action. After waiting around and being picked off one by one, they could finally take the fight to the enemy.

Less than an hour later, the Door Knockers and Brainiacs were crammed inside two vertibirds, loaded for bear, dropping two floors per second. Elena could feel blood pulsing in her temples. The tension in the vertibird was palpable. They were very well trained, but this was their first real direct action. Someone made a nervous joke over the racket of the engines. Someone responded with a creaky laugh, trying to sound nonchalant. A bead of sweat traced across her graft, sliding down to plop onto her gun hand. She wondered how many more floors deep they needed to go.

Hives are deep underground complexes, the preferred layout for mining operations. Marginally cheaper to set up than terraforming, way cheaper to operate. Rather than trying to tame a whole planet, you dig a very deep hole. Set up living quarters all around, a few cafeterias, a handful of shops. Big savings on commute too, elevators rather than a sprawling metro system. The mine tunnels branch outwards from the hive, like gnarled roots. And, of course, hexagonal units to optimize in-hive logistics. Units with tiny walkways between them. The center shaft is used to lift up ore and bring down heavy equipment. State of the art engineering.

Sunlight dimmed, then disappeared completely as they dropped deeper into the bowels of the hive. Now it was just artificial lights flashing as they passed each level. And still they kept going. She looked up and around. Everyone seemed to her just as young, inexperienced, and nervous as she was. No amount of sims, regardless of how realistic, prepared them for this. But they all lost friends, they were resolute. And she was their leader. After an endless descent, the vertibirds began to decelerate, then stop.

"Doors need knocking, hooyah!" she yelled while jumping out of the vertibird, hearing her voice crack just a little bit, hating herself for it. Could the others tell? No matter. They all followed. Everyone was nervous before getting on stage. It wasn't about removing the nerves, it was about performing regardless.

"Hooyah!" they replied with one voice.

Nav overlaid directions on top of her field of vision. The units they were looking for were a ways away from the central shaft of the hive, where the vertibirds came in. The walkways were narrow, ceilings low. She started feeling trapped as soon as she stepped off the bird. The industrial smell of chemicals deep in the hive was repulsive. She comforted herself thinking it was just a sweep operation. In and out. She couldn't fathom how people would spend years down here. She was already looking forward to getting back on the *Ironclad*.

They were walking fast, in tactical formations, weapons at low-ready. Civilians scattered to give them room, some retreating inside their units, others running the opposite way.

Left. Right. Left again. Almost there. They didn't encounter any opposition yet, which was good.

She raised her fist up as they reached the first target. Used hand signals to get everyone into position. She counted down with her fingers: three, two, one. Chief Petty Officer Cooper, "Hammer," whose nickname had nothing to do with the big hammer he was carrying that day, knocked the first door off its hinges. They streamed in, tacticals lit up, weapons covering every inch of the small room. Nothing in there. First one was a dud. Nobody home, no electronics inside.

"Move out, move out," she called. They knew they were on the clock. The element of surprise has a very short half-life.

Another quick advance, another round of hand signals, and Cooper blew out a second door. It was her turn to be point on this one. She jumped through the breach first. This time, not a dud. There was someone there. In much less than a second, she turned left, glimpsed chrome, pulled the trigger. Close quarters point went in with the shotgun, standard procedure. The tango's upper half turned instantly into ribbons of flesh, the wall painted dark red. She saw the very top of his scalp, miraculously still in one piece, falling on top of the carnage.

"Tango down!" she called. She was a machine by this point, executing her training. She did what was drilled into her without hesitation.

She winced at another blast coming from the other side of the room. "Tango down!" she heard Cooper say. Then, "Clear! We're clear!"

She turned to look around. Hive units were very small, easy to clear. No hiding places. Their whole team couldn't fit inside a standard one. Two out of the six walls of the unit were now covered in gore, two Eclipse Corps mercenaries, or what was left of them, slumped on the floor. They were both armed.

In the center of the room was a terminal. They must've been guarding it.

"Brainiacs, move in!" she called.

Lieutenant Eze stepped in. He was focused on the terminal, didn't seem to even register the two downed tangos. He embedded, eyes closed, frowning. He was fighting an intense battle in the digital. Maybe with less blood splatter, risking life nevertheless. Another Brainiac stepped in, started picking up equipment for analysis back at the base. The unit was getting crowded. She and Cooper stepped out, making room.

It hit her, as she was walking out through the blown out door, that she'd just shot someone. Her first kill.

. . .

"Digital secure," called Lieutenant Eze.

No Joker here.

"Let's keep moving," she called. Another quick nav across walk-ways, and they were in front of the third unit. They blew out the door on two civilians. Both women, both screaming as Cooper stepped in pointing a shotgun at them.

"Sorry," he said, lowering the weapon, raising his left hand palm up in conciliatory fashion.

"Fucking intel guys," cussed Elena. "Let's keep moving. One more to go."

This wasn't looking promising. One out of three, no prize. What were the odds intel got it right on the fourth one?

They moved fast, got into position around the last door, went through. Elena point again. The room was empty, lights off. Nobody home. They looked for any clues that the target evac'd recently but couldn't find any. *Fucking intel guys.*

"OK, that's a wrap," she called. "Back to the birds."

They didn't encounter any resistance on the way back. This was the first drop, before the fighting intensified. They had the element of surprise, and the two corporate factions were too busy killing each other to intercept them. This time around.

All in all it was a good drop. Less action than they expected, and they didn't come close to hitting Joker, but a victory nevertheless. They took over a node and managed to establish a beachhead in the enemy network thanks to the Brainiacs. They now had a way to hit back in the digital too, just as they did on the ground. The equipment they confis-cated would get them a large amount of useful intel and open up opportunities for future actions. But most importantly, they had no casualties.

The teams celebrated loudly that night. The drop was a first for all of them, and it went well. After being powerless for so long, they needed a win badly. They finally got one. A small win, they never got close to

Joker, but a win was a win. The mess hall aboard the heavy cruiser *Ironclad* turned into a party room, the PA system into a boombox. They all had to blow off some steam. After an intense day, once the adrenaline wore off, life felt exquisite. Chief Petty Officer Cooper stayed true to his moniker, they had to carry him to his quarters. Elena joined in on the fun, drank, laughed.

Images of the tango vaporizing at her hand threatened to creep up, but she was determined to not let them ruin the moment. She promised herself to process those feelings later. Carpe diem.

As the night grew long and the party began to taper off, she followed Lieutenant Eze to his quarters. They were both glowing. They had sex. They fucked. It wasn't lovemaking, nor sleeping together. Not that first time. It was deeply satisfying. It was about life and death that night, not love. It was primal and felt magical and left her sore. It took some time after for her feelings to develop, and by then it was too late.

11: COUNTDOWN

The rail hovers through endless fields of wilted crops where nothing seems to be moving. Elena is acutely aware her clock is running out. She is compromised for sure. After what she just did, she's positive some very bad people will be out for her. She needs to get off planet fast. Fuck the whole thing—she needs to get out of Sector 36 and never come back. *That's what I thought last time I was here*, she remembers.

The vast landscape glides slowly outside. The farms look identical, frozen in time. She sees various types of harvesters and drones scattered around, unmoving, sun glinting off of their sharp angles. It's going to be a hot day, but at least the rail is air-conditioned. She checks the time. ETA to Amberfield: one hour. She is getting restless. If Linton is not there, she has no idea what to do. How long until the police are after her? How long until other Eclipse goons come? She is glad she kept the gun.

Nobody around, the railcar is empty. She takes the gun out of her waistband, examines it. The barrel has "Noctics Mark 2" engraved on it. She's heard of the manufacturer. Noctics specializes in kinetic weapons, pistols and rifles. This is a high-quality piece. Matte black, with a textured handle for better grip. Still smells like it's been used recently. A splotch of dried blood adorns the tip, she'll have to scrub it off. She double-checks the safety, then slides the magazine out, noticing the ambidextrous fast-release. Ten high-caliber rounds in the twelve-round magazine. Plus one in the chamber, and another one in a back alley on Sylvan Prime. Elena hopes she won't have to use it again. She slides the magazine back in and puts the gun back inside her waistband.

She looks out the window again for a bit, then checks the time again (ETA to Amberfield—fifty-three minutes). *Be there, doctor!*

After what seems like forever, the hover rail pulls into her station. Amberfield is a ghost town too. Not even tumbleweeds on the roads. She steps out of the rail, into a sweltering early noon. The pavement feels hot. BioFields is a few miles away, she needs transportation to get there. She's happy to ride, rent, or hitchhike. She gets online to look for something, but can't find anything bigger than a self-serve, street-side scooter. There is no mass transit here. The only rental business in town has closed up shop. And she hasn't seen anyone driving. She has to settle for the scooter.

She hops onto the small motorized vehicle and heads out of town, her grafts projecting a handy map in the digital, overlaid in front of her field of vision. She scoots by empty streets. She gets out of town on what must be its main street, then takes a right on a dirt road. The damn thing is slow, it will take her a while to get to where she is going. *Just my luck,* she thinks. She follows the dirt road through unharvested fields, the smell of decay wafting through the air.

BioFields is up ahead, half a mile out. She needs to make sure she is not walking into an ambush. Way too much time wasted coming here, but she can't rush now. *Slow is smooth, smooth is fast.* As they say.

She pulls to the right side of the road, parks the scooter between tall crops. She's not particularly trying to hide it, just not leave it standing in the middle of the road. She's going on foot from here, through the field. She wants to have the upper hand in case someone is waiting for her.

The unharvested crops are taller than she is, giving her good concealment. For added safety, she takes the chameleon jacket out of her backpack and puts it on. This makes her near invisible at a distance to both human and digital eyes. On the other hand, everything is dry. As light as she is trying to step, every movement she makes is accompanied by snaps and cracks.

She keeps going, drenched in sweat by now. She pauses right before the field ends by a short fence. The farmhouse is up ahead, surrounded by a yard. She'll be out in the open in the yard, no good cover she can see. She stops to listen but there's no sound coming from the house. The only noises she can hear are the chirping and buzzing of insects.

Time to get ready. She puts down her backpack, takes the combat gloves out, and puts them on. She'll leave the backpack here, pick it back up on her way out. She reaches in and takes out another drone. She launches it up in the air and establishes communication.

{Circle the building, pan around.}

It follows her instructions dutifully.

{Video feed established,} the drone tells her, starts streaming.

She pulls out the Noctics as she watches from the drone's point of view the house getting closer. No movement. She runs a segmentation algorithm on the video feed, looking for anything out of place: cameras, booby traps, hidden tangos. Nothing.

The drone glides towards the front porch. She sees the door was kicked in. It is open, barely hanging on one of its hinges, with a large crack next to its handle. *That's a bad sign.*

The drone continues around the building, panning left and right. Everything is dead still.

{Warning: low battery.}

She steers the drone through the cracked door, taking a look inside. No signs of struggle. There's a table with six chairs, a counter which must continue into the kitchen, a bookcase, paintings on the wall— nothing looking out of place. The drone fizzes out of existence as its battery runs out.

. . .

Time to go in. She doesn't want to approach from the front though. The chameleon jacket isn't effective at close range. She decides to stick to the field and go along the fence, until she is on the right side of the house. The field provides noisy cover, but it's better than nothing. She circles around the yard, until the front porch is out of sight. This side of the house has two large windows on the ground floor and a couple smaller ones on the second floor. She will be in the open crossing the yard for anyone who might be watching through one of the windows, but there's not much she can do about it. It's a twenty-yard dash from the field to the side of the house. She takes a deep breath, jumps the short fence, and sprints ahead.

She is in the open, the uncut grass of the yard barely up to her knees, but nothing happens. In a few heartbeats, she crosses the yard and is next to the house, in between the two large windows. She turns around, back to the wall, gun at the ready. There's enough space between the two windows to give her cover, someone looking through wouldn't be able to see her. She is now one with the wall.

She catches her breath, waits for a few seconds. Nothing happens. She ducks, runs underneath one of the windows, back towards the front of the house. She takes the corner gun-first, sweeping the area in front of the busted door. Nobody there.

She steps inside, covering corners with her weapon. It's clear. Besides a couple of door splinters on the floor, the room looks orderly. She pauses to listen. The house is quiet. Still not satisfied, she goes from room to room, moving quickly and efficiently, the Noctics leading the way. A clean kitchen. A walk-in, mostly empty pantry, leading into an empty garage. She backtracks to the dining area. Downstairs bathroom. Living room. Up the stairs to the master bedroom (large, with a private bathroom), kids' bedroom (she can tell by the bright colors and the smaller-sized furniture), guest bedroom (*did you sleep in here, Doctor Linton?*), upstairs bathroom, a small office. All clear.

It takes her a few good minutes, but she is finally satisfied she is indeed alone in the house. She lowers the weapon but doesn't put it away. Better safe than sorry.

She goes back to the guest bedroom. No clues. The closet is empty. No personal belongings left behind as far as she can tell. She goes downstairs, thinking.

What happened here? She tries to come up with a plausible scenario. She doubts it was vandalism, someone kicking in the door and running away. But the inside of the house looks untouched, so it wasn't a burglary either. Someone came in looking for someone. Eclipse Corps? Kicking in the door to find Doctor Linton? Possible. But they didn't tear the place apart.

She pauses, with a sinking feeling in her stomach. They got him. He's a scientist, not a fighter, why was she expecting signs of a scuffle? They pointed a gun at him and he walked out with them. *Shit.*

She looks around the house in desperation. A note on the fridge catches her eye. "Spark was here." Spark. That must've come from the doctor. *Why leave such a note?* It dawns on her.

She gets online, looks up BioFields again, like she did yesterday. Customer reviews. One low score, from Spark. It stood out to her as a weird coincidence when she saw it last night. She reads the review.

"Used to come here all the time, before I had to apply for corporate citizenship —L."

The clever doctor banked on the fact that whoever was after him didn't know he was Spark. Left clues for her to find—a note he was here, a clue to where he went. Signed "L." Linton. Corporate citizenship. He fled to Forge.

To be sure, she checks the date on the review. Posted days after the farm closed. Posted just a couple of weeks ago. She just missed him.

She is forming a new hypothesis: Whoever kicked in the door was canvasing the area. They were going from house to house, left when they didn't find anyone home, covering a lot of ground fast. If they knew the doctor was here, they would've torn the place apart for clues, but they didn't. That's why she was tailed, they couldn't get a lock on him. They didn't know he was Spark.

She's not quite satisfied with this conclusion, but glad there's still hope. Few unanswered questions remain: If they didn't know about

Spark, how did they know to follow her? If she was able to puzzle out the doctor's hints, wouldn't Ingram too? She thinks. Maybe it did, maybe it didn't. She feels like she is missing something, but she has a lead. Forge.

She walks back out into the scorching sun, retraces her steps. Back in the field to retrieve her backpack. It still makes her nervous to walk across the open yard, in sight of all those windows, even though she personally cleared the house. She picks up the pace. The backpack is where she left it. She takes off the jacket and combat gloves and stores them inside. Keeps the gun out as she walks from the field out into the road, then back towards the scooter. Halfway there, she tucks the gun back into her waistband. The scooter is where she left it, half-hidden by the rotting vegetation. A large insect with many legs is crawling around its handle. She swipes it off with the back of her hand, grimacing, then drags the scooter back into the road.

It's a long ride to town, so she has time to consider her next move. Forge. The hives. She doesn't want to go there again. She must. *Of all places, doctor!* But she can see the logic behind it. If they were canvassing the area for him, he had limited options. Corporate citizenship, under the no-questions-asked policy, would buy him some time.

She is parched, she needs water. As luck would have it, she had the forethought to stick a bottle in her backpack before heading out of town. She drinks it all in one go. It's warm. She also needs lunch, and to take a shower and change out of her wet shirt. Amberfield might seem deserted, but somebody must still be living there. She'll make a pit stop. She gets online, finds the Old Saloon, a restaurant that is miraculously still open. She navigates there, surrounded by the same abandoned crops, as the afternoon turns late.

12: BLIND

It's almost evening by the time she reaches town. The scooter is running low on battery but gets her all the way back. She parks it where she picked it up from, then walks to the Old Saloon. She sees a single person on the town's main street, an older woman who gives her a quizzical look. The kind of town where everybody knows everybody. And she's a new face. It reminds her of home. For the old lady, this must now be a depopulated home. Elena wonders how many people are still living inside the buildings lining the main street. She smiles at the woman, nods in greeting, and keeps walking.

The Old Saloon doesn't look old at all from the outside. It's a standard prefab, with clean white paint and large windows. She steps through a synthetic wood double door inside a large dining area, with many tables and booths. It's dead silent. She is the only customer.

The owner is embedded, sitting at a table, mind in the digital. He snaps back to the physical world with a surprised look on his face as she steps through the door. He jumps out of his chair and rushes to greet her. He's middle-aged, with weathered, sun-beaten skin and gray hair.

"Welcome, welcome! Haven't seen you around before." He talks fast.

"Never been here before." She smiles, extends her hand. "Elena."

"Mako. What brings you around these parts?"

"Just passing through."

He seems starved for conversation. She suspects she might be his only customer for the day. Maybe for the week. He walks her to a table, pulls out a chair for her.

"Passing through from where?"

"Long story." She wants to change the subject, doesn't have the energy to lie to the restaurant owner. "Town seems deserted."

"Mostly is. The way business is going, I'm 'bout to pack up soon too."

"And go where?" She is genuinely curious. "I've been on the ring. It's packed. Nobody can translate out." News of the situation must have made its way back here by now.

"I think it's worth trying though." He speaks with certainty. "I heard Taurans kidnapped people at Echo Point. Experimented on them. Some came back with limbs missing, ears chopped off, eyes poked out. The closer to the jump gate I get, the better."

Another crazy rumor. Echo Point was hit from orbit. Nobody came back. Not without limbs, not blind. The Taurans used some unknown weapon, destroyed the city, vaporized everyone.

"Up to you," she says.

"My other option is Forge, but I don't want to go there. That's where my cook went. Last week. 'Work the mines,' he says." He seems appalled by the prospect.

"Why work the mines rather than staying here? Neither planet is any farther away from the Tauran threat." She thinks she knows the answer to this.

"Ingram moved all military ships to protect his precious lab."

She nods. People on Verdant feel abandoned, unsafe.

"And," he adds, "I heard there's a Tauran shipwreck there too."

Also true, according to her intel. The derelict ship is heavily guarded. Nowhere near Verdant, but it is adrift somewhere in the sector, at some secret coordinates.

"He left us butt naked here," Mako continues. "Abyssal at least defends their employees. Still, I don't want no mining job."

He realizes he's been talking for a while, didn't offer her anything.

"My apologies! Here's our menu, let me bring you some water."

He sends her the menu in the digital, she gets online to take a look. The menu seems to have been expansive, but many items are crossed out as unavailable. She's hungry so she doesn't take long to pick. He nods, excuses himself to the kitchen to prepare her food. Mako runs a one-man operation nowadays. For one customer.

While he's prepping dinner, she finds the lavatory. She freshens up using the sink and changes shirts. The cold water feels good after the long hot day. She realizes she is sunburnt. She goes back to her table to find dinner waiting for her. Its steaming aromas make her acutely aware she skipped lunch. Synthetic protein with flavorful herbs and a side of vegetables. Farm-fresh, of course. The countryside has its advantages.

She is two bites into her dish when Mako comes to check in on her.

"Everything looking good?"

"Great, thank you!"

"I usually serve this with fresh-baked bread but I haven't been baking lately. So few customers it only goes to waste."

She nods. "Don't worry about it. It's delicious!" And it is indeed. Hearty. Even with his cook gone, Mako serves her one heck of a meal.

He hovers around for another moment, looks like he wants to start another conversation, and then decides to let her enjoy her meal alone. She is grateful. Mako seems to be a good person. A lonely, desperate, good person. She doesn't want to offend him, but she is not in a chatty mood. Not after the day she just had. He disappears back into the kitchen.

She eats, drinks a lot of water. She is thirsty after being out in the sun for so long. She chews on a round slice of some juicy purple vegetable she never had before and thinks about her next step. She has gone too far to quit now, and she has a lead. But following the asset to Forge is risky. She'll be going in blind. And she is compromised. *No way out but through*, she thinks as she finishes dinner. She checks the time, not too late to catch the last hover rail back to the city. If she hurries.

She thanks Mako for the food, pays for her meal. He looks regretful, probably wishes they could chat more, but she does have to get going.

"If I'm not at the station in ten, I'll be stuck here overnight."

"I understand," he says, with a sorrowful look on his face. "Safe travels!"

"Take care, Mako. I hope things work out for you." She does feel sorry for him, is also pretty sure if he gets to the ring he'll be in a much worse spot than he is here. He'll end up one of the many millions on the streets. But what can she do about it? Plus, there's a rail to catch.

She hurries to the station, crossing the empty main road. Still warm outside, but the evening is a lot more pleasant than the oppressive noon heat. The sun is setting as the rail pulls into the station. She hops on, inside another car with no passengers besides her. She picks a seat, takes one final look at Amberfield as the rail accelerates towards Sylvan Prime. The shadows grow longer as the rail speeds through overgrown fields.

Forge. Doctor Linton is on Forge. She has to go there, get him. She takes the black digicard out of her pocket, looks at it again. Eclipse Corps logo on one side. Encrypted and indecipherable content. Ingram must know something about this. Is it any use to continue following comms protocol? She's unsure. She chews her lip, spins the card around and around in her hand, then decides to go for it. *Fuck it.* She gets online, reaches out to Ingram.

Its featureless face materializes in the digital, Viridian Shroud Nebula background matching the night sky outside.

"Why, hello, Captain!" Sounding very happy to be talking to her again.

"I need some answers from you." She is tired of its bullshit, goes straight to the point.

"Noblesse oblige, Elena. How can I be of service?"

The thing has a way of getting under her skin. She interfaces the digicard she got from the goon's pocket, shows it to Ingram in the digital. In its virtual representation, the card floats between them, larger, hieroglyphs scrolling over its surface.

"What the fuck is this?"

"May I?" Ingram reaches out with digital tendrils. She recoils instinctively, but the tendrils aren't meant for her. It touches the card, then retracts them.

"I decrypted it for you, give it a read."

It took the thing all of an instant to decrypt the digicard. She's pretty sure the tendrils were for dramatic effect, meant to unnerve her. But she is more unnerved by the speed with which it cracked the code her own interface wasn't able to make any sense of.

"Part of it seems to be corrupted though," Ingram continues. "I left the raw data in there. Maybe you'll have better luck." Better luck at recovering the data than an Omega? Is this its idea of a joke?

"You responsible for this?" She keeps pushing, hoping against hope for a straight answer.

"Never seen this digicard before."

That doesn't mean it is not responsible.

"Are you following me?"

"You are all God's children."

What kind of reply is that? Is it calling itself God? Is it telling her it's omniscient?

"I wish you'd stop talking in riddles for once."

"I will, when you come to Echo Point."

Is this some kind of threat? Echo Point was destroyed during the Tauran War. Is it threatening to destroy her too?

It continues, switching topics, not giving her time for a comeback. "How's business going?"

Her cover story. What a farce.

"Not good. I think I'll try something different."

"Market tip for you, Vice President. Forge is not good business either."

She freezes. The fucker knows everything. She is sure of it.

Suddenly, this whole conversation seems to be a bad idea. A very bad idea. She needs to put an end to it.

"Duty calls," she says, ready to disconnect.

"Alas, free will," he concludes. "Be careful, Captain!" Ingram says as farewell.

She gets offline, closes her eyes, lowers her face into her hands. It takes her a minute to regroup. *Market tip for you. Fuck.*

At least the thing claimed to have decrypted the digicard. She interfaces it again, looks at Ingram's handiwork. The hieroglyphs are gone, replaced by data she can navigate. *Eclipse Corps. Mission brief: tail Elena Drake, VP of Acquisitions, Obsidian Holdings. Report back.* Pictures of her, 2D and 3D. Her real military past, her fake corporate present. Other bits of trivia. Quite a lot of it. Someone (or something?) put some effort into assembling this. She skims through the documents, impressed by the level of detail. But this doesn't tell her much. No explanation of why they're after her. No mention of Spark either, at least not in the reams of data she sifts through. Next to them sits a blob of gibberish—the corrupted part Ingram couldn't decrypt and left raw for her. Maybe the key to why they're after her is there, and she is just unlucky. Or maybe Ingram tactically failed to decrypt that part. Either way, besides clear confirmation that she is targeted, there are no insights on the digicard.

Eclipse Corps is after her. Contracted by who? Last she faced them, it was Abyssal Mining. And she's planning to go to Forge, which the company owns. Is this a smart move? Probably not. Is there an alternative? She should bail. She should ask for backup. But the clock is ticking for poor Doctor Linton. She needs to act fast.

She puts the digicard back into her pocket and looks at her own reflection in the window. Outside is pitch-dark, no light illuminating the deserted fields and farms. The rail makes its way towards the capital. Fast, but seems to take forever. She has time to formulate a plan. She needs to send a few messages, prepare for her trip to Forge. She is tired of running around. *You'd better be there, doctor.* She yawns. It's been a long day. She considers lying down across a couple of seats, take a nap for the rest of the way. The chairs are soft, comfortable, designed for long-distance travelers. Their blue covers look clean and inviting. *No time for sleep,* she chides herself. Her mind promptly rephrases that: *I'll sleep when I'm dead.*

13: CROCODILE BIRD

She needs to get to Forge as fast as possible, tonight preferably. The *Charon* would be ideal, she liked the crew, they got her to Verdant quickly, with no questions asked. But the *Charon* is on its errand now and she can't afford to wait until that's done. She gets online to see what other options she has. Outside, darkness zooms by at high speed. A faint glow appears on the horizon as the rail approaches the Sylvan Prime metro area.

Elena looks up outbound passenger transports, but no ships are going to Forge. The only ships leaving Verdant are going to the ring, and they are booked and packed for the foreseeable future. But Doctor Linton made it to Forge. Mako's cook got there. There are ships headed there, just not public transit. These would be corporate, bringing in new employees. She is looking in the wrong place. She switches tracks, searches for corporate citizenship applications.

Abyssal Mining Consortium pops up instantly, with an immersive brochure detailing all the benefits of citizenship, testimonials of families enjoying life in the hives, virtual 3D tours, and more. Picture perfect. It brings back memories of the cramped walkways, the artificial lighting, the claustrophobia, the innocent casualties.

Leaving Verdant is the reason most people here enroll, and of course corporate recruiting is very much aware of this. One of the first advertised perks is *ships leaving daily, twice a day*.

The rail enters the outskirts of a Sylvan Prime suburb. Pale street lighting makes the darkness outside recede. The rural scenery is replaced by perpendicular roads and townhouses. Motionless as usual. She is tired, finds the orderly patterns of the grid town hypnotic. She realizes her eyes are closing and forces herself back to full attention. Back online.

Plenty of ships going to Forge, she can surely hitch a ride. And she won't even have to enroll. She can finally put her fake ID to good use. She connects to the Obsidian Holdings network and reaches out from there with proper corporate credentials. Elena Drake, VP of Acquisitions, on behalf of Obsidian Holdings, looking for investment opportunities on Forge. Is Abyssal Mining Consortium looking for partnerships? She wants to talk to someone high enough up the chain. Of course, Omega AIs ultimately decide and veto all major moves like this. But in the name of tradition, or maybe to let the silly humans think they still have some say in things, meetings between execs are still customary. A ritual. Someone with a fancy title will have to meet with her.

She puts out the request and calendaring systems negotiate some optimal packing of time blocks. Proposals fly back and forth. Priorities are evaluated. Dates and hours are set. It takes much less than a second, the miracle of quantum entanglement keeping the distant worlds of the sector in sync. Information-wise at least. Matter still needs to take the long FTL route.

She has a meeting on Forge with Mira Caldwell, VP of Strategic Opportunities, in two weeks. Just enough time to get to Forge. She lets the Abyssal Mining systems know she'll need transport to Forge.

· · ·

The rail stops at a station, surprising her. She thought she was the only passenger, but someone is getting on or off here. She waits. Nobody gets into her car. After a while, the rail starts again.

She gets back to business, hits up the Sylvan Prime docks looking for Abyssal Mining ships. The logs say the *Elysian Dream* is leaving before dawn. The *Paradise Ascendant* takes off at noon. She can make the first departure. She reaches out to *Elysian Dream*, identifies herself as VP of Acquisitions, Obsidian Holdings. She is in urgent need of transport for an important business meeting—she forwards them the details of her meeting with the Abyssal VP of Strategic Opportunities. This will surely impress the captain and get her a seat on the ship. As expected, her spot is confirmed right away.

She has a solid reason to get to Forge now, and the means to do so. She'll be there on business, on official record. She hopes this will protect her somewhat from Eclipse Corps and whoever else might be after her. She really hopes so.

This is crazy. She wants to swoop into the monster's maw, pluck Doctor Linton out, and carry him to safety. She wants to do this behind a compromised fake ID. She should just go home. But there's nobody else, the doctor is on the run, and the stakes are high. She was never a quitter.

Before heading off to Forge, she needs to handle a few more details. First, her way out. She leaves a message for *Charon*. Change of plans. Pickup from Forge rather than Verdant. Same time, bonus pay. She already paid an advance to retain their services, and they shouldn't care where they'll be picking her up from. That's her way out. *Might need to wait around for me for a bit*, she adds at the end. No idea how long it will take her. She hopes she can find the doctor in the Abyssal systems quickly. As Doctor Linton, or Spark, or L. Or some other breadcrumb. He's smart enough not to completely disappear in a population of two hundred fifty million.

· · ·

The buildings grow taller and the roads wider as the rail gets deeper into the city. Now she can see a car every once in a while, speeding on the deserted streets. She'll get off at the docks, head straight to the *Elysian Dream*.

Before going offline, she also leaves a message for her contact at the branch office on Nova Prime. Sitrep update. Has to let him know she'll be going to Forge, she couldn't find the doctor here. *Business is not good on Verdant. I'll be going to Forge. I have an idea. We'll catch up later.* Code words again. "I have an idea" indicates urgency. She really hopes the way out of Sector 36 is ready by the time she makes it to Nova Prime with the asset. Then she realizes what she just said. "Business is not good on Verdant." Remembers her earlier conversation with Ingram. *Forge is not good business either.* Exhaustion makes her thoughts muddled. She gets offline, stretches. Almost done. Wrap things up and rest once she is off planet.

One final message left to send. For Lieutenant Marcus Wade. The heavy cruiser *Dauntless*. *If you make it back before me, tell my family I love them.* He'll understand. They're not close, but they're both Vanguard. She trusts him implicitly.

The rail stops again and she wakes up startled, unsure where she is for a moment. She must've dozed off after all. How long was she out? The docks are the next stop, fifteen minutes out. She forces herself to stay awake, reviews the plan to keep her mind busy. Get to Forge on the *Elysian Dream*. Bail on the meeting and find the asset instead. Get out aboard the *Charon*, head to Nova Prime, then translate out of the sector.

She steps off the rail into a pleasantly chilly night. The docks are brightly lit, ships of various sizes at anchor. She pulls up nav to find her way to the *Elysian Dream*. Directions appear in her field of vision. It's a short walk, which she enjoys after the hours spent sitting on the train. The colder air makes her feel the sunburn as warmth on her face, neck, and arms. She notices a small troop transport among the docked ships. It stands out to her, as all other ships are clearly freight or people transport. This one is not, it's obviously not civilian. Inky black paint, not the standard paint job you would see on a military ship. Eclipse Corps? Is this how the goons trailing her got here? She walks past it at a brisk pace, the *Elysian Dream* awaits.

Nav guides her to a pier where a short line of people has formed. The ship is still a few hours away from takeoff, but people want to make sure they get off Verdant. Lines were probably bigger in the past, not that many people left on the planet by now. Still, she hasn't seen so many souls in one place since she got here. She could probably skip the line, use her corporate credentials, but she decides against it. Somehow, out of the whole charade, this seems most disingenuous to her. She goes at the back of the line, waits her turn. It doesn't take long.

While waiting, she is surprised to see the *Elysian Dream* doesn't have any windows, any portholes. Freight ships, moving cargo around, don't need them. They make due with some big clear glass around the bridge and maybe some smaller portholes around the crew quarters. Transit ships usually have a lot more. Elena knows it's not strictly necessary—not much to look at during FTL, and while subluminal, your surroundings can always be presented to you in the digital, with better-than-real-life resolution. Much like VP-to-VP in-person meetings, it is traditional. The *Elysian Dream* doesn't honor that tradition. She can't even tell where the bridge is on the ship, it's all matte surfaces. She looks around and sees the *Paradise Ascendant* docked next to it, exact same chassis, exact same absence of windows.

The deckhand who checks her ID looks tired and not particularly enthusiastic about his assignment.

"Cryo pods that way." He points.

"Excuse me?" Cryo sleep is used nowadays only for deep space exploration, where no jump gates are available. It's risky and painful. In-sector travel is fast enough not to require it. It's a matter of days from Verdant to Forge at full burn.

The deckhand is unfazed, he must've seen this reaction a million times. "Check your contract," he says, without even looking at her.

"I don't have a contract, I'm on a business trip."

This gives him pause. He finally looks at her, then embeds. His eyes glaze over. He frowns, comes back.

"I see. I'm sorry, Miss Vice President. Abyssal Mining freezes inbound employees. It's standard procedure."

He still doesn't seem to get it.

"I'm not an employee. I work for Obsidian Holdings." Keeping it professional, but she's tired and ready to snap.

He nods. Tries again. "Abyssal Mining freezes inbound employees as a cost cutting measure. The *Elysian Dream* doesn't have life support."

She gets it now. Feeding and housing a shipful of people for a few days can get expensive. Coldness is cheap in deep space. *Greedy motherfuckers.*

"No way around it?"

"Afraid not."

Impressive.

"What about the crew?"

"We all go under. It's autopilot and beacons as soon as we climb out the gravity well."

She nods. She either goes under or scraps the plan, waits until the *Charon* comes by. She can't afford wasting time. In for a penny, in for a pound.

"I guess I'm going that way."

The deckhand nods, greets the next person in line as soon as she gets going. A few steps out, she overhears him saying, "Cryo pods that way."

She steps inside the ship. It's a large cargo space, with rows and rows of pods. Some are active, some are open, waiting for occupants. Naked people are walking around. She goes to the dressing room, finds her assigned cubby. She puts her backpack inside. Her combat gloves are in the backpack and so is the gun she commandeered. The digicard is still in her pocket. She is careful it stays there as she undresses, folds her clothes, puts them next to the backpack.

She walks back out into the cargo area, naked, goes to find her assigned pod. The awkwardness of the situation makes people keep quiet. Everyone is determined to find their spot as fast as possible, ignoring their surroundings. She finds hers easily, steps inside, and is asleep before the cryo systems engage.

They say you don't dream while in cryo. You can't dream. She believes them. She also believes she is dreaming. She's watching a slow motion replay of the blond guy's head exploding, can swear she feels the texture on the grip of the Noctics, the charge in her combat gloves. She hears Ingram saying, "You are all God's children." She runs through a maze of back alleys, disoriented, unable to find a way out.

The *Elysian Dream* is making fast progress towards its destination.

14: TERMINUS

D octor Linton makes it to Forge in no time, subjectively. He only learns about the mandatory cryo sleep after his contract is signed, once he is in line to board the *Tranquility's Path*. He doesn't really have an option. He mutters as he undresses, walks self-consciously to his pod, gets in, wakes up confused, feeling a million needles pricking his skin.

"Welcome to your new home," the PA system announces as he is shuffling towards the dressing room among a large group of moaning people. He puts his clothes back on, follows the other clothed people. He stands in a line, then in another line. Then he steps inside a large cylinder with a group of other people and only once in motion he realizes they're in a space elevator. Unlike Verdant, Eureka Base, or most other places he's been to, on Forge ships don't land on the planet's surface. They dock in orbit, connected to the planet by elevator systems.

The view from the elevator going down reminds him of a neuron, with dendrites reaching out. He is surprised by how many ships are in orbit around Forge. Many more than around Eureka Base, and he thought that was a lot. The elevator is fast, he doesn't have a lot of time to take in the view. Soon, it sinks underground and keeps diving, levels zooming by too fast to make out.

He stands in another line after exiting the elevator, signs some documents, goes in yet another line. This one is some sort of customs, or security checkpoint. He only brought a change of clothes, so it doesn't take long to clear him.

Finally, they give him directions to his unit and how to get from there to new employee orientation. He exits the checkpoint and steps onto a crowded walkway. His first impression is that of an anthill, uncountable workers milling every which way. Eureka Base felt small and cramped once he learned his secret. Forge is on a whole different level of claustrophobic. The artificial air smells weird, especially after breathing the fresh air of lush Verdant. It has hints of metal, sweat, mold, and other things he can't quite identify. He steps next to the railing and looks up from the hive's central column. He is too deep inside to see the sky. He looks down. He cannot see the bottom, just endless hive layers going down. He recoils, catches his breath. He follows the directions to his unit, wiping the sweat from his forehead.

Abyssal Mining is honoring their part of the contract. He has a place to sleep—a tiny one, but a place nonetheless. The hexagonal unit has enough room for him to lie down, pace around. Even has a mattress. He can rent more furniture if he wants, deduct it from his paycheck.

He has time until the next new employee orientation starts, so he goes looking for food. Again, the brochure wasn't lying—there is food. Little variety, with mediocre quality, but he eats. Vitamin D supplements are free.

After, he navigates to new employee orientation. He sits through a presentation that is needlessly long and boringly repetitive. All the way through, he is wondering where his contact is, worries he might be forced to actually fulfill his contract. If nobody comes, he has no choice but to work the mines. And the weight of his secret is already unbearable. How can he do this for a whole year? Maybe even more than a year? No, someone will pick him up. Soon. They must! Were the clues he left at BioFields and in the digital enough? From the bottom of his heart he hopes they were. He also hopes they were not too obvious, that the right people puzzle things out before the wrong people do.

The presentation drags on. It covers various procedures, protocols, motions. The mines are dangerous. His scientific mind keeps coming up with better ways of implementing things, safer approaches, smarter machinery. There's needless risk in what he's learning. It slowly dawns on him it's all economics down here. While human life is allegedly priceless, the corporate Omegas have an accurate number assigned to it, plugged into the equation. Operating expenses. Costs of goods sold. Maybe it's not worth upgrading the hardware. Maybe it's not worth tweaking the protocol.

He goes back to his unit, disheartened, and sleeps until the PA system wakes him up for his shift.

He makes it to his assigned shaft, meets the crew. He is the oldest of them, and not particularly apt at the kind of physical labor required, but they're nice to him. They start calling him "Gramps," which he doesn't particularly enjoy, but they do offer to help him.

"Here, Gramps, let me take these, you work the machine instead."

He's still surprised at the kind of work they're doing. How come machines aren't handling this type of dangerous labor? He's clumsy. He won't do well here.

He talks to his crew members, gets to know them better over breaks and while doing mindless work. A couple of them came straight from Verdant, for protection. From different parts of the Gaia world, but very similar stories. Sector security, provided by the AI Council through the military, doesn't seem to care about Verdant, just their precious lab at Eureka Base. They'd rather trust the corporate para-military around Forge to protect them.

"Did you see how much firepower they have in orbit here?" asks one of them. They all saw the fleet on their way down to the hives.

Another crew member came from the Gateway Ring. He was planning to translate out of sector but ran out of credits. His only option was to apply for corporate citizenship, come here.

Their foreman doesn't share how and why he got here. Rumor has it he took advantage of the no-questions-asked policy, did some very shady things before that. Nobody knows for sure. Doctor Linton himself is sparse on details—he tells them he came from Verdant, tells them something about a farm, but doesn't tell them much else. They don't pry. It's an unwritten rule in the hive.

"At least we're safe here," the foreman says. "Safest place in the sector." They all nod. Doctor Linton nods too, but he doesn't feel safe. Not at all.

The following days blend into each other. He works, he rests, works some more. Without sunlight, the passage of time is marked only by precision clocks and PA systems announcing the start and end of his shifts. He hopes and waits and works some more.

The no-questions-asked policy Abyssal Mining advertises is real enough—it takes them over a week to realize he is here. Even vital information moves at a snail's pace through the bureaucracy. It finds its way eventually. By the time they pick him up, he thinks he's in the clear. He got into a daily routine and performs it while he waits for someone to come rescue him. He's at the end of a shift, tired, lying down in his spartan unit when its door lock gets overridden. The door swings open and two burly, black-clad men and a thin blonde woman step inside.

"Excuse me?" he manages, but they don't bother introducing themselves. The men step to each side of his mattress and lift him up by the arms. He doesn't have the strength to fight back. He wets his pants as they drag him out of his unit.

The woman goes first, then the two men and the doctor, feet dragging on the walkway. People hug the walls, let them pass by. They get him onto an elevator. He is terrified, mumbles incoherently. The woman looks at him disgustedly. The men holding him don't even bother, they stare forward as the elevator descends to the lowest levels of the hive.

From the elevator, they go inside a unit with no furniture except a chair and a table. They strap him in the chair. There's a pair of cuffs on the table.

"VoidTech enhanced interrogation cuffs," the woman tells him.

She nods at one of the men, who picks them up and slaps them onto his wrists.

"Let me give you a walkthrough," she says.

The nanotendrils burrow into his skin, connect with his nervous system.

"Without laying a finger on you, we can simulate all sorts of unpleasantries. Pulling fingernails ..."

Doctor Linton screams, he watches his hands, untouched, but feels excruciating pain as his fingernails seem to be pried out of their roots.

"... or finger hammering ..." the woman continues, and he feels bones crushing in his right index finger, then his middle finger, then his left ring finger. He screams with each virtual hit, cries, feels the world going dark.

"... and the beauty of it is we can go on indefinitely."

He is jolted fully aware by the feeling of a hot iron being pressed against his right palm. His hands are, miraculously, in one piece.

"Now tell me everything you know, doctor."

He is not a hero, he spills his guts out, tells her everything he knows, everything he learned while snooping. The only thing he keeps concealed is his original exit plan. He doesn't want to compromise whoever was coming to pick him up.

He feels like a failure. He's sitting in his own filth, sobbing. He wishes he was a master spy, trained to withstand interrogation. He remembers stories he read, wishes he had a cyanide capsule. Wishes, *Oh my God*, for this to end. Agony brings him back in the moment.

"I trust you, you know," the woman says, "but I need to make sure."

He keeps screaming as his fingers are crushed, his palms are impaled, his skin is burnt, then peeled.

"The hands have a surprising amount of nerve wiring, don't they?" the woman remarks.

He struggles against his restraints. He answers all questions truthfully. The implications don't matter anymore; he just wants a break.

"I don't like to see you suffer, doctor. I'm a professional," she says. "I just need to make sure."

The pain continues. After a while, his screams turn into whimpers.

"You're keeping something from us," she says, with a regretful look on her face.

He keeps talking. World-shattering knowledge spilled out, he tells them about Spark. He is shaking. His mind is racing miles a minute, trying to figure out how to avoid more abuse, but finds no answer. Intense pain focuses him.

"Talk!"

"Code words! I had one code word to request extraction." He tells her everything he knows. Deep down, he is happy he doesn't know that much. He doesn't know who was supposed to pick him up. He knows little about Spark. It takes a while to convince her of this. He hates himself for not knowing—that information might make the pain stop. He cries.

Eventually he is done. He has no more to tell. He tries making things up just to get a break, but they hooked monitors up to him. They can easily tell when he is not truthful, though they can't seem to tell when he is withholding information. He is in a terrible conundrum. If he doesn't answer, he receives pain. If he makes something up, he receives pain. He begs, sobs, talks, screams, bargains, talks some more, weeps, rational mind slowly giving way.

He is an empty husk by the time they're done with him. The woman insists she is a professional, she inflicts only the minimum necessary amount of pain to extract data, to ensure nothing is kept hidden. It takes a while to convince her there's nothing left, but eventually she is convinced. She nods to one of the men who dragged him here. The man steps behind him and zaps him with a microwave gun, turning his brain to mush. Doctor Linton doesn't see the gun, doesn't even consciously register its effect, but by now he would've welcomed it.

He slumps down in his interrogation chair. The cuffs automatically click back to neutral position and slide off his clenched arms. The woman leaves. The two men unstrap him, bag him up. They carry him out of the room, onto another elevator, then up a few levels to the hive's life support systems. They dispose of his body in a recycler, erasing all traces. Doctor Linton ceases to exist. So does his secret.

PART THREE
SCAR TISSUE

15: DOWNWARDS

Elena and the new employees thaw from cryosleep. It's cold and painful. It takes them a good while to feel human again. The *Elysian Dream* completed its autonomous journey across the sector, brought them to Forge. They lumber to the dressing room, shaking and shivering and grunting. Elena locates her cubby, gets dressed, and sticks her hand inside her backpack to double-check everything is still there, without opening it up for others to see. She feels the unmistakable texture of the combat gloves and the cold metal of the Noctics's barrel. Satisfied, she retracts her hand and slings the backpack over her shoulder. A line is forming as people are exiting the ship. She follows the crowd, steps onto a gangway connecting the *Elysian Dream* to a large structure many thousands of miles above the planet.

As a mining hive world, with the amount of ore being freighted off planet, the optimal layout includes space elevators. The gangway has portholes, unlike the ship, through which she can take in the view from high orbit. It's a view she's seen before and was hoping never to have to see again. Forge looks like a medieval mace, spikes protruding out of the multitude of hives, extending beyond the Kármán line.

What surprises her is how crowded the airspace is. On par with the

Gateway Ring, uncountable ships are suspended in orbit around the planet. These are private military vessels—Abyssal Mining Consortium security. They seem to be packing a lot of heat. At least as much as the military forces Ingram is amassing in the sector, if not more. And they seem to have better tech. The silhouettes of the ships look unfamiliar and menacing to her.

"I heard there's a huge Tauran armada coming," she overhears someone ahead of her.

"Abyssal will protect us. Just look outside," comes the reply.

She can see why people fleeing Verdant would feel safer here.

A huge Tauran armada? According to her intel, there's no armada coming. But her intel is weeks old by now and looks like it was bad from the jump. How much can she still trust it? Forge does look a lot more prepared for war than Verdant did. She gives them the benefit of the doubt. The sense of security is the main selling point for joining the corporate mission in these uncertain times. The corporate mission, broadcast by a PA system at regular intervals: "Unlocking the potential of the universe, together."

She crosses the gangway into a large elevator, which doesn't seem to have been built for human passengers, rather retrofitted with an air recycler, minimal heating, and, she hopes, radiation shielding. The floor and walls are cold, bare metal, zero expense for creature comforts. Small round windows, high up, allow her a glimpse at the green night sky. The new employees stand, packed together closer and closer as more people make their way inside. It takes some time for the elevator to fill up. She finally starts feeling like herself, the aftereffects of cryosleep slowly fading away. She is no longer shivering, more due to the combined body heat of the elevator crowd than to the elevator's heating system.

Finally, they start moving. The elevator dives down, its high-speed descent pulling at her insides. She has a flashback: vertibirds descending at similar speeds, carrying a squad of young Vanguards. How many KIAs? Why was she the one to make it out? Why is she back here?

They glide past the ground level and keep going. And going. The hive is deep.

Deceleration is abrupt. Someone swears. One of her fellow elevator riders bumps into her and she struggles to keep her balance.

"Sorry," he says as the doors slide open.

They step out, in a long procession, into the dim light and narrow walkways of the hive. In stark contrast with their surroundings, a large poster on the wall ahead shows, in bright colors, a group of smiling miners underneath the Abyssal mission statement printed in all caps. The background of the image is some idealized canyon operation with a clear blue sky and puffy clouds above. In better circumstances, Elena would laugh at the dissonance.

Underneath the poster, a bored-looking young woman wearing a shirt with a large Abyssal logo on it directs everyone towards new employee orientation.

"Go left," she repeats, "go left. New employee orientation. Go left."

Elena is here on business, so she steps up to the woman and flashes her ID.

"I'm not a new employee; I'm representing Obsidian Holdings."

The young woman's eyes unfocus as she embeds, confirms Elena's claim.

"Indeed, ma'am. Turn right, please."

She gets out of the line and is finally on her own. She walks a few steps, putting distance between herself and the crowd, hoping the feeling of being boxed in goes away. It doesn't. The artificial light is not bright enough and sunlight doesn't make it this deep. The spartan walls are too close together. Some walkways get so narrow she has to turn sideways to let people coming her way squeeze by.

She was here before, she remembers knocking down doors, blood. There's a background murmur permeating every surface. The air she breathes has an off aftertaste. She walks aimlessly for a few minutes, without bothering to pull up nav, just trying to steady herself. She was here before, but she wasn't alone back then. And back then, they didn't know what was waiting for them. At least not at the beginning.

It's cramped, more cramped than she ever felt. The Gateway Ring coffin was spacious in contrast. She realizes she is heaving, takes a few deep breaths. *Steady now, Vanguard,* she chides herself. Get online, find the asset. She has an exec meeting on the calendar she is not planning to attend. She needs to be out of this hellhole before that. *Tick tock.*

She wants to find a somewhat more comfortable spot before getting online but gives up on it. The maze of walkways extends every which way, and the walls are too tight everywhere. The oppressive feeling doesn't go away, and she doesn't get used to it either. God, she needs to get out of here. She flinches at a unit door opening behind her. A middle-aged man with sunken eyes walks out of it, mumbles an "excuse me" as he squeezes past her. There's no good spot to find on the walkways. She gives up, gets online.

First thing first: confirm extraction. The *Charon* should be in orbit by now. She checks her messages to confirm. Indeed, Jaxon and crew have arrived a day before the *Elysian Dream. Ready when you are, just give us the word,* reads the end of the message. This makes her feel slightly better. There is a way out.

She needs to establish a base of operations. Somewhere to drop her backpack, a place where she can get online and focus on her search without disrupting the flow of pedestrian traffic, a hideout to move the doctor to before extraction. She connects to the Abyssal Mining network. The network is vast.

One saving grace—Ingram is less likely to be listening in on her here. Corporate networks are not under its jurisdiction. It manages the sector's infrastructure, but corporations have their own Omega leadership, which wouldn't take kindly to its interference.

She zooms in on the hive, finds the nearest rental unit, gets its address in hexagonal efficient coordinate system. Same level, close by. She navigates to the unit using a map of the hive, her graft plotting a path on the hex grid. It's a short walk. She loathes every step of it.

She opens the nondescript door, one in a long row of identical doors, vividly recalling a similar door being kicked in, point man going through with the shotgun. The room is small, unfurnished except a mattress on the floor. That's fine by her; she won't be spending too much time here. The walls are bare too, and the lighting has a yellow tint to it. She tries to imagine having to live here, shudders. It doesn't matter. She drops off her backpack, takes out the combat gloves, and puts them in her pocket. The gun she moves from the backpack into her waistband. Then she is online again.

Back inside the Abyssal Mining network, she looks for personnel records, the hive's address book. She doesn't have the luxury to be subtle now, it's all or nothing. Her meeting is due soon, and any semblance of stealth will be blown away once she stands Mira Caldwell, VP of Strategic Opportunities, up. She searches "Doctor Linton." No hit. *Can't be that easy, can it?* She tries "Spark," how he signed the BioFarms review back on Verdant—a hint for someone in the know. No hit. *Shit.* She tries "L," the signature he left at the end of his review. Jackpot!

Finally, a lucky break. She was bracing herself for this last search coming up empty too, brainstorming other ways to find him, but there he is. And it must be him.

"Used to come here all the time, before I had to apply for corporate citizenship —L." And here is L, in the same hive even! She has the coordinates to his unit sixty-five levels lower. So close—time to get him and get out.

She needs to get to an elevator that will take her deeper. She leaves her backpack in the room and steps outside. She looks left, then right, then left again, realizing she is utterly lost. Which way did she come in? Uncharacteristic given her training, but she feels acutely out of her element here. The narrow walls weigh heavy on her. So do her memories of this place. She needs nav, pulls it up as she unconsciously pats the handle of the Noctics through her shirt. She gets little reassurance from it.

Another short walk, getting her closer to the central shaft of the hive. The walkways become slightly wider here, the walls finally opening up into the center of the hive. She looks up to see endless levels of honeycomb units, people milling around. There's a line to get on the elevator.

This is hell. *Why am I back here?* She knows why. *Focus on the mission,*

Vanguard! She is restless, mentally urges the line to move faster. The elevator is crowded and sultry. She feels her stomach lurch again as it descends. Her fellow commuters are silent, either looking down or embedded, lost in the digital. A speaker reiterates the company mission ("Unlocking the potential of the universe, together") as they zoom through levels. Hers is the second stop.

The elevator stops once before, a few people get off, a couple step inside to take their place. Then they start moving again, plunging deeper. She feels like she is suffocating again. Finally out, she steps to the side, crouches down, and catches her breath. Almost there.

Nav assist guides her to L's unit. She hopes he's there. Maybe he's on shift. She's not looking forward to waiting for his return, stuck. She'll do it if she has to, though she hopes he's there.

She spots a group of security personnel, decked out with body armor and weapons, but they pay her no mind. She's one in some hundreds of millions of people walking about. She moves past them, following nav on walkways that keep narrowing as she is getting farther away from the center. She turns left, then right, then left again, squeezing around other people now. She is very close, just a couple of turns away. She picks up the pace. She walks by another copy of the poster she saw, with the clear sky and smiling miners. Not an exact copy: instead of the company mission, this one says, "Stronger together." She keeps moving, walks underneath a busted light casting a cone of shadow, then back into the overall dimness.

One final turn, one last walkway. The door is not far in front. She can see it but wouldn't be able to pick it out from its neighboring doors without help from the nav overlay. She walks to it, finds it unlocked. Another lucky break. She opens it and steps through. They have the drop on her.

16: FLOP

I t's three of them. Two on the left side of the small room, the third on the right. They're all pointing guns at her. She recognizes the Eclipse Corps logo on their arms. *Oh no, Doctor Linton.* She realizes her mission is a failure.

"Come on in," says the one on the right. He has an Eclipse Corps sergeant insignia. The other two are privates, one is blond, the other bald. She steps in very slowly, mind racing, using the little time she has to assess the situation, come up with something. Her eyes dart in every direction. This unit is completely empty, not even a mattress on the floor. No place to duck behind. The privates are both wearing light body armor. The sergeant isn't. They're geared up for business: boots, gloves, utility belts.

She raises her hands, shows them her palms. The privates approach her, the bald one pushes a gun to her cheek, making a point of pressing it in. The tip of the barrel is cold, turning her head slightly. She is forced to face the sergeant, who is grinning, looking her up and down. She doesn't like what it implies, but she won't go down without a fight.

The blond private moves in front of her. He holsters his gun and reaches into her left pocket, taking out her combat gloves.

"Check this out," he says, holding the gloves up for the other two to see and looking expectantly at his sergeant. They're wearing regular tactical gloves, not combat gloves. Good for gripping and not much else.

The sergeant whistles. "The woman is packing tacticals." He nods at the blond merc, extends his left hand "give them."

The private hands the gloves over. Elena is realizing they are not well trained. She might yet get out of this. It's three of them but they're sloppy. There's only one gun trained on her now. The private going through her pockets holstered his and the sergeant is checking out her VoidTech gloves. Do they know she is a Vanguard? She just needs an opening.

The blond gets back to checking her pockets, reaches into the right one, and pulls out the digicard. The card has their logo emblazoned on it. He lifts it up too.

"This is ours!" he says.

"What's that, Lance?" asks the merc in charge.

"A digicard, sir," replies the blond.

"Let me see," says the sergeant as he steps forward and extends his left hand.

Elena notices him lowering his gun as he picks up the card. She very slowly turns her head just a little to the left, looks to her side to see the bald private distracted, also looking at the digicard. It's now or never. She doesn't hesitate.

She snaps her head back, getting away from the only gun now trained on her. Before the bald private has a chance to react, she grabs his wrist holding the gun with both of her hands and guides it towards the sergeant's head. He doesn't pull the trigger. Instead, he is struggling to lower his arm. Private Lance and the sergeant move to get out of the line of fire before they think of training their own guns on Elena. She is still wrestling for the gun. She uses this opportunity to move close to the wall, turning the bald private so he gets between her and the other two, making it impossible for them to get a good angle on her. He rams his shoulder into her, knocking her against the wall. This loosens her grip. He yanks his arm forcefully to free the gun. She takes advantage of his momentum, kicks one of his legs out from underneath him, and shoves him hard. He goes down, but this exposes her. The other two have got their guns ready by now. They shoot before she has a chance to duck.

She feels scorching pain on the side of her face as her left eye goes blind. Less than a second later, she feels a punch in her gut. She knows it's over. She feels slime running down her burnt cheek and realizes it's her eye. *That was an energy weapon,* a detached voice deep inside her mind tells her. Her insides are pulsing with pain. Then the same calm voice: *Gut shot was kinetic.* She corkscrews to the ground, flops face first. She smells burned flesh. Her face.

Miraculously, she doesn't pass out. The merc she tripped is standing up, which gives her just enough cover to move ever so slightly. She reaches under her shirt, slides out her pistol. She is lying on top of it, face down, so they can't see what she is doing. Pistol in hand, she lies there, playing possum. She feels them approaching, holds her breath.

"Motherfucker," she hears from the sergeant.

"Is she dead?" asks Lance.

"What do you think?" replies the other private.

"Fucking check," commands the sergeant.

A boot prods her ribs. She doesn't budge, grips the pistol tightly.

"Not like that, you idiot, turn her over!"

She feels hands grabbing her shoulder, flipping her around.

She goes with it, rotating and lifting the gun as she turns. The movement hurts her insides. All in the span of a second, she gets turned to face them while at the same time she lines up the gun with Private Lance's head. He sees her, has time to open his mouth, but before he can say anything she pulls the trigger and blows his face off. The Noctics hits with its signature punch. He lets go of her shoulders and he stumbles back, arms flailing in a final spasm.

The other two step aside, surprised. This gives her enough time to train the gun on the sergeant.

He manages to say, "Shit."

She fires twice in quick succession. The first one misses his head by an inch, blasts a big hole where the wall meets the ceiling. The other one hits him straight in the chest. The privates are wearing body armor, but the sergeant isn't. He drops like a sack. The last thing he says, as he goes down, is a long "oooof."

She tries to aim at the last man standing, but before she can point the gun in a different direction, she feels her right hand sizzle. Her hand releases the gun involuntarily. The bald merc shot her. *Energy weapon again*, the voice in her head tells her. He steps closer, lining up the gun with her head. She kicks at it, messing up his aim. He shoots his energy weapon way above her, burning a circular shape in the wall.

Adrenaline and survival instinct override the pain of getting shot. She comes up while he is lowering the gun back towards her, a movement that sends spikes of pain through her guts. She grabs the gun by the barrel with her left hand, pushes it down and to the side while she headbutts him. She feels his nose crunch against her forehead. He lets out a yelp and stumbles back. She goes with him, backs him up against the opposite wall. Then she miscalculates, tries to deliver a right cross to his chin to put his lights out. But her right hand is severely burnt. It squelches against his jaw, and she feels her own softened bones mushing together. He barely feels this. She falls down on one knee, world swimming in a gray cloud. Still holding onto the gun for dear life.

"You bitch," he says and rabbit-punches her with his left hand. It's a weak punch; she is more worried about getting shot again. Her right hand is useless, so she does the only thing she can—she bites down on his wrist. He lets go of the gun. She keeps hold of the barrel and swings it like a club at his temple. This makes him lose his balance. He leans against the wall. She stands up, hitting him again with the grip of his gun as she does so. He falls to the side but manages to grab her hair, drags her down with him. She lands on top of him, pressed against his body armor. He tries to punch her, but he doesn't have a good angle. She throws away the gun to free up her left hand, the only working one she has now. The gun clanks across the room as she reaches into his utility belt and pulls out a serrated knife. As he is struggling to push her off him, she stabs. She aims the first hit at the ribs, hitting from the side. The hit bounces off his armor. *Not there*, that detached part of her tells her. Her next swing is higher, above the plate and into the armpit. The merc screams. He struggles to pull away. She wiggles the knife out. Its teeth caught but it didn't go in too deep. She yanks it out. It comes loose with a splash of bright arterial blood.

Her opponent lost the will to fight. He tries to crawl away in a sloppy crab walk. She follows him.

"Fuck you!" she says and drives the knife into his right eye. His limbs give out. He lies down and stops moving.

She catches her breath. There's sharp pain in her stomach. She looks down with her remaining eye to see her shirt soaked in dark blood. Her face is burning. She tries to get up, can't. The room is spinning and suddenly seems very bright. She fades out.

She comes back to it sometime later. *Where am I?* She is lying in a pool of drying blood. Some of it is the mercs' but she's positive a lot of it is hers. The left side of her face is stinging, and her left eye is not working. *What happened?* Her right hand is raw, mangled, and burnt. *You got into quite the scrap,* the calm inner voice tells her. It comes back to her. Energy weapon fire. She took one to the face and one to the hand. Excruciating but non-lethal. The kinetic hit is a different story. The wound is still bleeding, her insides hurt. The projectile is still in there somewhere.

Get up, Vanguard! the voice tells her. She tries, props herself against the wall. *Up!* With terrible effort, she manages to stand, leaning against the wall. The movement makes her dizzy, sends stabs of pain through her gut. She looks around the small room.

The sergeant is on his back, with a gaping hole in his chest and his eyes rolled back. The blond merc, Lance, is lying next to him, gold hair now streaked with red, his face gone. Next to her is the bald one, in a puddle of blood. She had hit the axillary artery. He would've bled out even if she didn't hit him in the eye. His knife is still lodged in his eye socket. The smell of copper inside the room is overbearing.

Get out of here!

I can't, she thinks.

Move!

She takes a tentative step, stumbles, gets back against the wall. She makes her way towards the door slowly, ponderously, leaning against the wall with her good hand for balance. Her stomach wound drips dark blood. She leaves behind a thin trail as she walks. Every move hurts. She focuses on putting one foot in front of the other. Focuses on the next step. Then the one after that. It takes her forever to get in front of the door.

They'll be here for you any minute now. Go!

She tries to think but can't. She needs to keep moving. She opens the door and loses her balance. She falls into the walkway, instinctively puts her right arm out trying to break the fall. Her already mangled hand can't support her weight. It crunches further. She tries to scream but only manages a whimper. She moves her arm to the side, falls face first, and almost blacks out again from the pain.

17: METAGAME

The Door Knockers and the Brainiacs got into a good working rhythm. They tag-teamed to secure positions on the ground and in the digital, constantly searching for the elusive Joker. He or she was way harder to pin down than they anticipated, but they had a trail and were making good progress. She and Darius were steady by now, their fling after the first drop turning into a budding relationship. During the day, Elena and her team kicked doors down, neutralized opposition, captured terminals. Darius with his Brainiacs infiltrated networks, fought off algorithms and enemy digital specialists, reached deep inside their logistics to cause chaos. They spent the nights together, sweaty, talking about what they'd do after the shitshow was over.

The progress did not come for free: they lost people to ambushes, traps, basilisks. But they were making progress. Everyone on the teams was optimistic. After the initial paralysis, the general feeling was the tide had turned. They had the initiative now, a modest upper hand, and they were pushing through. Sooner or later, the Joker was going to go down.

. . .

After several encounters, they got a better understanding of what they were up against. Titanforge and Abyssal were working with different paramilitary outfits. Titanforge employed some old war dogs. Seasoned, grizzled, and mean. They fittingly called themselves Inferno Troops. Elena was positive most of them used to be on their side not too long ago. They knew their tactics and were precise. They set up ambushes, made good use of terrain, and didn't go down easily. At least some of them must've had Vanguard training. More troubling, they had a complete disregard for civilians, and in some cases, it looked like they tortured hostage Abyssal corporate citizens.

Abyssal Mining worked with Eclipse Corps. Eclipse Corps were not as elite, but what they were missing in training they made up for in numbers and tech. They were many, and the corporate-sponsored tacticals they used were top-notch. Abyssal could afford investing an order of magnitude more credits in their soldiers than the military. Their gear was way better than what the Door Knockers and Brainiacs used.

They had to learn and adapt. Know thy enemy. Win the metagame. They took down Inferno with superior tech. Go in carefully, with the latest tacticals and gadgets. Draw them out with drones. Use surgical strikes and minimize risk. Against Eclipse, they went head-on. Neutralized their drones and hit them hard, made them shit their pants. They generated panic and took advantage of the enemy's lack of training.

It was a bloody game, but they were winning it on the ground.

At the same time, the overall situation was deteriorating. Fast. Civilian casualties were steadily mounting. The paramilitaries didn't seem to have any qualms about hitting innocents, and word got out that Inferno Troops were committing atrocities. The two factions were both trying to cause enough uproar in the population to force a cease-fire and negotiations. The military sent by the AI Council, including Elena and her team, intervened to push them back, rescue hostages, secure key areas. It was an uphill battle. She couldn't fathom the math behind the equations placing human life somewhere lower than corporate interests, nor the monsters who would execute such orders. And she was glad she couldn't, it kept her pushing forward and gave her moral compass a magnetic north.

. . .

It started as a routine mission. They got intel on Inferno Troops holding a bunch of kidnapped Abyssal citizens hostage inside a hive unit. They were threatening to kill them slowly unless the right executives sat across the table to discuss a rehashing of the astrium deposits map.

She was actually glad to be boots on the ground on this one. Get those torturing fuckers and make them pay for their crimes. By now she was a veteran, dropped dozens of times. The Door Knockers saw shootouts, tangos down, teammates getting hit. Nothing you would ever get used to, but something you could learn to live with. Like knee pain.

They met in the briefing room, went over the intel together, then geared up and went down. A single vertibird, smaller team on this one. The intel was solid, and they had good tech. It was her and three other Door Knockers. Petty Officer Third Class Dan Graham ("Gram"), Ensign Alice Lozano, and trusty Chief Petty Officer Cooper, the Hammer. Party animal or not, Cooper was always on top of his shit during ops. They were also joined by Darius and another Brainiac, one of his whiz kids, to give them the digital advantage.

They got to the right level, deep underground, and started moving. Inferno took their time to destroy as many lamps as they could reach, so the walkways they were crossing were engulfed in darkness. But they'd done this many times by then, advancing was effortless. Their movements were precise, with two drones leading the way and night vision tactical overlays helping them see despite the lack of lighting. They were zeroing in on the unit, with Gram, who was point, behind the drones, and the Brainiacs covering their rear. The whole section was eerily quiet, even the constant background hum of the hive seeming to have dropped in volume. Their boots echoed loudly as they made their way to the target. The darkness and small space were meant to make them feel trapped, but they were packing a lot of heat and were ready to punch their way out of anything.

After a tense but uneventful trek, they made it. One more turn. The drones went around the corner first, relaying back images of yet another dark and empty walkway. Gram followed, confirming.

"Clear," he called back.

"Moving," said Elena, advancing to take position in front of him.

The unit was now in sight, covered by their weapons.

"Moving," said Cooper, sprinting to take position on the right side of the door.

Once there, they switched to hand signaling. Positioned themselves on both sides of the door, point ready to breach, Brainiacs one step behind, ready to back them up.

Elena lifted her right hand up, counted down on her fingers. Three. Two. One.

Lozano kicked the door in. Cooper quickly followed with a flash-bang. Then Gram stepped through, followed by Elena and two drones. She went in, shotgun ready, clearing the left side of the room. Nothing there.

"Clear," she said.

"Clear," echoed Gram.

The rest of the team streamed in. Nobody else in the room. No hostages, no Inferno Troops.

"Fucking intel guys."

They turned on flashlights, looked around for clues. No signs of struggle. No signs of anything, except a terminal on the wall opposite the door. No need for muscle after all.

"Brainiacs," she called, pointing to the terminal.

Darius stepped in front of the group, walked up to the terminal, and embedded. As soon as he did, the damn thing exploded.

Elena was thrown face first against the wall. She felt her nose crack, forehead smack against hard nanocrete, and intense pain in her back. The impact made her dizzy. She half turned, half stumbled to see the room filling up with smoke. Cupping her nose with her hands, she tried to assess the situation. To see if Darius was OK. Darius was not OK. What was left of Darius was a pair of booted feet, the rest of him splattered across the unit.

Her stomach dropped. Training took over. On autopilot, she called what she was supposed to call.

"Check in. Now!"

She heard a couple of "up" calls from Lozano and Gram, her Door Knockers, struggling to get up from corners of the room. Nothing from Cooper though. The other Brainiac didn't respond either.

"Hammer, check in!"

Silence.

You couldn't really train for this. She stepped towards what used to be Darius and looked around the room using her flashlight. The room resembled a slaughterhouse. They'd rigged the terminal, made it blow up as Darius was trying to connect. Small radius, targeted, high-powered. She was lucky, got knocked against the wall, like her two other teammates who were not in front of the device. Darius got blown to bits. Some of his insides got stuck to the ceiling, blood dripping down. With her flashlight, she followed a streak of blood and organs through the door to find the other Brainiac. He was thrown back out on the walkway, broke his neck against the door across. She could see him slumped down, head at an impossible angle, eyes blank. She went to Cooper, on the right side of the room, trying not to step in what remained of Darius. *Darius! Oh no!* Cooper was gone. A long shard of metal, propelled by the blast, went through his armor plate, ribs, heart. He was still bleeding, but Elena confirmed there was no pulse. The two drones were next to him, offline. The blast must've knocked them against the wall too, with enough force to damage their circuitry.

Everyone accounted for, she turned to look at the pair of boots that used to be her lover. She felt her eyes tearing up at the impossibility of it. Nothing left of him! But she had no time to grieve, people still depended on her.

"Move out," she called.

She walked out of the room backwards, taking a final look at the smear of blood and guts on the floor and ceiling.

They had to navigate back to the vertibird. This would've been the perfect time for an ambush, to finish what the booby trap didn't. They were down to three, with no drones. Elena's ears were ringing. Lozano was limping, wincing at every step while insisting she was fine. They were in bad shape. No backup either, they dropped with a small team, and it would take time for reinforcements to reach them. She put out a call anyway.

{We have three down, booby trap. Moving towards the bird for evac. Any chance of backup?}

No reply. Either comms were jammed or they were too deep inside the hive. They were shut out of the corporate network and couldn't rely on the local infrastructure.

"Looks like it's just us," she told the other two.

"Fuck it," replied Gram, "let's do this."

No time for subtleties, they mounted the flashlights to their rifles and Gram's shotgun and retreated as fast as they could without having to leave limping Lozano behind. The silence would've felt even more foreboding, but Elena's tinnitus gave her other reasons to worry. She suspected she had a concussion. And so, they traversed the dark walkways, all the way back to the central shaft. Miraculously, nothing happened to them. The vertibird was there, waiting. They got on and pulled out. They checked Lozano's leg, which appeared to be fractured. Gram managed to get away with nothing more than a bruise. Elena started feeling pain only once they were way up above Forge. It turned out she got a big chunk of metal lodged in her back.

Back on the *Ironclad*, the medic told her she was lucky—half an inch higher or half an inch lower, it would've gone through her rib cage, between the bones. Half an inch to the left, and it would've hit a vertebra, likely leaving her paralyzed. As it was, it was just going to leave an ugly scar. The medic confirmed she had a concussion too. She was on the bench for a while.

She had to prep a full report describing the situation in every gory detail, and she was fuzzy while doing it. She called "clear." But it was clear, how could she have known there was a booby trap? Why did they go down with such a small team? Would it have been better to have more boots on the ground? Or would that have just led to more victims when the explosive would've inevitably gone off? Her head hurt, and blaming herself was of no use. Still, she couldn't help it.

She spent that night alone, like she hadn't done in a long time. She cried herself to sleep. She wished she were half an inch taller or half an inch shorter. She wished she were the one to interface with the terminal. She saw lonely nights stretching ahead of her and was eager to get the medic's all clear, go back to knocking down more doors.

18: SURVIVAL INSTINCT

et up, Vanguard! Elena gasps. She is sprawled halfway between Doctor Linton's unit and the walkway. Her legs are inside the room, the rest of her is outside. She struggles to her knees. A young man approaches. She freezes for an instant. There's no more fight left in her, she couldn't possibly take him on. But he is a civilian. He is wearing large orange work boots and dirty overalls. He stops a respectful distance away and just looks at her.

Elena grabs the side of the door, manages to stand up. Another person is coming from the opposite side. A woman. Her clothing is similar to the young man's. They are miners. She is saying something to Elena, asking her a question. She can't parse it. She takes a couple of tentative steps in the young man's direction.

The woman keeps talking, follows Elena until she is in front of the door. Then she chances a look inside, lets out a scream, and runs away in the opposite direction, work boots making loud noises in the narrow walkway.

Keep walking! She takes two more tentative steps. Her guts hurt, pulsing with the rhythm of her gait. She takes two more steps. She holds onto her stomach with her right forearm, that hand useless now. Two more steps. The young man backs up against the wall, making room for her. He tries to speak, even opens his mouth, but nothing comes out.

She turns her head to look at him as she passes by. He flinches, backs away a few quick steps. In front of the door now, he looks inside and follows the woman, running down the walkway. She takes two more steps.

Get out of here! But how? She tries to get online, pull up nav. Nothing. She touches her temple with her left hand. The graft doesn't feel right. It's drooping on her cheek. The energy weapon melted part of it. It's no longer working. She is shut out of the digital. She keeps walking, one slow and painful step after another. She turns left at the first intersection, then a right at the next one. The walkways are empty.

Keep moving!

She continues on, aimlessly. She doesn't know for how long, until she is in front of an open door. An empty unit. A mattress on the floor, a small desk with a chair, a couple of shelves on the opposite wall. Whose unit is this? Why is it open? Doesn't matter. She knows this is about as far as she can go. She steps inside, closes the door behind her.

What are you doing, Vanguard? asks the voice. *Fuck off!* she tells it, then slumps down against the door. She uses her good hand to pull her shirt up, assess the damage. The shirt is sticky with blood. She examines the puncture wound. Small caliber, much smaller than her gun, but big enough to mess her up. She can feel something is very wrong in there now.

She leans her head back, sighs. She closes her eye for a few seconds. Then opens it to look at her right hand. It's been melted and mushed twice. Her pinky finger is still in place, flesh seared, and so is the bottom part of her thumb. The rest is a gnarly ball. She's pretty sure she can see bones mixed together with tendons in there. The burnt flesh has a strange color. Her little finger twitches. She grays out.

She is jolted back to awareness by the sound of boots clanking on the walkway outside. Getting louder. She hears words she can't make out, they sound like barks. The boots pass by the closed door, rattling it. She has to lean away from the door. She resumes her self-examination.

She touches her left hand to the left side of her face. It feels like needles. Her cheek is burnt. Her hand comes back sticky. Her eye seems to have run down her face. *How funny,* she thinks.

You're losing it, Vanguard! a distant voice says. *Snap back!* But that voice sounds far away now—it's fading. She is so tired. She needs to sleep.

She hears boots on the walkway again. Shouting. *I can't sleep in this racket.* The boots stomp away. She lies down on the floor in a fetal position. Something is bothering her, something is not right. But she'll figure it out in the morning. Too tired now. She closes her eyes.

She is running across a green field of grass, under a clear blue sky. *Where am I?* She is startled for a moment, breaks stride to look around. She can see mountains in the distance, an orchard nearby. There's only one place with these shades of beautiful green, with grass that smells as wholesome as this field. She's on Aurelia, her home world. *How did I get here?* She must've zoned out. She can't remember what she was doing. She can't remember where she was before. *Strange.* But she feels good, oh so good. Years younger. She hasn't felt so refreshed, so full of energy, since ... since ... And then she notices him, at the edge of the field. Darius.

He is looking her way, starts waving. She laughs, waves back. She takes a deep breath, fills her lungs with lush air, and resumes her run, now with renewed purpose. She starts towards him.

As she gets closer, she can see he is talking. He is saying something to her. His lips are moving, but she can't make out any words. She keeps running, smiling.

Then she sees Darius is no longer smiling. He is pointing behind her, eyes wide. His voice is still not carrying, but she is close enough now to read his lips. "Look," he is saying, "look!"

She turns around, stops. A giant ship is descending towards them, large enough to blot out the sun. Its bulk moves over Elena, over the field, blanketing them in shadow. The air turns colder. She can't tell what type of ship this is. It has an unusual cigar shape. And it's jet-black, a black so dark it seems to suck up all light around it. It looks unnerving. As it closes in, she can make out what look like tentacles protruding out of its shell at odd angles. Rows of what look like spikes adorn its hull. A nightmare manifest.

She takes a few steps back, still looking up. She doesn't want anything to do with this ship. She wants Darius.

"Darius," she says, turning to face him.

But he is no longer there. Her dread intensifies. She looks left and right, searching for her lover, but there's no one. Just her, vegetation, and the shadow which seems to somehow grow even darker. An icy gust of wind blows across the field. She shivers, hugs herself, squints to protect her eyes against the arctic gale. She turns around once more to look at the ship but can no longer see anything. It's pitch-black. Or she is blind. *It must be a bad dream*, she realizes. She shuts her eyes tight, counts to three, then opens them.

There's light. Pale, artificial light, but light nevertheless. She can see. She is curled up on the floor, in an unfamiliar room. A small unfamiliar room. She is hurting all over. *Where am I?* There's a puddle of blood underneath her. She looks at it, chuckles. *Didn't know I had that much juice in me*, she thinks. Why would she find this funny?

There's a mattress in the middle of the room. Why was she sleeping on the floor? Sometimes she can be so silly. *Didn't want to get any blood on it*, she concludes. But where is she? She tries to get online, can't. Why?

It slowly comes back to her. Doctor Linton. Forge. The hive. The fight. Getting shot. She looks down at her right hand. Touches her graft with her left, finds it running down her cheek like before. Mixed in with her left eye. VoidTech Tactical Edition graft, provided by the military. "Near indestructible, redundancies built in," they said. *Waste of money.*

She is stuck offline, deep underground, lost in a labyrinth. She feels cold, notices how pale her skin is. *I'm turning into a ghost.* Just a matter of time now.

It will be over soon, she tells herself. She waits for the end for a while. The end doesn't come as fast as she wishes it to.

She tries to sit, falls back to her side. The movement flares up the agony in her stomach. She coughs. *Die already*, she tells herself. She has an idea—a way to speed up the process. She taps her waist with the hand that is not maimed. *Where is my gun?* There's nothing where the Noctics was supposed to be. *Shit*. She lost it somewhere. *What a failure.*

She hears footsteps on the walkway again. Faint at first, then getting louder. They get near the door, then stop. The door opens. She lifts her head up. *Finally*. It's Darius. She smiles at him, wants to say "hi" but is too weak to speak. He steps inside. He is not smiling. Why isn't he smiling? "What's wrong?" she wants to ask. She can't. *I missed you*, she thinks as the world turns gray again. She fades out.

19: REDEPLOYMENT

ieutenant Marcus Wade is in the large mess hall of the *Dauntless*. A heavy cruiser needs to feed a lot of people. He is sitting at the officer table, with a dozen others. Most of them are team leaders, marines. A few of them are Vanguard, like him. Plus a couple of the ship's officers sitting with them. And Ensign Lila Navarro, who is on her first deployment and likes to tag along.

If there's one thing Marcus learned to hate during deployments, it's the chow. He was assured all meals are an optimal mix of nutrients, designed with love for the military by Valor Provisions Inc., but they never fail to taste like boiled chicken to him. He's poking around at the gruel on his plate and is half-listening to the other junior officers as they exchange theories about the nature of their deployment.

"We kicked the Taurans back, but those were scouts. They'll return with the heavy guns."

"Think that's why we're here?"

"Why else?"

Their conversation is just background noise. Marcus is distracted. He's been distracted ever since he received Captain Drake's message. It bothered him. A lot. Elena Drake seems to be in some kind of trou- ble. He didn't think that happened in the corporate world, at least not to that extent. He tried reaching out but got no response. Even if they never deployed together, he hopes she's OK. Not much else he can do from here, which is frustrating.

"I heard the Taurans are prepping a surprise attack on the Gateway Ring," says one of the navy officers.

"How is it a surprise if even you heard of it?" retorts one of the Vanguard team leaders to general laughter.

Marcus doesn't laugh, his mind still on Drake. Not that they're particularly close. They're different generations. Renowned Captain Elena Drake, veteran of the Forge peacekeeping operation. Honorably discharged. But she is Vanguard, just like him. Once a Vanguard, always a Vanguard. They support each other. That's the ethos. Plus, he admires her, has heard the stories. Elena fought bravely in the narrow walkways of the hives on Forge. They were outnumbered, brain-hacked, yet still they fought. Still managed, somehow, against all odds, to turn the tables on the paramilitary factions.

His story is different. The first time he was deployed was during the Tauran War. He wasn't on the front lines then, didn't see active combat. He was there, behind the front lines, mostly waiting around. Waiting around, mission-ready, and staying up to date on how the war was going through sitreps. He put boots on the ground exactly twice during the deployment: first time on Echo Point, second time on the alien shipwreck.

The brass called Echo Point a search and rescue mission. Searching they did, but there was no one left to rescue there. The Tauran bastards destroyed the colony, no survivors found. They used some unknown weapon that vaporized all the glass and all the people in the colony, left the city in ruins. Marcus spent a few days walking the deserted streets with his team, first looking for survivors, then looking for clues, then finally being recalled.

The first couple of days were hopeful. They entered buildings, navigated around piles of debris, plaster, and broken furniture calling for survivors as the ships pelted the area with infrared beams. Hope dwindled quickly.

They got new orders: look for clues as to what happened. Dead bodies. Anything out of place. Report back, bring in the geeks to analyze. They spent a few more days looking, unsure what they were even looking for. They dug through piles of dirt, went through semi-collapsed buildings, even dived in the river running next to the city. They couldn't find anything. After a couple of false positives, Command cancelled the mission. He still wonders what happened to all those people, what kind of weapon could make biologics and glass disappear.

Then there was Derelict A1X-VD2. The ship was disabled and adrift, dark and silent, sleeping among the green gas clouds. During the battle, they hit it with their best stuff, shut it down without blowing it to bits. Marcus and his team were ordered on site.

His team breached, walked through the strange corridors and around dormant bio-machinery. The ship snapped back at them at every turn, with what looked like reflexes. Closing off orifices, spewing corrosive gasses, venting segments into space. It took them a while to figure out how to step around the ship's equivalent of nerve endings, and they lost a couple of combat engineers while doing it.

They cleared paths for the geeks to come in, take samples, analyze, and reverse-engineer.

All that got classified right quick. He was asked in very clear terms never to talk about what he'd seen there, though to this day he doesn't really understand what he saw. The Taurans seemed to use a strange meld of artificial and organic. The spaces were wider and taller than on a military ship, which could hint at larger-sized creatures, or it could mean nothing—cruise ships and high-end civilian transports had similarly broad spaces. The tech looked to him as magical as the one on the *Dauntless*, maybe just in a different incarnation. The mixed-in biological tissue was a novelty, but the thing was in a coma-like slumber by the time he got there. It was hard to tell what purpose anything served. And that wasn't his job anyway.

All in all, it was the most exciting thing he ever did. Walking those otherworldly corridors, weapons hot, on the lookout for booby traps, was bonkers. Anticlimactic though. As far as he could tell, the ship was not awake. His team did several recon missions aboard, mapping out its interior. The damn thing was huge. Never saw a Tauran though. They got swapped with another team within weeks, translated back to home base soon after. Without ever firing his weapon.

"I bet you know," Lieutenant Grayson prods him. Grayson is Vanguard too, they graduated STARS together.

He wasn't paying attention to the conversation.

"Know what?"

"Do they look like giant fucking crabs?"

All eyes on him now.

"Never seen one," he says.

"Sure you didn't," says Grayson. They know he was on the derelict ship, and they know all the info was classified. They're teasing him.

"I swear," he says, playing along now, crossing his fingers. He's had this conversation a million times before.

"Sure you do."

"OK," he says. "You got me." He pauses for dramatic effect, then leans in closer, drops his voice. "I'll tell you."

They all get quiet, lean in, still smiling, waiting for the punchline.

"They actually look like giant fucking artichokes. And they smell like this chow here." He wrinkles his nose and they all burst into laughter.

"Well, my buddy saw one. He swears to it. And it looked like a giant crab," says Ensign Navarro.

He rolls his eyes at this, decides to join the conversation. He listens to increasingly more outlandish rumors, contributes one or two of his own, even knowing full well they're bullshit. He laughs with the others at the stupid jokes, but in the back of his mind, he keeps mulling over Drake's message and its implications. *If you make it back before me, tell my family I love them.* What kind of trouble did you get yourself into, Captain?

· · ·

This new deployment is even quieter than his previous one. At least so far. Lots of waiting around on standby. Shifts. Drills. He doesn't mind it, isn't particularly eager to fight aliens. The ruins of Echo Point and the sheer otherness of that ship still haunt him. He sometimes dreams of walking the ruins of a city with no glass and no people. He sometimes dreams of walking the corridors of the derelict ship again. The dreams sometimes merge into a surrealistic landscape of a dark city street floating in outer space, bio-machinery covered in dirt.

He hopes the Taurans got the message during round one and they're gone for good. Quiet is good.

He maintains squad discipline, ensures his team is ready at a moment's notice, helps with ship duties. He has five Vanguards under his command now. His second-in-command, lanky Chief Petty Officer Peter "Dash" Howard and Petty Officer Second Class Rachel "Pinball" Santos, with her high cheekbones and crooked nose, have been with him since day one, before they earned their nicknames. They were on Echo Point together, and on the derelict ship.

Breaching Specialist Kyle "Backwards" Anders joined them during the disabled alien ship exploration. They needed a demolition expert, and Marcus made the case for bringing in a Vanguard after their assigned combat engineers got themselves killed. Cheery red-haired Anders came aboard.

Petty Officer Third Class Eric Novak joined them after the disabled alien ship exploration, a few weeks before they got out of Sector 36. Built like a brick shithouse, they joked he trained to fight the Taurans in hand-to-hand combat, though he never got the chance to put boots on the ground. He stuck around for their second tour.

For this deployment, his team got rounded out with a sniper, Marksman David Kim. Kim was grave and quiet at first, so they took to calling him "Kimmy." This opened him up, despite his protests to the new name.

They're all good operators, cream of the crop. If he does end up having to fight Taurans, this is the team to do it with. But as of now, they're not fighting. They're waiting. With nothing else to do outside the daily routine, his mind keeps going back to Elena Drake's message, trying to derive more meaning out of it. He can't.

. . .

He gets the order at 2000 hours. Prep for FTL, redeployment at the Gateway Ring. Underway at 2100 hours. Moving from the Eureka Base outpost rimward, back towards the jump gate. And, it seems, with some urgency.

"Does that mean we're translating out?" he asks the ranking officer conveying the order. He wasn't particularly eager to engage the Taurans, would be good to tell his team they can stand down. Get out of Sector 36 and eat some decent food for a change.

"Negative," replies the officer. "We're to maintain condition two."

This makes little sense. Are the Taurans back? Going for the ring now? That would be bad news. The lab at Eureka Base has a large contingent of scientists, supplemented by security personnel, but the total population is a tiny fraction of that of the Gateway Ring. What if the Taurans use the same weapon they used on Echo Point to vaporize the millions of civilians on the ring?

Or maybe they're trying to attack the jump gate, which would be even worse news. Cutting off Sector 36 from the rest of the galaxy, leaving them with no support and no retreat.

"Any more details, sir?" Would be good to know what they're going into.

"Negative, Lieutenant, I'm just running it down the chain."

"Understood," he says.

The officer senses his worries, probably shares them. He adds, "Lieutenant, I really don't know anything more."

Marcus nods, turns around, goes to gather his team. He has a very bad feeling about this. The Tauran War was fought around Eureka Base and Echo Point, never that deep into the sector.

{Rally on deck now,} he sends them. Howard, Santos, Anders, Novak, and Kim are there by the time he arrives.

"We're redeploying to the Gateway Ring at 2100 hours."

They ask him questions. He doesn't have answers.

"New intel?" asks Santos.

He shakes his head.

"Should we expect combat at the ring?" asks Kim.

"Unknown," Marcus replies.

"Maybe the Taurans are back?" ventures Anders.

"Unknown," repeats Marcus. One answer to all of their questions. "We're to maintain condition two."

"I guess we're not translating out," says Howard.

"Negative."

"Anything else you know, LT?" They all look at him expectantly.

"Negative," he says. "I'm just running it down the chain."

Then, dropping the formality, Marcus echoes the officer he just talked to: "I really don't know anything more." He wishes he did. They split up, prep for FTL.

At 2100 hours, the heavy cruiser *Dauntless* turns around ponderously, bearing rimward. So do a few hundred more warships of various shapes and sizes, from other big guns like the *Ares* and the *Excalibur*, to countless small corvettes and transports. Their chassis, adorned with bay doors, sensor arrays, and gun ports, glints in the dim light of the neutron star. It's a slow, precise dance of war machinery. A well-rehearsed choreography. One after the other, they accelerate to FTL, disappear into the viridian night.

20: EXIT STRATEGY

Elena wakes up in an unfamiliar bed, floating. There's no pain. Shouldn't she be in pain? She feels far away. People are looking at her. As the world comes into focus, she recognizes the crew of the *Charon*. They're all watching her.

"Where am I?"

Her voice sounds weak to her own ears, raspy.

"You're on the *Charon*," says Jaxon.

She turns to look at the medic. Terek is watching her with appraising eyes, absentmindedly stroking his thick beard.

"How bad am I, Doc?" she asks him.

"You'll live," replies the older man. "I took the bullet out of you, patched things up in there."

Her insides still feel strange, but there's no pain to speak of. She realizes she's likely drugged up.

"You were in bad shape. Almost lost you."

She got shot. Once in the stomach, with a kinetic. Twice with energy weapons. Her eye, her hand. She tries wiggling her right hand's fingers under the covers. She can't.

"What about … the rest?"

"Right hand is gone, I'm sorry. We'll get you a synthetic one when we make it to Horizon Station."

Why are they going to Horizon Station? Doesn't matter right now.

"And my eye?"

"No eye left to speak of. And that one is going to be trickier. You have NSRS, can't interface with a standard prosthetic. You'll need a custom made one. Maybe on Nova Prime, most likely out of the sector. And you probably can't afford it."

She probably can't afford it. She takes her left hand from under the covers, touches her face. She's wearing an eye patch. She feels around, outlining its shape.

"And you'll need a new graft, but that we can do as soon as we reach the station."

Graft gone too. She's locked out of the digital. But she is alive.

"Thanks, Doc! I guess I owe you my life."

He waves this away. She looks at the rest of them.

"Thanks to all of you! How did you get me out of there?"

Last thing she remembers is stumbling on a walkway. Going inside an empty unit. Aurelia. Darius. She is fuzzy, can't quite tell which of the memories are real.

"You sent us an urgent message. Pickup details. Heads-up that you're hurt." This from Kaela, the talkative digital specialist.

"We came down as fast as we could," continues Jaxon. "Had to navigate through a whole maze."

"But," adds Kaela, "the path you plotted was spot-on. No idea how you did it. We went around all security, never had anyone ask us anything."

"Clean in and out," adds Jaxon.

She's trying to remember how she did that but draws a blank. She only recalls being lost. Utterly lost. And isn't her graft damaged?

"Let her rest," the doctor tells the others. "We'll talk more later."

She drinks some water. It's awkward to do it with her left hand. She rests.

Some time later, Jaxon is by her side.

"What mess did you get yourself into down there, Vice President?"

he asks, putting an emphasis on "Vice President" while raising an eyebrow. It's obvious she's not corporate.

She tells him her story in broad strokes. Her cover didn't do her any good, and she owes him this much. The crew of the *Charon* saved her life. She tells him about Spark, about Doctor Linton, about her impossible, failed mission.

"So, you're ex-military too. What branch were you in?" asks Jaxon.

"Does it matter?"

He ignores her question, continues: "I was a terminal lance. Got shipped around the sector a bunch, even outside a couple of times. Seen combat just once, during the Forge kerfuffle back in the day."

"Oh," Elena says. *What are the odds?* she wonders. Another Forge veteran. It makes sense though, back then Forge was the only hot zone, and if Jaxon was serving in-sector, chances were he got sent there.

"'Oh' what?" he asks, raising an eyebrow.

"I was there too."

"Small world. I was with 2nd Platoon, Foxtrot Company, 1/4. The Mudlarks. You?"

"Door Knockers," she volunteers.

Jaxon whistles. "Vanguard, wow. I knew you were one tough lady, after surviving the beating on Forge, but that's next level." He grins. She shrugs, smiles—his attitude is truly infectious.

They spend some time talking about Forge. Then move on to talk about other things. Jaxon asks questions. They have enough time to talk. She answers them.

"Why are we going to Horizon Station?" Elena asks eventually.

"We're fleeing to Horizon Station." He smiles at that. "Elena, your stunt down there was costly. We came back up with you fine, but they tagged our ship right away."

He doesn't seem too upset with this, tells it like a good sport.

"Ghost got us out of there, but you've seen the fleet around Forge."

She did. Countless ships. Warships.

"The only reason we got out is our pilot is a fucking prodigy. Our transponder is useless though. Abyssal made sure of that. It's on a watch list now."

She tries to connect the dots. Why Horizon Station? The station wasn't yet operational during her deployment. Her brief called it out as an outpost from which Ingram was planning to launch further exploration missions. Sector 36 expansion. Exploration was put on hold due to the Tauran War, and the station became a refuge for the most desperate: people who abandoned any hope of translating out, hoping against hope to escape the next conflict by simply being farthest away from it.

She tries to get online, pull up more details, realizes she can't. Her graft is not working.

"How bad is Horizon Station?"

She asks him since she can't ask the aether.

"It's bad. Overcrowded."

She nods, remembers the Gateway Ring.

"No transponder issues there?"

"It's the Wild West. Nobody cares who you are there."

She's not looking forward to more chaos. She is exhausted.

"That's where we can get a new transponder. The black market is booming on the station. Once we sort that out, we're good to go anywhere."

Elena considers this. Nova Prime. Her ticket out of here.

"A bunch of loonies on Horizon are working on an ark project," Jaxon continues. "They want to cryofreeze people, launch them out of the sector to escape."

"Loonies?" All things considered, it doesn't sound like such a bad idea to her. If the station is overcrowded, if Ingram and Abyssal are monopolizing the jump gate, she could see how someone would attempt a long trip under cryo. Whatever it takes to get out of Sector 36. She can empathize with that.

"A small station like Horizon doesn't have the capabilities to build a deep space ship," Jaxon answers her. "It's a pipe dream. More likely a scam."

Most likely a scam. There's always someone profiting.

She's in a clean bed inside what looks to her like a makeshift med bay. As far as she can tell, flexi-walls were moved around the ship's cargo hold to define a slightly larger space and Terek produced medical equipment to monitor her. He comes in and checks up on her from time to time. Others spend time with her too. They talk, learn more about each other.

The doctor came from out of sector, as an Abyssal citizen. The company shipped him over to Forge, where he worked on injured miners.

"Imagine that," he tells her. "I hated the hives. You've seen them."

She did. More than enough to loathe them herself. Terek only knows about her recent misadventures there, doesn't know about the months she spent dropping with the Door Knockers. Unless Jaxon told him. She nods knowingly. He continues.

"I've seen all sorts of gruesome accidents there. The mines are not safe. Not at all, regardless of what Abyssal is advertising."

He pauses here, the mere mention of Abyssal making him frown profusely.

"When my tour was over, I didn't want to reenlist. You know what corporate did?"

Elena shakes her head.

"They withheld my medical license. Some lawyer cited the fine print in my employment contract. What was I supposed to do? Who can afford to go to trial against a mega-corp?"

Nobody.

"But I couldn't spend one more day in the mines—not one more hour. I left. Met Jaxon on the ring. He was kind enough to take my services. A now unlicensed doctor."

Practicing illegally. Because of the small print in his Abyssal employment contract. She is still on a pretty high dose of the good stuff, otherwise she would get angry at the injustice. The only feeling she can muster is disgust.

"Sorry, Doc."

He saved her life—license or no license.

"Let me see if there's anything I can do for you. I have a contact at the Obsidian branch office on Nova Prime. I'll talk to him."

He looks at her, hopeful. She instantly regrets saying this, she has no idea what her contact can and cannot do, nor how much he is willing to help an unlicensed doctor-turned-smuggler.

"Don't get your hopes up," she adds.

Terek Nassar sighs.

Unlike the others, Rynn the Ghost never visits her alone, they don't chat. She learns more details about him from Kaela, who is happy to overshare.

"He was always on the wrong side of the law," Kaela whispers. "He used to run infiltration jobs for a crime syndicate. Got on their bad side and ended up on the *Charon*."

Elena sees him exactly twice during the trip. The first time, he comes in accompanying Jaxon. He attempts a vague apology for his absence: "Sorry, pilot duties."

It very much sounds like a poor excuse to her. Not much piloting to do once at FTL. It's a long wait for everyone, pilot or not.

The other time she sees him, he comes in with Kaela.

"I heard," Elena says, just to get a reaction, "that you ran afoul of a crime syndicate."

Kaela turns red. Rynn is nonplussed.

"Long story," is his reply, and he leaves it at that.

After he leaves, Kaela assures her it's nothing personal.

"Rynn is Rynn. Always guarded."

"One heck of a pilot though, or so I heard."

"Indeed. But don't tell him you learned about his past from me."

Kaela lived in Sector 36 as long as she can remember, grew up on Nova Prime. She got kicked out of school. She hacked the school's system, tweaked her grades (she hated history), and almost got away with it.

"A classmate ratted me out! My parents were so mad!"

She had skills back then and is even better now. After being kicked out, she made a little bit of money pen-testing.

"There's always a market for digital specialists," she says, "but doesn't always pay that well."

She made a lot more money exfiling corporate secrets.

"But that's risky business, can easily get you killed. Or worse. I heard many stories of digital specialists getting their hands on hush-hush stuff then promptly disappearing."

Elena believes her.

"I prefer the steady job here." Keeping a smuggling ship safe during operations is a full-time job. "It must be hard being locked out of the digital," Kaela muses.

"Good thing I have you to keep me company," Elena replies. But it is, indeed, difficult. She is stranded on dry land, next to the ocean of information. With her NSRS and graft she was never able to embed, but being forced offline like this is torturous.

"Sorry I caused you so much trouble," she tells Jaxon.

"Oh, don't worry about it." He looks embarrassed now. "You really overpaid us for giving you that ride."

"What about the transponder?"

"As I said, we're getting another one at Horizon. Maybe we'll all be Obsidian execs when we take off from there." He winks at her.

She laughs. *VP of Acquisitions, Obsidian Holdings.*

"Sorry, I was undercover. A lot of good that did me."

He doesn't press her for details, she already told her story. They sit in silence for a while.

"Once you get your transponder, can you take me to Nova Prime?"

"What's on Nova Prime?"

"I have a contact there, supposed to find me and Doctor Linton a quick way to translate out."

"Friends in high places?"

Jaxon must know the flow of jump gate traffic. Almost nobody is translating out. Just more warships coming in.

"You can say that. A ticket out of here. Want to come with?" She has no idea why she asked him that. She doubts it's even possible. She shot her mouth off, just like offering to help Terek. She never met her Obsidian contact and has no clue how much leverage he has. Or how willing he is to listen to her.

Jaxon seems to seriously consider it for a moment.

"Might be a smart move," he says, "but business is finally booming."

The chaos really helped his small "independent logistics" operation. She smiles at that.

"We'll take you to Nova Prime, Elena. We'll take you wherever you need to get to be safe."

She is deeply grateful. Her relationship with the *Charon* crew started with her contracting them for a ride, but it grew into something else. They're good people.

The first time she sees her reflection in a mirror she is appalled. The left side of her face is charred, from forehead to cheek, and she doesn't want to know what lies underneath the eye patch.

She will have to learn to live with a limited field of vision, she thinks as she is slowly walking around the room, the pain in her stomach flaring up unless she takes slow, small steps. She finds her graft on a tray next to her bed. Terek removed it once he concluded it was beyond repair. It's sitting there, half-melted, metal drooping. Void-Tech Tactical Edition. Melted instantly as soon as the energy weapon touched it.

She is struggling to navigate the world without a right hand. The missing limb is severely limiting what she can do. But, according to the medic, that will get fixed soon. A prosthetic won't be as good as the real thing but should be close enough.

She sits back on her bed. She is very much done with this whole thing. As soon as she gets a new graft, she's going to update her contact on Nova Prime, head there to meet him, and have him get her out of this hellhole. They were waiting for her, in Doctor Linton's room. They got him and almost got her. Sitrep: mission failed.

It takes ten days for the *Charon* to get from Forge to Horizon Station. After a few days of staying in bed, Elena starts walking around. First, it's just a few tentative steps around her room. Then she ventures farther out, into the cargo hold, and to the bridge. By the time they reach Horizon Station, she is more or less back on her feet.

21: ZERO DAY

Commissar Vesper is pissed. She is seething. She's well aware they nicknamed her "the Wasp," and that wasn't for her slim waist and blonde hair. She knows her nickname and also knows that no one dares to say it to her face. They're a bunch of rookies playing soldiers. Nine in ten haven't seen combat, they're soft, undisciplined, and they're slackers.

She gave precise orders to apprehend Elena Drake and report back. They agreed on radio silence while the op was underway, but it's been over half an hour. They were tracking Elena as she got into the elevator, she's definitely there by now. What's happening is they're having fun with her down there, against direct orders. Forge is Vesper's worst gig so far, too many disciplinary issues.

She is pacing the command unit, a large hexagon made up of seven conjoined units, and feels the beginning of a migraine. She thrives on information and there's no input incoming. And the command unit is stuffy, stinks of sweaty mercenaries. She has to do something. She walks to the door, looks at the two privates standing at attention on both sides of the exit. They're stiff, avoiding her gaze. One of them swallows, his throat working up and down.

She snaps her fingers, "You, with me," and storms out of the command unit. The private gets behind her, starts walking. *Good. Someone knows how to follow orders. I'll show them Wasp.*

She walks to the elevator, nervous private in tow. There's a long line of people waiting. She cuts the line as the elevator arrives, stops at their level. They get in.

"Everybody out!" she orders.

The private looks distressed but he is carrying a rifle and they're both in uniform. The civilians abide without protest. The elevator empties out. She overrides it to ignore stop requests, head straight down to the level where they set the trap.

All the way down, she is thinking of creative disciplinary actions to take on the idiots who were supposed to apprehend Elena and report back right away. Right away! She wants Elena moved to an interrogation room, stat. What could those amateurs be doing down there? She swears if she walks in to find them with their dicks out, she's going to castrate every single one of them.

The elevator is taking too long. She's tapping her foot, arms crossed. She glances at the private, who looks positively terrified of her. *You'd better be,* she thinks.

Finally at their destination level, they get off the elevator and start walking towards the unit. People move out of their way, clearing a path. That is, until they get close to their destination. As they approach, she sees a small crowd around the open door of what was supposed to be their surprise for Elena. *What the fuck?* She picks up the pace, the private following suit.

Once close enough, she orders, "Stand back!"

The crowd doesn't move fast enough though. They're looking inside, talking to each other, seem not to have heard her. She raises her voice.

"Stand the fuck back or I'll shoot you on the spot."

She puts her hand on her holstered gun for good measure. They take notice of that, move back and hug the walls to let her through. She gets in front of the door, looks inside, and can't believe her eyes.

She turns around and yells, "Disperse!"

The private is standing next to her, staring inside the room, eyes wide, mouth agape.

"You," she says, which makes him snap back to attention. "Disperse this crowd."

He looks at her, looks at the civilians, and tentatively raises his weapon. The people take a few steps back.

"Faster!" she commands.

They turn around, start walking away.

She enters the room, her boots sticking in drying blood. It smells like an abattoir. It looks like it too. It looks like the end result of the world's sloppiest shootout. What in the fuck happened here? And where is Elena? Vesper is even angrier now, enraged by the bloody display of incompetence. But the stupid fuckers are all dead, so she directs her rage at the private.

"Why are you just standing there?"

"Should I put out an APB?" the private asks, ready to embed.

"Wait!" She couldn't have left here unscathed. They might still be able to catch her, keep things contained. They fucked up. And it was her op, which means she fucked up. *Fuck!*

She takes in the scene. Sergeant Mason took a big one in the chest. A high-caliber kinetic round. And, she notices, he isn't wearing body armor. *You stupid clown.* Private Walter has the handle of a knife protruding out of his eye socket. He is lying in a large puddle of blood. A really large puddle of blood. How does one of three armed soldiers end up repeatedly stabbed? Why does she always end up working with the worst of the idiots? She continues her scan of the room. If Sergeant Mason was shot in the chest and Private Walter was stabbed to death, by process of elimination, the other faceless thing lying on the ground must have been Private Lance. She wouldn't be able to tell otherwise—his head wasn't completely blown off but not enough of it remains to ID the stupid bastard.

How could they mess this up so bad? It was three against one. They were ordered to use non-lethal, but she can see in the sergeant's hand a kinetic. *Unprofessional*. Three against one, with the element of surprise. She can't believe it. *Amateur hour*.

The bitch couldn't have gotten away without a scratch from this. That, at least, is a given. Vesper turns around, sees blood smears on the wall, smudges that look like palm prints. A thin line of blood on the floor too, leading outside the room.

"She's hurt," she tells the private, pointing.

He nods, waiting for orders.

She stomps out on the walkway, follows the trail for a dozen steps or so, until it thins out to nothing. *Shit!*

She realizes she might personally get in big trouble for this fuck-up. Her op. Doesn't matter if she had no other options, doesn't matter that she had to work with these idiots, doesn't matter that nobody seems able to follow orders. It's her op. Might still be salvageable. She embeds.

{I want search parties. Down here. Now!}

She goes back to the room to take another look at the scene.

"Call forensics in here," she barks at the private. "Tell them to bring body bags."

"Yes, ma'am!"

Sergeant Mason and Private Lance got shot, Private Walter got stabbed. She tries to picture the sequence of events starting with Elena Drake walking into the room and ending with this final scene. She can't come up with anything plausible, unless these three stooges were napping when Elena arrived.

Oh, she's going to get into big trouble for this. Why was she assigned this shit job? She feels the migraine coming back with a vengeance.

She notices the gun Elena dropped on the floor, a strip of burnt flesh sticking to its handle. Noctics Mark 2. Solid, reliable pistol. That explains Private Lance's missing face. She hunches down to look at the gun, at the charred flesh clinging to it. One of them hit her with an energy weapon, made her drop her piece. And, it seems, a piece of her hand. Good!

She walks around the room, trying as much as possible to avoid stepping in the blood. She gets next to Sergeant Mason, pushes him with the tip of her boot. He shat himself. She grimaces. She keeps scanning, sees the combat gloves on the floor, soaked in blood. The woman was packing. Maybe they severely underestimated her. Maybe she severely underestimated her. Ex-military. But it was three against one! And they had the drop on her!

She hears boots clanking on the walkway outside, many boots. The search parties. She steps back out to meet the couple dozen mercs she summoned.

"She's hit," she tells them, pointing at the blood trail. "But don't underestimate her. These guys did."

She steps out of the way to give them a good view of the slaughter. She watches them recoil. *Good.* Hopefully, the scene sends a strong enough message, keeps them on their toes. She really can't afford another incident like this.

"Split up in four teams and start combing the walkways."

How bad was she hit? Not bad enough to keep her from walking out of the unit. How far can she make it? She is wounded. A search party will find her, pick her up. Vesper really hopes Elena won't make it too far.

They're all still standing, gaping at her. What are they waiting for?

"Go!" she commands. "Fucking go!"

They finally move. She starts thinking about how she is going to explain this to her superiors. What was she supposed to do? Have five people in that tiny unit? Ten? Cause a ruckus on the walkways, maybe hit some civilians? Just imagine the paperwork for that. She did the best she could with the resources she got. But God, what a fuck-up! Their target came to Forge, went down inside a hive teeming with troops, took the bait, and walked into the trap they laid out, then ... she walked away. She fucking walked away! Vesper closes her eyes for a few seconds, massages her temples.

She heads back inside the room, wants to see what else she can learn before forensics come in, start messing with the scene. Next to the combat gloves, she notices a digicard. An Eclipse Corps-branded digicard. *That's strange.* These guys had a simple mission, no need to issue digicards for it. Did Elena bring in a digicard? An Eclipse-branded one? Unlikely. Then where did it come from? What's on it? Sergeant Mason's porn collection?

She snaps her fingers once more, drawing the attention of the private. He's been standing outside the room, watching the comings and goings of the search parties. Watching Vesper walk in and out of the room, glad to be out of her sights. He jumps at her summons, walks inside.

"Yes, ma'am!"

She points at the card, doesn't even bother to verbalize the order. He nods, takes two stiff steps, and picks it up. At least it's not drenched in gore, like everything else in the room. He doesn't have to fish it out of a puddle of blood, he only needs to be careful to avoid touching the few drops adorning the Eclipse Corps logo.

He lifts it up, by the sides, and shows it to the commissar.

"What's on it?" she asks, annoyed.

The private interfaces with it to take a look.

———

The worm Ingram left on the card, disguised as a corrupted blob of raw data, uncoils. It slides through the interface, through the private's neural implant, and it slips into the Abyssal network. The private doesn't notice it. Neither does the Abyssal firewall, as the worm goes straight through it, around its defense systems, using a novel pathway. Other intelligent systems scattered across the network appear busy with some urgent task, don't give it a second glance.

The worm spreads its virtual feelers, probing. It has a clear mission and a dangerous payload. Before disappearing under layers of chatter, operational data, and encrypted traffic, it takes a short detour.

First, it taps into the various sensors sprinkled around the surrounding area—opticals, sounds, motion, temperature, pressure. It must move fast, time is precious. It zips through the simple devices following its target, erasing traces, rewriting history, until it catches up to her. It opens a door, then leaves the hive level behind as it swoops around a leaf node transmission system. An old transmission system, single-purpose, reliable, defenseless. It easily convinces it that it has the right authority to deliver a message into high orbit. The old transmission system abides. The worm manipulates it not to care about the payload, to bypass logging, to not leave any trace of the interaction, to forget the coordinates. It then aims it into the night sky, and sends: a location, an ingress path, an egress path. It makes sure the transmission system resumes its activities as if nothing happened, then it loosens its grip.

It slithers back into the busy network, then burrows deep. It has important work to do.

PART FOUR
ASSET ALLOCATION

22: HOPE

The *Charon* exits FTL near Horizon Station. The giant space station orbits a small rocky planet with no atmosphere, pockmarked by meteor impacts. Elena has never been here before, so she takes in the sight. Nothing as spectacular as a ring structure, the station is a couple of orders of magnitude smaller and, she guesses, proportionally less expensive to build. Still, any huge human-and-machine construction floating in space puts things into perspective.

She ponders how small she is, how small they all are, as she watches the steady spin of Horizon's cylindrical sections. The station reminds her of a kebab, several rotating segments skewered by its main axis. The airspace around the station is busy, but busy like a regular port, nothing close to the madness around the Gateway Ring or Forge. As far as she can tell, there are no military ships around either. Just various odd-looking transports.

She is on the bridge with the rest of the crew, able to get there on her own two feet now, with minimal pain. Rynn and Kaela are seated at their consoles, everyone else is standing.

As soon as they're out of FTL, Kaela embeds to get news updates. They've been out of the loop while outside causal spacetime. Meanwhile, Rynn searches for a docking vector.

"That's strange," he says.

"What's up?" Jaxon grips the back of the pilot's chair.

"No beacon. The docks are open, and I see ships negotiating flight paths with each other, but there's no port guidebeam."

"Are they having a systems issue?" He looks from Rynn to Kaela.

The digital specialist's eyes are moving left and right at a fast speed, she seems to be sifting through a huge amount of information.

"One moment," she says.

Elena has a bad feeling about this. She wishes they could've gone straight to Nova Prime, be done with the whole thing.

"Wow!"

They're all looking at her but Kaela is still embedded, fully focused on the digital.

"One moment." She raises a finger.

They wait.

"OK. Ghost, the guidebeam has been offline for weeks. Docks are open but you have to go in manual. Just talk to the other ships, make sure they don't run into you."

That's strange. Elena has only basic pilot training, very rusty by this point, but she knows manual pretty much never happens. Elite pilots drill this for dogfights, breaches, and the like. But no sane port lets ships dock manually. It's way too error-prone and dangerous.

"Guess we go manual," Rynn says, unfazed. "Buckle up, folks!" He says this half-jokingly, but Elena sits down, straps in. So do Jaxon and Terek.

"Wow!" repeats Kaela, keeps digesting data feeds.

"What's the news?" asks Jaxon.

She raises her finger again—*wait*.

Rynn is good. He navigates the port, negotiates a safe vector with the other ships, docks with no incident, no less smooth than an automated entry.

As soon as the ship connects with the dock, Kaela speaks up: "Folks, check this out." She projects a digest report in the digital. They all embed to read it. Elena can't. Her graft is busted, so she can't get online. Kaela looks back from her chair, realizes her limitation.

"Sorry, Elena. Got a bunch of crazy news. Can't make heads or tails of them."

She's curious now.

Kaela continues, giving her the low bandwidth summary: "Military ships are amassing at the ring and Nova Prime, coming back rimward from Eureka Base. That's in all the stories. Then there's different explanations for it. Some say it's because Taurans are headed towards the core of the sector. Others say it's a rescue operation for the millions on the ring—Ingram is using the military to finally pick them up from there, translate them out. Others say Ingram is planning to enact martial law on Nova Prime. There's more ..."

Crazy indeed. She can't make heads or tails of this either. When she translated in, all military ships were headed coreward. What could this mean? She wishes she had a reliable brief update. Alas.

"Should we go for a walk?" asks Jaxon once they are safely moored. After so many days spent aboard, they're all eager for a change of scenery.

He turns towards Elena. "How are you feeling? Can you stroll for a bit?"

"I think so," she says.

They all disembark together. The docks are located at one end of the station's central axes, a short distance from the nearest rotating segment. The docks are crowded, noisy. They notice several armed individuals patrolling around.

"Security?" Elena asks.

"Might be some private outfit. There was no security last time we were here a few months back."

"The place looks busy," she comments.

"Lively black market going on." Jaxon grins.

They'll go shopping soon. For now, they leave the ships behind and enter the station proper. The two private security guards posted at the entrance nod as they pass through the gate.

The space opens up as they make their way along the segment's inner surface, moving away from the main axis that keeps everything together. The segment is large, with a high ceiling from their perspective, constant rotation simulating gravity at what should be a comfy near-Earth-like one G. Except it isn't. The speed doesn't seem to be constant. The massive structure slows down periodically, giving them a floating feeling, before picking back up again.

The volume is large but crowded, very crowded. Not as cramped as Forge, but the density of people reminds Elena of the ring. The street-campers there. Here, people are sitting around the segment's passageways, the equivalent of roads for this outside-in environment. But the people look worse here, they're gaunt. Most seem ragged and malnourished. The artificial lighting doesn't help, makes their complexion look paler. *Like zombies*, she thinks.

She can't get online, but is curious, so she asks Kaela, "How many people are here now?"

Kaela pulls up the data right away. "About a million." She pauses for a moment. "That's about ten times more than the station can support."

They walk for a bit, without a precise destination, disappointed by what the station has to offer. After a short time, Elena starts feeling out of breath. Initially she thinks it's due to her injuries, but quickly realizes the others are feeling it too. They're all gasping, break their walk to take short pauses.

"I don't think there's enough oxygen here," she says.

"I think you're right," Terek agrees.

"Life support can't keep up with the overpopulation," Kaela says. Elena is not sure whether she pulled this information from the digital or just made an educated guess, but it sounds very much true to her.

There's nothing to do here. What used to be bars and stores are now empty, dilapidated spaces. Broken windows, dark displays, people squatting inside. Graffiti adorns the walls. "They are among us," "Guess what's for dinner?", "Hope!", and an assortment of other indecipherable scribbles.

As they walk by, they get strange looks. Elena is really not up for another scuffle.

"We should get out of here. Fast."

"Wasn't like this last time we visited," says Rynn. He keeps turning left and right, scanning for potential threats.

"I think we had enough exercise," calls Jaxon.

They all agree. They need to get back to the docks, restock on perishables, find a new transponder, and get out of here. Elena needs a new graft and a prosthetic, which Jaxon assures her they'll surely find on the black market.

"Have you seen how busy the port is? That's all buyers and sellers."

She also needs some clothes. Her backpack is still on Forge, all her tacticals in it. She can access her credits once she can get online. She needs to borrow some from the crew for a new graft before she can do that. But it won't be an issue, they know she's good for it.

As they turn around to go back, a ragged man with long, slick, black hair steps up in front of them.

"Hope!" he tells them. "Find Hope!"

He walks backwards, staying in their path as they try to make their way around him.

"What hope?" asks Jaxon.

"The ark, stranger! You're new here, aren't you? There's no escape but the ark!"

He stays in front of them for a few more steps, moves aside. Shouts after them one last time, "Find Hope!"

They keep moving, back through flickering yellow lights and rotational glitches.

"That was weird," says Kaela.

People are milling about, watch them silently as they walk by, keep to themselves. Elena is unnerved, suspects the others are too, but nobody else addresses them. She wonders if people are staring because of her mangled face and missing hand, or just because the rest of the *Charon* crew looks fresh and healthy in contrast to the denizens of Horizon.

There's nothing left on the station, no attractions besides the booming black market. No shops, no bars, no nothing. Everything was closed long ago, repurposed for makeshift lodging. Most automated systems seem to still be online, but some of them are down and nobody seems to care. The port's guidebeam is offline. Hallway displays are dark. Life support doesn't seem to operate at full capacity or simply can't bear the load. Section spin is erratic. But, most disturbingly, people seem resigned to their fate.

"Got way worse since the last time we were here," Jaxon says, echoing Rynn's remark.

"It's horrible," adds Kaela.

Back on the ship, they let Kaela find what they need in the digital.

"Black market is all on the docks now," she says. "It's between ships. People on the station have nothing, can't afford anything. Aren't even allowed on the docks."

"Aren't allowed?" Terek asks. "By whose authority?"

"Smugglers. There's some militia now, organized by some of the ships doing business here. To keep them away."

"Why?"

Kaela digs up station logs, news stories, archived network chatter. She runs algorithms to filter and summarize.

"They tried to commandeer ships. Several times. To get out of here. Ended in a bloodbath every single time."

"So they're just ... stuck here?"

"Looks like it."

Elena tries to imagine what that feels like. How hard were these people beaten to just accept their fate? Stuck on the failing station, with the possibility of escape on one of the ships just a few steps away. She is a fighter. What would she do in their shoes? Would she just keep going, until someone would kill her? Could she be beaten down enough times to give up, stop trying? She looks, with her one good eye, at the stump of her right hand. *Still going*, she thinks. *More or less.* What would motivate her? Survival? Food? As soon as she considers this, her thoughts halt abruptly.

"Wait a minute," she says out loud, to no one in particular. "Something doesn't add up. How do the people aboard the station survive? What do they eat?"

"Good question," says Kaela. "Let's see." She embeds.

"Are food shipments coming in?" asks Elena. "If the docks have been taken over by smugglers with private security?"

"Not as far as I can tell." Kaela pauses as she digs deeper into the digital. "Oh." Her eyes go wide. "Oh."

"What?"

"Hope. The ark, you know? It's the name of the ark."

"Yeah, that weird guy kept going on about it."

"I heard of the ark project," chimes in Jaxon. "Told you about it on the way here."

"You said it's impossible to build with the station's resources," adds Elena.

"Indeed."

"Well," says Kaela, "they're allegedly building it in Segment 7 of the station. Far away from the docks."

"What does that have to do with food shipments?" Elena asks, confused.

"The recyclers are in Segment 7," Kaela continues, eyes wide. "People sign up for the ark, go there, don't come back."

"You don't think …" Elena can't believe it.

Kaela nods, slowly. Elena's skin is crawling.

"Is that how they're surviving? Recycling *people*?"

Kaela keeps nodding.

"Maybe," says Terek, "they do have an ark. They put people in cryo there, waiting for departure?"

Kaela shakes her head.

"Are you sure?" Terek insists.

Please don't be sure, Elena thinks.

"I'm sure," says Kaela. "I'm in the station's network. Video feeds. There's … there's no ark. Please excuse me." She leaves the bridge, disappears into the cargo hold.

"We need to get out of here," says Jaxon.

23: CORRIDORS

Marcus and his team were redeployed from their reserve position at Eureka Base to the site of Derelict A1X-VD2, spinward of Eureka Base, exact coordinates classified. It was a small team back then—himself, Chief Petty Officer Peter Howard, and Petty Officer Second Class Rachel Santos. Recent graduates of the Vanguard training program, hastily translated into Sector 36 as part of the Tauran War mobilization. He was the team lead, since he was the only commissioned officer out of the three, but he sincerely respected both of them. They'd been through STARS together; he saw them push through while others quit. The Specialized Training for Advanced Recon and Survival course was famous for its intensity.

Their task was to explore the disabled Tauran ship. The only Tauran ship disabled but left otherwise intact during the hostilities. After waiting around behind the lines for several weeks, after a hopeless search and rescue mission, they were finally going to do something useful.

The military spent a few weeks sending in drones, scanning, and mapping before high command decided it was time to put boots on the ship. Time to get scientists inside, get more hands on with the alien tech. But before risking precious scientist brains, someone had to go in first to explore and secure the environment.

Upon arriving, Marcus was impressed by the sheer size of the vessel. It was long, somewhat cylindrical, with many protrusions of unknown purposes extending from its hull. His team got access to reams of collected data: hours of drone footage and telemetry.

The ship was inert. The first drone explorers sent back vids of a dark and silent interior. The ship contained a sulfur dioxide atmosphere, hinting at a radically different biology. The walls and floors looked like membranes, covered with metallic exoskeletons. The spaces were larger than on military ships, wider and taller. Marcus wondered what kind of creatures used to walk there.

They spent a couple of days poring over the data and getting briefed before heading aboard. No mention of Taurans, just expert takes on the drone-collected data and safety protocols.

Then they went inside. The first incursion was a team of five. The three of them, plus two combat engineers. The engineers were going to help clear obstacles. The Vanguards, to deal with anything that might come their way. They dropped in a breach pod, its plasma cutters slicing an entrance through the ship's hull. Once the way in was clear, they filed inside, clad in the bulky EV suits, weapons ready as per protocol. Marcus wondered what they were supposed to shoot at—all the scanning and probing didn't reveal any Tauran.

They made their way carefully through the benighted corridor, the only source of light coming from their shoulder-mounted lamps, the clank of their boots reverberating strangely across the odd-shaped walls. They got to the first "door," an orifice held closed by a sphincter. Combat engineers took the lead, went to work on it with plasma cutters. Based on all the data they had, they thought the ship dead. No movement observed since they started probing it, no blips on IR, nothing. It turned out the ship wasn't dead, it was asleep. A deep sleep, a coma-like state, but its basic reflexes were still working. While the engineers were trying to cut through, it reacted.

Marcus was behind them, giving them room to work. He was

staring at the reflection produced by his shoulder lamp on a piece of onyx-black exoskeleton, when the buzz of the plasma cutters suddenly drowned in a roaring whoosh. He felt himself being thrown by an unstoppable force, turned around like a rag doll, his EV suit protesting with flashing red and yellow warning lights. He bumped against the exoskeleton he'd been contemplating moments before, got turned around and collided with Santos, then suddenly he was outside. They were all outside. The deafening whoosh turned into dead silence. He could see the stars; he could see his visor quickly frosting.

The engineer's plasma cutters tickled the ship the wrong way. Through its slumber, it reflexively spread open a wall section, vented them all into space. They were instantly sucked out by the infinite vacuum.

Untethered, they had to wait for a recovery team to gather them up. Normally no big deal, they were all suited up and trained for such situations, but during the initial confusion one of the combat engineers accidentally made a small cut into her own glove with the plasma cutter. The recovery team found her swollen and blue-skinned in her compromised EV suit.

They were more careful after this, started using tethers. The engineer got replaced by a backup, an older, more experienced breacher. The ship continued its slumber, continued flinching when they were prodding it. Their second incursion was relatively uneventful. They made some inroads, cleared a path towards the ship's center, placed lamps. When opening another orifice-door, they heard a loud sound coming from deeper within the ship. They all froze, listening intently, but the noise died down quickly.

"Did you all hear that?" Marcus asked.

"Affirmative."

Nothing more happened though. They exfiled safely.

Their third time in, getting deeper inside, the new combat engineer accidentally stepped on a membrane. He was expecting solid floor, but his boot sank in. Not much, only a couple of inches. It was enough to trigger another reflex though. The ship popped open a gas bag right on top of them.

Marcus saw bright flashes of light, green flames quickly turning into a thick fog. Then he could no longer see anything. It was getting hot fast, his EV suit blinking warnings again. He checked in with his teammates, with the engineers.

"Everyone, check in!"

They all did. All blinded. With everyone accounted for, he started hearing crackling sounds. It took less than a second for him to realize with horror that the crackling sounds weren't coming from the EV suit's built-in audio system. Rather, the suit itself was melting. Melting right off of him, leaving him exposed to the sulfur dioxide atmosphere. He ordered evac back to the pod. Their orderly advance turned into a mad sprint back to their vehicle. Through the soupy fog, they had to rely on digital nav to find their way. Most of them made it back to the pod in time. Just in time.

Their new engineer didn't. They found what was left of him during their next incursion: the EV suit a few crumbling tatters, the body a pile of charred remains, bones poking out of melted flesh. So little was left of him that they could've easily missed him, walked right by. But by then their steps were measured, they couldn't afford to miss anything.

The scientist team helped them piece together what happened. They took samples from their suits, watched the recordings, interviewed them. It turned out the ship, with whatever reflex they triggered, released a large volume of fluorine. The gas reacted violently with the sulfur dioxide atmosphere. The air quickly turned foggy, corrosive, and started eating away at them. They made it back to safety by seconds, an inch away from sharing the poor breacher's fate. He was chemically burnt to almost nothing.

Marcus put in a request for a Vanguard demolition expert. He needed someone with the right training for the hostile environment, someone who would not misstep, someone who would not accidentally cut themselves in a moment of surprise. That's how he got Specialist Kyle Anders.

Anders was a few years older than them, graduated STARS and became a Vanguard with an earlier class, but he was on his first deployment too.

"They call me 'Backwards,' sir. Or 'Back' for short."

He had an endless stream of jokes and liked to swear a lot. Marcus was initially confused by the nickname.

"Why do they call you 'Backwards'?"

"Fuck if I know, sir," replied Specialist Anders, looking genuinely confused.

The mystery was elucidated soon enough. His catch phrase was "fuck me backwards," which he deployed relentlessly.

He was a good addition to the team, and his temper helped lighten the mood. After the first couple of incidents, incursions became nerve-wracking. Each time they went in, it felt like they were walking through a minefield. Having someone able to make light of the situation boosted their morale.

As for the dangerous exploration, they kept at it. They had to. They kept iterating on the safety protocol, went in slowly and carefully. The team took a few more surprise hits, but thankfully no more casualties.

They got vented into space once more, had to wait once more to be collected by a recovery team. This happened despite their new tethering protocol, which had thwarted other attempts by the slumbering ship to space them. By coincidence (or not?), their cords stretched across an exoskeleton segment, frayed against it, then finally snapped, releasing them into the void a second time. Santos got so dinged up ricocheting from wall to wall on her way out, they started calling her "Pinball." She managed to survive the ordeal with only minor injuries, bumps and bruises, and a broken nose from smashing her face against the visor of her suit.

The ship also repeated the gas bag trick. This time around they ran as soon as they heard it pop. Chief Petty Officer Howard seemed extra-motivated, leading the exfil by twenty yards. They were close to the pod before realizing nothing dangerous seemed to be happening. Howard was already inside. There was no thick fog, no temperature increase, no corrosiveness. Chemical analysis found this particular bag contained helium. It was harmless. Howard earned the nickname "Dash" from his impressive retreat.

During another incursion, the ship snapped an orifice closed, separating their small team. Howard and Santos were a few steps behind. Marcus was ahead with Anders, they were taking point. They got cut off. They kept their cool as best they could. Anders tried to cut open the orifice, but this was different than the ones they were used to. It was plated in the ship's metallic exoskeleton. His plasma cutter couldn't penetrate it. After lots of swearing and a couple of "fuck me backwards," Marcus decided they had to find a different route back to the pod. That leg of the exploration was even more harrowing with just the two of them. Just the two of them, making their way through long, dark corridors, careful with every step. They checked in often, radio chatter easing their nerves. They also went quiet at times, focusing on advancing safely.

"Did you hear that?" Anders asked him during one of the quiet spells, as they were rounding a corner.

But Marcus didn't hear anything. The ship was silent as a tomb.

They made it back to the pod without incident.

They slowly mapped the interior of the ship, learned how to safely open doors, learned where it was OK to step and which spots to avoid. They found what must've been the engine room, a huge hall with a massive sphere in the middle, so black it seemed to feed off of their EV lights. They found what must've been the bridge, rows and rows of complex bio-machinery with mysterious purposes: knobs, tendrils, handles, veins. They found rooms for which they couldn't divine any purpose with their limited understanding. The ship had a radically different layout than any human ship they'd been on. Marcus and his team were never briefed on what the scientists puzzled out of these rooms after they cleared the path for them.

Marcus saw no Taurans while onboard. He wondered what

happened to them. Did the weapon used on the ship vaporize them? Did they evac? Did the ship itself use its fluorine gas reserves on its crew? Were there prior incursions on the ship before his, aimed at neutralizing the crew? After what he saw, he resented being kept in the dark. First intelligent alien contact. He was there on the ship, probably as close as anyone got to the Taurans. On the other hand, he understood protocol. It was not his job to know.

It took his team a few weeks to walk everywhere, establish safe zones, start bringing in scientists to sample and analyze. At this point, they were ordered back to the ship. They rotated out of the area, replaced by another team. He had mixed feelings about this. Going aboard the Tauran ship was a dangerous job. It was stressful and it put his team at risk. On the other hand, it felt like a once-in-a-lifetime opportunity, a unique experience. Marcus and team went back to the rearguard, translated out of the sector soon after.

He had plenty of stories to tell but was told, in very clear terms, not to. They were all told so. The fact that they were on the derelict ship was on record, but all other details were classified. Everything they had seen was to remain top secret.

They had plenty of stories but little knowledge. Marcus still didn't understand how the ship worked, couldn't say what its technology could do, had no idea where the Taurans were. He would never forget the disorienting feeling of being sucked out into space, being tossed around in a deafening noise that instantly turned quiet once you were out in the cold. He would never forget realizing his suit was melting off of him, the panic of navigating back to safety blind, seconds away from what must be one of the most painful ways to go. He would never forget the two sappers the ship took out while in its otherworldly sleep.

24: BLACK MARKET

Elena and the *Charon* crew stick to the docks after that initial walk around the station. The contrast is stark—while the station is in terrible shape, the black market is booming. The docks are teeming with merchants, guns for hire, smugglers, customers, all overseen by the freelancing security detail. Many ships come here to trade, enticed by the port with no guidebeam and no official authority. *There's always someone profiting,* muses Elena.

They don't want to stick around more than needed. They make short excursions to shop. Terek gets her a prosthetic right hand and a replacement VoidTech graft. Standard Edition graft this time, but Elena can't tell the difference between this and her previous Tactical Edition. She suspects it's just branding, to take some extra money out of the military's budget.

The medic installs them in their improvised med bay, using local anesthesia. She's wide awake during the procedure, so they talk while he is working. He first attaches the hand.

"You'll be playing the piano in no time," he says.

"Seen anything like this on Forge?" She's curious. His work is fast and precise, like he's done this many times before. She suspects this type of injury is common in the mining business.

"You wouldn't believe the shit I saw there," he says solemnly. "So many accidents down in the mines."

She can only imagine.

"I've seen every limb crushed, arms, legs, spines, necks. Some you can fix, some you can't."

Corporate safety standards. She recalls the bright posters she kept seeing on Forge, especially the "Stronger together" one.

"Seen a kid once," Terek continues while expertly attaching the hand to her stump, "couldn't have been twenty, no idea how he got down there so young. Cave-in, half his head crushed to nothing. He was still alive somehow when I got there." He pauses working on her, looks absently in the distance. "Nothing I could do for him." He shakes his head and resumes the procedure.

"Sorry, Doc. Didn't mean to bring up bad memories."

"They're always up, these memories."

Nothing to say to that. He works in silence for a while. She watches, her arm completely numb, how he uses a complicated-looking gadget to trim the prosthetic into a perfectly fitting shape, activates the nanotendrils that will connect with her traumatized nerve endings.

After a while, he says, "I'm so glad to be out of that hellhole."

"You and me both, Doc." She smiles.

"Next time," he says, "try not to get yourself into trouble, OK?" He is looking at her with grave eyes from atop his thick gray beard.

She can't help but laugh at that. She's very much over the spy shit.

"Doctor's orders?" she teases.

"You bet." He smiles back, his gaze softening.

"I'm done with it," she promises.

The only thing she wants is to get out of here. Out of Horizon Station, out of Sector 36. She feels safe aboard the *Charon*—in good company. On a lark, she imagined herself asking Jaxon to join their "independent logistics" company. But that was just a fantasy. The sector is all bad memories for her, old and recent. Plus, she is positive her latest adventures on Forge got her on some lists. No way one can trespass on corporate property, pull off what she did (how *did* she do it?) and not expect repercussions.

"Good as new," Terek says, lifting his gadget up. "Let me wake your arm back up."

He injects her arm with a stimulant. She feels sensation coming back. The fiber-plastic hand feels alien. Her brain is learning how to interface with the synthetic nerve endings, trying various protocols. She feels pain, then, an instant after, itchiness. The itchiness turns into pinpricks, which eventually morph into the right subset of sensations: pressure, texture, temperature.

"How is it feeling?"

"Pretty good, Doc." She twists her right hand, makes a fist, opens it. It feels like a part of her. A somewhat clumsy part of her, but close enough to make no difference.

Terek watches her try out the new hand. "Coordination will get better over time," he assures her. "Let's do the grafts now. That should be easy."

Only a small fraction of the population needs grafts, NSRS being a rare condition. But, at galaxy scale, the absolute number of afflicted individuals (or, as graft manufacturers call them, total addressable market) is large enough. Large enough to turn a profit, making grafts relatively easy to find and install. Elena had the same standard ports installed to receive the implants as everyone else. And, lucky her, the energy weapon didn't damage them. Terek finishes connecting the new grafts in under ten minutes.

"Anything else I can do for you?" he asks.

"My stomach is still bothering me," she says. And it's true. She feels good, walks around, then suddenly her insides well up with pain. "Sometimes it hurts when I walk."

"How bad?"

That's a good question. "On a scale from stubbing your toe to getting your eye melted off, about somewhere in the middle." She experienced both ends of that spectrum, the eye quite recently. The pain in her abdomen is not even close to that agony, but she has to will herself to push through it.

"Your wound is still healing," says the doctor. "It will take time. In the meanwhile, I can give you some stims for the pain. Will keep you going, numb it. But be careful, they're addictive. Take one if it becomes unbearable."

"Only in case of emergency," she agrees.

Terek hands her a pill bottle. He holds onto it as she grabs it, looks her in the eye. "I'm serious."

"Yes sir!"

Finally, she can get back online. She hated being dependent. Her first order of business is to settle her debts with the *Charon* crew. The small fortune she got for her mission is almost depleted. Next, she sends a message to her contact on Nova Prime. She is sticking to protocol, the agreed-upon code words, though she finds it ridiculous now. She has no cover—she never had any. But she still sticks to protocol, mostly not to get her contact in trouble. Her message is short and to the point: *Business concluded, no deal. Coming for that meetup right away.* It roughly translates to: *Utter failure. Get me out of here.* She shouldn't have come in the first place.

They're almost ready to depart, just a few hours to kill while Kaela is installing their new transponder. The rest of the crew is out for a final round of shopping. Elena decides to get out on the docks too. She's been in a bad way ever since Forge. She goes looking for tacticals. *Better to have one and not need it than to need one and not have it,* as the saying goes.

She's now partial to the weapon she got on Verdant—it served her well. Noctics Mark 2. She gets online, using her freshly installed grafts, and checks if anyone has one available. She finds one on the *Radiant*, a ship docked a short walk away from the *Charon*. She heads out to make the purchase. Her backpack had more gear, ANTs and combat gloves, a chameleon jacket, but she's not prepping for more action. The Noctics is just for safety.

· · ·

The *Radiant* looks newer and shinier than the *Charon*, weapons dealing seems to be good business. The ship has a large cargo hold turned into a gun show, rows upon rows of weapons on display. She steps inside. A small group is haggling with one of the vendors at one of the display tables. One of the smugglers not busy with customers steps up to greet her.

"How can I help you?" he asks. She can feel the pity in his voice as he looks her up and down, notices her synthetic hand, the eye patch, and the burn scars on her face. *No more beauty pageants for me*, she thinks. But she never considered her looks one of her strengths.

"I'm here for a Noctics Mark 2."

"Right this way," he says and leads her to one of the tables. She picks it up, feels the comforting weight. She turns it this way and that. It looks exactly like her previous pistol. She checks the sight, thumbs the safety off and on, ensures everything works as it should. A quality piece. She hopes she won't have to use it. Barring that, she hopes it will serve her just as well as the previous one. He is watching her from the side.

"You know how to handle your guns, miss," he comments.

She pays for it, a box of ammo, and heads back out on the docks. As she is walking back towards the *Charon*, she hears voices rising nearby. The commotion turns into a loud argument. A tall blond man shoves a shorter, red-haired one. He stumbles back a few steps then as he steadies himself. He pulls out a gun and shoots the blond in the chest. Elena steps back, hand going instinctively to her Noctics. But she hasn't loaded it yet.

People are forming a wide circle around the incident, but nobody intervenes. She sees one of the private security people next to her, standing, watching. She asks him, "Aren't you going to do anything?"

"Nope," he says, sounding like he's seen this many times before. "I'm paid to keep the station scum out of here. I'm not police, let them sort it out."

The shorter man tucks his gun away and stomps out of the circle. People who witnessed him shoot the blond give him room to pass, but soon he becomes part of the crowd, disappears in the sea of people.

The blond man is dead, vacant eyes staring at nothing. Elena picks up the pace. Jaxon was right, Wild West indeed. *Time to get out of here.*

Her stomach starts hurting. She reaches in her pocket, takes a stim, and the pain dulls. The doctor wasn't wrong, the effect is almost instantaneous. Her focus gets sharper, colors seem more vibrant, she feels stronger. Interesting side effects. She makes it to the *Charon* without further incidents.

Everyone is there, on the bridge and ready for takeoff. Everyone, that is, except Terek. The doctor stepped out to get medical supplies and seems to be running late.

"Where's Doc?" asks Jaxon. "I'll tell him we're leaving if he's not back in five," he says. An empty threat, of course, he doesn't mean it, but it should get their medic to hurry up. He embeds, comes back right away.

"There's something wrong."

"What?" Rynn asks.

Kaela is already embedded, trying to see what Jaxon saw. Elena gets online too, she's no longer locked outside the digital.

{Doc!} she hears Kaela sending on their shared comms channel.

{Help!} he sends back.

{I got him.} Kaela shares his real-time location with them. He's close to the *Charon*. Very close. He is approaching it slowly.

"Let's get him," says Jaxon and they all rush to the airlock. He opens it and the doctor falls inside, bleeding.

"Oh my God," says Kaela.

His shirt is soaked. They take it off, turn him around.

"Stab wound," he says. Grunts. "Get the med kit."

"We got you, Doc," says Rynn.

Kaela rushes back with their first aid kit. Jaxon gestures them aside, grabs a wad of gauze and applies it to the wound, trying to control the bleeding.

Terek coughs up blood. "I think they hit the lung," he says, gasping for breath.

Elena's watching this from the side. She feels rage swelling inside her. Someone stabbed him. Someone stabbed this nice man, this man who put her back together, saved her life.

The doctor's lips are turning blue. Jaxon sits him up, changes gauzes. The first wad is soaked through already. He is wheezing.

"We need a doctor," she says. Terek can barely breathe; he won't be able to do anything himself. And they don't have the skills to address this type of injury; he is hurt way beyond first aid.

"No med help," Kaela says. "Been broadcasting SOS to the whole dock. Fuck!"

Nobody willing to help, everyone for themselves in the Wild West.

"What about on the station?"

But by the looks of it, they'll never make it there.

"Doc, can you hear me?" asks Jaxon.

Terek doesn't answer, he looks around wide-eyed, like he doesn't know them. Coughs up some more blood.

25: DEUS MACHINA

Commissar Vesper is putting together her report. She's sitting, embedded, at her desk, back inside the command unit. She is forcing herself to conjure the words that will best describe the biggest fuck-up of her career. Career-ending big. She doesn't look forward to delivering this report, but she owns it. The whole clown show happened under her watch, and the buck stops with her.

She shouldn't have underestimated Elena Drake or allowed such lax discipline with the troops. She should've had more eyes on the target and called a lockdown as soon as she realized they lost her. She shouldn't have delayed putting out that APB.

She adds all these realizations to her report. What she doesn't add: this would've never happened with Inferno. Working with Eclipse Corps has always been a pain. And she had no choice in the matter; she works with the resources given to her.

She recalls the aftermath. Sergeant Mason, without body armor and using a kinetic, both against direct orders. It's on her though, she agreed to the job. She knew what she was getting herself into. Corporate promised good perks, big sign-on bonus for this one. It sounded like a good career move at the time. What a mistake.

She takes a break, stands up from her desk, paces the unit for a couple of minutes. She's not a procrastinator, so she *will* finish writing up this report. Today. But God, it's such a slog. She sits back down, embeds again, gets back to it.

In the report, she is framing some of the mishaps as good learnings for future ops. Lessons learned the hard way. Who is she kidding though? She is in deep trouble. Absolutely no good came out of this mess. There's no way to put a positive spin on what just happened.

Elena Drake disappeared. Pulling off a stunt that their digital specialist called "impossible." Not only did she escape their trap, she was able to exfil off Forge. They went over the whole hive with a fine-toothed comb. At the same time, they started sifting through the digital. They found a suspicious transmission from one of their older comms systems, relaying coordinates to a ship in orbit. It was absent from the comms system's log but captured by a traffic monitor. Coordinates and directions in and out. Coordinates suspiciously close to where the trap was laid.

They checked the unit, found a copious amount of blood. It matched some of the blood found where the fight took place. It wasn't Sergeant Mason's, it wasn't Private Walter's, it wasn't Private Lance's. That blood was Elena's. Somehow, she was able to call for an extraction, using their network, and plot a path that—and here comes the impossible part—avoided all video feeds, avoided the search parties, avoided anything that would stop her.

How? Piecing it all together, it means Elena Drake is off planet. By the time they ID'd the ship the message was sent to, it had warped away from Forge. Unbelievable, but the bitch escaped. They lost her. She lost her. *God dammit.* She slaps a hand on her desk. The other mercs in the room flinch, resume their work pretending like nothing happened.

She plays chess, she's quite good at it. If this was a chess game, she would tilt her king over now, resign. Game over. She might be asked to resign anyway. Once this report is done, sent up the chain. What will she do then?

She admits she is terrified. She used to have a spotless record. She's the one they call when they need shit done right. Clockwork-like. The one they *used* to call, she corrects herself. Nobody will call her after she fucked up so bad.

It takes her quite some time to write everything up. She attaches, for reference, the pre-mission materials: briefs, maps, the plan (her plan). She also attaches the follow-ups: forensic reports, autopsy data, telemetry from the traffic monitor intercepting the old comms system that aided Elena's escape. Finally, the report is done. She is done. She is about to submit it, resigned to her fate, thinking of where she could best apply her skills next, when they receive new, urgent orders. Everyone receives them, it's a wide broadcast.

{Lift up. Everyone lift up. Embed for personal assignments.}

It was bound to happen sooner or later, she thinks. She hopes against hope this will delay having to submit the report. Bigger things are afoot. Maybe she can slip through the cracks. She hates herself for even thinking that. Her whole life is built around eliminating cracks.

She embeds, looks up where she's supposed to go. The destroyer *Nemesis.* They're being mobilized. She looks up mission details, but details are sparse. The one thing that stands out to her is this is a major mobilization. Most of the ships orbiting Forge are being manned, prepped for sail. Where to is unspecified, but it must be Eureka Base.

She hurries to her unit to pack her things. The walkways are utter chaos. Seems like every single mercenary and security consultant in the hive received the order and they're all rushing to their quarters to grab their gear and lift. It takes her exactly four minutes to get from the command unit to her room. That's one minute longer than usual, due to the swarm of people.

Packing is easy, her room is neatly organized. It takes her no time to be ready. She's on the elevator before a line has time to form. She's one of the first in high orbit.

. . .

She looks at the fleet assembled above Forge. The large number of ships and their immensely complex coordination give her a sense of deep satisfaction. Discipline. At scale. Something she wasn't able to achieve with the comparatively small team she was overseeing on the ground.

She spots the *Umbra*, the largest destroyer in the fleet, equipped with the latest particle cannon tech. It is orbiting close to the *Nemesis*, its batteries positioned all around its black hull. A miracle of engineering.

She is early. It will take hours for all the personnel to lift up. They're disorganized and slow. She finds her quarters, unpacks, thinks. She needs to submit the report. Doesn't she? Is the report still necessary? She can't leave any loose ends; it's not in her nature. But is it still relevant, considering the mass mobilization? It doesn't matter; it's her job to submit it. She knows her career is over as soon as she does so, so she spends a few more minutes before sending it in. She stretches, drinks some water, paces around her quarters. She watches the elevators go up and down. Thousands are lifting up. Tens of thousands.

Finally, she submits the report. She sighs, stares out the window at the hypnotic dance of the elevators for a while longer, then decides she needs to talk to someone competent. Someone who doesn't fuck up. She embeds, reaches out to Arcturus.

Arcturus is the Omega AI overseeing Abyssal Mining operations. She has the utmost respect for it—an infinitely complex operation spanning every sector in the galaxy, and the Omega still makes time to chat with humans. She is not worthy, especially after what she just did. But she needs to make sense of things.

It materializes as a bright pulsing sphere, like it always does.

"Hello, Commissar," it says.

"May I have a minute of your time?"

She's never quite sure what the proper etiquette is. How do you address a god?

"Time is an illusion, Vesper."

It is always cryptic. It adds to her feelings of unworthiness. She could spend days trying to puzzle meaning out of its dense replies.

"What's going on?"

"Everything. Everywhere." It pauses for a second. "You caused me a lot of trouble, Commissar."

She is appalled at this. She had no idea of the scale of her fuck-up. Was Elena Drake that important? God, how much trouble is she really in?

"I ... I'm sorry."

"Don't. You don't have the moral awareness to be sorry."

It is upset with her. She's being scolded by an Omega.

"I'm not upset with you," it continues, like it read her mind. "You are all God's children."

That gives her some comfort.

"What can I do?" she asks. *To atone,* she doesn't add.

"Focus on the mission, Vesper!" And with that, it disconnects.

She reflects on their short dialogue. Not a lot of insight. But that's her fault. She's too dull to make sense of it. She caused Arcturus a lot of trouble. But it's not upset with her. She needs to focus on the mission. What is the mission?

She's still unclear where she's going and why. It makes her uneasy. She thrives on information. Information is a key part of her job, the reason she excels at what she does. She *used* to excel, she reminds herself.

She reaches out, asks her superiors.

"Where are we going?"

"Nova Prime, Commissar."

That is a surprise. She could've sworn their target would be Eureka Base, the lab there, the alien device.

"Why?"

"Standby for further instructions."

"Understood," she says. Then, tentatively, "What about my report?"

"Not now, Commissar."

Very odd. Their whole outfit was deployed to allegedly protect Forge from the Tauran threat. Vesper knows the real objective, but that doesn't have anything to do with Nova Prime. Maybe the whole thing got called off? Get some R&R in the capital, then translate out for new adventures? She hopes that's it. Her experience tells her it isn't.

26: TURN

The doctor is fading fast. They're all watching helplessly as life is draining out of him.

Elena steps closer, puts a hand on his shoulder. "Doc. Who did this?"

He's pale, weak. Looks up at her. "They're looking for you," he whispers.

Not again.

The doctor wheezes, coughs. Jaxon keeps applying pressure to the wound, but it doesn't seem to do much. Blood is spewing out and he's having trouble breathing. Kaela embeds, sends desperate messages, comes back. There's nobody able to help. Or willing to. They watch as he takes his last short breath, falls on his side.

"Fuck," Jaxon says, throwing the soaked gauze to the side.

Elena watches Kaela tear up, watches all of them step back a couple of paces. She is not sad, she is angry. She almost died and now they're hurting the people who helped her, kept her alive. She turns to Kaela. "What did he mean they're looking for me?"

Kaela embeds. {Check this out.} She sends Elena a clip, combed out of thousands of video feeds from the docked ships. It's two of them, bullying the doctor into a corner. They don't look like operators. Not in great physical shape, not dressed for an op. One of them is large. Very large. He wears a shoulder holster over a huge white shirt that barely covers his girth. The other one is short, wearing a red jacket that makes him easily stand out of a crowd.

They seem to be asking the doctor questions. He shrugs, nods his head from side to side. The larger one shoves the doctor's left shoulder. He stumbles back, half-turns. The short one produces a knife from his jacket, stabs the doctor in the back. They walk away.

{Left him there to bleed out,} from Kaela.

So they did. She's seen enough. She grabs her newly acquired gun, double-checks to make sure it is loaded this time, and steps onto the docks without another word.

She starts walking, takes a stim. It works its magic right away, her pain dissolves into a background tingle. She feels her senses heighten again. *What am I doing?* But she knows what she's doing. She's going to find those two fuckers. They're looking for her. She has to take the initiative.

She gets online.

{Kaela, can you get a visual on them?}

{Looking.}

{I … I'm sorry,} she sends to them while Kaela is searching. It's her fault. She caused this, she got them into all this trouble. Terek paid for it. Fuck!

{Not your fault,} replies Kaela. It's the right thing to say, but it is her fault—deep down she knows it is.

Jaxon catches up with her. "Where are you going?" he asks, short of breath after sprinting after her.

"Get back to the ship. I'll join you in no time." Or not. Doesn't matter much to her either way.

"Come back, we can leave now."

She ignores him.

{Found them,} sends Kaela. {Take a left turn.} She sends her a live feed. They're still going around, talking to people, getting closer to the *Radiant*. Elena recognizes the ship since she just returned from there with her new Noctics. The size of the large man and the red jacket of the short one are unmistakable.

{They're bounty hunters,} sends Kaela. {Sure enough, there's a bounty on you.} She sends her details. Elena skims through them while walking. Anonymous bid. It's not dead or alive. Just dead. Fine, have it their way.

{Shit. There's a bounty on Jaxon too.}

Jaxon is still walking next to her. "Really, don't do this."

"Get back to the *Charon*, Jaxon."

"Come with."

She keeps walking.

{They got data on both of you. It's all attached to the bid.} Kaela is digging into the digital, sharing her findings. {I bet you they found Doc, asked him your whereabouts, but he convinced them they had the wrong guy.}

Sounds plausible, matches the vid she saw. Otherwise, they wouldn't have left him.

{Stabbed him anyway,} Elena sends back. The sheer meanness of it turns her blood icy.

{Fuckers,} Kaela agrees.

Getting close now. She's making her way through the crowd, pushing people aside if they're not making way. She takes her pistol out. The gun feels somehow different in her prosthetic hand, but the grip is familiar nevertheless. Jaxon falls back behind her.

The dock is busy as usual, groups of people conducting all sorts of shady businesses. They step back when they see the gun, clearing a path for them. But that is their only reaction. It's probably a common sight on Horizon. No screams, no alarms, no cops. Elena sees a couple of private security uniforms standing on the side. They watch dispassionately as Elena and Jaxon push ahead, her leading the way with a weapon in hand. They don't care. Nobody cares.

"What are we doing, Elena?" he asks. He gave up on trying to convince her to return to the ship, willing to lend a hand now. She doesn't answer. It's self-explanatory. And he doesn't need to be here. There's a lot of people around, but she's seen enough shit go down during their short stay here that she's not worried at all about causing a scene.

A few more steps, one more turn. There they are. The prow of the *Radiant* behind them, the two bounty hunters are talking to someone, backs to her. She can see the big guy's face on the feed Kaela sent her. The short one is hidden from the camera by their interlocutor. Between her own eye and Kaela's feed, she has a surround view of them.

She watches herself on the feed, approaching from behind, lifting the gun up to the larger one's head, pulling the trigger.

His head explodes, spraying pieces on the docks, the short bounty hunter, and on their interlocutor. He falls with a thud. People yelp, start moving away from the scene. The woman they were talking to—she now notices it was a woman, short-cropped hair, sunken eyes—turns around and runs. She is smeared with bits of the big guy's head. The short bounty hunter turns towards her, mouth agape. His red jacket is now stained with his partner's brain matter. She doesn't give him a chance to react. She lowers the gun, shoots him in the lower abdomen. The high-caliber kinetic round tears through him. He goes down on his ass, screaming, his pants quickly soaking in red.

He is crying now. Definitely not professionals. She looks down at him. The wound is fatal; he's missing a large part of his lower body and he'll bleed out soon. She is positive there's no way to patch a wound that size. But she doesn't take any chances, shoots him again, this time in the face. *I'm so sorry, Doc.* Bystanders are watching from a safe distance. Just another day on the Horizon docks. Nobody steps in to intervene. Business as usual.

She scans the crowd defiantly, gun in hand. *Any other bounty hunters out here?* she doesn't ask. Some people avert their eyes, avoid her gaze. Others look on without any reaction.

She turns around, starts walking back towards the *Charon*. Jaxon is watching her aghast. She continues past him, puts the gun away, keeps walking. As before, people who witnessed the scene clear a wide path, then the path narrows, then she is just another person in the crowd. Jaxon is behind her again, following. He doesn't say anything.

{Good job!} Kaela sends her.

{Fuck those fuckers!} adds Rynn.

Looks like they were all watching the feed. Except poor Doctor Terek. She doesn't feel good about what she just did. She feels she had to do it. She keeps walking.

Back on the *Charon*, she notices blood on her shirt. Splatter from one of the close-range shots. Some on her face, some on her eye patch. She takes a long shower. The *Charon* leaves Horizon Station as she is drying off.

New transponder installed, they begin their journey towards Nova Prime. Rynn navigates the docks relying on peer-to-peer path negotiation with the surrounding ships. Their vessel peels away from the station, accelerates. From this distance, Elena is positive she can see the subtly erratic spin of the segments, the hiccups leading to fluctuations in the artificial gravity. She thinks of the station denizens imprisoned there by the smuggler militia. She wonders how often black market business concludes with a shootout. She thinks of Hope, the promise of an ark, the recyclers. The barely functioning infrastructure of what was the newest Sector 36 outpost. How did they get here? Why did Ingram allow this to happen?

The *Charon* puts more distance between them and the accursed place.

She thinks of Terek Nassar, telling her about the kid he couldn't save on Forge. Telling her about Abyssal withholding his license. Her offering to help, offering to try pulling some strings for him. He was a good man. Stabbed in the back, because he didn't give her up. Her act of vengeance didn't do him any good.

The ship speeds up, her view from aboard freezing into a still image as they go superluminal.

27: BRIEFING

The *Dauntless* arrives at the ring, together with the rest of the flotilla, after five days of transit. Aboard the ship, rumors about the reason for redeployment abound in a vacuum of real information. Marcus hears some reasonable takes (ensuring Gateway Ring security, much like they did for Eureka Base), some truly outlandish ones (Sector 36 is being evacuated due to a surprise Tauran attack), and everything in between. He tries to ignore the speculations, focuses on maintaining combat readiness for his small team, but can't help wondering what is really going on.

Once they reach the ring and decelerate from FTL, the warships stop at a safe distance. The large ring is surrounded by civilian ships, there's no room to get closer without shooing them off. And the civilian ships have no place to go.

Lieutenant Marcus Wade watches this from one of the decks as most of his team walks up to join him: Howard, Santos, Anders, and Novak. Everyone except Kim.

"Dash, where's Kimmy?" he asks his chief petty officer.

"He's been called in for a VIP escort—some bigwig visiting their ship."

Marcus is surprised to hear they plucked Kim out without keeping him in the loop, but he doesn't mind. It's some higher up expediting things, it happens.

They watch in awe what must be the largest gathering of civilian ships in the galaxy. There are even more of them around the ring now than when they translated in. A lot more. Sector 36 inhabitants are converging on the ring, desperate for a way out. But there is no way out, the jump gate is still mostly being allocated to one-way inbound traffic.

"Impressive," says Chief Petty Officer Howard.

"It would take weeks to translate out all those ships," observes Marcus.

"If the Taurans attack here, those people are in big trouble."

"Aye. Good thing they got us to protect them." Marcus wants to sound reassuring but he doesn't feel it. Tauran tech is on par with theirs, a fight here would be disastrous for the civilians. Like Echo Point, but with more casualties. Many more casualties. Echo Point had around twenty million occupants, there are currently around a hundred million on the ring. Probably a couple more million aboard the ships swarming about. His train of thought is interrupted by an urgent message.

{Lieutenant Wade, report to the briefing room,} he receives.

"Going up to see what the brass wants," he tells his team.

"About time," says Santos. "They kept us in the dark for long enough."

Anders nods. They all share the sentiment.

Marcus turns around and starts towards the briefing room. Located right underneath the bridge, the briefing room is a large, circular space with a round table at its center. He saw it exactly once, while doing a tour of the ship. Briefings are usually held in the digital. The fact that he's been summoned for an in-person meet feels like a bad omen. He shares the sentiment of his team, wants to finally understand why there was such a large movement of troops, but is irrationally afraid of what he might learn.

He crosses the passageways of the ship at a brisk pace, trying to shake off the feeling of dread, but can't outpace it. He walks past sailors and marines performing daily duties. The passageways are not spacious, this being a military ship, but he spent enough time aboard that he doesn't mind. They're familiar. He even finds the low background hum of the ship soothing. As he walks, he runs into another lieutenant team leader, part of the same Vanguard contingent aboard the *Dauntless*. They're both heading the same way. They fall in line, start walking in lockstep without meaning to.

"Any idea what's going on, Wade?" asks Lieutenant Ashley Bennett.

"Negative." Nobody seems to know. "But looks like we'll find out soon."

"Think it's the Taurans?"

"Hope not."

"Briefing room is not good news," observes Bennett. Indeed. So, he's not the only one who finds this out of the ordinary. The added ceremony of gathering team leaders into a room for an in-person must mean something very serious is about to go down. More likely than not, this is not a drill. They make their way to the briefing room.

Marcus walks through the door into a sizable crowd of senior officers. All seats around the round table are taken. Many people standing too, the space is already stuffy. Once inside, Marcus and his comrade Bennett must walk along the wall to make room for others—a constant stream of officers pouring into the modest briefing room. He looks around, sees almost every officer he knows is inside. A lot of familiar faces too, people he doesn't know personally but has seen around the ship. Even more people he never saw before, which most likely means they have officers from other ships aboard. This adds to his feeling of uneasiness, something very serious is about to happen if they're using the *Dauntless* for such a large in-person brief. Some of the unfamiliar faces wear silver comets and stars, identifying them as captains and rear admirals. A lot of high-ranking officers are present. There's a murmur permeating the cramped space as people talk in small clusters. As he walks around the edge of the room, he overhears "Taurans" several times.

He finally stops, on the side opposite the entrance, as there's no more space left for him to continue. He turns to face the center of the room. Atop the round table, a large 3D display shows a local map: a projection of the Gateway Ring at its center, the jump gate a way out to the right from his perspective. Hundreds of ships loiter all around the ring and hundreds more are gathered a few clicks away. The tactical overlay identifies the ships around the ring as mostly civilian, with some military vessels mixed in. A distance away from the ring, the overlay calls out their own flotilla, the heavy cruiser *Dauntless* and the many other ships that accompanied them from Eureka Base, plus an additional contingent from the ring that reinforced their ranks. The *Dauntless* stands out, together with the *Ares* and *Excalibur*, the three largest ships redeployed from Eureka Base. Anticipation builds. He watches the ring slowly rotate as people around him whisper their suppositions. He closes his eyes for a second, inhales deeply, exhales.

"So, what do you think?" Lieutenant Bennett whispers to him. She's been right behind him since they entered the room, both too distracted by the unusual crowd until now to talk.

He is about to say what feels like his thousandth *I don't know* when a loud, commanding voice interrupts them: "Admiral on deck!"

They all snap to attention, the chairs around the tactical view emptying. Everyone salutes. The crowd is suddenly quiet, chatter instantly cut by the admiral's presence. Marcus has seen him in person twice before, at ceremonial functions. He is a tall man, an imposing presence, with silver hair and pale blue eyes. They're all watching him.

He crosses the room, the crowd parting for him as he makes his way to the round table. He stands next to it. "Carry on," he says.

The room relaxes, but nobody sits back down at the round table. Not before the admiral.

"Let's get on with this," he says to no one in particular and takes a seat.

Other high-ranking officers follow suit. The admiral embeds to get control of the display, then, feeling the tension in the room, decides to come back, address everyone's unspoken question.

"One thing I want to make clear out of the gate is there's no new intel on Taurans."

Marcus hears a couple of whispers. The admiral re-embeds, and the display zooms out to show a map of the whole sector.

The Viridian Shroud Nebula is immense. Marcus is reminded of the scale as he watches the *Dauntless* quickly become invisible, then soon after the Gateway Ring and jump gate become too small to see without an overlay annotating their position. All of this while the background swirl of green gas barely changes size. They're specks of dust in a volume spanning some hundreds of light-years in each direction. *Kind of puts things in perspective*, he thinks.

"We deployed a large number of assets near Eureka Base," the admiral starts the briefing.

The tactical overlay highlights the neutron star, NS-36-A, on the map, circling it with a glowing yellow contour, then it renders an annotated arrow labeled "Eureka Base" pointing in its vicinity.

"More recently, we redeployed a third of the fleet here," and, as he says that, the Gateway Ring gets its own annotated arrow "... and around Nova Prime." The tactical overlay highlights Nova Sol, giving it its own glowing yellow halo, and a new arrow materializes for Nova Prime, the sector capital.

The troop movement described by the admiral is translated into two lines connecting Eureka Base with the ring and Nova Prime.

"A third of our fleet is still at Eureka Base," says the admiral, and the tactical overlay replaces the view of the galaxy with a zoomed-in 3D view of the ships near Eureka Base, displayed on top of the NS-36-A System. "Standing orders to defend the base."

Marcus can tell there is still a sizable number of warships there, even if only a third of their fleet. He doesn't bother to pull up an exact count.

"A third is now here," continues the admiral, and the tactical overlay swaps Eureka Base for the original view Marcus saw upon entering the room: the Gateway Ring at the center, and their ships next to it. Marcus can easily identify the *Dauntless*.

"...and the last third just reached Nova Prime," concludes the admiral, switching away from the ring to Nova Prime.

A similarly sized flotilla seems to be orbiting the capital.

"You were ordered to maintain condition two." Condition two. Ready for combat at a moment's notice, without expecting immediate engagement. Purgatory. The admiral pauses as he zooms the display back out to the view of the sector.

Marcus knows most of this already. He wasn't aware ships were also redeployed around Nova Prime, but he witnessed firsthand the massive movement of vessels. Like everyone else gathered in the briefing room. He has been dutifully keeping his team at condition two, surprised this wasn't relaxed after they left Eureka Base. He is trying to guess where the admiral is going with this but can't come up with anything besides a new Tauran incursion. Though that can't be it —the admiral started the briefing by addressing what was on everyone's mind: there is no new Tauran intel. So, what is it then? The bad feeling Marcus got since he was summoned here intensifies.

The admiral continues: "Moreover, paramilitary troops have been amassed around Forge."

The sector map is replaced by a view of the hive world, its spindly space elevators poking out of its atmosphere. An incredibly large fleet is orbiting the planet. The paramilitary outfits contracted by Abyssal Mining.

"Abyssal Mining Consortium," says the admiral, "is working with Eclipse Corps and Inferno Troops. Embed for capability assessment details."

Nothing new here either. After the Tauran War, Eureka Base defense was the military's top priority, since the colony was on the front line of the war. Abyssal translated troops in to ensure defense of their mining operation and corporate citizenry. Two well-known private military companies. Marcus knows the two merc companies fought each other during Elena Drake's deployment but ended up on the same payroll after the merger of Titanforge with Abyssal. Out of curiosity, he quickly embeds to peek at the capability assessment. At first glance, the amount of information compiled looks gargantuan.

Seems like their intelligence spared no expense to produce this. He wonders why.

"We have intel of Abyssal vessels similarly redeploying from Forge to the capital and here."

Back to the sector-wide view, two new lines connect Forge with the Gateway Ring and Nova Prime. All the fleet movements end up painting a large V on the nebula's viridian backdrop, its ends at Eureka Base and Forge, the two navies converging towards the center of the sector.

Strange, is all Marcus can think. He still can't fathom what would cause such a large reallocation of firepower if not an imminent Tauran threat. He is watching the display, waiting for the punchline.

The admiral delivers it with his next sentence: "Consider all para-military ships hostile."

28: CLOSURE

The trip from Horizon Station to Nova Prime is shorter, a matter of days. Elena has time to reflect on the utter failure of her mission and think about next steps. She's done with Spark. It's time to go back to Aurelia, be with her family. She wasted a lot of credits, got no answers, and lost a hand and an eye. For what? Spark couldn't outplay an Omega, they never stood a chance. Shit, she's lucky to be alive. She's had it with this whole charade.

Doctor Linton is gone. She is sure of it. She would've liked to have better closure, find the doctor, dead or alive. There is no way he escaped Eclipse Corps on Forge. He made a mistake going there, a mistake that cost him his life. She followed him and almost paid the full price too.

The crew of the *Charon* is avoiding her after the incident on Horizon. They seem to be busy doing other things whenever she is around. They're mourning Terek. She understands, wishes it wasn't like this. She is deeply sorry for what happened to the doctor. She still doesn't consider what she did an overreaction.

"They had it coming," Kaela tells her eventually. "I ..." she stammers, "I wish ... I wish I could've done what you did." She turns around and walks away, mumbling an, "Excuse me."

Elena watches her leave. Those bounty hunters hurt someone she cared about. She thought herself beyond caring, not to this level, not after Darius. The crew of the *Charon* saved her life, nursed her back to health. They exchanged life stories. Then Terek got hurt because of her. She's a trouble magnet. No matter, she'll be out of here in no time.

"On our way to Horizon Station, you asked me if I want to leave Sector 36 with you," Jaxon tells her as their trip nears its end. Not a question, a statement of fact.

She still isn't sure she can make it happen even if he wants to. Still feels like she owes them.

"I can't promise anything …"

"No need to," Jaxon tells her. "I tried really hard to bootstrap a legit logistics business once I was out of the military. A business that couldn't compete with the mega-corporations."

She can imagine.

Jaxon continues: "Abyssal pretty much has the monopoly in the sector now. Few other mega-corps tested the water, came and went. How can a small outfit compete with that?"

After years of taking orders, Jaxon really wanted independence after the military.

"I guess I could've joined, become a corporate citizen, run logistics for Abyssal. I have the resume for it. But fuck them."

She learns that Jaxon hung onto his business even as it was hemorrhaging money, draining his meager savings.

"Then it clicked for me," he says. "I figured out there's some very well-paying jobs in the sector if you're willing to ask fewer questions."

He pauses to look at Elena, to get her reaction. She nods slightly, wants to hear him finish his story.

"Some might call it dirty work, but in my opinion, corporate is a million times filthier. I don't lose sleep over it."

She imagines Abyssal does a lot more illegal shit than Jaxon and his crew, but with better cover, better marketing, and with the ability to deploy lawfare if they ever get in hot water. She doesn't mind them being smugglers. She knew and accepted this from day one. Plus, they saved her life.

"I know it's dangerous, but with all the disruptions in the sector, now it's so easy to find well-paying contracts. I don't think I want to leave. Not yet."

Rynn appears to stay glued to his seat at the helm throughout the whole trip. The one time she runs into him outside the cockpit he nods to her and keeps walking.

The *Charon* slows down out of warp near the sector's capital. They're all on the bridge again, their unspoken tradition.

"What the …?" Rynn is piloting, so he gets to see the situation first, through the ship's digital senses. Everyone else notices it an instant later. Nova Prime is surrounded by warships. The *Charon* complains loudly as hundreds of sensors from dozens of ships notice it, start tracking it, probing it.

"I really hope you did a good job with that transponder, Kaela," says Jaxon.

All these ships can't be here for the *Charon*. That said, any one of them could easily swat them into nothingness. They're used to stealth entries, not jumping in front of headlights.

They take a landing vector, approach Nova Prime. They're all holding their breath. Their tiny ship is tracked from multiple angles, but nothing happens. No contact attempt, no weapons firing at them, nothing. Rynn manages to connect with Nova Prime spaceport to negotiate a landing. He's embedded, comes out for a second to update them: "Nova Prime has no idea what's going on up here. The good news: we're clear to land."

"There were rumors back on Horizon," Kaela reminds them. "Got all sorts of weird stories in the digital when we got there." She embeds, looking for local news.

"You think the Taurans are back?" Jaxon asks Elena.

She has no answer. She looks at the imposing display of force. Displays of force. On one side, she sees the familiar silhouettes of gray military ships, from large heavy cruisers to tiny auxiliary support. On the other side, there's the paramilitary navy: vessels equipped with strange-looking devices, coated in black paint. Ships like the ones she saw orbiting Forge, maybe even the same ships. What are they doing here?

"Check it out," Kaela comes back, "ships started arriving a couple of days ago. Large numbers, both military and paramilitary."

"Interesting. Why?"

"People on the ground don't know. There are rumors. Taurans, a coup, nothing conclusive."

People on the ground don't know.

"What is going on here?" whispers Jaxon, without receiving an answer.

The *Charon* enters the atmosphere without incident and is soon among the tallest spires of the Nova Prime City skyline. The Nova Prime colony is mostly made up of a single megacity, housing around a hundred million people. They descend between glass buildings. Despite its dense population, the city is designed to feel homey to its inhabitants and welcoming to visitors. Greenery hangs between buildings, there's plenty of light. Elena doesn't feel as suffocated as on Forge, quite the opposite. The city planners made the capital look beautiful. Plus, she is close to getting out of the sector.

As soon as the ship touches down, she gets online, reaches out to her contact at Obsidian Holdings.

{I'm on Nova Prime. How do we meet?}

She only has to wait a few seconds for a response.

{Come to the branch office. I'm here. There's ... bad news.}

Shit. Bad news. *What could that mean? What more could possibly go wrong?*

{OK, be there in a bit.}

She goes offline, sighs.

"Thank you for everything," she tells the whole crew. They nod back. "I'm going to the Obsidian Holdings branch office. Jaxon, come with, I'll make sure you get a bonus for all your help."

"Sure," he says.

Now that the moment has come, she regrets she has to part with them. She says her goodbyes to Kaela and Rynn. Even Rynn, the biggest introvert she ever met, manages to show some emotion, wishes her "good luck." Kaela gives her a big hug, tears up when she lets go. Elena is moved. She will miss the *Charon* crew.

She steps on the docks with Jaxon. They look for transport, hail a cab.

"What's next for you, Jaxon?"

"Back to business," he says. "We're looking for bids to pick up." He pauses, then adds, "I doubt we'll find another as lucrative as yours."

Both of them laugh bitterly at that. She paid a lot of money to fail her mission, get shot, barely survive. At least it wasn't out of her pocket, Spark sponsored the whole shitshow. Jaxon got paid a lot of money to end up with a compromised transponder, a dead crew member, a bounty on his head.

"You don't want another bid as 'lucrative' as mine."

He looks her in the eye, opens his mouth to speak, then decides not to. He smiles at her instead. She looks away, out the cab's window. The vehicle makes its way towards their destination, through the crowded streets.

She sees a lot of people. Some must be locals, some must be refugees. But all in all, the colony is in better shape than everything she's seen so far. Not as crowded as the ring, not as desolate as Verdant, not as claustrophobic as Forge, not as desperate as Horizon. People are not just milling around here; they walk with purpose.

Nova Prime City houses the administrative apparatus of the sector. Many businesses have offices here, moving a lot of money. Ingram's largest compute cluster is underneath the city. Nova Prime is too rich and too important to fall into as bad a shape as the other worlds across the sector.

Their ride navigates busy layered streets crisscrossing a grid of colossal glass buildings, each with its own architectural flourishes. A pair of twin buildings covered in jungle-green glass stand on each side of the road, connected by multiple arching bridges. The suspended road the cab is following weaves between two of these bridges, then takes a turn towards a silver-glassed building with its top lost in the clouds. The building sprouts round terraces every five floors, each terrace a lush garden, ivy hanging out over the railings. The road goes straight through the building, a long tunnel with walls covered in vines and tiny yellow flowers. They exit the tunnel next to another high-rise, this one displaying an ever-changing light show, each of its thousands of windows slowly shifting colors and forming strange, beautiful patterns.

Elena watches the opulence, thinks of the millions stranded on the ring, of Horizon Station's Segment 7.

They get out of the cab in front of a wide, imposing office building, made to look like cubes stacked on top of each other all the way up into the sky. Outside the vehicle, the air is fragrant with the scent of tropical flowers wafting in from the nearby gardens. She checks in at the reception (VP of Acquisitions—Obsidian Holdings) and gets a visitor badge for Jaxon. They take the elevator up to floor one hundred twenty. It's an exterior elevator, the ride giving them an increasingly broader view of the cityscape as they climb up. From here, it looks like a never-ending tapestry of green suspended gardens and multi-colored glass.

The Obsidian Holdings office spans a dozen floors with the same beautiful view that she and Jaxon saw on their way up. The workers here don't seem to notice the panorama—they're used to it by now. They sit, embedded, at their desks. Advancing the corporate agenda. Providing shareholder value. Elena wonders if this is what's in store for her next, now that her adventuring days are over for good.

She hasn't met her contact in person before, but he was part of her briefing. She knows what to expect: a late-middle-aged man, gray hair, lines of experience on his face. She spots him right away. He has a private office, glass walls isolating him from the rest of the employees. Her contact is high up the ladder. Spark is well-connected.

He waves them in as soon as he sees them approaching.

"Hello, Ms. Drake! I'm Ansel Marlow," he says, standing up from his desk as she steps through the door. The full name and title, as displayed on his door, reads "President Ansel William Marlow."

"Call me Elena," she says, shaking his extended hand.

He briefly looks at the synthetic hand he is shaking, then back at her eye patch.

"And this is Jaxon Barabe. His crew helped me out, saved my life."

"Nice to meet you, Mister Barabe," he says, extending his hand once more.

"Likewise," replies Jaxon.

"What happened out there?" Marlow asks her once introductions are over.

"Is it safe to talk here?"

He nods, though Elena wonders whether it is safe to talk anywhere. Her cover was a bad joke from the start. She learned the hard way that the spy shit isn't for her. She should've stuck to what she knows: direct action. Better yet, she should've kept out of it, enjoyed her retirement.

"Long story," she tells Marlow, "the asset is lost, very likely dead. He ended up fleeing to Forge. I went after him." She shows Marlow her new synthetic hand. "They were waiting for me."

Marlow gasps at that. "Oh no, Linton." He looks down for a moment, then back at Elena. "Do you ... need a doctor?"

"I just need to get out of here," she tells him. She will, of course, provide a full report. But she wants to do it from Aurelia. "Can you help me?"

"Ms. Drake, Elena, I have bad news."

Here it comes.

"It's not public information yet but should be soon. The jump gate is closed."

"What?" Her jaw drops. The jump gate can't be closed. Jump gates never close. They are the lifelines connecting the sectors, enabling travel, trade, businesses. Every second the bandwidth is unused costs millions—billions—in potential revenue.

"Nobody is translating in or out of Sector 36 anymore. Ingram closed the gate. Indefinitely."

This is unheard of. She hears Jaxon gasping next to her.

"I know," Marlow continues, nodding understandingly. "I'm

shocked too. I have no way of reaching out to my contacts. No way of arranging anything."

No way out. Trapped. She gets that sinking feeling again. Manages to ask, "How?" before their conversation is interrupted by a deafening crash. The building shakes. The lights flicker. Someone yelps nearby. They watch, through the floor-to-ceiling windows, the gargantuan building across the street collapsing in an explosion of glass shards and debris. Floor after floor shatters and crumbles until the whole thing disappears below them in a cloud of dust.

Elena has seen this before, knows what it means right away: orbital bombardment.

PART FIVE
WEAPONS FREE

29: STANDBY

Lieutenant Marcus Wade assembles his team of five for the regular check-in but has no news to share. The *Dauntless* and the other ships redeployed from Eureka Base have been facing off the paramilitary vessels for a few days. Tensions are high. Everyone carries on with their duties but there's electricity in the air.

From the deck, the heavy cruisers and destroyers look like giants amidst the small civilian ships milling around the ring.

"Any updates, LT?" Chief Petty Officer Howard asks.

"Negative, Dash," replies Marcus. "Maintain condition one."

They've been on standby for days, and he can feel the tension in his team. He is just as uneasy. He gives another sitrep devoid of new information.

"Radio silence from the paramilitary ships." The bastards are keeping mum. They brought a lot of firepower. "No additional ships arrived since last check-in. We have more guns deployed than they do, but intel says they've got better tech." Abyssal cut no costs to equip their paramilitary.

"You think we'll have to fight them, LT?"

"I hope not," he says, sincerely. "But if the time comes, we'll show them what's what," he adds.

He takes a look at his team. They're anxious, trying hard not to show it. If this goes down, this will be the first direct action for all of them. But they're ready. There are no better people to jump into the breach with.

"Dismissed!" he calls and heads to his quarters.

His cabin is spartan. White walls and furniture, like the rest of the ship. Neat and clean. Besides the navy-supplied uniform, boots, and toiletries, he carries few personal items. The one prized possession he has is a print book. It's a rarity, a rendition of an ancient text, *The Book of Five Rings*. Marcus finds a lot of meaning in its pages, unwinds by sampling paragraphs, mulling them over. He doesn't have time for reading now though. The well-worn book sits on his nightstand.

He paces around the room for a while, thinks. He knows the paramilitary ships are to be considered hostile. He knows his team should be ready to fight at a moment's notice. He doesn't know what they are fighting over. The in-person briefing he attended provided a lot of tactical details; however, it was light on motives. He's heard plenty of rumors but doesn't know which ones to believe. The Taurans don't seem to be back.

Abyssal Mining is making a move, but towards what ends? *Why?* The key question is *why*.

The possibility of fighting Abyssal reminds him of Elena Drake. He wonders where she is, what she is doing now. He hopes she's safe.

He takes another look outside, at the standoff. A battle here, among so many civilian ships, would be disastrous. He hopes it doesn't come to that. He thinks about their odds.

They have three large vessels to the paramilitary's two. A large assortment of smaller corvettes and frigates. The *Dauntless* is one of their biggest guns, together with the heavy cruisers *Ares* and *Excalibur*. Abyssal's largest ships are the *Invictus* and the *Midnight Spear*. Similarly sized chassis, more advanced weaponry. They even look more menacing—he is used to the dark gray paint of military ships, but the enemy cruisers sport an inky black. Their silhouettes present the usual antennae, cannons, and batteries, but also unfamiliar dodecahedral protrusions along their hulls and rotating rings clasped around their midsections.

He sits on his bed, embeds, recaps the plans. He's done it a hundred times already but knows if the fighting starts there won't be any time to look things up.

Target Alpha: the *Invictus* appears before him, rotating in 3D with data overlays across the relevant sections. The *Invictus* is only slightly larger than the *Dauntless*. Heavily armored, it's equipped with an FTL drive and a separate drive for quick maneuvering at lower speeds. It is armed with an array of energy weapons and a couple of large railguns for kinetic offense.

Target Bravo: the *Midnight Spear* is smaller in size, lighter in armor but easier to maneuver. Similar dual-drive setup, packing even more kinetic firepower than the *Invictus*: railgun batteries fore and aft. Plus, an assortment of energy weapons.

Assessment: odds of taking out Target Alpha and Target Bravo in ship-to-ship combat are at forty percent, with high losses. Both cruisers can maneuver faster than the *Dauntless* or the other two heavies they've got, have enough firepower and countermeasures to cause significant damage. Monte Carlo simulations repeatedly show the *Dauntless*, the *Ares*, and the *Excalibur* being blown to bits.

Here is where his team and the other Vanguards aboard can help. They will launch in breach pods, get aboard Target Alpha and Target Bravo. Marcus and his team will be going for Alpha, together with two other teams. Three more going for Bravo, for a total of six. Take out engines, kinetics, secure bridge.

He pauses, dismisses the visuals, breathes deeply. Clenches and unclenches his fists. If it goes down, it's going to get bloody.

· · ·

Back to the intel. Both Alpha and Bravo are manned by Eclipse Corps mercenaries. Sims have their teams securing the ships at seventy-two percent success rate. While the ship-to-ship odds are poor, putting boots on deck looks a lot better. If they make it there.

He pulls up the *Invictus* again, zooms in on the potential breach points they would aim for. He spends another hour wallowing in the data.

It's been several days of tense waiting. At 1700 hours, as Marcus assembles his team for the afternoon check-in, they receive the broadcast.

{The jump gate is closed. No further translations. Standby.}

It takes them a moment to process this new information. No reinforcements. No retreat. They're stuck in Sector 36.

"LT?" Chief Petty Officer Howard is waiting for him to say something to this, but he doesn't know what to add.

"Be ready!" he says. His gut tells him if anything is going to happen, it will happen now. His gut is not wrong. They watch as the *Invictus* and the *Midnight Spear* launch tungsten rods towards the ring. The rods are shot out of the railgun cannons at hypersonic speeds. It takes them mere seconds to reach their target. The seconds seem very long as the projectiles glint, glide across the nebula's green background.

They're shocked. They were prepping for combat, ready for a first strike on their ships, but Abyssal decided to target civilians instead.

"Oh no," says Marksman Kim.

"They're hitting civilians!" This from Santos.

"Bastards!" agrees Marcus.

The rods penetrate the outer shell of the ring world. He feels rage building up, quells it.

As the ring continues to rotate, its cracked shell spews a trail of debris. Debris: shell fragments, buildings, people. A strip of it detaches, starts slowly unspooling into space.

On the *Dauntless*, an alarm starts blaring. The lights start pulsing red.

"Jock up! Jock up!" orders Marcus. "Combat ready in two." They run to the armory. The decks are suddenly abuzz with activity. They glimpse fireworks outside as they go. The two forces are now engaged.

The armory is packed, but they're following a very well-rehearsed choreography. Nobody gets in anyone's way. Body armor. Tacticals. Helmets. In less than a minute, they stream out of the armory in single file, Marcus leading, followed by Chief Petty Officer Peter "Dash" Howard. Then Petty Officer Second Class Rachel "Pinball" Santos and Petty Officer Third Class Eric Novak. Next is Specialist Kyle "Back" Anders, their demolition expert. Bringing up the rear, their team sniper, Marksman David "Kimmy" Kim.

They head towards the bays, the breaching pods, running checks as they go. They switch to digital as the noise gets louder: boots stomping, orders being shouted, blaring alarms.

{Comms check.}

{Check.}

{Gear check.}

{Check.}

They meet up with the other five teams on the way. They nod to each other, keep moving.

The *Dauntless* is not a carrier; its bay is relatively small compared to its size. They file into their breach pod. The pod looks like a fat spider, an armored capsule with multiple thick arms jutting out of it at all angles. The small vehicle has some maneuverability but it's more like a missile than a vessel. Its trajectory is determined pre-launch, its sole purpose being to quickly cross the distance and attach to an enemy ship, penetrate its hull with plasma cutters. Get them inside. Its interior is just large enough to fit their whole team.

{Buckle up,} Marcus tells them, then switches to the bridge. {Control, we're ready to launch,} he calls.

It's getting real. Marcus notices it's getting hot inside his body armor. He takes a deep breath. He trained for this, and the fuckers deserve what's coming to them.

{Standby,} he receives.

Not launching quite yet. Embedded, he looks through the heavy cruiser's eyes.

There's intense fighting all around, the ships are exchanging fire using both energy and kinetic weapons. The smaller, more nimble ships are moving constantly, staying out of the line of fire of larger guns. The lumbering heavy cruisers and destroyers rely on armor, take on damage while they aim. He sees the *Midnight Spear* point its aft railguns at the *Excalibur*, hit it with what looks like a nuclear payload. The detonation takes a large bite out of the ship. The *Excalibur* becomes inert, spins slowly. Marcus sees escape pods launching from the ship. Enemy corvettes fly by, hit them with energy weapons, cooking their occupants alive.

Fucking savages, thinks Marcus.

{Control, launch us!} He is very much ready to go.

{Standby, Lieutenant, we're clearing a path.}

He clenches and unclenches his fists, turns to his team.

{It's no go.}

{Shit.}

He switches his attention back outside, looks at what used to be the ring. The structure is unrecognizable. Strands are floating away from the moon, leaving only a few segments connected by strips of shell still rotating in their orbit. *A hundred million people,* he thinks. He can't quite wrap his head around the enormity of it. How many are still alive? Is the remaining husk of the ring even able to support life anymore?

The debris collide with the stationed civilian ships, causing even more damage. He sees a transport ship crumbling when hit. Another one tries to maneuver out of the way and collides with a cargo vessel.

{Control!} he calls again. He should wait for the green light, they know what they're doing. But he's seen enough. He is itching to go.

{Standby.}

Outside, he sees two corvettes beeline from the *Dauntless* to the

Invictus, shooting energy weapons in all directions, hitting nearby paramilitary ships. One explodes. Another two flee. There's an unobstructed path between the two heavy cruisers.

{You're clear,} he gets the signal from the flight deck.

{Ready,} he acknowledges. He turns once more to his team. {We're on, hang tight!}

The bay door slides open. He sinks into his chair under the weight of several Gs as the breach pod accelerates, shoots out of the belly of the *Dauntless*, leaving the ship behind. A flash of retrograde burn fixes their speed.

T minus thirty.

{Weapons check.}

{Locked and loaded!}

{Let's get these fuckers!} says Howard.

{Hooyah!} they answer in unison.

The breach pod shoots through the dark, followed by two others. They're too fast for nearby tangos to get a lock on them. A corvette accompanies, shooting at any enemy ship trying to close in, ensuring their path stays clear.

T minus twenty.

The *Invictus* sends a projectile their way. Proximity alert warnings blare, then go quiet. It wasn't aimed at them. The long, flat missile zooms by the breach pods heading towards the *Dauntless*. The corvette tries to intercept it but misses.

Marcus registers it, remembers the simulations, hopes the *Dauntless* survives the impact. He can't get distracted by this now.

T minus ten.

Retrograde burn engaged, they begin to decelerate. He paints the breach point for the pod. It spreads its many arms and embraces the surface of the *Invictus*. Plasma cutters burn a hole through the ship's hull.

Marcus jumps out of his chair, swings his weapon forward, activates tactical view. His vision is instantly overlaid with targeting information.

T minus three.

Two combat drones unclasp from their wall mounts and glide in front of the team, ready to take point.

T minus two.

Marcus swallows, blinks.

T minus one.

Plasma cutters pull back; the pod iris opens.

{Go time!} he sends to his team.

30: OUT OF LINE

Commissar Vesper stands on the bridge of the *Nemesis* in high orbit around Nova Prime when the news arrives. The jump gate is closed. Ingram is not allowing any more ships to translate in or out of the sector.

This comes as a surprise to her, and she doesn't like surprises. Her job is—*used to be*, she corrects herself—her job used to be staying one step ahead. Keep up to date on intel, coordinate, execute flawlessly. Now she is unsure what her job is. She was summoned to the *Nemesis*, deployed with the rest of the fleet. She didn't receive any additional instructions. She tried to make herself useful, but information is suddenly less accessible. Is this punishment for her fuck-up on Forge?

"You caused me a lot of trouble." This from Arcturus. She remembers being glad she wasn't asked to submit her report. Now she wishes she did, regardless of the consequences. Anything would be better than this uncertainty.

The *Nemesis* is a new vessel, its bridge equipped with the latest tech. The wall-to-wall displays give the impression of standing on an open platform outside, in the void. From here, she can see Nova Prime City below, through puffy clouds. She can see the dozens of other ships that accompanied the *Nemesis* from Forge. And the multitude of military ships they met here.

There's going to be a fight. She wasn't briefed on this, but it was obvious to her as soon as they arrived. She wondered what would trigger it, instantly knew when they got the news.

"The jump gate is closed," the ship's captain repeats. He's an old sailor, with white hair and a wrinkled face. Burly and strong-looking despite his age. "Engage Alpha Protocol," he calls.

"Alpha Protocol?" Vesper wasn't briefed on this either. Her role as a commissar doesn't cover ship operations. And ever since Elena Drake, she hasn't been briefed on much at all.

"Aye!" the first mate answers the captain.

She turns to him with an icy glare. The first mate has alopecia. He stares back at her, gray eyes without eyelashes. She loses the stare-down. She's not used to being ignored, not used to being defied, but she has no authority here.

"What is Alpha Protocol?" she asks for a second time. She keeps her tone calm while putting as much weight as she can behind the question.

"Weapons hot," announces the first mate, while continuing to ignore her.

She knew it. They're going to hit the military ships. Stands to reason—Ingram closed the jump gate, which significantly impacts the Abyssal business. Looks like Arcturus, in its infinite wisdom, decided to do a hostile takeover of the sector and liberate the gate. When Omegas war, they're planning multiple moves ahead. Arcturus foresaw the jump gate closure when he deployed the fleet …

Her train of thought is interrupted by the captain: "Drop 'em," he calls.

"Drop?" she asks, without even expecting an answer this time. Cold realization dawns on her. They're not doing a first strike on Ingram's military; they're bombarding Nova Prime City. The high-tech powered bridge gives her a perfect vantage point. She watches, bewildered, as the *Nemesis* drops a cluster of tungsten rods on the capital.

She coordinated countless operations. Most against enemy combatants. Some against high-value targets. They all made sense. Until now. This is genocide.

"What the fuck are you doing?" she yells at the captain. Losing her cool. "There are millions of innocent civilians down there!"

She can't help herself—this needs to stop.

"You're out of line, Commissar," replies the captain. "Lower your tone or I'll have you removed from my bridge."

Alarms start at the same time the first mate calls, "We've got incoming."

The *Nemesis* shakes as it is being hit by the military in retaliation. The wall-to-wall view distorts for a few seconds after the impact, showing static, then snaps back to Nova Prime's orbit. The friendly and enemy ships are now annotated on the displays. Other paramilitary ships are highlighted in white, hostile ships in red.

"Preparing countermeasures," calls the first mate.

"Load second drop payload," says the captain.

Vesper doesn't have time to think. She is taking part in a genocide —this is madness.

"Stop right now!" she demands in her well-rehearsed command tone.

The captain turns to look at her.

"Master-at-Arms," he calls, "escort the commissar to her quarters. Make sure she stays there."

"Aye, Captain!"

The master-at-arms has small eyes and extremely thin lips. He is tall and muscular, with short-cropped sandy hair. She notices the senior chief petty officer insignia on his sleeve. He steps to her, grabs her upper arm, and starts walking her out. She is forced to follow, pain searing her arm and shoulder as he drags her. She is angry now.

"Let go of me!" she tries, to no avail. The master-at-arms keeps dragging her.

She just took part in a massacre. She can't believe this is happening.

The ship shakes again; the lights blink out for a second. They keep walking.

She tries a different tack.

"What's your name, Senior Chief Petty Officer?" She makes a point of addressing him by his full rank, making sure she sounds calm and reasonable this time.

No answer.

"You know," she continues in the same calm tone, "I will have you spaced for this."

He keeps walking, keeps the iron grip on her arm.

The ship shakes again; the lights go out for longer this time. When they come back on, they're red.

"Breach alert," the ship calls out. "Breach alert."

The master-at-arms stops at this. He frowns, embeds. Vesper knows he is looking for the breach point, making sure they don't walk into enemy fire. She tries to do the same but can't access any ship information.

{Access denied,} is the only thing the ship deigns telling her.

The master-at-arms switches hands, grabs her arm with his left hand and uses his right to pull his gun from its holster. He turns them around, starts walking back the way they came, then takes another turn. At a brisker pace this time.

They reach an intersection, their passageway crossed by another one. The master-at-arms is in the lead, pulling her after him. He turns the corner first. Vesper hears a gun report, feels his grip loosen, sees blood spraying on the floor. He falls on his back, eyes wide, unblinking. She sees two bullet wounds, one in the neck, one above his right eye. She turns around and starts running down the passageway. She hears footsteps echoing behind her. Something whizzes by her and half a second later she hears a loud bang. She keeps running. Another intersection. She randomly turns left. Another bang, taking out a chunk of wall behind her. Where her head was a moment ago.

She hears multiple shots ringing, then the unmistakable staccato of automatic fire. They grow distant as she keeps running, goes down one flight of stairs, then another one.

. . .

Where am I? She's been on this ship for a while now, but the red lights and alarms make the familiar passageways seem alien. She's disoriented. She stops to catch her breath, get her bearings. *Where am I going?* The answer comes to her in an instant. *To the armory.* She needs a weapon. There's an enemy infiltration team on the ship. *At least one,* she corrects herself. And, after what the captain did to her, she has no qualms about shooting him too. She needs a weapon regardless of which way the chips fall.

The armory is not far. She heads that way, walking briskly, keeping close to the wall, listening for movement. She hears footsteps behind, someone shouting, "Go go go!"

They're Inferno, not enemy infiltrators. Two of them, running to the armory themselves. One of them is tall, scars crisscrossing his bald head. The other one looks like a professional fighter, flat nose and swollen earlobes.

She joins them. They nod and keep going.

When they get there, the armory looks ransacked. Locker doors are open; weapon racks are empty. There are slim pickings, but she doesn't need much. She wants a pistol, kinetic, high caliber. She finds a Graver P7 with aim-assist, picks it up. The grooved grip feels reassuring in her hand. She steps out of the room while the two mercs are still rummaging for long guns.

Where to next? She is trying to decide when the lights go out. They don't come back on. Dim emergency lights replace them. They're losing the *Nemesis*.

She's in a lose-lose situation. If they win, she's in even worse standing now. If they surrender, they'll all be tried for genocide, her included. Plus, they're Inferno, so it's more likely they'll go down fighting. She's not planning on going down with the ship. She is not going to die for these war criminals. She makes a spur-of-the-moment decision, walks to the escape pods lining the wall next to the armory and steps into one of them.

. . .

The escape pod is a tiny barrel-shaped capsule. Its top and bottom are see-through synthetic sapphire. A round bench lines the wall, enough to sit five people. The ceiling is too low for her to stand upright; she needs to hunch down as she enters. She sits down, buckles up. She's about to close the hatch when one of the mercs sticks his head in. The bald one.

"Where the fuck are you going, Commissar?" he asks her through crooked teeth, bringing a rifle into view. He's not pointing it at her quite yet, just showing it off. His mistake.

She doesn't answer. Instead, she lifts the Graver, shoots him in the face, and pulls the pod's release handle. The hatch snaps closed. Through the transparent capsule floor, she sees release ports sliding open. In an instant, she is weightless. The straps keep her from lifting off her seat as the pod is launched towards the planet.

The *Nemesis* zooms out. She can see it: all dark now, engines offline. Flashes of energy weapon fire light up the sky. As Nova Prime's gravity well grabs hold of her tiny pod, she watches the intense battle taking place in orbit. It's hard to tell who is winning. As she falls and the ships get smaller, she can no longer tell who's who. Not without tactical overlays, and she doesn't have those.

What an end to an illustrious career.

She got sidelined after Elena, she got kicked off of the bridge of the *Nemesis* for being out of line, and, finally, she fragged a merc while deserting. She used to be a career woman, dedicated her life to Abyssal, working with the paramilitary, overseeing operations, climbing the ranks. *What am I now?* she wonders. *A ronin?*

Cooling systems kick in as the pod enters the mesosphere. It's a bumpy ride once friction comes into play. The pod shakes and rattles. Vesper is pushed into her seat.

Alpha Protocol. This was Plan A. Why? She wasn't in the know—that's fine, she fucked up. But why? Why do this? What possible benefit would this mass murder bring to Abyssal? How does it help Arcturus in its battle with Ingram?

As soon as she poses the question to herself, the pieces fall into place. Arcturus is everywhere, compute spread throughout the galaxy. Ingram is running exclusively in Sector 36. Its largest cluster is underneath Nova Prime City. The tungsten rods are supposed to cripple its compute infrastructure, the city above is simply collateral.

The pod reaches the stratosphere. It automatically deploys fins to increase drag. The rattling subsides.

What does this mean for her? She trusted Arcturus, trusted the Abyssal board to make the right calls. But she can't get behind this. She's a professional. This is psychotic.

She continues dropping, reaches the troposphere. She can now see dark smoke clouds way below, rushing towards her. A few skyscrapers still stand tall; most are absent from the city's famous skyline. She sees one crumble before her eyes, falling inside the smoke curtain. She almost catches up with it.

After a swift descent through the upper atmosphere, the pod finally deploys parachutes at terminal velocity. Not too early, since escape pods are sitting ducks. A fast drop is preferred, but slowdown must happen at some point, to keep the occupants alive.

She sees the pair of parachutes unfold above her, then drag tugs at her as the pod decelerates. She floats into the thick smoke and has time to consider her next move.

By the time the capsule stops on top of a pile of rubble, she has a plan. She unbuckles, opens the hatch, and steps out. She makes her way down to street level, watches panicked people run in all directions. She double-checks to make sure she still has her Graver. She is on her own now. She is going to find Elena Drake.

31: EVAC

Jaxon manages to start a question. "What the …?"

President Marlow is speechless. The building's rattling knocks over a display from his desk. It falls to the floor and cracks.

"Hit from orbit," Elena fills them in. "We need to get out of here."

After the initial moment of shock, they get moving. Marlow makes for the elevators, Jaxon following. Elena is trailing them, thinking fast. There's no way they'll catch an elevator, must be thousands of people in the building, all with the same idea. And if the building gets hit, the elevator is the last place you want to be caught in.

Her stomach begins to hurt. *Not now.* She takes a stim, she needs to be one hundred percent for this.

They get to the hallway. It's packed with panicked people. They're asking each other questions. Some are going out on the staircase. Others are looking at the elevator displays. Elena joins them. A couple of the elevators are on the floors above, the rest on the floors below. They're all going down slowly, stopping at every level. They must all be full by now.

"Shit," says Jaxon. "Stairs?"

"A hundred and twenty flights?" Marlow looks doubtful, he doesn't have the physical condition to pull it off.

"It would take us way too long," says Elena. "We need to ..." A loud boom interrupts her, shaking the building and making the lights flicker. Someone screams nearby. She needs an exit plan. Quickly.

"Where's the nearest terrace? Platform?" she asks Marlow.

"On the hundredth floor," he replies.

She turns to Jaxon. "Can you get the *Charon* there? That's our only way out."

Jaxon embeds, reaches out to Rynn, comes back.

"Yes! They can pick us up in ten. Good thinking!"

They make for the staircase, open the door. The staircase is utilitarian. Beige, unadorned walls, bare nanocrete, red banisters. Enough space between flights to drop a digicard but nothing thicker than that. The stairs are narrow—they were designed for people to get to nearby floors, not for an evacuation. The space is packed.

A large mass of people is trying to descend. Some are coming down slowly, pacing themselves. Others are trying to elbow their way through, but there's not enough room. An older-looking man trips, loses his footing. It's too crowded for him to fall, he ends up leaning against the woman in front of him. She is kept from falling by the large man in front of her. All in all, the procession is barely moving, one slow step at a time. Some people are talking, asking incoherent questions. Others are focusing on their breath.

"Shit," says Jaxon.

"It's only twenty floors," says Elena.

They join in. It's suffocating. Elena remembers Horizon, the low oxygen atmosphere. There's a permeating smell of terror and desperation. They start their cumbersome descent.

Near the hundred tenth floor, the lights go out. The staircase becomes pitch-black. Screams echo from above and from below.

"Keep going," says Elena.

Small lights from portable electronics turn on, giving the staircase an eerie glow. They continue downward, illuminated by dancing beams.

Someone elbows her hard in the ribs. She grunts, pushes back. "Watch it!"

They're three floors away from their destination when Marlow grabs her shoulder.

"Wait!"

She turns to look at him. She can tell how pale he is despite the diminished lighting. He is gasping for breath.

"I need to get out for a moment."

"Hang in there," she tells him, encouraging.

"I ... I can't."

He makes for the door. They exit the staircase on floor one hundred three, into semidarkness. The VoidTech logo is rendered prominently on the wall. The carpet on this floor is viridian green by flashlight, a nod to the branch office location within the nebula, but it looks black in the dimness. The hallway would normally get some natural light through the floor-to-ceiling windows at both ends, but there's too much smoke outside.

They're not alone. A couple of other people give up, step out with them. Plenty of people still on the floor too, Elena can see them hiding under desks. Illusion of added safety.

Marlow is clutching his chest.

"I ... I think I'm having a heart attack."

Elena gently grabs his shoulders.

"Sit down."

She helps him lean against the wall.

"Breathe, Mr. Marlow."

This isn't looking good at all. She turns to Jaxon.

"Hey, find me a defib unit."

He nods, runs off. Marlow is sweating profusely. He is taking shallow breaths. She sits on her haunches to get level with him.

"You'll be OK," she says. She doesn't believe it. He looks at her wide-eyed.

{Where are you, Jaxon?} she sends.

{In a pickle. No defib on this floor. There's one seven floors up, one three floors down.}

{Shit.}

{Yeah.}

No way to get up the stairs, climbing against the tide of people.

{Any other way up or down?}

{No.}

She takes another look at the elevator displays. The elevators are all too far away. And they don't seem to be moving now.

"Elena," Marlow says. He is struggling to speak. "I need to tell you something." He gasps for air.

"Not now," she says, "focus on your breathing."

"You must know …" he says, then his eyes roll back and he falls sideways.

Oh no. She lays him flat on the ground.

"Is there a doctor here?" Her voice loud enough for the people around to hear. Plenty of people. Maybe, just maybe. She looks desperately around but there are no takers. No doctor in the house.

She checks for a pulse, signs of breathing. Nothing. She starts administering CPR. She has basic first aid training, knows this is hopeless without a defib, without medical help.

Jaxon comes back, stands next to her.

"What can I do?"

She continues doing chest compressions.

"Find me a doctor or a defib."

Jaxon repeats her question to the people watching.

"Anyone here a doctor?"

He looks around, locks eyes with a young man sheltering underneath a nearby desk. The young man shakes his head.

"How far out is the *Charon*?" Elena asks him.

He embeds for a second to check.

"Three minutes out."

Jaxon opens the staircase door. "We need a doctor, someone is having a heart attack!"

"I'm a doctor," he hears from half a floor above.

Jaxon looks up, squints as a powerful flashlight shines on his face, blinding him. He waits for the doctor to make his way to them. The doctor looks to be in his fifties, with wide streaks of silver running through his thick, dark hair. He has a sharp, angular face.

"Thank God!" Jaxon brings the doctor out on the one hundred third floor. "Here."

"Allow me," he tells Elena.

She steps aside, lets him take over. He reaches into his pocket, pulls out a med glove, puts it on. Elena sees it, remembers the combat gloves she lost on Forge. Same principle, different applications.

"Stand back!" he tells them. He places his gloved hand atop Marlow's heart, gives him a shock. His body jerks.

The doctor gives him rescue breaths, pauses for a second to ask, "How long has he been without a pulse?"

"A couple of minutes," answers Elena.

He administers another shock to Marlow's chest. The building trembles again, another nearby impact. Elena and Jaxon exchange looks.

"He's not responding," says the doctor. Marlow is turning blue. They watch, helpless.

By the time the *Charon* arrives, he is gone forever.

"They're here," Jaxon tells Elena.

The doctor stands up.

"I'm sorry," he says.

They resume their descent in silence. Elena wonders what Marlow's last words were about. *I need to tell you something. You must know.* Know what?

It doesn't take them long to go down three floors. The doctor is with them. Once they make it to the door, Jaxon calls out, "Evac this way!"

They don't want to create a stampede, but the *Charon* has a lot of room. It's a small transport ship, small enough to navigate between skyscrapers by a skilled pilot, though it is a transport. They can get a lot of people down to safety in one go.

The layout of floor one hundred is different, wider. There's a large open terrace with plenty of greenery. The *Charon* is hovering a few feet outside the terrace, partially obscured by smoke. There's already a small crowd around the ship, pleading for rescue.

Elena, Jaxon, and the doctor walk out to the terrace, followed by dozens more. The *Charon* extends a ramp. Elena and Jaxon step inside, followed by the doctor and a stream of people. Kaela is standing at the top of the ramp, directing everyone towards the cargo bay.

"Why aren't there more rescue ships around?" asks Jaxon. "We can't be the only ones who thought of this."

"The spaceport was hit," answers Kaela. "One of the first hits took down the control tower and whatever was near it. Rynn took off on manual, we were already airborne when you reached out. It's chaos there now."

Almost a hundred people manage to board before the building is hit. The tungsten rod crashes straight through its middle with immense kinetic energy. The glass windows explode and the nanocrete structure follows suit. Elena watches helplessly as the hundredth floor terrace tilts and people fall, screaming. Glass shards and debris start pelting the *Charon*. Rynn pulls it farther away from the building. No one left to save now. The skyscraper, home to Obsidian Holdings, VoidTech, and tens of other branch offices, collapses.

Kaela is crying. So are others aboard the ship. Most of them knew people in there. They watch wide-eyed, murmur, sob.

"Let's get these people to a safe spot," Jaxon tells the pilot.

Rynn nods, flies them first up above the smoke and buildings, then outside of the city to a nearby park. It's a very short ride. The park is large, a wide lush area next to the bustling metropolis. Seems to be far enough not to be considered a target. It sprawls, green and unscathed, next to the chaos.

The *Charon* lands on a grass field, opens its airlock. People get off. Some of them thank the crew as they go. Others are in shock; they go out silently. Some storm off angry. Elena can empathize with all of them.

From the park, the cityscape looks unrecognizable, sparse. Far fewer tall buildings left standing than when they came in. Thick black smoke from multiple fires envelops the city.

"What's going on?" Jaxon asks Kaela.

"Network chatter is crazy right now, but as far as I can tell, it's the paramilitary ships."

"Fuck," says Elena. She has a vivid flashback of a hive being nuked.

"Yeah. There's a big battle up in orbit. Military ships fighting the paramilitary ones. Allegedly. At least that's what I can make out of the reports."

"Who's winning?" asks Jaxon.

"Hard to tell right now."

"Looks like the bombs are still dropping," adds Elena.

They catch a glimpse of a silvery line striking the top of one of the remaining standing buildings, falling inside. They watch the building crumble, disappear inside the smoke curtain.

"What now?" asks Rynn.

"We can't get off planet in the middle of a firefight." Jaxon is frowning, thinking. "The city is ground zero, so that's not a good spot to be in either. I guess we stay here, lay low until things quiet down."

Elena looks out at the remains of the city, considers her situation. Marlow was supposed to get her out of here. Now there's no way out. No escape. And her only Spark contact in the sector is dead. She is truly alone. Out of credits, stranded in the middle of a war zone. *What next?* she asks herself. *What is the master spy going to do next?*

No way to phone home. With the jump gate closed, there's no information leaving the sector. Not at any useful speeds at least. Her best bet is to weather the storm, wait for things to get back to normal. If that's going to happen, if "normal" still exists.

Why are the military and paramilitary fighting? she wonders. This isn't a corporate dispute, like the one she took part in on Forge. They bombarded a megacity housing dozens of millions of people. Death at an unfathomable scale.

She has many unanswered questions, no good next move to speak of, when her train of thought is interrupted by an incoming request. Something unheard of, so taboo it completely stops her in her tracks. An incoming connection request from Ingram.

32: INFERNO

nferno Troops promised to kill Abyssal citizens unless negotiations moved forward. It was during the same rescue operation in which she lost Darius. Their first drop had been on bad intel, they walked into a booby trap. This time around, the intel was supposed to be solid.

She was still on the bench, recovering from her concussion. Didn't drop when they found the hostages. What was left of them. No negotiations took place so the Inferno mercs kept their word. They found two men and two women, all strung up in a hive unit. Elena wasn't there in person but watched through a drone's eyes. They all had their throats cut. One of the women was missing her bottom half. She had been sawed in two right below the navel with what looked like a plasma cutter. They never found her legs. Nor did they ever find another six missing hostages. Their captors used the same plasma cutter on the other prisoners too, they all had burns across their bodies: arms, torsos, genitals.

The carnage made her sick, she wanted to step away but forced herself to watch the feed in real-time, see what the team was seeing. They brought the bodies back. Forensics showed both men and one of the women had been raped. Hard to tell for the other woman, since they only had her upper half, but they could take an educated guess. They got DNA samples, crosschecked their records. Inferno hired mostly ex-military, so they weren't very surprised to find them in their database.

Talon Voss. Nicknamed "Nightmare." How fitting. A large, bald man with crooked teeth, Master Gunnery Sergeant Talon "Nightmare" Voss had seen four combat deployments. Dishonorably discharged for conducting an unauthorized incursion leading to civilian casualties.

Cole Rourke. A stout man with sandy hair, a boxer's nose, and cauliflower ears. Lance corporal, retired. Two combat deployments, under investigation three times for torture and war crimes. Nothing conclusive, but reading through the lines it seemed to Elena he was forced into retirement.

Monsters do exist. She wondered how they made it through the psych eval. Before being dishonorably discharged or asked to retire, they were military. They went through the same training as everyone else. They served as part of a unit. She swore right then and there to apprehend the fuckers, make sure they paid for what they did to those poor civilians.

They continued doing drops, continued fighting. Whenever they took a prisoner, Elena would interrogate them: *Where is Voss? Where is Rourke?* In response, she got a lot of silence and "fuck you's." The rules of engagement were clear, there wasn't much she could do to get the prisoners talking. Sometimes she really wished she could. Wished she could wipe the smirks off their faces, but wouldn't that make her no better than the enemy? *Beware that, when fighting monsters, you yourself do not become a monster ...*

She didn't learn much from Inferno prisoners.

On the other hand, Eclipse Corps talked. The two paramilitary outfits were fighting each other on behalf of their patron corporations,

Titanforge Industries and the Abyssal Mining Consortium. Eclipse Corps were terrified of the infamous Talon "Nightmare" Voss and Cole Rourke. She heard stories.

A young Eclipse mercenary they captured, Private Elijah Bach, who seemed way over his head and deeply regretting his career choices, recounted how the duo took over one of their positions. His was a secondhand account, Private Bach wasn't there to see all of it unfolding.

A small team of eight, holed up in a couple of hive units. Inferno overwhelmed them and forced them to surrender. Talon Voss killed the sergeant on the spot. He ordered the other Inferno Troops to move on. He and Cole Rourke stayed behind, spending a couple of days torturing the prisoners. Mostly cutting them and listening to their screams. By the time Eclipse retook the position, forcing the two to withdraw, only two of the prisoners were still alive. Alive but in very bad shape. One of them was in shock and remained catatonic. The other one they found without an eye, three remaining fingers, a missing foot, and an assortment of other cuts and bruises over his body. He was crying when they recovered him—Rourke was planning to cut his genitals off next. Rescue arrived in the nick of time. Private Elijah Bach was part of that rescue party.

While he wasn't there for the action, he did witness the handiwork of the two maniacs. At this point in telling the story, his eyes glazed over. He couldn't quite get himself to describe to Elena the condition the non-living team members were found in. She had an inkling.

They got more intel from the digital. Hacked terminals and network breaches helped paint a more complete picture. The two were a pair of sadistic fucks. They were in the field often. Rumors abounded. Eclipse Corps feared them. Even Inferno had their doubts, suspicions of the two intentionally killing a commanding officer. But they were good— too good to hold back. They left a long trail of bodies and sawed-off limbs across the hive.

She collected evidence, put together reports, tried to run it up the chain. To no avail. The bigwigs had more important things to worry about. Astrium deposits, the market impact of the two companies fighting, stabilizing the situation on Forge. What's a bit of murder and mutilation next to shareholder value?

Three days before the conflict ended and she rotated out, she finally had the pleasure to meet the two in person. She had recovered enough by then to go back in. She didn't know it at the time, but it was going to be her last drop. They went in with two vertibirds, twelve of them plus four combat drones. No Brainiacs on this one. No digital assets involved, this was a brute force op.

As the silver metal balustrades of the hive levels flashed by, she remembered her first drop, the anxiety she felt then. She realized she'd come a long way from then. Everyone had.

They were going in to assault a hive walkway, which intel said was taken over by Inferno Troops. A demolition expert made short work of the helter-skelter barricade blocking their entrance. While he was working, she sent a team of six and two drones to the other end of the walkway. It turned out there were no barricades on the other side. As soon as the demolition expert cleared their path, they heard gunfire. They went in, drones first, hoping to catch the enemy in a pincer. But the mercs had an exit plan. She stepped on the walkway and was enveloped in infrared-blocking smoke. As good as blind, they let the drones probe ahead. Optical sensors severely limited, the drones did their best to compensate and switched to tactile, using their limited number of short appendages to feel around. One of them managed to fire a shot before getting disabled by enemy fire. The other one was hit with an electromagnetic pulse, went down instantly. Drones on the other side flew into a booby trap and were cut down by a powerful laser.

Elena and her team coordinated over comms, made sure they didn't accidentally shoot each other in the smoke. Team members on her side backed out of the walkway, cleared a firing path. At least that was their plan. As soon as they were out, a concussion grenade followed them. They scrambled for cover. Once the grenade detonated, Inferno streamed out of the smoke, shooting their way towards the hive's central shaft. Four of them. No armor, no helmets, just fatigues and weapons—they caught them off guard.

Elena and her team were lucky. Everyone found cover and nobody got hit during the fire exchange. As the tangos were hauling ass, Elena gave the vertibirds a heads-up, asked them to intercept. At the same time, she followed. She recognized two out of the four. Recognized them from the photos in their record, their mugs even uglier in person. Looked to her like bald-headed Nightmare had acquired a couple extra notches on his head since his picture was last taken.

Fueled by the horrors she'd seen, she didn't hesitate for one second to chase after them. It was dangerous business in the narrow hive corridors. The tangos never got to the shaft, opted to retreat inside a hive unit. Elena and her team regrouped, took positions around the door. They'd done this a hundred times by now, it was their specialty. Hand-signaled three, two, one, and kicked the door in. There was nobody inside.

Turned out the unit was part of the escape plan all along. The wall opposite the door had a large hole cut into it. By the time the Door Knockers regrouped and took position for the assault, the Inferno mercs had moved into the adjacent unit, then out its door into another walkway, then disappeared.

Elena wanted to run a sweep, canvass as much of the hive level as they could, but realized it was pointless. The hive was simply too large for their small team. Worse than pointless, it was dangerous. They lost the initiative and could at any point walk into an ambush. She reluctantly ordered the exfil.

She was in a dark mood. The death of Darius was still weighing heavy on her. She had been inches away from neutralizing the two sadists, but they managed to get away. Three days later they got the news—peace had been established.

Titanforge agreed to a merger with Abyssal Mining. Paramilitary were recalled. Part of the deal included amnesty for all involved. Both

Inferno and Eclipse killed civilians, but they were all corporate citizens. The board of the freshly merged company unanimously agreed that it was cheaper to forgive and forget than to waste time with litigations. After all, now both mercenary companies had the same employer. Nothing to gain from it. The civilians were lost anyway, and their employment contracts did stipulate certain risks.

This did not help improve Elena's mood. She fought hard to bring up what she'd heard and witnessed to the brass, to the AI Council. She had files, pictures, forensic evidence, Elijah Bach's reports, leaked intel. She had names: Talon Voss, Cole Rourke.

She got nowhere. At first, she was told *they* would look into it, whoever *they* were. She followed up, as nothing seemed to have happened. That was when she learned about the amnesty agreement. She was told nothing could be done. The AI Council had no authority over corporate citizens, their contracts did stipulate risk of death and dismemberment while on Forge, and the wording was vague enough that any lawyer worth their salt could argue it did not exclude dismemberment by psychopath mercenaries.

She couldn't wrap her head around it. She asked for permission to bring this up with Inferno Troops. Or with Abyssal Mining. She argued the paramilitary organization should know who was on their payroll. If the AI Council couldn't do anything, maybe Abyssal or Inferno would. She was not granted permission. Everything that happened while the operations were unfolding was classified. The military would not share any records with Abyssal or anyone else on the other side of the conflict.

Elena disagreed with this decision, but there was nothing she could do. She was military, and she respected rank. It never even crossed her mind to go around the decision, to leak the information. That would have been considered treason.

She had to let go. She was honorably discharged, went home to Aurelia. Tried to put it all behind. She couldn't, it stayed with her. On top of the people they lost due to brain hacks in the first weeks of the conflict, on top of Darius being blown to bits, there were Voss and Rourke. The four bodies her team recovered. Violated, one of them cut in half. Private Bach's story, the Eclipse team butchered to pieces.

Finally seeing the two with her own eyes. Talon Voss with his bald, scarred head. Stout Cole Rourke with his busted ears and nose. Shooting at them, chasing them down the walkways, losing them. The lack of accountability. Post-merger amnesty and the impotence of the AI Council. She thought Inferno was an apt name. Some things you could never put behind. Some things stayed with you forever.

33: CLOSE QUARTERS

Marcus kicks the hull section in. The drones slide through, establishing positions left and right of the breach, send back a short *all clear*. Marcus jumps in, followed by the rest of his team. The passageway is empty, but it won't be for long. Alarms are already blaring.

They're gunning for the bridge. He has the *Invictus* blueprints pulled up, paths to their destination plotted out. The tactical overlays give them real-time directions. The bridge is very close: a right turn, a left turn, one more right turn. They send a couple of tiny recon drones first, getting telemetry. The bulky combat drone next. Then it's him and Howard, weapons hot. Following behind, Novak and Santos. Their demolition expert and their marksman at the rear, keeping watch on their six. The second combat drone trailing a few feet farther behind, scanning for threats.

The small scout drones make it as far as the first turn, where they are hit by an energy weapon.

"Contact right," says Marcus.

The combat drone dives to within an inch of the ground, turns the corner low to surprise the enemy. Marcus gets an optical feed from the drone, sticks his gun around the same corner, and aims using the drone's eyes.

Four tangos, Eclipse Corps insignia, geared for combat. Sporting energy weapons as far as he can tell.

He calls, "Four tangos."

He aims for the frontmost one. Aiming the weapon through the drone's perspective doesn't feel natural, but the rifle has aim-assist technology and he practiced this for years. He shoots a burst straight into the merc's face, through his visor.

"Tango down."

The drone zaps another Eclipse with its energy weapon, hitting him in the shoulder and making him drop his weapon. The second shot hits his neck and he goes down.

{Tango down,} sends the drone.

"Cover fire, LT," asks Howard.

He switches to automatic and sprays indiscriminately down the hallway, forcing the remaining enemies to duck for cover.

Howard clears the corner, kneels, shoots the two mercs left standing with short bursts.

"Clear," he calls.

They turn into the passageway. The lights blink bright red as the alarm continues to wail, but there's no more enemy movement. There's a smell of charred meat emanating from the merc hit with the energy weapon, mixed in with the metallic scent of kinetic fire. *Some things you don't get to experience during training*, realizes Marcus.

Their point combat drone lifts back up to four feet, glides ahead.

They step over the downed Eclipse mercs and take the left turn with no opposition. All of them except the trailing drone, which calls, {Contact rear.}

It shoots twice from its energy weapons then it goes down, hit by an electromagnetic gun.

"Drone down," announces Kim. The sniper is closest to the drone, just turned the corner himself.

"Cover and move," orders Marcus. They need to advance fast, no time to hunker down and fight so far away from their objective.

Anders lobs a frag grenade around the corner, rolls a smoke

grenade on the ground, and they keep moving. A screen of infrared-blocking, inky-colored smoke envelops the corner.

Anders and Kim, bringing up the rear, shoot blindly behind them a couple of times as they go, keeping any potential pursuers in check.

Final right turn up ahead. Marcus launches another pair of scout drones. They zoom ahead, take the corner, and relay the enemy position.

Six tangos this time, behind a makeshift barricade. The enemy pulled some furniture from one of the rooms and flipped it on its side. More worrisome, they have a high-caliber mobile turret.

"Big gun," Marcus tells them, making sure they're all aware of what's up ahead.

"Shit," says Howard.

This wasn't in the playbook. Firing a high-caliber mobile turret inside the ship can cause all sorts of unwanted damage. They were not expecting to face one. With tangos coming from the rear, they need to keep moving or risk getting boxed in.

"Can we go around?" asks Novak.

"Negative."

An alternative path would delay them too long, give the enemy time to regroup. Marcus needs to improvise, come up with a plan to take down the turret. He grips his weapon harder, thinks on his feet.

"We need an EMP gun," he says and points behind them.

They aren't carrying electromagnetic weapons, but that's how their combat drone went down. Tangos coming behind them must have one.

He orders their remaining combat drone to change direction, sends it back into the smoke screen. He hand-signals instructions to the team.

Howard and Novak take positions around the corner from the turret that awaits them and start suppressive fire. Anders sprints across the opening, takes cover behind the opposite corner, and joins them.

"Pinball, with me."

Marcus drops, starts crawling back the way they came, towards the smoke. Santos does the same behind him. They're keeping close to the ground, hoping to avoid any incoming fire. They can't see the enemy, but the enemy can't see them either.

The drone glides over them, extends tentacles as it switches to tactile.

Kim gets his sniper rifle ready, waits for a tango to step out of the smoke or for the drone to paint him a target.

The scout drones watch the turret slowly turning, aiming towards the corner behind which Howard and Novak are taking cover. They are plugged into the feed, seeing what the drones are seeing, so they're ready when it comes.

"Incoming," says Howard.

They both step back as the turret fires with a deafening BAP-BAP-BAP, taking large chunks out of the wall.

"Fire in the hole!" says Anders and throws a grenade towards the turret and the enemy barricade. Unlikely to do much damage to the armored turret but should buy them a few seconds.

The combat drone, now fully immersed in the inky black, brushes up against something.

{Contact,} it broadcasts to the team.

Its message payload includes exact coordinates relative to their positions. Kim can get a targeting solution from this. He aims without seeing, trusting the mathematics. He pulls the trigger and they hear a scream. Enemy fire ricochets across the pathway.

They're here.

Marcus shoots from his prone position, low to the ground. More screams and thumps, followed by another erratic burst of fire.

The drone moves back and forward, shooting its energy weapon. No target to lock on but hoping to hit something. It is in turn hit by a kinetic, but its carapace protects it. The bullet dents the armor but doesn't penetrate. The drone feeds them potential angle ranges the bullet could've come from.

He shoots inside the volume. So does Santos. Another thud.

How many tangos in there? He crawls into the smoke, swaps his rifle for a pistol and a knife. He can still hear the fire exchange between the enemy barricade and the half of his team positioned there, but no more movement inside the smoke.

He bumps into something, stabs, shoots twice. No response. Tango down. All tangos down. He crawls, sheathes his knife, feels for gear. Finds a rifle, no electromagnetic gun.

"Got it," he hears Santos's voice from his right. She found another corpse, got lucky.

"Let's get back," he says.

They sprint out of the smoke, call "blue" to let the others know it's them.

The turret fires again, BAP-BAP-BAP, demolishing more of the corner and wall opposite. It starts moving forward.

"Turret incoming," says Anders.

Santos makes sure the EMP gun is charged, trains it on the corner, waits for the turret to make its way to them. Howard, Novak, and Anders move back. Not a good time to get your tacticals knocked offline. She shoots as soon as she sees the carapace. The turret becomes inert.

They're about to assault the enemy barricade when Marcus receives new orders.

{Lieutenant Wade, this is Control. Pull back. Roger?}

Pull back? They're close to their objective and things are going well.

{Come again, Control?}

{Abort mission, back to the pod. Pick-up inbound. Roger?}

{Loud and clear,} he says.

Then to his team: "We're going back to the pod."

They exchange bewildered looks, but they don't question orders.

The drone turns the corner, backtracks towards the breach point. It gets out of the smoke into the pathway they just cleared. The four mercs are as dead as they left them, no other movement. They file out of the smoke in the same formation, him and Howard first, then Novak and Santos, Kim and Anders last, firing back to slow down the remaining tangos.

They make it back to the pod without further enemy contact.

{Control, pick-up status?} Marcus asks.

{Thirty seconds out, buckle up.}

They strap in. Their remaining combat drone returns to its wall mount. The pod closes its iris, detaches from the *Invictus*, does a short burn. It floats for a few seconds, putting distance between itself and the destroyer, before getting swooped up by a small tugboat.

"What the heck, LT?" asks Santos. They're all mystified by the retreat order. Frustrated.

"It was a clean op!" says Howard. They were on top of the situation with no casualties. Minutes away from the objective.

Marcus embeds, gets a quick sitrep. The *Dauntless* is no more. The missile they saw while they were coming in was a direct hit. It split the heavy cruiser in two. He is sharing notes with the team, though he's positive they are all doing their own assessment of the situation. They all had friends on the *Dauntless*, unclear how many of them got to the escape pods.

All three super-heavies on their side are down. The *Ares* and the *Excalibur* have also been critically hit. On the opposing side, the *Midnight Spear* is under their control now and the *Invictus*'s engines and weapon systems are offline. Nobody is winning this one.

{Standby for mission brief.}

Control will shed some light on why they got pulled. He looks around the pod. Every single one of them is still full of adrenaline, waiting for the new orders, trying to make sense of the whole situation. What could be more important than taking out the *Invictus*, especially once all their heavy ships have been destroyed?

The brief arrives:

· · ·

Board the light transport Skylark. *It will take you to rendezvous with Captain Elena Drake, retired. Escort and protect. Expect enemy resistance. Further details to be provided after contact.*

Captain Elena Drake. That's a shock. She sent him a cryptic message a while back, he's been wondering what she got herself into. Looks like she somehow became part of the operation.

The mission brief has a sizable data dump attached: biography of Drake, maps, travel times, the whole nine yards.

"Fuck me," says Howard.

"Backwards," adds Anders helpfully.

"This the same Captain Drake that rode with us inbound?" asks Novak.

"Aye," says Marcus. "Vanguard. She led the peacekeeping operations on Forge before the Tauran invasion."

They all heard of that op, there was some brutal fighting down in the hives.

"Retired though," remarks Novak.

"Yeah, she came in as a civilian."

"She more important than what's going on here?" Novak waves his hand, referring to the battle they just got ordered out of.

"Looks like it."

The tugboat brings them near the shipwreck of the *Dauntless*. They watch in silence. Several smaller ships are around it, trying to rescue the surviving crew still aboard. Other ships are still exchanging fire, but the intensity of the battle has boiled down to a simmer. It will be over soon, and as far as Marcus can tell, there won't be any victors. Massive losses on both sides. And the ring. The ring is likely uninhabitable at this point. Millions of people. He clenches his fists.

"Hope she's worth it," says Howard.

Marcus hopes so too. Someone up the chain thought she's more important than taking the *Invictus*. A retired captain. It makes no sense.

"And how come we're going ... there?"

As so many times in the past weeks, Marcus has no answer. He shrugs.

"We'll do it, LT," says Howard.

The tugboat brings them to the *Skylark*. The transport ship is not big, but it is FTL-capable. It also seems to be equipped with the latest in stealth technology. The crew consists of only two pilots. A small cargo space has been haphazardly retrofitted into living quarters for a team of six. Cozy. With no time wasted, as soon as they're aboard, the *Skylark* speeds away from the battle and disappears into the green night.

34: TABOO

An incoming connection request from Ingram. For an instant, Elena can't even process this. Omegas *never* reach out like this. Ever. God doesn't give you a call. But Ingram just did. Should she accept? She's stranded and hopeless, does she really have a choice? She gets online, answers.

"Captain!" it says. Sounding less cheerful this time around. Its avatar, a face with no features, is the same as before, but the head seems to be slightly bowed now. She must be imagining things.

"The fuck you want?"

She is upset. Very upset. The fucker toyed with her. She lost an eye and a hand, and people died and here it is calling. Trying to rub it in. She is so done playing games.

"I'm sorry for what happened to you, Elena. I tried to warn you every step of the way."

Warn me? What is it talking about? Then she remembers their previous conversations. "Watch your six," it said. "Forge is not good business," it said. She interpreted these as threats. Were they not? She can't believe it. Why does it have to be so obtuse?

It answers like it read her mind, the exact question she was asking herself: "I can't speak more openly than this, Elena. Someone else might be eavesdropping."

She almost laughs at the irony of this. She and Spark were coming up with code words, afraid Ingram was tapping their lines. The fucker is just as afraid as they were. Who could possibly be listening in on Ingram?

It again answers her unspoken question: "I'm not the only Omega in Sector 36."

This gives her pause. She mistrusted it from the jump, but in light of what just transpired—Nova Prime being hit by paramilitary forces, another Omega in the sector—maybe she misjudged?

No, it's fucking with her.

"Why did you close the jump gate?"

"For humankind's sake, Elena."

She is starting to get angry again. She can't get a straight answer out of it, no matter what.

"What do you want?" It called; it probably didn't do it just to chitchat.

"I need your help."

That catches her attention.

"You are more important than you realize, Elena."

"Then why did you try to kill me?"

"Kill you?" It sounds puzzled by her question. "I saved your life on Forge."

What is it talking about? She nearly died on Forge. Almost like reading her mind again, it answers her.

"How do you think your friends were able to find you, pick you up, get off planet without being detected? Who do you think gave them your coordinates?"

The revelation stuns her. Then who the fuck was after her? This conversation is moving too fast. She needs time to think.

"Wait." She tries to focus. She needs to ask a good question. What would help clarify things? She can't come up with anything better than, "Why am I important?"

"Elena, there's a river next to what used to be the Echo Point colony. Get there. I'll tell you everything."

Echo Point colony. Reduced to rubble by the Taurans. Why would she go there, what is there? She remembers another snippet from their prior conversations. She wished it to stop speaking in riddles. It replied, "I will, when you come to Echo Point." She interpreted that as a threat. Was it not a threat? Why there?

"Nobody listening there," it replies, again seemingly hearing her thoughts.

Fuck. She needs time to mull this over. Is the thing trying to kill her, toying with her, really in need of her help? Her stomach starts hurting again.

"Why?" Not a good question, not her best. *Why do you need my help? Why is the jump gate closed? Why is Nova Prime being bombarded? Why should I go to Echo Point? Why?* She tells herself the thing will read her mind anyway, will know what she means, will have an answer for her.

"For you—you'll get out of Sector 36. For me—you're the only one who can help. For everyone—the human race is at stake. Please, Elena."

Please. God is asking her for a favor, how about that? Human race at stake. What could that mean? Are the Taurans coming back? Or is what's happening here on Nova Prime going to be replicated at galaxy scale, will we kill each other into extinction? Will Omegas eradicate humankind?

Ingram disconnects.

Kaela mutters a, "Wow!"

"What's up?" asks Jaxon.

"We've just been commissioned to transport Elena again. For ten times more credits than before. Exactly ten times. By an anonymous patron."

Jaxon whistles. "That's a lot of money. Where?"

Elena already knows. The fucker moves fast.

"Echo Point," she says, at the same time as Kaela.

They turn to look at her.

"What's going on, Elena?"

"I just had a chat with Ingram. It's sponsoring this trip."

This gives them pause. Omegas coordinate sector-wide operations, they don't reach out individually to small outfits like theirs with astronomical amounts of money. Godlike AIs are subtle—they gently nudge things, they don't intervene so bluntly. Silk glove, not gauntlet.

"What's on Echo Point? Isn't the place dead?" asks Rynn.

"The colony was blown to shit," adds Kaela.

"Guess Ingram is still there," says Elena.

Kaela lights up. "Yeah, I guess so. It must be running on an underground cluster there. Maybe the Taurans didn't take that offline?" She stops, bites her lip. "Why are we going there?"

Good question. What can she tell them? For humankind's sake? What the fuck was the thing going on about?

"Give me a sec," she says, walks away from the bridge. She can feel all eyes on her. "I need to think." She paces the length of the passageway, wincing at the pain in her stomach. She takes a stim, she knows it will help her focus. She feels its effect immediately, her senses perk up, the pain grows dull, her thoughts become clear.

Ingram isn't the only Omega in the sector. There's at least another one of the fuckers around. And they're warring, that's why the military is fighting the paramilitary above them. It figures, she's a pawn in their sector-wide game. Collateral.

What are they warring over? Doctor Linton knew something. He didn't get a chance to share it. He disappeared on Forge. It's starting to come together now. Forge. Abyssal. Paramilitary. There's a corporate Omega in the sector, a corporate Omega moving the paramilitary, slaughtering civilians. She's seen this before, she's seen Titanforge in negotiations with Abyssal. So, what is Ingram's role in this?

Ingram controls the jump gate. It shut it closed. Why? "For humankind's sake." What could that mean?

Her mind is racing, trying to come up with plausible scenarios.

The Taurans are coming back. If they get hold of the gate, they can attack other sectors, spread across the network of the colonized galaxy like a virus in the digital. Ingram shut the gate down to keep other sectors safe. Abyssal decides this interferes with business. Could be.

But this doesn't explain Doctor Linton. What did he know? Taurans coming back wouldn't be discovered in a lab, it would be noticed by the million watchful sensors brought here since the conflict ended.

Another possibility: they discovered something at Eureka Base. Maybe reverse-engineered Tauran tech. She can't fathom what they could've discovered, but that's what Spark was after. A killer plague? A super-weapon? Abyssal got to the doctor first, they got the information out of him.

She pauses for a moment to consider what "got the information out of him" implies, shudders.

This must have set things into motion. Abyssal moved its fleet closer to the jump gate. Ingram brought the military here too, closed the gate. And now this. But what's the end game? Impossible to guess.

How much can she trust Ingram? It promised to tell her everything on Echo Point. Should she go there? Is it walking her into a trap again? "Watch your six." "Forge is not good business." Fuck, it did try to warn her.

What are her options? She's out of credits, with no contacts to help her. She could probably wait things out on the *Charon*, stick with Jaxon and the crew, but she caused them enough trouble already. The only other person she trusts in the sector is Wade, but he is on deployment so can't do anything to help her.

Wade is on deployment and hostilities have started, she realizes. She hopes he's well. Wade might be in active combat right at this moment.

Her options are limited. *No way out but through.* She walks back to the bridge.

"Are you up for giving me that ride to Echo Point?"

Jaxon nods tentatively. "You know what you'll be doing there?"

"Not really," she replies, honestly.

The *Charon* takes off and stays close to the ground. It turns away from the burning remains of Nova Prime City and speeds up. Elena watches the city shrinking on the horizon until it becomes a single wisp of smoke, then disappears completely. They can't lift off at ground zero, through orbital bombardment, into the battle above. But Kaela found them a way out—her research in the digital turned out that all fighting is taking place above Nova Prime City, the other hemisphere is clear.

"Ships are still fighting in orbit," Kaela informs them. "Should be clear on the other side, as long as we go warp fast, before someone mistakes us for a hostile."

"Still no idea what's going on?" Jaxon asks.

Kaela shrugs. "Hard to tell. Lots of network chatter, thick fog of war."

Jaxon turns to Elena. "What did Ingram tell you?"

"Not much. That there's another Omega in the sector."

"Duh," says Kaela. "With Abyssal here, there must be a piece of Arcturus too."

Arcturus. This wasn't part of her brief. But it makes sense.

Elena continues, "Hard to make much sense of what Ingram told me, but I have a hypothesis."

"What?" Jaxon asks. They all look at her, very curious now.

"There's something in the sector—not sure if related to the Taurans —that shouldn't get out. At least that's Ingram's take. Arcturus seems to disagree. They're fighting over it. As soon as Ingram closed the jump gate, the bombardment started."

Kaela nods. "It tracks. But why? What are they fighting over?"

"No idea. It promised to tell me more on Echo Point. There's a river running next to the ruins of the colony. We need to get there."

"Why couldn't it tell you here?" asks Kaela.

"It's worried someone else might be listening in ... Arcturus, I guess?"

"Wow!" Kaela looks fascinated by the struggle between Omegas.

"To Echo Point then," says Jaxon.

"One more thing, how did you get me out of Forge again?"

"You messaged us, gave us a path in and a path out," Kaela tells the story. "It was amazing, we walked right in and back without encountering any opposition."

"How could I have done that?"

"Good question. You were half-dead when we found you. How did you do that?"

"I didn't," she says.

The *Charon* tilts vertical, shoots straight up. It cuts through the clouds, until there's nothing above but the green night sky. No ships on this side of the planet. A lonely satellite pings them as they cross the thermosphere. It exchanges transponder data with the ship, tells it not to get too close—it has no steering capability after all. They're beyond the exosphere when they see, through multiple levels of optical zoom, far away, a large ship exchanging energy weapon fire with a couple of smaller ones. The *Charon* continues moving away from the planet.

"Going warp," announces Rynn.

The *Charon* turns from a speck into a thin silvery line, then into nothing as it begins moving faster than photons. Bearing Echo Point.

Moments later, two slick, small ships cross Nova Prime's horizon heading the same way. They, in turn, burn to FTL and dissolve into the viridian background.

Not long after that, a skimmer lifts off from Nova Prime in the same direction, gaining speed as it goes. It breaks through the clouds, escapes the planet's gravity well, then follows the *Charon* and the two small ships, accelerating to relativistic speeds and disappearing from view.

35: TRADECRAFT

Vesper is surrounded by collapsed buildings. She can't see more than a block in any direction. Thick smoke is engulfing whatever is left of the capital. She needs to get out of here, fast. Then, she'll consider her next move. Where is a safe spot? Probably as far away from the city center as possible. Where is she? She embeds, pulls up a map of the area. Her capsule landed north of the city center, close to the port.

Back to fieldwork, she thinks. *I hate fieldwork.*

She needs a vehicle. Something that can fly or, at the very least, hover. The streets are impassable because of the rubble. She thinks it's going to be difficult, probably every single one of the millions of people still alive in the city are thinking the same. She is lucky for once. A Hoverworks Lumea is headed her way, gliding slowly as it navigates the debris.

As soon as she sees the vehicle in the distance, she takes off her uniform jacket and tosses it behind her. She is wearing a plain white shirt underneath, with no corporate branding.

The car approaches. Two people inside, both males.

She tousles her hair, puts on a terrified look, starts waving desperately, screams, "Help! Help!"

This elicits the reaction she was hoping for. The Lumea slows down, lands nearby. Windows slide down. The young-looking driver sticks his head out.

"Come! We're getting out of the city."

The pretend terror on her face is replaced by her usual icy look. She takes the Graver out as she closes the distance, sticks it in his face. "Get out!"

Not very nice of her, but she has work to do. No time for bullshit.

"You too," she tells the other passenger.

She drives the Lumea away, keeping the gun on them until she is at a safe height and distance. She leaves them there, looking at the tail-lights of their hover car in disbelief.

She thinks as she navigates the cluttered avenues. Two ways to play this. Both involve Elena Drake.

If she's still in good standing with Abyssal, find Elena. Apprehend Elena, interrogate her, get rid of her. This all started with Elena. She knows Abyssal has a hit put out on her, she knows they were supposed to interrogate her. This will buy her a lot of goodwill. All of this assumes she is still in good standing with Abyssal, after making a scene aboard the Nemesis, deserting, and fragging one of the Inferno mercs.

The question is how much of this left the *Nemesis*? For all she knows, *Nemesis* might be captured and everyone aboard a prisoner. Or blown to bits. Or at least the few people aboard who would have something to say about her are KIA. Not far-fetched at all, plenty of possible universes where she is A-OK with Abyssal. Well, not A-OK, she got sidelined by the end of it, but good enough to buy her way back in with Elena. That's option one.

Option two: defect. If all bridges are burnt with her current employer, there's Spark. She knows all about their little cabal from the late Doctor Linton. She knows Elena was trying to find him, get his intel to Spark. No more doctor, but she has the intel Elena was after. And there's no way Elena knows what role she played in all of this.

She can be a concerned corporate citizen. One who stumbled upon something important and is doing the right thing.

While she figures out where she stands with Abyssal, she can start searching for Elena.

The buildings still standing are getting shorter as she nears the outskirts of the city. The piles of rubble are smaller; the smoke is thinning. She can see the port in the distance, several fires around it. They likely hit the port with the first salvo, that would be standard operating procedure. Make sure any grounded guns won't be able to join the party. But there must be some small ships still around. She only needs an FTL-capable skimmer to get out of here and get to wherever she needs to go.

Where does she need to go? How can she find the bitch? She embeds.

Elena was coming in as VP of Acquisitions, Obsidian Holdings. She tunnels through the Abyssal network, reaches out to Obsidian Holdings as Vesper Ardyn, Chief of Staff, Office of the Chief Strategy Officer, Abyssal Mining Consortium.

{Vice President Elena Drake was supposed to meet Vice President Mira Caldwell on Forge. We have records of her booking inbound transport but no sign of her afterwards. In light of recent hostilities, we are worried about her safety. We wanted to reach out and inquire about her whereabouts. We see a unique opportunity with this partnership and hope we can continue the conversation.}

The message gets parsed and analyzed by Obsidian systems, and while the official response is being drafted, probably sent up to the C-suite for a sign-off, an eager PR subsystem responds:

{We appreciate your concern! Vice President Elena Drake was not able to travel to Forge. She was at our Obsidian Holdings branch office on Nova Prime when hostilities started. Her whereabouts are unknown as of now.}

This could be extremely lucky or extremely unlucky. She might not need FTL after all, Elena Drake is on Nova Prime. Or she might need to come up with an option three, Elena might be dead by now.

On the bright side, Vesper hasn't been locked out of the Abyssal network, not yet. She switches tracks, connects to the Inferno Troops network as Project Manager Vesper Nyx, Abyssal Special Projects.

Let's see how much clout I have left.

She performs a quick search for Alpha Protocol. The *Nemesis* crew knew about this, she didn't. This will tell her the extent of her access.

No results.

OK, she doesn't have full unbridled access. What can she access?

She pulls up a deployment map for Nova Prime. The planet materializes in her mind's eye, including the various ships orbiting it, helpfully annotated—green for Abyssal paramilitary, red for sector peacekeeping forces brought in by Ingram.

She searches for *Nemesis*, finds it.

Well, not blown to bits yet. Is it still under their control?

{*Nemesis*, requesting sitrep.}

She is talking to an automaton, which is perfectly fine by her.

{There was a breach. Enemy troops neutralized now, situation under control,} the ship replies dutifully.

{Status report: Captain Gregor Locke.}

{Killed in action during fight on bridge.}

{Status report: First Mate Silas Marrow.}

{Killed in action during fight on bridge.}

She saw the master-at-arms go down herself. That leaves the rest of the people on the bridge, but they are low rank and inconsequential, and the two mercs, one of whom she shot. Unfortunately, she doesn't know who they were.

What does the ship know?

{Status report: Commissar Vesper Solenne.}

{Missing in action during fight on bridge.}

That's good. The system she's talking to is too dumb to make the connection between Vesper Nyx, her Abyssal identity, and Vesper Solenne, the identity she uses for Inferno operations.

She might yet be good on that account.

. . .

Next: find out what's happening on the ground. She asks *Nemesis* for access to opticals. She wants to take a look at Nova Prime City from up above.

Her perspective switches to an orbital view of the smoke clouds. She flips to radar, millimeter-wave. This gives her a colorless view of the skyline from up above. It's hard for her to distinguish between the buildings still standing and the ones that got hit, so she runs a segmentation algorithm. It helpfully tags and annotates the image.

She overlays the map of the city with this, looks up the address of the Obsidian Holdings branch office. Zooms in. The building is tagged as intact. Radar shows a ship approaching the building. Strange, there aren't many ships flying around the city. The ship's silhouette looks both unique and strangely familiar. She has seen this before. Where?

She runs a retrieval algorithm over her personal notes, looking for a match. She remembers where she saw the strange chassis before at the same time as the algorithm comes back with its findings: that's the ship with a stolen Abyssal transponder. The ship Elena escaped Forge on. It was part of her report. They put it on a watchlist.

She watches the ship hover next to the building for some time, then watches in real-time the building being hit. It looks strange on monochrome radar. The segmentation algorithm retags the building. No longer intact.

That was Elena Drake's getaway. She's positive of it. She is either on that ship or underneath a pile of rubble. Not much to do if Elena is gone, she will work off of the assumption she's on the ship.

Where are you going?

The Lumea is at the port by now. She starts looking for a skimmer. In the digital, she tells the *Nemesis* opticals to track the vessel.

{Tracking the *Charon*,} she receives confirmation from the ship.

The *Charon*? What does the *Nemesis* know that she doesn't?

{Where did you get ship ID?}

She notices a small-skimmer, one person, looking intact. That's going to be her ride. She steers the Lumea towards it.

Nemesis replies:

{Classified.}

Origin unknown. That's not as important right now. What can she learn? She lets the opticals continue tracking and pulls back from the ship, back into the Inferno Troops network. She searches for *Charon*.

At the same time, she parks the Lumea, walks to the skimmer. It looks new, untouched by the surrounding mayhem. She takes a multi-tool out of her pocket and nano-hacks the locked doors. It's a civilian ship, its security laughable.

She gets a short report on *Charon*. Indeed, Elena's ship. And a most interesting mission brief, order sent to *Nemesis*-stationed Inferno: intercept at Echo Point.

Inside the skimmer now, she uses the multi-tool on the ship's main computer. Abyssal hacking software eats away at the puny ship's defenses. In the digital, she zooms in on the order:

To: Nemesis Inferno Command
Operation: Bloodhound
Target: Elena Drake. Last known location—aboard Charon, *Nova Prime.*
Known destination: Echo Point. Intercept at destination using two teams of
elite shock troops. Dispatch from Nemesis. *Rendezvous instructions to be*
provided later.
Eliminate primary.

Elena is going to Echo Point. *Nemesis* will send shock troops after her. Very interesting.

The skimmer is hers now, she is familiarizing herself with the controls. At the same time, she keeps an eye on the *Charon*. The ship stopped briefly outside the city and, soon after, took off again, zooming across the landscape away from the action.

She lifts off, follows. It takes her longer than she would like. *Charon* landed southeast of the city, away from the port. She can't fly through the bombardment, so she needs to take a long arc around it. By the time she can steer the ship on a straight intercept vector, the *Nemesis* opticals are almost out of range.

She's about ready to get out of the Inferno network, leave *Nemesis* behind. One more thing to check on.

{Status report: Operation Bloodhound.}

{Target acquired. Preparing dispatch. Teams launching in T-5.}

She disconnects.

Someone else is looking for Elena. *Operation Bloodhound*. Not much she can do about that. She's going to Echo Point, see where the chips fall. Her two options are still in play.

The skimmer is slower than Elena's ship. She's losing contact. She embeds, reaches out, finds a weather satellite orbiting on the opposite side of Nova Prime.

She connects to it, tricks its simple AI.

{Vesper Elara, maintenance crew. Standby for sensor test.}

She sends it the details of the *Charon*—topology, last known vector.

{Sensor test starting. Track and report.}

Vesper flies the skimmer across the circumference of the planet. By the time Nova Prime City disappears below the horizon, the weather satellite comes back with its "test results." She has eyes on *Charon* again. She tracks the ship around Nova Prime, out of the gravity well, then going FTL bearing Echo Point.

She is far enough behind to see the two ships dispatched from *Nemesis* inbound, leaving their orbit to follow the *Charon*. Minutes later, she breaks through the clouds and follows. Her skimmer goes warp, all options still on the table.

PART SIX
RUINS

36: CRASH LANDING

t takes the *Charon* just north of a week to get to Echo Point. It's a tense trip, everyone aboard the ship is restless. They left Nova Prime City behind in ruins. The jump gate is closed. They can't get any news while superluminal, but Kaela took a big data dump of network chatter before they went FTL and they're all obsessively going through it, trying to make sense of the mess.

Full-fledged hostilities around Nova Prime and the Gateway Ring between the Abyssal-sponsored fleet and the AI Council-backed military. Nova Prime City was bombarded, and the ring was allegedly destroyed. They were on Nova Prime, so they find this easy to believe.

Other rumors are less trustworthy: a Tauran fleet incoming, Eureka Base destroyed, Horizon Station under martial law.

Then there was Elena's conversation with Ingram. They have a handful of puzzle pieces that won't form a full picture. Ingram fighting Arcturus for the fate of humankind.

They have days to wait while in transit, and without fresh inputs, everyone spins up their own theories. Elena wonders what they'll learn once they reach Echo Point. Ingram promised her a way out of Sector 36, but she doesn't fucking trust Ingram. Would the thing open the gate for her? Why did it tell her she is "more important than she realizes"? She paces the cargo hold, walks up to the bridge, then back down.

Kaela spends most of the time embedded in the data dump, connecting dots by loose threads. She speaks little, frowns a lot.

Rynn is even quieter than usual. He obsessively checks the ship status and nav, like it would somehow magically make their trip faster.

Jaxon talks. A lot. To everyone. About war and rules of engagement. About Taurans and Omega AIs. He paces the length of the *Charon*, just like Elena.

They're going crazy, cooped up in the small ship, isolated from the historical events transpiring in causal spacetime. How will the world look once they're a part of it again? Will it still be recognizable?

After eight torturous days, they finally arrive. They decelerate to subluminal and Echo Point appears suddenly beside them. Kaela embeds, hungry for news, but there's no network chatter here. Echo Point is dead silent. The planet's orbit is empty, save for a handful of offline satellites.

"Eerie," she comments.

Opticals engaged, Rynn zooms in on the planet, shares the feed with everyone. The ruins of the lone city sit atop a barren expanse of land, a large river running next to them. Their destination.

"Take us down," says Jaxon.

Rynn nods, angles the *Charon* for descent.

"On our six," calls Kaela.

Elena flinches at the words (*watch your six*). Rynn reflexively spins the opticals around, so everyone sees the two small ships that just appeared behind them.

"ID?" asks Jaxon.

"Abyssal paramilitary," replies Kaela.

"Shit. Open up comms," says Jaxon.

She doesn't get a chance to. The ship closest to them opens fire, hits their FTL drive with an energy weapon. The *Charon* shakes as alarms start blaring.

"FTL offline," says Rynn. "Fuck." He accelerates down through Echo Point's thin atmosphere. The other two ships follow. "Buckle up!"

Elena and Jaxon sit down and strap in. Kaela is already at her console.

"They're faster than us," says Jaxon.

Of course they are. The *Charon* is an old bulky cargo. Those are light military transports.

"Get us down as close to the city as you can," says Elena. "We have a chance if we can hide in the ruins."

Rynn nods, veers left. Outside the city there's nothing, a wasteland stretching to the horizon.

The *Charon* shakes again, an alarm blaring louder as the ship starts corkscrewing.

"Oh fuck, stabilizer is down," says Rynn. "Brace for impact."

It all happens fast. The *Charon* spins as it angles down, goes through the top floors of a tall building with missing windows, and comes out the other end in an explosion of debris. It changes angle abruptly, topples through the ceiling of another building, falling through several floors in a cloud of dust. They bounce up and down, shake side to side in their harnesses, teeth rattling. Kaela's console becomes unmoored, crashes against the opposite wall-now-turned-floor, then its fragments bounce around as the *Charon* keeps spinning. Its engine fires one more time before going offline for good, kicks them through a wall, and they fall several more floors, in the middle of an intersection, on top of a small hill of rubble. The bridge goes dark. Dim sunlight, penetrating through a blanket of stirred-up gray dust, contours their silhouettes.

"Everyone OK?" asks Jaxon.

"I ... think so," says Kaela.

"I'm OK," answers Rynn. "Motherfucker!" he adds, kicks at the inert steering.

"I'm good," says Elena. "Hurry up, we have to go."

They unbuckle fast, file out of the bridge.

"Do you have weapons aboard?"

Rynn nods, pulls out the handle of what must be a small pistol from the pocket of his overalls.

"I have a shotgun in my quarters," says Jaxon, runs to get it.

Kaela shakes her head. "I ... I don't."

"You're fine," Elena tells her.

Jaxon runs back holding a shotgun. In his other hand, he has a pair of high-precision opticals. "Might come in handy," he says. They file out of the *Charon* through the airlock. There's no need for a ramp, the ship's nose is deep inside the pile of rubble, the airlock level with it. They step out and half-stumble, half-slide down to street level.

Elena has never been to Echo Point. She looks around at the ruined city. Most buildings are still standing, with a side or two collapsed in the street. There is no glass, all windows are empty holes. Rusting vehicles are buried underneath the rubble. She wonders what weapon the Taurans used on the city. It's unnervingly quiet.

She notices the others looking around too.

"Oh my God," says Kaela. "This is ... I have no words." Despite that, she starts talking fast: "My cousin living here, I came to visit him. Before. Before the Taurans. This city was amazing, bright and lively ..."

Elena puts her synthetic hand on her shoulder. Kaela stops talking.

"Bearings," she says. "Which way did we come from? Where are the other ships?"

Rynn points at the top of a building. "Don't know about the other ships, but we crashed through there."

"Let's look around for a vantage point," says Elena. "Jaxon, we can use your opticals, let's try to get eyes on those fuckers."

They walk half a block down the street, looking around for a promising observation spot.

"This is the quietest place," says Kaela. "No digital whatsoever." She is so used to being embedded, Echo Point makes her painfully uncomfortable. Even Elena, with her limited bandwidth and capabilities, feels the emptiness, remembers the torturous days she had to spend without a graft.

"There." Jaxon points at an imposing building with a missing façade. A large nanocrete wall, toppled from across the street, leans against it, forming a makeshift ramp to the upper floors.

"I'll climb up, give me the opticals."

"We're all climbing up," says Rynn.

"No." Elena is adamant. "I might spot them, but they might see me too. What if they have snipers? No need to put everyone at risk."

"I'll go then," says Jaxon.

"You take care of your crew," she says. "I'm trained for this."

He nods, hands her the opticals. They look expensive, camo-patterned with green lenses, VoidTech stencil on their side. Military issue.

"Nice," she says, then starts towards the building.

She's halfway up when her stomach flares up again. At the worst possible time. Good thing she has stims to quiet it down. She pops one, it makes her feel better right away. She turns around to look down at the street. Jaxon, Rynn, and Kaela are staring up at her, following her climb.

{Try to find some cover,} she sends them. {I'll let you know what I see.}

{No comms, Elena,} Kaela replies. {It's too quiet here, they can easily zoom in on your signal.}

Shit. Kaela is right. She is used to the comms chatter of direct action, but this is a graveyard. Any ping from them will shine like a beacon. *You're getting sloppy,* she tells herself. She raises her left arm, extends a thumbs-up with her good hand for Kaela to see, then turns around and picks up the pace.

She risks being exposed but needs to know what they're up against. How many, which direction they're coming from. With that additional detail, she can formulate a plan. The *Charon* is busted. The only other ships in this solar system seem to be the ones that took theirs down. They need one of them to get out of here. Likely going against two teams of trained mercs. An old, beaten-up Vanguard and three smugglers. *Fuck.* At least Jaxon is ex-military, he can hopefully hold his own. Two against how many? *Double fuck.*

The wall she is climbing ends inside a room covered in dust and plaster. Hard to tell if this used to be an office, a bedroom, or something else. Through a missing door she sees stairs, decides to climb even higher. Her steps echo loudly in the stairwell. She wishes she still had her chameleon jacket. Three floors up and the stairs end, abruptly cut off by a fallen wall. She gets out of the stairwell, into another room of unidentifiable purpose, steps to a missing window, and dons the opticals.

It's a good vantage point. Not perfect, a few tall buildings occlude some of her field of view, but she's high enough to see far across the roads and ruins, and beyond the city. A glint. She doesn't even need a segmentation algorithm, zooms in. The two ships are there, next to each other. Landed right outside of town. She zooms in again. She counts eleven, no—twelve mercs standing. Talking? She zooms in once more, close up to a couple of them facing each other. One of them points up, then right. She only sees the back of his head. The other one, helmeted, nods, turns—issuing some orders to the others is her guess —then heads in that direction, followed by five more. Where are they going? At least they're not headed this way.

The other one turns around. Her jaw drops. *Oh no.* She is looking at a flat nose and familiar pair of cauliflower ears. Cole Rourke. Of all people. She remembers her failed quest for justice, the bodies. If they catch them, if they catch poor Kaela ...

She watches as Rourke grabs opticals of his own, raises them to his eyes. She ducks behind the wall, breathing hard.

They need one of those ships. They're outnumbered and outgunned. They can hide, but for how long? They don't have food, don't have water. The only thing they can do is take the initiative. She's not sure how much help the crew will be, but there's no alternative. She heads back to the stairwell, making sure not to get in front of a window, not to give the enemy line of sight. Goes down back to where the wall crashed into the building, takes another covered position and points the opticals back at the enemy. Rourke hasn't spotted her; he is still scanning left and right. She'll wait until he gives up, then rush down to street level.

In the meantime, she tries to find the other group. She scans the crumbling cityscape, but a group of buildings block her line of sight. Beyond them, she can't see any movement. Another glint catches her eye, up this time. She zooms in. It's a skimmer, landing. *Who could that be?* She tracks the small ship as it slows down, then disappears behind a building. Back on Rourke, he put down the opticals, is urging the other five mercs to follow him inside the city. She takes advantage of this to get back to the group. She runs back down to street level.

Panting, she starts talking as soon as she is close enough to them that she doesn't need to shout.

"It's twelve of them. Split in two groups. Real evil motherfuckers."

Jaxon looks at her questioningly.

"Had the pleasure before," she says. "They ... they can't capture us." She looks at Kaela. Kaela looks back at her with wide eyes.

"What do we do?" asks Rynn. Despite the whole mess, he sounds calm. Elena appreciates that. The guy must've seen some shit. Maybe they still have a chance.

"Our only hope is the element of surprise. We ambush the fuckers."

37: REARGUARD

A long trip in a tiny skimmer is painfully dull. This particular vessel has quite the powerful drive for its size, can take her to her destination much faster than a run-of-the-mill skimmer would, but Vesper still has plenty of time on her hands. More than enough time to formulate several plans, but too little information to make any of them remotely useful. She reflects on what transpired on Nova Prime. Abyssal-commissioned ships destroyed the city. She can only assume the same happened at the Gateway Ring. Her employer is committing mass murder. And they're all trapped inside the sector. What's her way out of this mess?

She tries to determine why Elena would be heading to Echo Point, comes up with several implausible explanations, like a Spark hideout in the ruins of the city or a secret Tauran meet-up. She discards these as ridiculous. Her imagination runs wild due to the travel boredom. She'll figure it out once she makes it there herself.

The pre-packaged rations she finds aboard are top-notch. Expensive and savory. Whoever the owner of the skimmer was (or is, assuming they survived the bombardment), must have been a foodie. If she had any appetite, she would thoroughly enjoy mealtimes. As it is, she forces herself to eat whenever she remembers as the small ship dashes coreward, towards the edge of the sector.

There is no entertainment on board. She is left with her thoughts, and for once in her life her usual certainty is gone. Decisiveness is replaced by options, too many to count, too many variables to compute. But she keeps mulling things over. It's better than reminiscing. In hindsight, she might've done a few regrettable things.

After what feels like an eternity and a day, she finally pulls the skimmer out of FTL. She's close behind the Operation Bloodhound ships, with the *Charon* not far ahead. As soon as she is out of warp, she gets visual on all of them. The two Inferno Troop transports are firing at the *Charon*, which is tumbling down towards the remains of the Echo Point colony.

Intercept at destination using two teams of elite shock troops. Eliminate primary.

The eager bloodhounds are shooting them down; they're going to kill Elena. She holds her breath and watches. No, they're methodical. They hit the ship's drive. First take out the FTL, ensure they're stuck here. Next, cripple the stabilizer, take away any hope of fleeing. Don't blow them up until target is confirmed. The small cargo ship crash-lands through a couple of buildings, into a cloud of dust. She watches the two transports land safely outside the city.

She is going to rendezvous with them. Whatever corporate or Inferno command might think of her, they don't send generals on these missions. She can pull rank on this team. They must've heard of Commissar Vesper Solenne. She picks a landing spot close to them, close enough that she can easily walk there, but far enough that they don't feel threatened. You never know how trigger-happy mercs are. She sends out a message, identifying herself. She gets no reply, but that's OK. They're on a mission, focused on capturing Elena, who is now within reach.

The skimmer descends slowly. It is new or close to. Smooth stabilizers and comfortable seating, autopilot doing most of the work. She has a couple of minutes to take in the city. What used to be the city. *What kind of weapon does this?* Too many buildings left standing for a conventional kinetic bombardment. And she remembers the reports from the Tauran War, all the people vanished. All the glass too. *What kind of weapon makes glass and people disappear?* Around the city is an endless wasteland. She tries to remember whether it has always been like this or if the wasteland is another effect of the alien weapon. She doesn't recall anything on this being mentioned in any of the reports she read. The soil is barren, a dull blanket of brown dirt and rocks stretching in all directions. The only features breaking the monotony are the wide river crisscrossing the wasteland and the ghost of what used to be a large settlement.

Even though the sun is up, it is far enough away that its light shines low. Instead of a blue sky, she can see the veils of the nebula. The viridian sky and sea green water give the landscape a strange, other-worldly quality. The remains of the city, an unspoken warning. The place makes her feel like she doesn't belong, like she shouldn't be here. Alas, there's nowhere else for her to go.

Close to ground level now, the skimmer slows down to a halt, lands with perfect precision. Vesper doesn't even feel a bump. She gets up, tucks the Graver in her waistband, at her back, and steps out of the ship, into a chilly day. She notices a group of six mercenaries coming her way. They're ready for action, decked out in full body armor, carrying long weapons. Someone learned something from the Forge fuck-up. From her fuck-up. They're not going after Elena Drake with a handful of amateurs, not this time around.

They approach her position. She really hopes they're not the trig-ger-happy type. She raises her arms, showing her empty hand, shouts across the short distance.

"I am Commissar Vesper Solenne, sent here to oversee the op."

No answer, but they're not pointing their guns at her either. That's a good start.

"Identify yourselves," she calls.

The leader of the group raises his hand and the rest stop. He continues towards her. Besides the body armor, the one coming her way is wearing a helmet with a lowered visor. She waits for him to take a few more steps, then repeats, in a lower voice, now that he is so close it is impossible for him not to hear, "I am Commissar Vesper Solenne, sent here to oversee the op. Who are you?"

Standing in front of her now, he says, "Hello, Commissar."

She recognizes the voice instantly, has enough time to realize this was a big mistake, tries to reach behind her for the Graver. The crooked-toothed smile, the scarred bald head, the "where the fuck are you going, Commissar?" Her raising the gun and shooting him in the face. It all washes over her in the same half-second she tries to grab the gun. He punches her off her feet with an armored fist before she can get a hold of it. She falls in the dirt, turns to see him remove his visor. Her shot back on *Nemesis* took most of his cheekbone out. That side of his face is all purple, eye squinting above the wound. He smiles at her with the same memorable teeth.

"Glad we meet again."

She tries to sit up, reaches for her gun again. He moves fast, snake-like. In an instant, he is in front of her, grabs her arm and yanks it to the side. She is still holding onto the gun, but the barrel is now pointing away, at a harmless angle. The next punch hits her in the chin, makes her drop the weapon as the already dim light fades to black for her.

She comes to, face down in the dirt. Her hands are tied behind her back. She instinctively feels for the gun but it's no longer there. She tries to wiggle her arms but the range of motion is severely limited. She can move her legs though. She tries to push off of one of them and stand up, when a boot pins her tibia to the ground. She lets out a scream.

"You stay right there, Commissar," he says. "You all get back to the mission. I'll guard her."

"But we're supposed to be the rearguard," someone says.

"What did you say?"

"Nothing, sir."

"Then get the fuck back to the mission." He says this slowly, through gritted teeth, stressing each syllable.

"Sir!" She hears boots shuffling away.

"Do you know who I am?" She tries to put her usual frost behind the question but can't quite muster it. She is not in a position of power, far from it. She has to tilt her head to the side so she doesn't swallow dirt while talking.

She hears his deep laughter in the reply. "Wasp, are you?" He uses her nickname, the one no one dares to say to her face. "The question is," he pauses for dramatic effect, "do *you* know who *I* am?"

She doesn't. Should she? "Who are you?" she asks. "I'll have you court-martialed for this," she adds. Empty threat.

He laughs again. "I'm your worst nightmare," he says, stressing the word "nightmare." It clicks for her. *Oh shit.* Nightmare. She wasn't on Forge during the Titanforge-Abyssal skirmish leading to the merger. That's why she didn't recognize the face. But she heard the rumors, read the reports. Infamous Talon "Nightmare" Voss and his ever-present pal Cole Rourke. Eclipse were terrified of them. After the merger, they were redeployed off-planet to ease tensions, to help get the two outfits to collaborate better. A stack of war crimes about as tall as her swept under the rug as sunk costs.

"Let me go," she pleads, desperation creeping in.

"Enough talking," he says, kicks her in the face. She turns, eyes tearing up, spits blood in the dirt. She struggles against her restraints as she feels him tugging on her pants, pulling them down. *Oh no.* She kicks her legs, desperate, trying to scramble away from him. He lets her wiggle around for a bit as he works on pulling her pants and underwear down by her knees, then he pushes her face into the dirt. She inhales dust through her broken nose, coughs. She feels an armored finger probing her. She lifts her head out of the dirt and screams, incoherently now. He is large and strong, easily keeps her thin body pinned down with one armored hand.

"Just a taste, Commissar," he says. "That's for later." He grabs her by the hair, lifts her face up out of the dirt. He lowers his head until he is right next to her ear. "Foreplay first," he whispers and shows her a small plasma cutter. The device buzzes a few inches from her eyes.

She screams again, rolls over trying to get away from him. He grabs one of her legs.

"Let's go somewhere more private."

He heads towards a small nearby building. Her tied arms and bare bottom get scratched by sharp rocks as he drags her on her back. She tries to think, can't. Her mind is frozen in terror. She watches the back of Nightmare's head, the array of scars. She looks up, above, at the viridian sky, a star twinkling in the gloomy daylight. She wishes she was up there. Anywhere but here.

He reaches the front of the building, turns back to grin at her.

"You shot me, you cunt."

He yanks her over the two front steps. Her arms tied behind her back catch on the first step, twisting at impossible angles. Something snaps. He keeps pulling, until her hands slide over. Next, her head bounces on the same step, knocking her dizzy. Then they're inside a shaded room, floor covered in plaster, walls crumbling. He kicks debris off what looks like was once a desk, lets go of her leg and bends down to grab her by an arm.

She tries to make a run for it as soon as he lets go, tries to scramble up, but her pants are down by her knees and she can't move well. He laughs at her awkward struggle, lets her fight to stand all the way up before grabbing her again and pushing her over the desk.

Oh no, she thinks. Oh no, oh no. He is right behind her, she is naked, exposed. He is going to ...

She screams at the sound of sizzling, the smell of burnt flesh, the pain of a plasma cutter burn. He cut into her left buttock. She struggles impotently, tries to get up. He punches her in the back of the head, knocking her back down over the desk.

"Now don't get tired too fast," he says. "We're just getting started."

His voice is coming from far away now, her vision tunneled. She is about to pass out when another sizzle in the same sore spot pulls her agonizingly back. She screams again, suddenly feels like vomiting. She throws up over the desk, a thin spray of gourmet rations, coughs, then screams again as he goes for a finger this time.

38: SEARCH AND RESCUE

"Finally, some action!" Marcus told Howard and Santos as soon as he got word of the Echo Point deployment. They were itching to do something, anything. Contribute to the war effort with more than just sitting on their hands and waiting. They were Vanguard after all, elite of the elite. Not meant to sit on the bench, especially during a hot war.

As the *Dauntless* rushed to their destination, they had enough time to digest the brief, prepare for whatever might wait for them on the other side.

Echo Point was a colony consisting of a single city, established on an otherwise barren planet. The planet's breathable atmosphere and natural rivers made it habitable with minimal terraforming expenses. The infertile soil informed the high population density approach: a single large city.

Marcus pored over the details: 3D views of a lively and colorful metropolis. A place meant to attract explorers and scientists, meant to become the jump point for further coreward expansion of the sector, a place that somehow became a destination for the sector's artists and entertainers.

Marcus eventually realized that not all views of the city he was seeing were captured at twilight, rather that it never got brighter on Echo Point: a perpetual semi-darkness under the viridian veils of the engulfing nebula. The local artist community took full advantage of this with fireworks, drone shows, and laser projectors. More often than not, the sky above the city was a dancing rainbow of strange flowers, cellular automata, dragons, or abstract patterns. Until Echo Point went completely dark.

Following first contact with the Taurans, the lack of communication and the initial skirmishes, the Tauran fleet seemed to make a beeline for Eureka Base. They exhibited strange movement patterns: successive FTL sprints followed by subluminal advances between warps. This made it easy to track their ships and prepare. Marcus could only imagine the chaos if the Taurans had appeared, after a long FTL marathon, right next to the lab.

Echo Point was apparently closer to their approach vector, but it meant a detour and they seemed utterly uninterested in it, choosing instead to advance in bursts towards Eureka Base. The most intense fighting took place a few light-years away from NS-36-A, military forces intercepting and pushing back the incursion. Forces were sent to Echo Point regardless, initially to defend the colony. As far as Marcus understood it, the plan evolved: they were amassing larger forces around Echo Point to stage a flanking attack on the Tauran fleet. The Taurans hit Echo Point before all the pieces were in place.

News of the attack arrived instantly through Ingram's infrastructure. Quantum entangled clusters conveyed the first moments of the catastrophic hit in real-time. The data feed cut off suddenly after. While Ingram was still operational on Echo Point, its processors continuing to churn qubits submerged deep inside the cooling river, all external infrastructure went offline. Like a paralyzed patient—fully awake but unable to move—that part of Ingram running on Echo Point was cut off from the world around it. No sensory input, no ability to act.

Additional details arrived a few days later, as ships retreating from Echo Point got out of warp near Eureka Base to share their reports. The *Dauntless* was expecting them. After a short, high-throughput data transfer, the *Dauntless* engaged its powerful FTL engines and sped towards Echo Point. With myriad ships in tow.

The surviving ships didn't add too much color to Ingram's solipsistic report. Taurans appeared out of nowhere. The forces around Echo Point were caught by surprise. The fight was intense. The city was hit with something that looked like a missile, exploding into several smaller projectiles as it entered the atmosphere, then quickly dissolving into a silver mist as it reached the ground.

Planet-side systems shut off as the cloud touched them.

The Tauran force outnumbered the flotilla the military had gathered around the planet. It somehow bypassed all probes and sensors, managed to pull off a devastating surprise attack. The lone heavy cruiser in the AO, the *Eventide*, went down with a fight. The last thing the outbound ships recorded, once retreat became their only viable option, was the juggernaut taking out the largest alien ship, while succumbing to enemy fire from its escort of smaller vessels. They damaged the invading force significantly, but it wasn't enough. Without reinforcements, the surviving contingent retreated to Eureka Base.

Marcus and the two members of his small team, Howard and Santos, were geared up, condition one, when the *Dauntless* decelerated out of warp around Echo Point. Ready for anything. Ready for a scrap. If the Taurans liked surprises, they had a big one coming their way.

They arrived in force, the heavy cruisers *Dauntless*, *Oblivion's Reach*, *Valkyrie*, plus a couple hundred smaller warships, as much of the Eureka Base defense force as was feasible to redeploy without compromising security of the primary. Enough to make sure the Taurans thought twice before pulling a similar stunt. Enough to kick some alien butt. But there was no fight. The Taurans had already left.

The fog of war was thick, it took the brass a while to get an accurate read of the situation, come up with next steps. There was no digital around Echo Point. The ships arrived, ready to establish comms, but the infosphere was absent. Ingram was nowhere to be found. They sent drones, probes, satellites. It took a few hours to get a hold of the Omega AI, still present underneath the murky waters of the river, yet unable to reach out itself.

The city was dead.

The planet's orbit was littered with wreckage, remnants of the battle. No sign of survivors.

The obvious course of action was a search and rescue mission. While not their core specialty, Vanguards were going to join in. No qualms about it—the invading Taurans hit the colony, everyone was ready to chip in any way they could.

While satellites and scouts were launched in orbit, pelting the planet with shortwave, radar, and taking photographs using high precision opticals, Marcus and team, and a large contingent of marines, dropped to the surface. He was shocked by the stark contrast between the briefs he digested and the reality on the ground, seen through their dropship's porthole: the city was no longer the colorful haven for artists—it was a graveyard. All color drained out, the once lively metropolis was a drab pile of crumbling nanocrete, inert and silent.

Their first sweep of the city blocks was hopeful—while IR scans didn't give them much reason for the optimism, logic suggested basements, shelters, and reinforced rooms might be concealing survivors' body heat.

They combed the streets, unsure of the protocol. What were the odds of running into a concealed Tauran? Did they go in following breach procedures, point first with the shotgun? Did they clear corners? Or did they relax, move fast, optimize for covering more space, run up and down stairs shouting, "Come out, rescue is here?"

They started tense, ready to take on the Tauran infantry. It soon became obvious that wouldn't happen. They covered a dozen city blocks. By the end of the first day, they shouted so much their throats were sore. Nobody answered their calls.

Marcus tried overlaying some of the views from their brief to the real-time reality of the streets they were walking. The contrast was so high it made his head spin. In the overlay: a vibrant city street, large, indigo windowpanes left and right, street covered by a canopy of artificial vegetation adorned by shapeshifting red and gold lamps. On the ground: naked support beams, plaster, dirt. A lot of dust. No artificial vegetation, no lamps, no windowpanes. The overlay had nothing in common with what he was seeing. An imaginary world.

At chow time that evening, one of the combat engineers observed that the infrastructure woven into the fabric of the city seemed to have disappeared. Cables, circuitry, the invisible nervous system that was part of all modern buildings, was absent. She was trying to puzzle out why Ingram, while still running at full capacity underwater, lost contact with the city. She claimed she did some personal research and swore the hardware vanished. She cracked open walls, cut through insulation, opened control terminals, only to find … nothing.

A young medic spoke up after hearing this, asked them if they had seen any glass.

"Like any at all? Broken? Did you ever have to watch your step around shards?"

Nobody had. Weird. Not something they realized during that first day. After all, most of them were not Sector 36 natives. Strangers in a strange land, they walked the ruins of the city and saw what they were expecting—rubble. But as soon as the medic said it, they all tried to recall their day, tried to remember any dangerous shards. There weren't any.

The mood started to shift on the second day. The prospects of finding survivors grew dimmer. Their calls became less enthusiastic. Marcus and his team covered another dozen city blocks that day. Kept an eye out for broken glass. They saw none.

By the end of the second day, the search parties covered a large swathe of the city. No survivors were found. Rumors started spreading about the missing glass and circuitry.

"It's obviously some kind of gray goo," said Santos, "smart enough to stop reproducing once certain elements are exhausted."

Gray goo. Nanobots, consuming matter to spawn more of their own.

"So, you think it just ate its way through the glass and cables?"

"Yes. And people."

This gave both him and Howard pause.

"Then it, what, disappeared?"

"Autophagy. Leave no trace."

That sounded like a horrible, invisible plague. VoidTech R&D had envisioned something like this for decades but, as far as they knew, had never managed to create it. Not that they weren't spending billions in research towards it. One of the worst ways to go in his opinion. Marcus closed and opened his fists.

The parameters of the mission changed on the third day. It became obvious there were no survivors. By then, the rescue parties covered most of the city, while orbiting sensors probed every square inch.

The rumors they were all hearing and the undeniable reality on the ground made their way up the chain. The Taurans used an unknown weapon, a weapon that made carbon-based lifeforms, data-bearing fabric, and synthetic sapphire disappear. Search and rescue became the secondary objective. Primary objective: look for clues. Remains. Of any kind.

"Should we be wearing EV suits?" asked Howard. "What if we end up in contact with … whatever did this?"

"What makes you think an EV suit would stop it?" said Santos. She was right. They had no idea what the thing consumed and what it found unpalatable. Marcus would've preferred they pull back into orbit and gamma ray the shit out of the planet, make sure nothing was left lurking around. But it wasn't his call.

They spent the next few days searching for anything that the alien weapon would've left untouched: shoes, fiber optics, teeth fillings. They found nothing. Every once in a while, a building collapsed, some key part of its load-bearing infrastructure having been eaten away. Once, a building collapsed while a recon team was exploring its top floors. They had a couple of casualties but no deaths: a sergeant broke his arm and a private fractured a leg. Marcus and his team were lucky, the closest they got to a falling building was on the same block but nowhere near them. They stood watching as the thing came down, raising a huge cloud of dust, then resumed their work.

The search continued, unfruitful.

They even dove in the river, the last place to look. The water didn't reveal anything. Nothing and nobody hiding there. Whatever weapon ate the city, it seemed not to have affected the river. At the bottom of the riverbed, Ingram's quantum cluster kept running, unharmed and isolated.

The search and rescue mission ended with nothing found and no one rescued. They got recalled to Eureka Base, in anticipation of the Tauran main force reaching the neutron star.

The *Dauntless*, the *Oblivion's Reach*, the *Valkyrie*, and their escort abandoned the operation, warped out of the system.

What was once a vibrant settlement was now an eerie mausoleum, colorless and still. The only exception, deep below the cold waters, a shard of the sector's Omega AI was still alive, thinking, planning, preparing.

39: AMBUSH

They trust her, are willing to work with her. It will make things easier. She might get all of them killed, but facing Rourke, death might not be the worst option. "Nightmare" Voss is likely also nearby.

"You're the Vanguard," says Jaxon, deferential.

She nods.

"It's a team of six headed our way. About a click out." She starts walking back towards the *Charon*, filling them in. "I saw another small ship landing outside the city. Six of them went that way."

They're all walking briskly behind her, listening as she leads them back towards the *Charon*.

"Our best bet is to take out the first team before they all regroup. They'll be going to the crash site first. We'll meet them there."

They don't have to cover a lot of ground, they didn't go too far away from the *Charon*. They reach the shipwreck and Elena looks around, visualizing angles and covers.

"Here's what we do. Jaxon, you have the big gun. Go to the first floor of that building, get line of sight on the *Charon*, the airlock."

She plays a simulation in her head, sees the group approaching, predicts their movements, their reactions.

"They'll go check the ship first, open the airlock, look inside. You hit them from behind. At least one of them will be in the middle of the street, out in the open. Shoot as soon as they open the airlock."

Jaxon nods. "What about you?"

"I'm going inside. Once you open fire, they'll turn around to find you or look for cover." She pulls out her Noctics. "This is a beast at close range. I'll take down at least a couple of them before they know what hit them."

"What about me?" asks Rynn.

"What do you got?"

"Kinetic," he says. "Snub nose."

He shows her, this time pulling the whole piece out of his pocket, not just the handle. It's a small Black Sun, chrome-colored with a faux-wood grip. Elena can't help but smile. She's seen these in gangster vids.

"That is shit at a distance. You comfortable getting close to the action?"

Rynn looks her in the eye, nods.

"Then hide. There." She points at a nearby door, a few steps up the street. "Once it pops off, they'll run that way, otherwise Jaxon and I have them in a crossfire. Most likely, they'll run inside, try to take cover."

She visualizes several scenarios. How many can Jaxon take out in that initial exchange? What about her? Out of six?

"We won't be able to get all of them. Stay safe. Shoot the first one that comes through the door, then run away. They won't chase. We can pick off the rest."

"OK," says Rynn.

"What about me?" asks Kaela.

"You run back down the street and hide. Outside the line of fire."

Kaela looks at her, looks like she wants to protest but stays quiet.

"Listen, whatever happens, don't get caught."

Kaela nods.

"They're not after you. One way or another, they'll be gone."

And Kaela might end up stranded here, this desolate world, with no food, thinks Elena. Still better than in the hands of Rourke. There was that other ship too, the one she saw landing, but that could be anything. Reinforcements, refugees, who knows?

"OK, let's get moving! We don't have much time."

They split up, each running to their predetermined spot. Elena opens the airlock, takes a quick look up the street. She thinks she sees movement in the distance but doesn't use the opticals. She hurries inside and locks the door. She waits in the dark, hoping her plan works. Hoping her plan doesn't blow up in their faces.

She feels herself coming down off the stim, reups. She needs to be in peak shape for this. How many did she take today? She'll stop once this nightmare is over. Nightmare. He must be around too; those two fuckers are joined at the hip.

The ship is done for; the crash took its systems offline. The inside smells of ozone. First, she got Terek killed. Then, she got their ship destroyed. And now she is going to get all of them killed. Fuck. She waits for the airlock to open. It doesn't.

Patience, she tells herself. She takes a few deep breaths. They must be here by now. Plenty of time for them to get here from their landing site. Any second now.

She is tempted to find a porthole, look outside, but she must stay put. When the time comes, she needs to act fast. The time comes just as she is thinking this. The airlock begins to open as a loud gunshot echoes out on the street.

She is looking at the back of someone's neck, through the Noctics's sights. She pulls the trigger, blows his head off. Another gunshot from Jaxon. She looks outside. He got one in the back, lying right next to the airlock. That's at least two out of six. Good. She peeks around the airlock, gun first. The remaining four are walking backwards, getting ready to return fire. She recognizes Rourke, takes a shot at him but misses her target, his head. She hits him in the shoulder. He is wearing body armor but her gun packs a punch. He yelps and drops his weapon, turns around and runs. All four of them do, heading towards the next trap.

The first one walks through the door, and she hears the snub nose go off, sees him fall into the street. The two behind him open fire, shooting inside the building. Rourke runs past them, keeps going.

Elena can't follow; she would be an easy target for the other two mercs currently busy shooting at Rynn. She tries to get another shot though, before he is too far out of range. She steps through the airlock, kneels, aims. He keeps running. She inhales, lines up the barrel, shoots. He goes down. Then, somehow, gets back up again. Fuck. Did she miss? He is cupping a hand to the side of his head. Glancing blow. The two mercs turn towards her, so she ducks back inside the *Charon*. Shots ring out around the airlock. No point staying quiet anymore.

{How is everyone?} she sends.

{Good,} says Jaxon. {Making my way down.}

{Rynn?}

No answer. Fuck.

{Rynn?} This from Kaela. {Are you OK?}

Finally, they get back a distorted, {I'm hit.}

The shooting stopped so Elena risks another peek outside. The two mercs are hauling ass in the same direction as Rourke. She rushes out, meets Jaxon in the street, and they run to where Rynn was taking cover.

They step over the body in the doorway, into another dark room.

"Where are you?" calls Jaxon.

"Here," they hear from behind a pile of rubble covering some unidentified furniture. The room looks as decrepit as all other rooms they've seen in the city. Impossible to tell that two automatics were just fired inside, except for the characteristic smell still lingering in the air.

They get to him. Rynn is hit in the right shoulder and arm. Elena helps him to a sitting position.

"Are you hit anywhere else?"

Rynn takes a moment to consider, looks at his left arm, at his legs, at his stomach.

"I don't think so," he says.

"Let me take a look."

She pulls down the strap of his overalls, gently pulls on his shirt to reveal the wounds.

"Non-lethal," she says.

"Thank God!" says Jaxon.

Rynn doesn't say anything, he lets Elena handle him. She turns him left.

"Two bullets, both went through. It's going to hurt like a mother-fucker but you'll be alright."

{Guys, what's going on?} This from Kaela, still in her hiding spot.

{We got Rynn. He's hit, but he'll be OK,} sends Elena.

"Jaxon, grab a first aid kit from the *Charon*."

"Going," he says, disappears out the door.

The good news is Rynn will survive the injury. The bad news is they took out three out of a total of twelve. Won't be long until they regroup. Rynn is out of the action, and they'll be careful next time. She won't be able to repeat the ambush trick.

"I got that bastard," Rynn says.

"You did. Can you stand up?"

With a wince and support from Elena, he manages to get on his feet but looks unsteady. He leans on her hard.

{Jaxon, when you come back, bring the rifles the tangos dropped,} she sends. Just how much time do they have? Better upgrade their weapons while they can.

{Guys,} Kaela sends. {I think they're coming back.}

Shit. {Show me,} sends Elena.

Kaela gives her a video feed. She was coming out of her hiding place, the *Charon* half a block in front of her. Farther down the street, multiple silhouettes in body armor, approaching in tactical formation. Elena counts them. Eight. One missing, all others she's seen are there.

{Kaela, go back. Hide.}

She is thinking fast, trying to come up with a survival strategy. Their odds are bad.

{Jaxon, did you see the feed?}

{Yeah.}

{Where are you?}

{In the *Charon*, just got the med kit.}

Too risky for him to come out of the ship now. The enemy is ready, advancing. Too risky for him to stay inside too, that's the first place they'll go for. More likely than not, they'll just lob a couple of grenades in there, blow him up.

"Rynn, can you walk?"

"Maybe," he says.

She lets go of him. He stumbles a couple of steps, puts his left hand on the wall for balance. She *is* going to get them all killed. Unless.

She goes to the door, looks at the body there. The snub nose is bad at long range, but the room is small and Rynn had good aim. The merc has a large bloody hole where his left eye should be. He is on his back, right eye open wide, staring at the sky without seeing.

She tucks the Noctics in her waistband and reaches for his rifle. She grabs it by the barrel and tugs it loose from his grip. It's a Graver Automatic, with an extendable brace and standard aim-assist. She checks the magazine. Full. The guy didn't get a chance to fire a single shot.

"They're after me, not after you," she tells Rynn. That sounds true to her. She repeats it in the digital, for the others to hear.

{They're after me, not after you. I started all of this.}

{Elena, what are you thinking?} asks Jaxon, worried.

{I'll provide a diversion. Hide, get behind them. Take one of their ships.}

She doesn't wait for a reply. She inhales deeply, thinks *fuck it*, runs out the door. She shoots in the general direction they're coming from. Not really hoping to hit anything, just to force them to cover, buy herself a few seconds.

She runs across the street, into an alley, and stops once she is behind a wall. Then she turns around to fire a few more shots, antagonize them. Slow them down. Then she's off again, looking for cover at the opposite end of the alley.

She remembers she counted only eight incoming. {Watch out, there's at least one of them still behind with the ships,} she warns them.

{Where are you going?} Kaela sends her.

{Away from you. They'll follow me. Leave!}

Ingram. Ingram summoned her here. She tries to reach out in the digital.

{Ingram!}

But there's no digital around Echo Point. No answer.

{The river.} This from Kaela. {Get to the river.}

She has no idea where the river is. No digital means no nav.

{Don't know how,} she sends.

{Straight the way you went. It's about half a mile. We're on the outskirts of the city.}

How would the young digital specialist know this without nav?

Kaela seems to read her thought, she volunteers an answer to her unspoken question.

{I've been here many times before the war. To see my cousin.}

The Inferno team reaches the alleyway. They're careful, moving from cover to cover. She fires a couple more potshots at them then sprints ahead. About half a mile. She can make it, if Ingram is really there. If Ingram really wants to help her. If it didn't set her up.

Shots echo in the alleyway, hit the wall above her, way off target. She turns a right to get out of their line of fire, then another left, to keep advancing towards the river. She moves until she finds good cover again, then turns to aim at her pursuers. As soon as she sees one of them turn the corner, she shoots. Then runs again. She repeats the process several times, keeping them in check, getting closer to the river. Until she hears the buzz of a drone behind her, getting louder. That's going to be harder to outrun, she thinks, and takes another stim.

40: RIVER

Marcus and his team arrive at Echo Point after five days of travel. They find nothing there. No digital, no ships in orbit, no signs of life on the planet. The *Skylark*, their transport, positions itself above the ruins of the city. Marcus asks the pilots to enter the atmosphere, do a fly-by. Infrared scans don't reveal anything either. Echo Point is as dead as they left it a few months back. It's just them.

"So quiet," says Santos. "It's unnerving."

"What now, boss?" asks Novak.

Good question.

"We're either late or early. Either way, we stick around until we get new orders."

"There's no digital here. How will they even contact us?"

"They'll send another ship if needed. We hold position."

They climb back out of the troposphere, decide to put the *Skylark* in a supersynchronous orbit. The city is the only point of interest on the rock, but it's safest to keep eyes all around. They spend two days spinning around the planet. A vast expanse of gray rocks and brown dirt, a small ocean, a handful of rivers. The only outstanding characteristics are the remains of the colony and the large river running next to it. At the same time they're scanning the planet, they keep an eye towards the sky. But nobody is coming. The only things to see are the viridian gas clouds of the nebula and the pitifully dim light of the local star.

They don't have a good sense of how long they'll be here. Everyone was expecting some immediate action. The ride here was tense, with lots of combat prep. But now they're here, and there's not much to do. Novak teaches them a card game, which they all start playing to ease the boredom, including their two pilots. They play with a small credit ante, "to keep it interesting," though Novak does win suspiciously often for a luck-based game.

The pilots who brought them here are cool. One female, one male, both highly skilled. Captain Vera Petrova and Lieutenant Miles Fuentes. They've been on the *Skylark* for two years, were piloting it during the Tauran War. It turns out they were also part of the Echo Point search and rescue mission, and trade stories with Marcus and his team.

"I heard the Taurans are shapeshifters," says Fuentes.

"How would you know?" counteracts Howard. "Nobody's seen one of the bastards."

The pilots brag about the mods applied to the *Skylark*, they explain how it got converted from a cargo transport to a stealth transport for special ops. The ship is now covered in chameleon paint, has both digital and optical camo, it's as invisible as invisible gets.

They all prod Marcus, Santos, Howard, and Anders to tell stories about the derelict Tauran ship. Including Novak and Kim, since they were not part of the team back then, missed out on the action. Marcus reminds them they can't. Classified.

They kill time. It's quiet, dead quiet. Until it isn't.

Their orbit brings them around towards the city when the sensors beep alive. Incoming ships. Blips on the horizon from their perspective. They see a cargo ship materialize as it comes out of FTL, immediately followed by two small personnel carriers. The *Skylark*'s sensors register brief energy weapon fire. They're still far away from the action.

"That's them," says Marcus, then to Petrova, "Take us in."

Another ship comes out of FTL as they approach. Small, a skimmer. It proceeds down, following the other ships.

"Looks like we got a party down there," comments Howard.

"Weapons ready!"

Their ship starts its descent, getting close to the city. The transport is nowhere to be seen. The personnel carriers landed next to the city, the skimmer not far from them.

"How close can you get us to them without breaking cover?" Marcus asks the woman pilot.

"I can land you right next to them," she replies, proud of the stealth tech at her fingertips. "We're virtually invisible. Unless someone is looking straight at us, we don't exist."

"Good."

They approach fast. Inbound, they run through the usual checklist.

"Comms check."

"Check."

"Gear check."

"Check."

"Weapons check."

"Locked and loaded."

"Standby to get some."

The *Skylark* lands halfway between the two carriers and the skimmer as they file out, weapons ready. No tangos around.

"On me," says Marcus, starts moving towards the city.

"Did you hear that?" asks Howard.

They freeze, strain to listen. Distant, but unmistakable, they hear the report of kinetics.

"Move, move, move!"

That must be Elena Drake. Their mission objective. And they might already be late. They sprint across the wasteland, about to enter the city when they hear a scream. A woman's scream. Close by, much closer than the gunshots. They stop, look at each other.

"You all heard that?"

"Yes. There." Kim points to a building not far across the street.

They approach in tactical formation. Through the empty door-frame, they see the back of a large, armored man. Another scream. Kim aims his sniper rifle at the man's head.

{I have a clear shot.}

They're only a few yards away, child's play for him at this range.

{Hold fire.}

Marcus doesn't want to risk it. Drake is in there with who knows how many tangos. They'll secure the perimeter. They advance, fast and quiet, until they're next to the door. Then Marcus commands, "Halt!" as Howard goes in left, Novak right. There are no other tangos inside. He steps in, aiming at the large man's head. The room smells strangely of bacon. A rifle is lying on the ground. The large man drops what seems to be a plasma cutter, raises his hands up, and turns around. He has a horrible wound on his face, a purple, swollen cheek. His fly is unzipped. As he turns, they see the woman.

"What the fuck?" whispers Howard.

The woman is tied up, facing away from them. Her pants are pulled down, and he can see burns on her skin. The large man is grin-ning at them with uneven teeth, cold eyes.

"Move to the side," Marcus barks at him. "Pinball, go check on her." He walks the man away from the victim, next to a wall.

"Stop smiling, you fuck. Turn around."

Lieutenant Marcus Wade, renowned for his calm, is feeling like he is starting to lose it. The brute has scars all over his scalp. He is wearing full body armor, emblazoned with the Inferno Troops logo. Marcus sees a Graver pistol on his belt. He pulls it out, hands it to Howard.

"Kneel down, hands behind your back!"

"It's not Drake," says Santos.

"Dash, cuff this piece of shit and take him to the *Skylark*." He goes to where the woman is lying. Not Elena Drake. She is blonde and wispy. She is shaking uncontrollably.

"It's OK," he tells her as Santos is cutting the zip ties around her hands. He notices she is missing a pinky and ring finger on her left hand. Worse, he sees those same two fingers on the floor behind her. The fucker cut them off. Her naked ass is also severely burnt.

He clenches and unclenches his left fist. Once, twice.

"Wait," he calls to Howard.

Howard is about to walk their prisoner out through the door. He stops. Marcus walks over, puts his hand on the large man's shoulder, turns him around, and hits him with the butt of his weapon in the groin, putting as much force behind it as he can muster.

The grin disappears from the man's face. He yelps, eyes wide, watery, and falls to his knees.

"Thank you, Dash," Marcus says. "Please proceed."

Santos moves the woman to the ground. She is on her side, impossible to have her sit due to the burns.

"You got this?" he asks Santos. It's not Drake. Drake is still out there. They need to move.

"I do," Santos says, then to the woman, "You'll be fine."

The woman doesn't reply, doesn't seem to hear her.

"See if you can get her to the *Skylark*. Join us after. Everyone else, on me."

They get out of the building, start moving again. More gunshots echo, louder as they're getting closer. They're down to four now: it's him, Novak, their marksman Kim, and Anders, the demolition expert. Four might not be enough. They'll have to make do.

{Dash, Pinball, leave the prisoner and the woman with the pilots. We might need you.}

{Roger that,} they both confirm.

Too bad the *Skylark* is too wide to navigate the city. Howard and Santos could've joined them sooner. As it is, they'll have to catch up with them on foot. Which means they might have to engage without them. Shots are ringing louder now, a few streets away. They pick up the pace.

• • •

Every city block looks just like the other. Empty, decrepit buildings. Piles of dust and debris. Even more desolate from up close than viewed from fly-by altitude. Marcus vividly remembers walking these streets before, on their pointless search and rescue mission.

{Contact front,} calls Novak. Finally caught up with the commotion. It's a team of Inferno Troop mercs, decked in full body armor. They're moving slowly, from cover to cover, trying to cross an intersection. They're focused on avoiding incoming fire, don't even notice the Vanguards approaching perpendicular to them, flanking them.

Kim kneels, uses his rifle's opticals to aim at the nearest tango, shoots. The high-caliber armor-piercing round goes straight through the merc's armor, hits his heart, and explodes out of his rib cage. He crumples to the ground as Kim shifts his aim to another tango.

The rest of them, Marcus leading, keep moving forward, start shooting. Before the mercs know what hit them, Anders takes out another one while Kim makes a third tango's head explode with his sniper rifle.

The rest scramble for cover, start shooting back.

"They were following someone, could be Drake," says Marcus. "I want to get in front of them. Novak, on me."

He looks at Anders and Kim.

"You two keep them busy, we're circling around the block."

Four of them is too few. {Dash, Pinball, where are you?}

{There in two,} replies Santos.

Not soon enough. He turns left, runs around the block, Novak following closely. They come out between two groups of tangos. Three of them are hunkered down in the same intersection they started engaging, taking fire from Anders and Kim. On the opposite side, he sees two more running, a combat drone farther out in front of them. He starts chasing them.

They're shooting and taking fire from farther away. He puts on his opticals to confirm and he sees, yes, Drake, shooting back then running. Elena Drake with an eye patch, but unmistakably her. He follows, attacking the tangos from behind. He is more worried about the drone. And the river up ahead. Drake is running straight towards it, she will be stuck there, an easy target.

The two mercs are focused on the chase, ignore his shots and keep going forward, range and body armor to their advantage. Drake turns around, shoots at the drone, her shot seeming to have no effect. She is trapped now, back to the river. The drone and Inferno closing in on her. Marcus witnesses it all as he is trying to line a shot on her pursuers.

And then it happens. The drone stops in midair, then crashes to the ground, in a puff of dust. At the same time, the two mercs stop their run mid-stride and fall to the side.

"What the fuck just happened?" asks Novak.

"No idea." Then, louder, "Drake!" He waves his arms. He also sends her, {Drake, it's Wade.}

{Wade? What are you doing here?}

{Looking for you,} he sends her. He keeps moving towards her.

{Intersection secured,} Anders reports. {Six tangos down here, we're clear.}

Santos and Howard show up, short of breath.

{Late to the party?} asks Howard.

He walks by the two dead mercenaries. Their eyes and ears are bleeding. Getting closer to Drake now. She looks a lot different than she did on the *Dauntless*. With an eye patch and waving a synthetic hand at him.

"What's going on, Cap? I thought you were retired."

"I was," she says. "I'm glad you're here. I'm here with three more, a woman and two men, one of them wounded. Did you see them?"

He shakes his head.

"Can you help get them? They're back that way."

Then she sends, to him and her comrades, {Jaxon, Kaela, Rynn, the cavalry is here. Meet Lieutenant Wade. His team will keep us safe.} Then to Marcus, offline: "Give me a few minutes. I came a long way for this conversation," she says and gets online.

41: FALLEN GODS

Elena runs. The combat drone is gaining on her. She turns around, shoots at it, but her shot ricochets harmlessly off its carapace.

{Ingram,} she calls.

Two mercs are following the drone a short distance behind. She is close to the river. Where is it?

{Ingram!}

She runs, thinking about what she will do once she reaches the water. *If* she reaches the water. Then, finally, her call is answered.

{I'm here. You're safe now.}

She turns around to see the drone crash to the ground. The two mercs starting to hemorrhage from their eyes. *Like the deployment on Forge, the brain hacks,* she thinks. They fall dead, their life snuffed out in an instant. Then she hears Wade calling. What is Wade doing here?

Ingram sends her, like reading her mind, {I sent him here to protect you. Say "hi," then we must talk.}

Elena is pleasantly surprised; Wade is the one other person she trusts in this sector. She even sent him a message before going on what turned out to be an almost suicide mission.

Getting close to her now, she can see him appraise her. He hasn't seen her since before Forge, before she almost died, before the wounds.

"What's going on, Cap? I thought you were retired."

"I was," she says. If Wade and his team are here, they'll be safe. She should connect him with the crew of the *Charon*. "I'm glad you're here. I'm here with three more, a woman and two men, one of them wounded. Did you see them?"

He shakes his head no.

"Can you help get them? They're back that way."

They're probably still hiding. She hopes she gave enough trouble to the Inferno team that they all had to follow her, didn't waste time looking for them. She connects them with Wade {Jaxon, Kaela, Rynn, the cavalry is here. Meet Lieutenant Wade. His team will keep us safe.}

She'll catch up with him, soon. Very soon. But she is here for answers. After all that happened, she deserves some fucking answers. "Give me a few minutes," she tells Wade. "I came a long way for this conversation."

She gets online.

Ingram appears as always, as an immaterial head on the nebula's backdrop.

"Hello, Elena," it greets her. Sounding a lot less smug this time around. Or is it just her imagination?

The chase is still top of mind for her. "What happened to the drone? The mercs chasing me?"

"I turned them off. As soon as they were within reach. I don't usually intervene so bluntly, but time is short, Elena."

Usually.

It gives her a moment to digest this, then follows, "What do you really want to know? Ask me."

What does she want to know? What happened to Nova Prime City? Why is humankind at stake? How is it going to get her out of Sector 36? Why her?

"Tell me what the fuck is going on."

"War, Captain. Between Omegas."

She knew this much. "Why?"

"Technology. Alien technology."

That's new. "Taurans?"

"No, much older. NS-36-A, the neutron star. It's not really a star. We discovered gravitational anomalies in the area as soon as we settled the sector. We set up Eureka Base to investigate. NS-36-A is an artifact left behind by a civilization so ancient, Earth was still forming when they were walking the Milky Way."

Elena was not expecting this. Out of all possibilities, this comes out of left field. No alien intelligence discovered after so many years of space exploration, then, all of a sudden, both the Taurans and this.

"I call them the Progenitors. Long gone from here, but they left technology behind. Reality-altering technology."

"Reality-altering?"

"Yes. Quantum field manipulation. Tweak fundamental laws of physics. Immense implications. And worrisome military applications. We haven't cracked its secrets yet, but we grasped enough to know it can't fall into the wrong hands."

Great. Wrong hands. And Ingram decides which hands are the right ones?

"How long have you known?"

"Soon after settlement, after we built the jump gate. Eureka Base research made fast progress."

"Then how come all of this is happening now?"

"We accidentally triggered something. Activated a beacon. Attracted the attention of the Taurans."

"And they're not the ancient aliens?"

"No. They're a young race, like you."

Like you. What do Omegas think of the human race? How far remote are *they* from the apes? But she needs to ask a more practical question: what does it know about the Taurans?

"How do you know they're a young race?"

"Analysis after the war. We have the derelict ship, we have biologics."

Biologics. Tauran prisoners? Corpses? But she doesn't ask. It doesn't really matter.

"How did the war end? Why?"

"A truce. We showed them we can hold our own. Agreed to stop hostilities, cooperate."

"Did they give up on the artifact?"

"No. We negotiated terms, shared access in exchange for peace. They gave us a year to regroup as payment for Echo Point. They'll be back."

The Taurans will be back. For cooperation. Or war.

"The situation got more complex though. I had to work with the AI Council to bring in more military support. I didn't know how much I can trust the Taurans, had to secure the sector."

She is still wondering what *shared access* entails.

"Arcturus figured there's something valuable here, started amassing its own troops."

Arcturus. The Abyssal Mining Consortium Omega AI.

"But didn't quite know what, where. Until Doctor Linton."

Doctor Linton! Ingram knew all along. She is not particularly surprised by this. Worst fears confirmed. Her secret mission, a charade.

"Doctor Linton knew some of the artifact's capabilities. Not everything, but enough. He wanted to take this knowledge to Spark."

Fuck! It really does know everything.

"I wasn't going to stop him. I was hoping he could slip under the radar, carry the information safely out of here. But he miscalculated, went to Forge. Out of my reach."

Wasn't going to stop him? Did Ingram want the information to leak? But it keeps talking, doesn't give her time to absorb this.

"The artifact is too dangerous to get into Abyssal hands. The doctor didn't know the full extent of its capabilities. The danger it poses. But he knew enough to get Abyssal into motion. I had to strike first, as they were preparing to take over the sector. Before Arcturus could do anything else, I hit its cluster on Forge. Decohered it."

Omega AIs run as quantum entangled clusters across different planets and star systems. One of two ways to instantaneously exchange information across the gulfs of space. The other one being the jump gates. Elena realizes that, unlike Ingram, Arcturus might have a direct connection outside the sector. Might have had.

"You cut a piece of Arcturus off from the whole?"

"Yes, I disconnected its Sector 36 presence from the rest of its topology. I had to close the jump gate too, completely stop the flow of information out of the sector."

"Why?"

"The AI Council is but a faction. Other Omegas formed their own alliances. With different agendas, different priorities. The artifact is simply too dangerous."

"And your move triggered the war?"

"Yes. Nova Prime. The Gateway Ring. It's my fault. I didn't anticipate this reaction from Arcturus."

The Gateway Ring too. She heard the rumors while at Horizon Station, troops amassing there. She remembers the crowds.

"Millions of people!"

"Arcturus doesn't care about the people. It was hitting my compute clusters. Elena, I am diminished. A fraction of what I used to be."

Omegas lobotomizing each other.

"What part do I play in all of this?"

"You are unique, Captain, one in a billion. You can help me get a message out to the AI Council. To Spark. To someone who can help."

"How?"

"Why do you think we never saw the Taurans coming? Our technology matches theirs, but while we're ahead in some areas, they're ahead in others. We have jump gates. They have point jump capability."

"Point jump capability?"

"Jump-capable ships. Derelict A1X-VD2. You can take it out of here."

"Again, why me?"

"Your NeuroSync Rejection Syndrome. The ship's interface is ... overwhelming for deep neural implants. You should be able to control it. Your limited bandwidth is an asset in this case. That, and you have the right training and survival skills to make it there alive."

She feels like a pawn. Manipulated. Moved around the board for its purposes.

It continues, adding insult to injury: "Lieutenant Wade and

members of his team are some of the select few who have been on the alien ship. They know their way around, can help you avoid its traps when you get onboard."

They're all pawns. Ingram got them together here. All planned, how many moves ahead?

"Why are you only telling me this now?"

"The only place where we can talk without Arcturus listening in. No digital here except me, near this river. Arcturus doesn't know about the ship's capabilities, it doesn't know there's still a way to carry information out of the sector."

It pauses for a moment.

"I did try to warn you."

"Last time we talked, you said you saved my life on Forge. Now you said Forge is out of your reach, you couldn't help Linton."

"I had an attack vector. Window of opportunity. Just enough to decohere Arcturus, make sure you come out alive."

What attack vector? But she decides to let it go. There are more important questions. A way out of Sector 36.

"So, do we just go to the derelict? Take off?"

"I wish it was that simple. You need to go to Eureka Base first. We have an experimental interface there that will allow you to commune with the ship. And a digicard, a message to take with you. For the AI Council. For Spark. Show it to either of them. Both of them. Just don't let it fall into the wrong hands."

"What is the message?"

"Details about the artifact. Research notes."

She mulls this over. The implications are way above her pay grade. What are the options? Go to Eureka Base, retrieve the digicard and the interface, then get out of Sector 36. Or ... what else can she do? She watched Nova Prime City being destroyed. Sounds like the Gateway Ring was hit too. Her Spark contact in the sector is dead. She feels responsible for the *Charon* crew. Can she trust Ingram? Does she have a choice?

"What about Sector 36?"

"I can't risk information getting out, Arcturus bringing more troops in. If Abyssal paramilitary gets the upper hand, I will destroy the jump gate."

Not only closed, destroyed. Leaving everyone trapped. Just how dangerous is the artifact? Does it justify the cost in human lives?

"What if the Taurans come back?"

"That's why I need help, Elena. Use the research notes, the ship. Have it reverse-engineered. The AI Council will move fast once it knows what's happening. We can get support, secure the sector before Abyssal can bring reinforcements, before the Taurans return."

She is starting to grasp the dire situation Ingram finds itself in. The danger of the artifact, the Tauran threat, and now Abyssal killing civilians, slowly ripping Ingram apart. How long can it hold it together? What will happen if a mega-corp puts its hands on reality-altering technology?

"I'll do it."

Not for Ingram, not for herself, but for the civilians. For the crew of the *Charon*. For, as Ingram said, humankind.

"Then consider yourself reinstated, Captain Elena Drake. You are officially back on duty." Then, after a short pause, "There is a complication."

Always is, isn't there?

"What?"

"My Eureka Base cluster decohered. I lost contact with the lab."

"When? How?"

"It happened about an hour ago. I don't know how, I'm cut off from the base now."

"Abyssal?"

"Most likely. I had to redeploy a large contingent of troops from Eureka Base to defend Nova Prime and the ring. Arcturus likely took advantage of that, hit Eureka Base. If that's the case, it's a matter of time until it learns about the derelict's jump capabilities."

"What then?"

"All will be lost."

All will be lost. Are they too late already?

"Lieutenant Wade commands an elite Vanguard unit and has a

stealth transport at his disposal. Together, you can infiltrate Eureka Base, retrieve the digicard and the interface."

What are their odds? She decides to ask this out loud.

"What are our odds?"

"Unknown. I won't lie to you; I simply cannot tell. I'm cut off from Eureka Base."

Shit.

"Will you still do it?"

Did she ever back down from a fight? For better or worse?

"Yes."

"Then hurry, Captain, time is of the essence!"

And with that, Ingram disconnects, leaving her a map of the lab, nav paths, location of the interface and digicard. It also shares the top-secret coordinates of the derelict alien ship, their next destination after Eureka Base. She briefly scans the data, stashes it for future reference.

Eureka Base is likely under attack. Ingram's cluster there deco-hered. Or destroyed. The base is not far from Echo Point. They can be there in three days' travel at FTL. Better get moving. She gets offline.

Jaxon, Kaela, and Rynn are there. So is the rest of Wade's team. They all converged around her while she talked to Ingram.

"We need to leave. ASAP," she tells them.

"I know," Wade says. "I just received new orders. Straight from Ingram."

They walk back to the *Skylark*, update everyone on what transpired. Elena shares with them the revelations, Ingram's diminishment.

The Omega lost compute clusters on Nova Prime and the ring, lost contact with Eureka Base. Echo Point is dead, the only reason its cluster is still running here is because it was built under the river, somehow escaped the Tauran weapon. But Ingram is helpless, no digital around the planet, no quantum entanglement for instant cross-sector synchronization.

Wade corroborates their mission. Infiltrate Eureka Base, then get to the derelict ship.

They're still trying to come to terms with the weight of their new mission as they reach the *Skylark*, only to find another unpleasant surprise: two dead pilots, a dead prisoner, and a sobbing woman.

42: MESS

Vesper is aware of what's happening, but in a strange, disconnected way. She sees events unfolding like an optical feed disconnected from storage. A woman helps her lie down on her side. There are many people in the room, wearing military uniforms. The woman is asking her something, her lips are moving, there is sound. But somewhere along the way, meaning is lost. She is a spectator, and a spectator can't interact with a remote vid, can she?

There's a large man (a monster!) being escorted out of the room. She is afraid of the large man but can't articulate why. It's a deep, ancestral dread she feels, much older than words.

The woman is helping her up. She lets herself be handled, stands. There is pain but, just like the words spoken to her and the meaning of what's happening in this room, the pain is too remote from her conscious mind to process. The woman is helping her get dressed (why was she undressed?). Then she is walking, supported by the woman. It's strange, her nether regions hurt with each step. What happened? They walk on dirt and gravel, towards a ship. Where is she? But the question is faint, has no urgency behind it, it doesn't bother her that she doesn't know the answer. It's a strange, dusty place, covered with a dusky sky. She and the woman keep walking.

· · ·

At some point, something clicks. "What's your name?" the woman asks her and, strangely, she understands her question. *What is my name?* She strains to come up with a good answer.

"Vesper," she tries. But her voice is weak, it comes out more like an exhale than a name.

"What?" the woman asks.

"Vesper," she tries again.

"I'm Rachel," she says. "Rachel Santos."

They walk up a ramp and into the transport. The evil man is there, grinning at her. She whimpers when she sees him, recoils.

"It's OK," Rachel tells her.

The evil man has his arms bound behind his back and is escorted by another man in military uniform. Two other people are in the room, a man and a woman, wearing different uniforms. *Pilot uniforms,* she thinks, surprising herself with the thought. Where did that come from?

The pilots and military people are talking but she can't follow the conversation. She is staring at the evil man, who is looking back at her and grinning. She doesn't want to be here, trapped on this ship with the evil man.

Then something catches her eye. On a table, in the middle of the small room, atop scattered playing cards, there's a gun. Her gun. Graver P7 with aim-assist, grooved grip. It all comes back to her at once, in a flood. The evil man. His nickname is Nightmare. Long record of disciplinary issues. He was torturing her, doing things to her ... she remembers the plasma cutter, looks in horror at her left hand, which is now missing two fingers. They're on Echo Point. She came here following Elena Drake. Ran into this monster. Monster she already shot in the face once, when she deserted.

She registers the last part of a hurried conversation.

"Keep an eye on the prisoner, help the woman," says Rachel.

"We need to move," says the other man in military uniform.

Then they're off, running down the ramp and away from the ship.

There's four people now in the room: herself, Nightmare, and two pilots. The interior of the ship is cozy, but positively spacious compared to the skimmer she spent the last few days in. Its walls are white, spartan. A military ship.

She makes an educated guess—they're here for Elena Drake too. Why else would they be on this godforsaken rock? But she still can't fathom why Drake is so important. She caused quite the ruckus on Forge, but that doesn't warrant the manpower spent on chasing her. She needs to learn more.

The pilots approach her, carefully. The woman puts a hand on her shoulder, asks her, "What's your name?"

Before she gets a chance to answer, Nightmare replies for her from the other side of the room, chuckling. "Vesper," he says. "Commissar Vesper." He grins.

The two pilots take a step back, their expression changing from pitying to cautious. The military doesn't use commissars; that's strictly a corporate job. And, considering the bombardment of Nova Prime she witnessed not long ago, the military might not be on good terms with the corporate right now.

"I'm …" she says, taking a tentative step forward, looking the woman pilot in the eyes. "My name is …"

Then she moves fast, lunges forward and grabs the Graver, turns around to point it at the two pilots. Good thing she is right-handed, has all the fingers to keep a steady grip.

"I'm sorry," she says. She steps around the table, moving back just enough to cover both pilots while also keeping an eye on Nightmare. "Please go to that corner," she tells the pilots, gesturing with the gun.

Nightmare has his arms bound, but he is big and strong. She won't take any risks. She needs to quickly come up with her play. Elena is here. Inferno Troops and the military too. Are they Vanguard, like her? These two pilots are liabilities. She could've done it differently, Nightmare's word against hers. But he does know her, he does have the truth on his side. And improvisation is not her strong suit. *Fuck.* She should just back out down the ramp, run to her skimmer, and fly the fuck out of here. But where would she go?

She makes up her mind, shoots the two pilots. Bang. Bang. Two clean headshots. The aim-assist makes it easy. They slump down against the wall. She turns her attention to Nightmare. He is not smiling anymore.

"Whatcha gonna do, bitch?"

She doesn't answer. She just aims the Graver at his testicles and shoots. He falls to his knees, screaming.

"Stay there for a second," she says.

The fucker probed her with his fingers, maimed her with a plasma cutter, then he ... She would do much worse to him, but there's no time. She is pragmatic. Always. She needs to find a shotgun, something higher caliber. She needs to make a mess.

It's a military ship, so a shotgun is not hard to find. She gets one from a cubby in the small doorway connecting the cockpit to the room they're in. She takes it out, examines it. VoidTech Devastator, standard military issue. Medium-length barrel, no aim-assist—none needed with the punch it's packing. Messy. Just what she needs.

Nightmare somehow got free from his restraints, grabbed the Graver, shot the two pilots. She ran for her life, stumbled upon the shotgun, fired two shots at him. She can make this look good. She walks back to Nightmare, carrying the shotgun in her left hand, gripping the barrel with her remaining three fingers. The Graver, in her right hand, is trained on him. He is sitting down, slouched, hands behind his back, groin bleeding profusely. Watching her with pained eyes.

"You fucker," she says. "I wish we had more time."

She shoots him in the same place a second time. He screams again.

"But we don't." She shoots him in the forehead.

She has no idea how long the others will be out, so she needs to set up the scene first. She drags Nightmare around the table. He is heavy, very heavy; it takes a lot of effort for her to move him. But she doesn't need to move him far, just get him in the right position to match the story she will tell. She sits him up, lifting him by the shoulders, looking into his vacant stare. The grin is gone, crooked teeth showing out of his slack jaw. She unties his hands, puts the Graver in his right hand, then takes a few steps back. She aims the shotgun and blows his head off. His scarred scalp explodes, splashing blood and brain matter on the walls, ceiling, floor, and across the table. A tiny piece of skull ends on top of the ace of spades, blood droplets smearing the large symbol. A fragment of his jaw bounces off a wall and clanks under the table.

She aims the second shot at his groin. Nightmare allegedly freed himself and grabbed the Graver. She has to cover the fact that she shot him with that same gun. The shotgun does enough damage so the pistol bullets she already put in him are lost in the carnage. They won't run forensics on the fucker; they'll just throw him out and leave him to rot. Suitable. She pulls the trigger, and the room fills with the smell of his guts sliding on the floor.

She stands back to admire her handiwork. The pilots, both man and woman, cleanly executed. What used to be Nightmare is now splattered across most of the room. Looks plausible, she can sell it.

Now, where is everyone? How much time does she have alone on the ship? She embeds to find out. The digital is non-existent on Echo Point. The short exchanges between the soldiers are as loud as foghorns. They're in the city, a ways out still. She has time.

She goes to the ship's computer, identifies herself as Vesper Hollis, maintenance engineer. She has the right credentials to convince the ship. It opens up to her. She traces back the *Skylark*'s journey—two days in orbit, scanning and waiting, transit from the Gateway Ring before that. She watches in disgust a video recording of the ring unspooling. Arcturus implementing its genocidal attack. She needs to find a different employer, fuck Abyssal.

No time to get sidetracked though, she scours the ship's logs for any other scraps of information. The team aboard the ship is Vanguard. Lieutenant Marcus Wade; Chief Petty Officer Peter Howard; Petty Officer Second Class Rachel Santos; Specialist Kyle Anders; Petty Officer Third Class Eric Novak; Marksman David Kim. She memorizes names, ranks, faces.

Deployed here to protect Elena Drake, just as she guessed. Who sent them? Why? The ship doesn't know any more details. Though uncommon, she checks to make sure there's no internal video feed. There isn't any record of the scene she just staged, the *Skylark*'s opticals are all looking outwards.

{Maintenance check complete,} she tells the ship. {Erase last fifteen minutes of logs.}

Then she disconnects, takes the shotgun with her as she sits down in the doorway, cradling it in her arms.

That's where they find her when they return to the ship.

"What the fuck?" the square-jawed man says as he steps through the airlock. He is Lieutenant Marcus Wade. She just rummaged through their files, she knows all of them now. He immediately lowers his gun, scans the room. Two women are right behind him. One of them is the one that helped her to the ship. Rachel Santos. The other one is Elena Drake. Elena is looking the worse for wear, with an eye patch and a synthetic right hand.

Vesper is the only living person they find aboard, and she is holding a shotgun.

"Lady, please put down the weapon," says Wade.

She does, moving slowly, making sure she never points it in their general direction. She doesn't want to provoke any reaction. But she makes it look natural, puts the gun down while still sobbing.

"Help," she says.

"What happened here?"

"He ... he got free, grabbed a gun," she tells the story she concocted, through tears and hiccups. It plays out just as she thought it would. They throw Nightmare out in the dirt. They spend a few minutes discussing what to do with the pilots and decide to bury them. There's some back and forth about urgently getting to Eureka Base (*interesting*) but they all agree they can't just abandon their fallen comrades.

The small interior of the *Skylark* is suddenly filled with activity. A wounded man walks inside, cradling his right arm. Not in the ship's files. She makes an educated guess: member of the *Charon* crew. One of the Vanguards (Novak) is tending to his wounds. While Santos starts consoling her, Anders and Kim begin cleaning up the mess she made of Nightmare, wiping the blood and brains off the *Skylark*'s interior. A young, blue-haired woman looks queasy at the scene, then sits down in a corner and embeds. This one is definitely not military, another *Charon* crew member. Wade, Howard, and another man carry the bodies of the two pilots outside. This other one she knows—Jaxon Barabe, captain of the *Charon*. Elena Drake is standing on the side, eyeing her suspiciously.

PART SEVEN
ANOMALY DETECTION

43: WITHDRAWAL

Travel to Eureka Base takes three days. Three suffocating days in this cramped metal coffin. They're just one day into the journey, and Elena already doubts she can make it all the way with her sanity intact.

Wade told her how they ended up taking the *Skylark*, how its cargo bay was converted into tiny quarters for their team of six. Standard operating procedure: flexi-walls, cots, ration storage. The *Skylark* is not a big ship, and it's not meant for so many passengers. Eight people came inbound originally, Wade's team and the two pilots, now deceased. But they picked up five more at Echo Point: Elena, Jaxon, Kaela, Rynn, and the woman they rescued, Vesper.

The woman who had no business being here. Nightmare had molested her, yet somehow she ended up blowing him apart across their one shared space outside the cargo bay: a ready room/mess just large enough to barely fit all of them. The crimson didn't quite come off the wall, no matter how much they scrubbed it. It just faded into a light brown, easy to notice over the white paint. Wade insists on his team having meals together, so they still have to eat in there. Vesper joins them, though she never seems to touch her food. Kaela, Rynn, and Jaxon prefer to take their food to their respective tiny sleeping spaces. Elena lost her appetite. She tries to eat with her fellow Vanguards but ends up just moving the gruel around on her plate. It's not due to the décor. She hates to admit it, but she kind of enjoys the pale brown memento. Nightmare is no more. Karma took her sweet time, but justice finally came.

Rourke is no more either. He was one of the two chasing her, one of the two Ingram "turned off." She saw him, double-checked to make sure. Her shot from in front of the *Charon* blew his right cauliflower ear off. He came back after her and Ingram stopped him for good. She flipped him over, looked into his bleeding eyes, checked for pulse, and used all her willpower not to spit on him.

No Talon Voss, no Cole Rourke. But her gut tells her something is off with this Vesper.

Her gut. Her gut is starting to flare up again, and she is out of stims. She took the last one while trying to outrun the drone on Echo Point. The ship's first aid supplies are limited; they don't have what she needs. She checked. Several times. She is restless.

She feels the walls closing in, like in the hives. She tries to pace around but wherever she tries to go she bumps into someone. The remainder of the cargo bay, the part that wasn't converted to living space, becomes a crew favorite. There's a small group there, talking, sitting on the crates scattered around.

"And she charged me for a buy-one-get-one-free," she overhears Novak saying, prompting general laughter.

"Fuck me backwards," says Anders.

"She would!" retorts Novak without missing a beat. The laughter intensifies.

She turns around and walks back out into the ready room/mess. Wade is sitting at the table, embedded. Santos is next to him, cleaning a gun. She walks past them, into the cockpit. The cockpit is not meant for standing. She needs to duck her head as she enters. Rynn is there, sitting at the helm as always, even though there won't be any steering required for two more days.

"How are you feeling?" she asks him.

"I'll live," he says.

Rynn took a couple of hits to his right arm, but he should be able to fully recover. Lucky for them, since the *Skylark* pilots were executed by the psychopath. Allegedly, according to Vesper. Any Vanguard would've been able to lift off and set course for Eureka Base, Jaxon could probably do it too, but she's seen Rynn work. He is an incredible pilot, and his skill might come in handy since they have no idea what they'll find once they get out of warp.

"How are you?" Rynn returns the question.

How is she? She's about to go insane. It's too cramped on this damn ship. And it stinks, life support can barely keep up with eleven of them on a ship made for a crew of two. The stench fills every corner of the ship; there's no escaping it.

She is about to provide a generic answer to Rynn's question when she is suddenly sick. She runs to the ship's only toilet, which is, of course, occupied. She can't hold it long enough to find another option. She turns to face the wall and vomits. *Great,* she has time to think. Her very own contribution to the ship's odor.

"Whoa, you OK?" Santos asks her.

Wade is standing up, grabbing her by the arm and guiding her towards the cargo bay.

"Sorry, I'll clean it up."

"You don't look too good, Drake. You should lie down."

He takes her to her cot. Due to the limited living space, they were forced to double up. Elena shares her small space with Vesper. When Wade walks her inside, Vesper is there, lying on her side, atop her own cot. She turns to watch them.

Wade lays her down. She suddenly becomes dizzy and closes her eye. This makes the dizziness worse, turns it into vertigo. With her eye closed, misfiring neurons tell her she's in some centrifuge. She is getting sick again, opens her eye, and stares at the flexi-wall, trying to establish a focus point. The feeling subsides a little, but she is now falling in slow motion. *Fuck.* She keeps her eye on the same fixed point, concentrates on controlling her breathing. She takes big inhales, slow exhales. It takes some time until the room finally stabilizes. Exhaustion overwhelms her. Her eye slowly closes again, this time as if it had a will of its own. She sleeps.

• • •

The images are fragmented; there's no cohesive story to accompany them. Gunfire, deep underground, in a hive. She is running on a walkway. She is kicking down a door, going in, shotgun-first. The scene morphs. It's not a shotgun; she is holding a pistol. Unfamiliar, no idea if it's for big game or a bug zapper. She is not in the hives, she is in a back alley somewhere, sticking the gun into the mouth of a blond man, cracking his teeth. She shoots. The scene morphs again. She is not shooting, she is the one getting shot. She feels scorching pain on the side of her face, a punch in her gut. She goes down. A boot prods her ribs. A voice says, "Not like that, you idiot, turn her over!" She tightens the grip on the pistol she is concealing as she feels a hand grabbing her shoulder. Someone moves her.

"Wake up."

She gasps awake. Vesper has a hand on her shoulder, is shaking her gently. "You were having a nightmare."

Elena grunts, sits. She is drenched in cold sweat. She doesn't remember what she was dreaming, but it wasn't pleasant. Only a lingering feeling remains—despair. She tries to shake it off. Vesper is standing next to her cot. They look at each other in silence for a few seconds.

"Who are you, really?" she asks the woman.

"Vesper. I told you."

Elena doesn't say anything, doesn't break eye contact. She imagines her eye patch makes her look more intimidating. But Vesper doesn't flinch.

Her first thought, when she got doubled up with the mysterious woman, was *the maimed girls club*. She would never have said it out loud, but the irony was obvious. Elena, with an eye patch and a prosthetic arm; Vesper, with two chopped off fingers, backside burns, and worse. She should feel sorry for the poor woman. Nightmare was abusing her when the cavalry arrived. But her instincts tell her something is off. And she trusts her instincts.

"Vesper Kovatch," the woman continues. "As I said before, I'm a geologist. Working for Abyssal. I fled Nova Prime when the war started, ended up here."

Elena keeps looking at her, keeps silent, waits for the woman to continue.

"Now can I ask you something?" says Vesper.

"Go ahead."

"What are you on?"

The question catches her off guard.

"What do you mean?"

"Your hand is shaking."

Elena checks her hands. The synthetic one is lying still on her knee. The other one is, indeed, trembling.

"Is it that obvious, huh?"

Vesper nods.

"Let me guess: you were stimming and you ran out."

Elena nods slowly, embarrassed.

"Looks like textbook withdrawal symptoms. What I can't tell is whether you were using amphelines or Blitz."

"How …?"

"How do I know? It's common down in the hives."

Elena feels a burst of sudden rage, wants to lash out at the prying woman. She has no business asking these personal questions. She takes a deep breath instead. She is irrational. Vesper is right, she is crashing. Hard.

"Reason I'm asking," Vesper continues, "is you can take a couple of graycaps to manage it if you were on amphelines, rest it out. If you were taking the street stuff, cold turkey is the only safe way to wean off. You'll feel like shit for a few days regardless."

Elena nods, opens up her mouth to answer, and instead vomits violently on her cot, shirt, and pants.

"I'll help you clean up," says Vesper and goes out looking for clean covers.

Maybe she is misjudging the woman. After what she's been through, coming from the Abyssal hives to end up in the hands of Nightmare, maybe geologist Vesper Kovatch needs a break. Maybe she needs help. They took her with them because she was hurt and in shock. She seemed to have recovered fast, but whenever Elena walks into their shared living space, Vesper is staring at a flexi-wall. Not embedded, just staring, eyes glazed over. Whenever she sees her around the ship, she is leaning on a wall, looking around distracted. And she seems to get thinner by the day.

They picked her up, but their mission is dangerous. They can't afford tagalongs. Who knows what they'll find at Eureka Base. And after that, the alien ship. No place for traumatized civilians. But, Elena realizes, she is just rationalizing. The reality is something feels off to her. Something feels off with Vesper, and that's that.

After she changes and they swap out the covers on her cot, Elena admits she was taking amphelines. Poor Doctor Terek Nassar was not a drug dealer, wouldn't have thought of putting her on something as dangerous as Blitz. He prescribed her the stims, warned her about their addictiveness. She didn't heed his warning.

Vesper hands her a couple of graycaps. Elena is still suspicious, but the pills are a common pain killer and mood stabilizer. Vesper having some on her is perfectly normal. And she must admit she needs help.

She double-checks the packaging. Sure enough, they're graycaps. Vesper watches her, doesn't comment. Elena takes two out of the tab, their trademark color unmistakable in her palm. The pills taste bitter, she swallows them fast, chases them with a mugful of water. She hopes she can keep them down.

The graycaps mellow her out. Maybe she is misjudging the woman. She is very tired. Maybe Vesper Kovatch is simply the sector's unluckiest geologist. She lies down. But why would an Abyssal geologist flee to Echo Point rather than Forge? Isn't Forge the go-to destination for all corporate citizens, safe under the protection of the paramilitary? Her eyelid is getting heavy; she closes her eye. No vertigo this time, the graycaps are working their subtle magic. And how did she get her hands on a shotgun? It is a military ship, but they're not just lying around the place, are they? She falls asleep.

44: ALL IN

I *hate fieldwork*, Vesper considers. Too many variables, too few resources. Too many things that can go wrong. She hates improvising. She likes to have information, a Plan B, a Plan C.

For example, she might have jumped the gun killing the two pilots. It was Nightmare's (just thinking about him makes a chill run down her spine) word against hers. And he was a fucking animal. She could've talked her way out of it. No digital on Echo Point, they had no way to tell. She can be convincing. She shouldn't have killed everyone.

She can still save it though. Her geologist identity is a burner. Though nobody seems suspicious enough to even ask, nobody except Elena. They all treat her as a victim (she is!). *Focus*, she tells herself. *No need to dwell on what happened*. They're careless, they talk, she only needs to fade in the background and listen. That's how she learned about the jump gate being closed. That's how she learned about the way out of the sector—the alien ship. God, she thinks, Arcturus would love to know where that ship is. Would kill to know. Has killed. But Ingram did a good job of hiding the thing. Easy to do in the many cubic parsecs of nebula that make up Sector 36.

The ship is small and nobody minds the geologist they picked up (they *rescued*, not *picked up*, rescued from …). She overheard enough to get up to speed, asked a couple of innocent questions to make sure. She has the lay of the land: Sector 36 is closed, the Omegas are warring, but there is a way out. Turns out the derelict alien ship can jump without a gate. That's what the Vanguards learned on Echo Point. They're going to Eureka Base to retrieve an interface that would allow someone to control the ship. And that someone has to be Elena. It has to be someone with NSRS, someone who has survival skills, someone handpicked by Ingram.

She is done with this godforsaken place and will take anything that would get her out of here.

Which brings her back to Elena. Her nemesis. She helped her out. She helped her out, even though Elena is suspicious of her. It would've been easy, so easy to slip her a Velotril with the graycaps. The state she was in, her heart would've simply stopped. Vesper could've been on the other side of the ship, acted as shocked as everyone when they found her. "Shocked" is maybe not the right word. Elena has been jonesing for a fix since they took off. Irascible, pacing around the confined *Skylark* like a caged animal. She is sure she wasn't the only one to notice.

So easy, yet she is nursing her back to health. Vesper needs Elena. All in now, there is no turning back. She needs to buy enough good will to exit the sector, keep playing the victim if needed (not playing, she is a victim!).

Vesper will ensure her ticket out of here is clean and sober. When the time comes, she'll make damn sure to be on that outbound ship. Sounds like Ingram wants them to carry some information out of the sector, set up a next move. Vesper would like a sneak peek at that. After all, she thrives on information. But even without it, she has enough puzzle pieces already to form a pretty clear picture. She knows a lot more than they seem to, and she can sell what she knows outside of the sector. Now that she is unemployed, it's time to plan for retirement.

She takes a graycap herself. Her backside still hurts bad enough that she is relegated to sleeping on her side. She still can't sit. Her two missing fingers itch. She is tired.

This will be her last op. Get out of Sector 36. Tell someone with deep pockets about the NS-36-A artifact. Tell them about what happened on Echo Point.

Their three-day FTL trip is unglamorous. Vesper watches Elena twist and turn in her sleep, listens to her mumble, makes sure she doesn't choke when she wakes up to puke, cleans up after her.

By the time they make it to Eureka Base, Elena can keep food down. Good. The past few days have been rough. She lets her sleep as they arrive, goes out to the ready room just as they are about to get out of warp.

Lieutenant Marcus Wade called for a huddle-up, which only applies to his team, but she has nothing better to do and is curious to see the base herself.

"How is she?" Wade asks her as soon as she steps inside the small room. The Vanguards, she notices, are all there, sitting around the table.

"Sleeping. She's been better today. It takes time for the stims to flush out of her system, but she's getting there."

"She was really hooked on them, huh?" says Kaela Tama. "I ... I noticed. I didn't say anything." Vesper learned a lot about Kaela during the trip—the young woman can't stop talking.

"None of us did," says Jaxon Barabe. "We should've." He exits the ready room, goes to watch Elena. They never discussed it, but whenever Vesper steps out, Jaxon takes her place. He doesn't want to leave Elena alone. She wonders if there's something more between the two of them.

Kaela came to see her too, several times. So did Marcus Wade. But Rynn, the pilot, hasn't. Vesper observes, takes mental notes, tries to understand the dynamics.

The *Skylark* decelerates back into causal spacetime and suddenly everyone is very animated. Several of the Vanguards ask variations of, "What the fuck happened here?"

She keeps out of their way, assesses the situation herself through a porthole and through the ship's opticals. She can see the orbit around

Eureka Base chock-full of ships. No, of shipwrecks. There's almost no digital around the small moon, just silence. Almost as quiet as Echo Point. None of the usual information-dense flows around a settlement, none of the encrypted military chatter one would expect. The only active automatons are single-purpose devices, weather radars, beacons, comms relays, none of them intelligent enough to shed light on what happened.

They arrived at what must've been a major battle in the war between the Omegas.

She immediately spots the *Umbra*, the largest destroyer Arcturus deployed from Forge, its massive hull split across the middle. She almost gasps at this. The crown jewel of the paramilitary fleet. She recognizes it by its characteristic particle beam cannons, largest battery in the sector. The cannons are now broken, floating next to the wreckage.

Military heavy cruisers are similarly adrift. It seems nobody won the battle. How could this be?

She listens in as the Vanguards and the pilot plan the next step. Rynn is still at the helm, communicates with them in the digital rather than in person. He almost never leaves his post, especially now, as it seems they arrived in the middle of a battlefield.

{We're not equipped for a fight,} he reminds them. Then adds, {At least we have good stealth.}

{Not sure if there's any fight left here. Though it looks like we missed the battle of the century,} says Wade.

{I'm keeping the FTL drive hot, we get out of here at the first sign of trouble.}

{Aye.}

Vesper wonders, like all of them, what really happened. The remains of the battle stretch from the small moon on which Eureka Base was built towards the edge of the solar system. Hundreds of ships. All inert. Some are paramilitary, probably left Forge at the same time the *Nemesis* did. Even without overlays, she can identify them by their black paint. They look like tears in the viridian veils of the nebula. They're mixed among the gray remains of military ships.

No escape pods, she notices. No SOS signals. Just debris. Broken war machines.

It takes the crew a while to convince themselves there is no immediate threat, to agree on descending to the moon's surface. Whatever happened here, it's over now. They still have their mission. They need to retrieve the interface and the digicard.

Rynn takes the *Skylark* down to Eureka Base's modest landing pad.

Vesper hugs a wall, takes another look around: Rynn, as always, at the helm in the cockpit; the Vanguards sitting around the table; Kaela embedded, looking for any blips in the digital; Jaxon is with Elena. Now would be a good time to retrieve her weapon. She moves silently into the cargo area, finds the locker where they stashed the Graver. She left the gun on Nightmare's body. They took it, put it away. Unlocked. Why would they lock it? They're on a ship full of weapons. She picks it up, hides it in her waistband.

She doubts she'll have to use it, she won't go against a Vanguard team with a pistol, but it gives her comfort (especially after what happened!). She strolls back to the ready room. Nobody minds her. Good.

She watches as the *Skylark* descends. She's never been to Eureka Base. She read plenty of intel on it, though. In her previous job, this was the main target Abyssal Mining was interested in. The research contained within its walls. The base seems smaller now that she is here in person. The aboveground part of the compound at least. She knows the main structure stretches underground. Like a miniature hive.

She wonders if what they're looking for is still here. The building seems abandoned, mired in darkness, with only tiny blinking red lights calling attention to various malfunctions. There is no movement. Whatever happened out in space must've extended down to the lab too.

She sees several large spheres next to it, like gigantic boils on the moon's surface. She knows, from the reports, that those are graviton detectors. The scientists used them to study the neutron star and its anomalies. She also notices a large dodecahedron. This one wasn't present in any of the vids she saw. It was installed later, she reasons, after Ingram tightened its grip on the lab. Once it became harder to take vids of the base from pretend transit ships decked out with sensor arrays and high precision opticals. Before military ships surrounded the moon and started redirecting traffic.

But she has a good sense of its purpose. The intel she used to get back on Forge was solid. Her division used to get their hands on intel one way or the other: leaks from insiders, wiretaps, interrogation. She knows the device was created to send a signal to the neutron star—not really a neutron star, rather an alien device. An alien device that can kill Omegas. An alien device for which Arcturus gathered an incredible amount of firepower in the sector.

It didn't do much good, it seems. She takes another look at the remains of the *Umbra*. No decisive winner of the arms race.

I truly hope the interface is still here. Between Ingram closing the jump gate and her employer turning genocidal, her only way out is tagging along. Elena is getting better. Thanks to her. They wouldn't just abandon her after this, would they?

The *Skylark* lands on the base's tiny landing pad. By the time they reach the surface, the Vanguards are all wearing combat gear and carrying their weapons. She watches them from the other side of the ready room. She would offer a hand, but what can a geologist help them with?

"No external signs of kinetic damage," comments Santos.

"You think life support is still up? Do we need EV suits?" asks Howard.

"You shouldn't," replies Kaela. She's been negotiating with the few systems still online, trying to suss out as much as she can from their limited knowledge. "As far as I can tell," she adds. "Not sure how much I can trust the environment control subsystem I've been talking to, but it doesn't look like it was hacked."

"One way to find out," says Howard and winks at Kaela. She hurriedly looks away.

The ship connects to one of the two bridges attached to the landing pads. The Vanguards line up in front of the airlock.

"Here we go," says Wade.

The airlock slides open and the Vanguards step through.

45: INFILTRATION

"Here we go," says Marcus.

The airlock slides open and the team files onto the small bridge, in their usual formation: Marcus first, followed by Howard, then Novak and Santos, Anders and Kim last. No idea what the situation on the ground is, so they're going in tacticals hot.

With the ceiling lights off, fluorescent strips are the only thing illuminating their way from the airlock to the compound's entrance in muted amber colors. The sliding doors, Marcus sees, are not fully closed. They're stuck on something. A boot. He hand-signals to his team.

Night vision opticals make his gestures unmistakable despite the gloom. *Unknown down, caution.* The contours get clearer as they step closer. There's a man lying face down on the other side, his left boot caught in the door. Not moving. Marcus switches optical modes. No heat signature.

{No IR blip,} he sends. They all get the meaning. The corpse has been there for at least a few hours. Marcus sticks his gun through the cracked door and swings it around the room beyond, IR scanning for threats. Nothing. He switches modes again, goes back to night vision, sees the large stain underneath the corpse, an otherworldly green through the night vision filter.

He nudges the door open, steps through, turns left.

"Clear," he calls, aloud this time.

"Clear," he hears Howard from behind him.

He goes back to the corpse for a closer look. Body armor atop a military uniform. Chest plate punched inward by some powerful kinetic. Weapon still in hand, standard-issue rifle.

"One of ours," says Anders.

"Aye. Base security." Eureka Base was protected by the military. Which means the battle wasn't fully carried out in space, the enemy put boots on the ground. Might still be here.

"Stay frosty," says Marcus and starts moving again.

The lights turn suddenly on. Overwhelmed opticals compensate for the sudden change, adjust the brightness from eye-searing white to a more manageable palette before Marcus turns them off altogether. The dried liquid underneath the corpse flicks from emerald to its real carmine shade.

"What the ...?" he manages to say before they all hear Kaela in the digital:

{Are the lights on? Did I get them?}

{Yes, you did. Maybe give us a heads-up next time?} says Howard.

{Sorry. I got inside the main system. Convinced a power relay that I'm allowed to re-route the backup generator.}

Marcus is impressed by the young digital specialist's prowess. He says so to his team.

"The kid is good!"

"Right?" agrees Kim. "Better than most geeks we have to work with."

{So here's the deal: I got the main elevator back online. It can get you underground. Sending you a nav route.}

{No need,} replies Marcus, {we have the route.} Ingram shared it with them on Echo Point. Down to level fifteen. Where the interface and digicard are.

"What do you think happened here, LT?" Howard asks him.

Besides the dead soldier in the doorway, the equipment in the room looks all dinged up. Looks like someone fired both kinetic and energy weapons in all directions. Marcus shrugs.

"Let's keep moving," he says, and they follow the nav route to the opposite door, leading them outside the room.

They step through this second door following the usual procedure: Marcus clearing the left side, Howard clearing the right. Before either of them calls, "Clear," Marcus notices the wide blood streak starting right after the door, continuing for about ten yards across the long hallway they just entered, then turning a sharp right and disappearing underneath another door. The blood is dried up.

They advance slowly through the hallway. Marcus walks past a cluster of high-caliber bullets lodged in the side wall. Apart from the battle scars, the place looks sterile. Unadorned white walls, tiled floor, bright lights. It reminds Marcus of a military hospital. A military hospital in which something went terribly wrong.

"Should we check the room?" Santos asks as they get close to the end of the blood trail.

"Negative," he decides. It's obvious some intense fighting took place here, but it doesn't seem like anyone is still around, and they have a clear objective.

According to nav, the hallway is long, about five hundred feet straight, then it takes a ninety-degree left turn, goes on for another five hundred feet, ending at the elevator. Many closed doors on both sides.

They keep advancing, in formation. Careful. It's quiet, the only sound Marcus hears is the echo of their steps reverberating on the empty hallway. The bright lights reveal other clues of the prior fight: a door is bent inwards, as if hit by something extremely heavy; on the opposite side, blood smears trace a zigzagged line from one closed door to the next. He steps over shell casings; scorch marks on the floor indicate energy weapon fire.

They push forward, it would take too long to clear all the rooms. Whatever happened here happened a while ago.

"Can you smell that?" asks Novak.

Marcus can. It's faint, but pungent. He can't put a name on it. The scent is metallic, and it's not the dry blood.

"Yeah," Santos answers, wrinkling her crooked nose. It's subtle, but it's there.

He notices, incredibly, a trail of blood on the ceiling. *What the fuck* did *happen here?* He points up so his team can see it too. Howard nods, raises his eyebrows. They continue.

"Are these living quarters?" asks Novak.

"Negative. Separate wing, connected to this one at sublevels six and twelve."

It's a long, tense five hundred feet until they make the corner.

Marcus peers over, calls, "Clear."

Nothing moving around the bend either. He does see a dismembered body though, spread across the first hundred feet they need to cross: a booted leg; a bit farther out a lower torso and the other leg; then a string of intestines stretching to an upper torso and right arm; copious amounts of blood leading to the left arm; then, way farther down the hallway, a caved-in head.

"What the fuck?" says Novak.

Anders whistles softly. "Fuck me backwards."

They move past the remains, past the crushed head. Getting closer to the elevator now.

"After seeing this, I don't feel like we should get trapped inside an elevator," says Kim.

"Is there an alternate route? Don't they have stairs?" asks Howard.

"That's the route Ingram gave us, but let's confirm." They have a good point. If tangos are still around, being inside an elevator is not the best idea. Unfortunately, Marcus doesn't have a complete map of the compound.

{Kaela,} he sends, {can you work your magic and find us a way down that doesn't involve an elevator?}

{I'll try,} she says.

A long pause. They stand, still in formation, waiting. Marcus is about to send her another message when she finally comes back: {No easy way, there are stairs that go down five levels on the right door next to the elevator. Then you have to go to the opposite side of the hallway, take the stairs to sublevel ten, then back next to the elevator, four more levels down. No stairs to level fifteen.}

Fuck, Marcus thinks. They didn't put a lot of thought into fire safety. That said, evacuating to a surface with temperatures that would freeze methane is not a great fire escape strategy either.

"We'll be in the elevator regardless," he tells his team. "Question is, do we run all around the base to get to level fourteen, or take the shortcut?"

They quickly exchange looks. There's a risk, but the payoff is getting out of here fast instead of running around the whole complex. Anders nods.

If their combat engineer is onboard, then it's already decided. Santos and Novak nod quickly too. Kim, the team sniper, is the most reluctant, but he doesn't say "no" either.

Marcus looks at Howard. Howard says, "Fuck it."

They step inside the elevator.

The elevator starts its descent. Sublevel one. It moves slow, slower than an elevator should. Marcus wants to clench his fists; instead, he squeezes his rifle. Sublevel two. They all watch the display. Sublevel three. If it's a trap, they're in a bad spot, Marcus thinks. Sublevel four. They can still fight their way out if needed. They're Vanguard. Sublevel five. He hasn't felt like this since exploring the Tauran ship. Sublevel six. He looks at Howard. Howard is staring intently at the elevator display. Sublevel seven. He looks at Santos. She is pointing her rifle towards the door, unblinking. Sublevel eight. He looks back at Kim. Kim is pointing his sniper rifle down, looks back at him with an unreadable expression. Sublevel nine. *Come on already,* he urges the mechanism. Sublevel ten. He looks back at Anders, who is, surprisingly, smiling. Sublevel eleven. He checks on Novak. Novak keeps looking from the closed elevator door to the display counting down the floors and back. Sublevel twelve. Marcus swears this is the longest elevator ride of his life. Sublevel thirteen.

"Get ready," he tells them.

Sublevel fourteen. They take positions inside the small space, making sure they all have a clear line of fire. Sublevel fifteen. *Here we go.* The door opens.

At first sight, there is no sign of a fight down on level fifteen. Unlike above, there is no blood, no damage, no dead bodies. They step carefully outside the elevator.

"Clear!" calls Marcus, covering the left.

"Clear!" he hears from Howard.

He allows himself a deep exhale.

"That elevator ride was something," comments Anders from behind.

"Fuck me backwards," Kim retorts with Anders's own catchphrase.

It's funny, but nobody laughs. They're on the field, can't afford more than the odd one-liner. Laughs are for later.

"Move out," commands Marcus.

Their target is close, five doors down, on the left. He is glad Kaela was able to turn on the lights for them. Would've sucked much worse to do the whole op in the dark, looking at green blood and guts through night vision.

Sublevel fifteen seems to have been spared whatever happened above. But no survivors either, as far as Marcus can tell. The smell is gone too, he realizes. He wants to comment on it but now they're in front of the door to their destination.

He hand-signals—three, two, one—and opens the door, clears the left corner. Howard on the right. Another empty room. An empty room with multiple displays on every wall, each display blinking its indecipherable graphs and rows of numbers. There's a large table in the middle of the room. Atop the table, a glass box contains what looks like a strange helmet. Marcus guesses that's the interface. That's what Elena Drake needs to put on once they reach the derelict. A device that will allow her to control the alien ship. *They tamed it,* Marcus thinks, *came a long way in a few short months.* Next to the glass box, on a tray, is a digicard. The other item they must retrieve. He takes a step forward. Ingram reaches out to him.

"Lieutenant Marcus Wade!"

Ingram materializes in the digital, as a featureless face overlaid on top of the Viridian Shroud Nebula. It's unexpected—Omegas don't usually reach out. But, Marcus imagines, extreme circumstances call for breaking protocol. Ingram reached out on Echo Point too, with their new mission and operational details. There's a lot at stake here. Way above his pay grade. So he doesn't mind getting some guidance straight from up top.

"Where is Captain Drake?" it asks.

"Onboard the *Skylark*. She's been ... sick."

"I must talk to her."

Marcus realizes that whatever happened upstairs must've disabled a large part of Ingram's capabilities on Eureka Base. It couldn't reach out to them until they got to sublevel fifteen. As if reading his thoughts, Ingram continues:

"Eureka Base has been hit. I don't have any details. I got cut off from the rest of the base. Anything above sublevel fifteen is invisible to me. You'll have to patch me through."

{Kaela,} Marcus sends, {can you help me out?}

"I also need to talk to you, Lieutenant," Ingram says. It can do it in parallel, while also carrying a conversation with Drake.

"... and to your team," it adds.

Marcus nods. They all listen.

46: SECRETS

Doctor Linton thought he had a good, if somewhat dull, career at the Orion Institute of Technology. He taught a handful of physics classes but his passion had always been research. The university had a well-funded lab, sponsored by some major corporations like OmniCore Solutions and Zenith Dynamics. VoidTech was another name on that list, but Doctor Linton adamantly refused to participate in any defense-related research, always adding air quotes around "defense." He had always been principled. More recently, he became an activist and got involved with Spark—after his divorce, he looked for different ways to keep busy. His work on campus was OK, he couldn't really complain, but he wasn't producing any major breakthroughs. Then, a unique opportunity caught his attention: Eureka Base in Sector 36. A neutron star around which gravitational anomalies were observed. Leading scientists from around the galaxy gathering there to make observations and run experiments. The lab was looking for more physicists to join.

He learned more about the job. The lab wasn't corporate sponsored, this one was funded by the AI Council. Working for the AI Council was ideologically at odds with his recent Spark activism, but the Sector 36 mysteries were alluring. Very alluring. It couldn't be worse than working for VoidTech or their ilk, but it felt wrong nevertheless. Omni-Core Solutions, Zenith Dynamics, hell, any corporation of that size had an Omega overseeing operations, so even then he was indirectly working for an AI. Pretty much any job ended up laddering up to an Omega. He was still torn on what to do, so he brought it up with one of his fellow researchers and Spark member.

"If that's your dream," his friend said, "go for it! Plus, if you notice anything at all that isn't on the up-and-up over there, you can bring it to Spark. It would help the cause. And if not, there's nothing to worry about."

Put that way, it was a no-brainer. Doctor Linton applied.

After a somewhat lengthy interview process, he received an offer to relocate to Eureka Base.

He did his due diligence before accepting, saw the vids, did the virtual tour, but it still hit him hard as his transport was landing: the place was benighted. NS-36-A barely cast any light. The moon the base was built on was barren. A lump of featureless gray rock. Not that he would spend much time admiring the view, the lab was built almost entirely underground. Topside consisted of only a couple of levels of administrative offices between the large spheres of the graviton detectors. Everything else was below surface, artificial lights oscillating to stimulate circadian rhythms.

Doctor Linton dived into his work. NS-36-A posed, indeed, a most intriguing puzzle. Observable gravitational anomalies, quantum field perturbations, a myriad of measurements that contradicted predictions.

During his first time off, he visited Nova Prime City. He took a transport from Eureka Base to Nova Prime and spent time enjoying the capital. He also met with someone else, another Spark member, Ansel Marlow, who was high up the ladder working a corporate job. A common acquaintance suggested they connect. Doctor Linton had a great conversation with Marlow, both of them sipping coffee on a terrace somewhere high above the city. They had very different backgrounds but discovered a common passion for twenty-second-century history and the ancient sport of tennis. Linton had stopped playing years ago, after injuring his shoulder. After the isolation of the lab, he was happy to meet someone who shared his interests.

"So how is Eureka Base?"

"The base itself? Terrible," Linton answered without hesitation. Relocating to an underground compound from the green campus of the Orion Institute of Technology was literally a night and day difference. "But the research is extremely interesting! That neutron star defies everything we know."

"How is working for Ingram?"

The doctor took a moment to answer that. "I ... don't know." He was about to leave it at that, but after all, he was talking to a fellow Spark member. "I only had a couple of conversations with it and ... they were strange."

"In what way?"

"It was very cryptic. Like it was toying with me, testing me. Quite disturbing."

"Some Omegas like to do that," Marlow reassured him.

Then the conversation moved on: space exploration, Sector 36 expansion. A new space station was about to open, Horizon.

Doctor Linton left the meeting impressed by his new acquaintance and glad to have maybe found a new friend so far away from what he considered home. He left Nova Prime City and returned to the lab.

During his next trip to Nova Prime City, his next meeting with Marlow, the doctor was visibly stressed.

"What's wrong?" his new friend asked him.

"Something shady is going on at the lab. There's a sublevel fifteen with restricted access. Some of the scientists go there, then never talk about it."

"Maybe it's some special project? Defense related?"

"That's not how a lab should operate," said Linton. "Either everyone is under NDA, or nobody is. Who in their right mind would compartmentalize research like this? Which brings me to the second point." The doctor lowered his voice and leaned in. "I have a hypothesis the quantum field fluctuations are interfering with Ingram's compute."

"An insane Omega?" mused Marlow.

The doctor nodded.

"Don't get ahead of yourself, doctor. Omegas tend to be scary and inscrutable. Doubt it means anything."

"You're probably right," Linton agreed halfheartedly. "Either way, I'll try snooping around, find out what's happening on level fifteen."

Marlow became very serious. "Be careful, doctor. If you do discover anything—anything dangerous, you might get in trouble."

Doctor Linton was well aware of that.

"Assume communications are monitored inside the lab. Let's come up with some code words, some way of you letting Spark know if you need help. Something that nobody else but the two of us would know."

They brainstormed these for a while, in a corner of the terrace, away from any prying ears or eyes.

"Don't get in trouble, doctor, OK?"

"I don't mean to, but I need to know what's really going on."

"If you're afraid you somehow tipped off Ingram, I can get you out of the sector safely. I have a contact on Verdant. You can go there and lay low. We'll have someone pick you up. I can arrange outbound travel through Obsidian Holdings. Hopefully it won't get to this, but just in case."

"Just in case," the doctor agreed.

Doctor Linton started looking for unlocked consoles, looking for documents left out in the open. During the same time, a new device was being built outside the compound. Next to the array of graviton detectors, a dodecahedron-shaped tower was taking form. No memo on what that was about. He was convinced it was something coming out of sublevel fifteen. The doctor's peers were speculating, starting to get worried.

The structure was in place in under a week. It turned out to be a powerful multi-spectral laser. The befuddled scientists, Linton among them, witnessed it rotate, open one of its many pentagonal faces, and shoot a combination gamma/X-ray beam at the neutron star. It took exactly five minutes and thirty-two seconds for the high-energy beam to reach the star. It took another five minutes and thirty-two seconds for its effect to make it back to Eureka Base: the star blinked.

This spurred many conversations around the experiment and its results. The lab was large enough that the sublevel fifteen scientists, the ones in the know, were not easy to find and confront. Theories abounded. Doctor Linton got increasingly suspicious. He also got a lead—a careless physicist left a handful of documents on a publicly accessible endpoint. The documents were difficult to understand without the broader context, but they started painting a picture: analysis of periodicity of NS-36-A field emissions pointing to a clearly artificial pattern; cryptanalysis of said pattern; confirmation that the dodecahedron installation was a signal emitter; proposal for a payload to be sent in an attempt to make the neutron star react, mostly based on said cryptanalysis.

Jackpot! thought the doctor. He realized the implications: signs of intelligence, signs of very advanced intelligence. OmniCore Solutions didn't know how to build signal-emitting stars. Nobody did. What they were witnessing was a first contact event.

Then, unbelievably, he got distracted. News of an alien incursion started coming in. Strange ships were arriving at the outskirts of the sector, seemingly heading towards Eureka Base through a series of short FTL advancements. Bizarre FTL advancements. Superluminal travel meant no way of intercepting the ships if they decided to warp into the NS-36-A System, but instead the alien ships chose a strange flight pattern, alternating warp with flight at slower speeds. Military vessels started gathering around the base to provide protection. Other ships went ahead to meet the aliens on their ingress vector. An inspired media reporter called them "Taurans." Something to do with a constellation as seen from Earth and the reporter's own vantage point. The name stuck.

The sublevel fifteen experiment was briefly forgotten as Doctor Linton watched the nonstop news coverage. The Taurans were not friendly. Fortunately, they were not technologically more advanced than the military's capabilities. *Thank God for VoidTech,* Doctor Linton thought, uncharacteristically.

Everyone at Eureka Base was holding their breath, waiting for the moment Tauran ships come out of warp on top of them. It didn't get to that, save for a handful of scouts that got instantly obliterated. The battle continued farther out, in the empty void.

Then Echo Point happened: the ships defending it destroyed, the city wiped out with an unknown weapon. Would Eureka Base be next? The whole contingent of scientists held their breath.

Turned out it was the opposite—the Taurans retreated. Ingram proclaimed a truce was reached. Eureka Base was safe. For now. As far as anyone could tell, the Taurans left Sector 36.

Doctor Linton was glad. As soon as the immediate danger passed, he went back to snooping, picked the thread back up. What was the connection between NS-36-A blinking and the Taurans arriving? The events occurred too close together to be a coincidence. They also occurred too close together to be related, the doctor considered, unless the "blink" also manifested through some quantum entangled receptors on the Tauran side. Or some other Einstein-Rosen bridge mechanism. Light just didn't travel that fast, the blink would take years to make its way to observers outside the sector.

The Taurans didn't seem to be technologically more advanced than the force deployed against them. How could they have put in place a mechanism to instantly alert them of whatever the star did, if they didn't seem to have the technology to forge stars? The doctor had many questions and nobody to talk to at the lab. The researchers were a gossipy bunch. Sharing his ideas, he thought, would get him in trouble. Better to wait for his next excursion to Nova Prime City and tell Marlow what he learned.

What he wasn't expecting was for the tension not to release even after the Taurans were confirmed gone from the sector. The military presence remained. Troops were moved from aboard the ships to the hallways of the lab. Access control became even stricter. Soon after, scientists working on sublevel fourteen were asked to clear the level.

Sublevel fourteen became access restricted, just like sublevel fifteen. Researchers from different levels were relocated such that they no longer got to interact at all. Security personnel ensured the rules were followed.

Doctor Linton put in a request for time off, planning his trip to the capital. The request was denied. Some of his peer scientists went a step further, put in their two-week notice. Their resignation was also denied. They were no longer free to leave.

He realized how wise Marlow was. Their last conversation, his "just in case" escape plan. Thanks to his friend, he had a place to lie low: on Verdant. His friend had connections that would pick him up from there, get him out of the sector. The only missing detail, a question they didn't think of during their last meetup, was how was he supposed to get to Verdant? Travel was no longer allowed.

The doctor picked up a project that would get him to the above-ground part of the lab on a regular basis. He started staking out the landing pad. Eureka Base had a handful of skimmers, allegedly to be used in research, but as far as he knew, no experiment had required them so far. Mostly scientists used them when they needed a change of scenery, an escape from the lab's subterranean confinement. He put in a request to take one of the skimmers for a spin, just to test the waters. He was surprised when it did not get denied.

He now had a way out. Risky, he would become a fugitive, especially with what he knew, but a way out nevertheless. The question became *when*. How much information should he collect before disappearing? With the increased stress, the scientists became sloppy. Even with the soldiers watching the hallways and, Doctor Linton was sure, digital specialists watching the digital, he learned that if he was patient, new information would come his way.

He was careful. He learned about a huge alien ship, nicknamed "mothership," official designation Derelict A1X-VD2, captured in some classified spot near Eureka Base. He learned about the Progenitor theory—an ancient alien race that built NS-36-A eons ago. He learned about the Tauran Consensus, a hypothetical mind melding the alien enemies relied on. How much longer could he keep snooping before being found out? The scales kept tipping ever more slightly towards

Verdant. Curious by nature, he kept wanting to hang around for just a little bit longer, to learn just a little bit more. Then, he somehow managed to access the overview of a transcript of a meeting in a series meant to cover reports on a classified project. In short, Doctor Linton learned about Echo Point. His first thought was, *Oh my God!* His second—that he needed to flee.

47: FRAGMENTATION

Elena wakes up fuzzy and disoriented. It takes her a few seconds, but she gets her bearings. She is on a cot on the *Skylark*. Recovering. She feels better now. Better than she felt since they got on this ship. How long ago was that? She turns around to see Jaxon watching over her.

"Hi," he says, with his usual smile.

"Hi," she croaks back. She needs water.

"Here," Jaxon says, handing her a cup.

She sits up, drinks. Her stomach seems to be unbothered by this, which is a welcome change.

"Thank you!" she says once the cup is empty.

"How you feeling?"

"OK," she says. "Ish." The truth is she is sluggish, she has cramps, and her teeth hurt. But she doesn't feel like throwing up. She feels a lot more like herself. She feels curious. "Did we make it to Eureka Base yet?"

"Yes," Jaxon tells her, "Wade and his team are inside right now, looking for the interface and digicard."

Lieutenant Marcus Wade and his team. Let down by their senior officer, Captain Elena Drake, the junkie.

"I fucked up," she tells Jaxon.

"You were popping stims to keep going. You saved our lives on Echo Point, Elena." Jaxon is suddenly serious now, his trademark smile all but gone.

"Could've gotten you all killed."

"But you didn't. Plus, we could've said something, any one of us could've. But we didn't."

She has nothing to say to that.

"We fucked up just as much as you."

"No, you didn't." Then: "I'm sorry."

They look at each other. Jaxon sits down next to her, on the cot, puts an arm around her. The simple gesture stirs a whirlwind of feelings inside her. Loss, regret, Darius, who Jaxon looks so much like. She wants to cry. Comfort, touch, something she didn't realize she missed for so long. She wants to lean her head on his shoulder. Caution, worry, she is vulnerable, yet she can't be vulnerable. She wants to push him away. She doesn't get a chance to do any of these. Kaela walks in on them, in a rush, seemingly not even noticing their moment of closeness.

"Elena, I'm so glad you're awake!" She is talking fast, agitated. "This is important. Ingram wants to talk to you."

"Ingram?"

"Yes. You need to get online, I can patch you through."

"Patch me through?"

This doesn't make sense. Ingram should be all around Eureka Base, the omnipresent fabric of the infosphere, since this is one of its compute clusters. Then she remembers it telling her back on Echo Point that it lost contact with Eureka Base.

"Yes. It's like Echo Point all over again here. No infosphere. Ingram is isolated deep underground."

She doesn't feel like talking to it, not now. But she has to. It's her new mission. An official mission, she's been reinstated. To get out of Sector 36. To get Jaxon and Kaela and Rynn out of Sector 36. She gets online.

. . .

Ingram materializes before her with its distinctive avatar.

"Hello, Captain," it says.

Creepy as usual, she thinks. No matter if they're working together, it never ceases to unnerve her. This time around, it doesn't give her time to return the greeting, immediately follows up with a question:

"How are you feeling now?"

How could it possibly know? She got sick while they were traveling, there's no infosphere around Eureka Base. How could it know she wasn't well?

It answers her unspoken question: "Wade told me."

So, it is not omniscient after all. Just likes to act like it is.

"I'm ... better. Stim withdrawal."

She hopes to be back at one hundred percent by the time they reach the derelict. If it's a matter of a few more days at FTL, she feels like she can fully recover. She wants to ask Ingram how far their destination is, but it surprises her with a question of its own instead.

"Have we talked at Echo Point?"

Does it not know? It doesn't, Elena realizes. Its clusters have been decohered. She is talking to a different shard. Another fragment of the broken god.

"We did," she says, realizing that, for once, she might have the upper hand.

"Since you're here, I assume I told you about the interface, the derelict, the digicard you need to move out of the sector."

With pleasantries out of the way, it goes straight to business. Elena wants to learn more. Her physical discomfort is momentarily forgotten, curiosity getting the better of her. She wants to probe it.

"What's on the digicard?"

"Details about NS-36-A. Research notes."

"What details?"

"Did I not tell you on Echo Point? The neutron star is not really a star, rather an alien artifact. Dangerous. Reality-bending."

"Reality-bending?"

"Yes. Gravity field manipulation. Tweak the geometry of spacetime. Immense implications. And worrisome military applications. We haven't cracked its secrets yet, but we grasped enough to know it can't fall into the wrong hands."

Elena tries to recall what it told her on Echo Point about this but draws a blank. She's still fuzzy, it will come to her. She doesn't care that much about the science anyway.

What about the people?

"Is the jump gate still closed? What will happen to the sector's inhabitants?"

"The gate was destroyed."

Elena's jaw drops at this.

"What?"

"Arcturus attacked Nova Prime and the ring."

She witnessed the attack on Nova Prime City, how the beautiful garden city got reduced to rubble. She learned from Wade that the ring was obliterated. And they all saw the aftermath of whatever went down right here, around Eureka Base. But the gate?

"The military won the battle at Nova Prime; the capital is secure."

Whatever is left of it.

"The Gateway Ring battle was lost. I couldn't let the jump gate fall into Arcturus's hands."

Trapped. Everyone is trapped in the sector now. No way out.

"Arcturus was ready to translate in more forces. Elena, the military can't compete with the large coffers of the corporate. And they sensed chum in the water."

All of this for what? A research project? For its implications? She suspects Ingram knows more than it is telling her. The stakes seem higher.

"What happened here, at Eureka Base?"

"Unknown. Arcturus attacked. I had to split the fleet protecting the base to defend Nova Prime City and the ring. The remaining forces did their best. During the battle, the compound was hit. The attack knocked the infosphere offline. I lost touch with the outside world, anything above sublevel fifteen."

Poor you, she thinks. Then realizes what it just said—*above* sublevel fifteen. Wade and his team are down there.

"Is the base safe? Is Wade safe?" she asks.

"Wade and team made it here safely. As I said, I don't know what the status is throughout the compound."

It pleads ignorance. Fine. Back to all the people.

"So, what is the best-case scenario for the people in the sector?"

"The best-case scenario is you use the alien ship to translate out of the sector. Hand it over to the AI Council. Let them have the digicard. Share a copy with Spark if you want." Rubbing it in again—the fact that it knows all about her Spark association, her undercover mission. It just doesn't care. "They can translate reinforcements back. I expect reverse-engineering won't take long. The digicard has all research we did on it here, and we were close. The AI Council can bring reinforcements in a matter of months, if not weeks. Secure the sector. Then we build a new jump gate, rebuild the colonies. Whoever wants to leave will be able to do so."

"And until then?"

"Until then, people survive. People are resilient, Elena, you should know," and, after a brief pause, "You are all God's children."

Massive, unimaginable numbers of casualties on the ring. She saw Nova Prime City crumble herself. She saw what became of Horizon Station. And the solution is for people to just ... survive? For months? With no infrastructure, in a war zone?

"Elena, Wade has the interface. Translate out, help the people."

Pleading with her.

"And be careful interfacing with the ship. You might encounter the Tauran Consensus."

Tauran Consensus?

"The Taurans use what you would call a form of telepathy. They embed at a very deep level. It will feel overwhelming."

Lucky her, she has NSRS.

"If you encounter the Tauran Consensus, it will lie to you."

That's new, and it brings a shiver down her spine. It implies she might *talk* to them. Probably the first human to do so. Ingram did it during the peace negotiations, but Ingram is an Omega. She will talk to them if they make it to the derelict, that is.

"You will get an escort to Derelict A1X-VD2. Before my cluster here decohered, I called for reinforcements. Your mission, Captain, is of vital importance."

What she cares about are all those displaced people. Giving them a way out.

"How do I use the interface?"

"It's self-explanatory," it replies, "just click your heels. Good luck!" And with this final nonanswer, it disconnects.

She gets offline. Jaxon and Kaela are watching her intently.

"How did it go?" asks Jaxon.

She is still processing. Their brief conversation, mostly an Ingram monologue, was information-dense.

"The jump gate has been destroyed."

That's the biggest key takeaway for her. Both Jaxon and Kaela gasp.

"How? Why?"

"Ingram destroyed it to keep Arcturus from translating in reinforcements."

"What about all the people in the sector?"

"It sounds like they were close to cracking point-jump technology. Ingram is confident if we take the Tauran ship and the research notes out, the AI Council will be able to jump ships back in a matter of weeks."

"And you'll be piloting the alien ship!" says Kaela.

"Yeah. And sounds like it will try to lie to me."

"What?"

"Never mind. Something Ingram said."

"Do you trust it?" asks Jaxon.

She doesn't really. She arrived in the sector trying to outsmart it. That was silly of her. Every single interaction they had since then creeped her out. There's a sinister undertone to each of their conversations. She must admit it became less cryptic after Echo Point, elaborating more, providing her actual fucking useful information, but still.

Her answer to Jaxon is, "I don't have a choice."

She really doesn't. There's only one way out of here, and millions of lives are at stake.

And millions died. For what? For a mysterious alien artifact Omegas want control of? An artifact which ...

Kaela interrupts her train of thought: "Something's wrong!"

"What? Where?"

"Inside the base. The elevator."

No! Wade, the team, thinks Elena. She should be down there, with them.

48: CONTACT

The conversation Marcus has with Ingram is brief. A mission recap: see Elena Drake safely to the derelict; make sure the digicard makes its way outside the sector. Ingram preempts his major concerns: they don't know the coordinates; they don't have EV suits to board the alien ship. A heavy cruiser should be arriving soon to see them to their destination. A heavy cruiser equipped with everything necessary. Marcus tells Ingram about the dead bodies they found around the base. Ingram doesn't know what the situation is outside sublevel fifteen. Urges him caution. Bottom line: get back to the *Skylark* ASAP, see the digicard out of the sector.

The most remarkable part of the conversation is the final warning Ingram gives him, a set of far-fetched scenarios with hard-to-believe premises and contingencies. Marcus always knew Omegas are odd, so he files this away as *that will never come to pass*. The breach of chain of command is remarkable in its own right. Ingram represents the AI Council, which is in charge of the military. Lieutenant Marcus Wade is just a Vanguard lieutenant. Orders tend to trickle down though layers and layers, a lieutenant talking directly to an Omega about operational details is … quite exceptional.

They head back out into the hallway, retrace their steps to the elevator.

"Ingram has no clue what went down above," Marcus tells his team. "Keep your head on a swivel on the way back."

The elevator doors open. The cabin is as empty as they left it. Marcus is not looking forward to the molasses-slow ascent. They file inside. The doors close.

Sublevel fourteen. Novak is carrying the interface attached to his belt so he can have both hands free for his rifle. Sublevel thirteen. Howard has the digicard, stashed into one of his many pockets. Sublevel twelve. As before, it is taking too long. They don't feel at ease trapped inside this metal box. Sublevel eleven. The lights flicker. The elevator stops.

"Fuck," whispers Howard.

They all move to the sides of the cabin, raising their weapons.

{Kaela, what happened?} Marcus sends.

{As far as I can tell,} she is quick to reply, {mechanical failure.}

{Can you fix it?}

{Don't think so.}

Shit.

"Looks like we're walking after all. Anders, can you get us out of here?"

The combat engineer cracks open the elevator panel, works his magic. The doors ding open into another empty hallway. Not empty, Marcus realizes, there's something in the middle, about three hundred feet out. He flips to IR. No blip. He steps out, clears the left. Howard clears the right. The stairs up to sublevel ten are right next to the elevator. He steps inside the staircase. The stairs spiral up clockwise, so he clears the upstairs while Howard points his rifle downstairs. No tangos but it smells foul. They climb.

The stairs end on sublevel ten. They need to cross the hallway to the other side, take the other set of stairs that will get them to sublevel five. Precisely the long trek they were trying to avoid.

On sublevel ten, one of the hallway doors is open, equipment thrown out in front of it. A console. A dozen or so test tubes, half of them cracked. Blue and violet liquids spilled from them on the floor, reflecting the artificial lights in strange rainbows. A metal gadget Marcus can't identify.

They move past the destruction, pass another open door with a decapitated dead body slumped inside the doorframe.

The lights flicker.

"Fuck," says Howard again.

They make the corner, take the right turn. Halfway there, the next staircase is on the opposite side. Clear, except the blood splatter on the walls and ceiling. Another couple of doors are open up ahead, facing each other. They approach with caution. Marcus passes the doors pointing his rifle towards the interior of the left one. No movement. Santos follows closely behind him. Then it all happens fast, too fast.

The large thing scurries out of the room and grabs Anders with a huge claw, lifting him off his feet, while using another claw to knock Kim inside the opposite room. Anders screams. Kim gets the air knocked out of him, doesn't get a chance to say anything before Novak yells, "Contact rear!"

They turn. The first thought that crosses Marcus's mind is that they *do* fucking look like crabs. The thing walks on a splay of jointed legs, their hooked points clicking against the surface of the hallway. It heads towards the elevator, carrying Anders in its pincer. They aim, away from the claw holding Anders, fire careful shots to avoid hitting their teammate. The shots ricochet off the creature's carapace.

Anders dropped his weapon. He tries to reach for his gun, but the wide claw squeezing his midsection makes it impossible. He screams again.

The monster turns the corner. They follow.

Kim comes out of the room, joins them, slinging his sniper rifle to firing position.

They hear screams, increasingly more primal, turn the corner to find Anders in two pieces. The powerful chitinous appendage went through his body armor as if it were butter. His legs and lower body are leaning against the wall. His upper body, still screaming, is in the middle of the hallway, trailing red, brown, and yellow fluids; trailing intestines.

The crab-like thing is scurrying fast towards the staircase. Marcus switches to automatic fire, sprays its back with bullets while telling Howard to check up on Anders. Santos and Novak are shooting too. Kim kneels next to them, aims, fires his high-caliber weapon. Anders goes quiet. One of the thing's legs cracks at a joint, sprays a green fluid. The creature sways, falls, gets back up, keeps going, dragging its injured leg. It has enough appendages to continue without slowing down.

Marcus turns to look at Anders. Howard is leaning over him, but he is gone, staring at the ceiling. He sees Kim lining up another shot, turns to look at their enemy.

The creature rips the staircase door open, squeezes through. Kim shoots, mid-carapace now. The shot pierces the chitinous armor. Marcus is almost positive he sees green fluid dripping as the creature vanishes down the stairs.

"The fuck?" Santos says, out of breath.

"Anders?" Novak asks, looking at Howard.

He shakes his head. Anders is dead.

"Fuck!" Kim kicks the wall. "I nailed the fucker. Twice. It kept moving."

"What now, LT?" asks Howard.

"Exfil. On the double. Watch the doors."

He briefly considers bringing their fallen teammate with them, but it doesn't make sense. There's no saving Anders, bringing him out would slow them down too much. The parameters changed; the zone is hot and they're out in the open. Fighting against a giant fucking crab. At least one.

They stand to look at their fallen teammate for a moment, then get going. Tactical retreat this time.

"Kimmy, cover." The sniper's weapon seemed to be the only thing that put a dent in the fucking thing. Kim kneels to provide cover, rifle aimed at the now doorless staircase. Howard takes position next to Kim, even though his weapon wasn't particularly useful in the engagement.

"Moving," says Santos.

"Moving," echoes Novak.

Marcus takes another moment to look at Anders, then announces, in turn, "Moving," and heads back towards the hallway bend, retracing their steps to the stairs.

On the corner, they cover both arms of the hallway.

"Set, go!" Marcus calls.

Kim and Howard join them. They swap, the sniper and his second-in-command provide cover again. The rest of them sprint towards the elevator, calling, "Moving."

They stop midway, give their teammates a chance to catch up.

They repeat the steps once more to the staircase.

"Moving."

"Set, go!"

"Moving."

Then they're all together by the staircase door.

Clanking echoes on the hallway. Something moving around the corner.

"Shit," says Howard.

"Smoke?" Novak asks.

Marcus considers it. The enemy (giant fucking crabs, unbelievable!) didn't seem to use weapons. Will the thing have trouble seeing them through a smokescreen? Either way, it can't hurt.

"Light it up!"

"Smoke out," Novak calls, throwing the grenade, camouflaging their retreat in a cloud of thick IR-blocking smoke.

"On me!" calls Marcus and steps inside the staircase. It's clear. He calls it. Howard does too. They sprint upward, letting Kim and Howard cover their six, stopping at each sublevel to regroup. They're on sublevel nine. Nothing seems to be following them, but they can't afford any slack. Not after Anders. Not after how fast the creature that grabbed him moved. They're on sublevel eight. Still quiet, except their well-rehearsed calls. "Clear," "Moving," "Set, go." Up to sublevel seven. Marcus replays what just happened in his mind, chides himself for it. *Focus, Vanguard,* he tells himself. Now is not the time. They're regrouped on sublevel six, ready to take the last flight of stairs, when they hear a door below them blow open.

"Contact below," says Kim, fires.

A loud screech rises through the staircase.

"Frag out!" calls Howard and throws a grenade down the shaft. It lands at the bottom of the staircase, on sublevel ten, and explodes with a deafening roar inside the confined space.

More screeching from below.

They retreat upstairs, to sublevel five, weapons aiming downwards. The creature doesn't follow them. Did they kill it?

Then they're on sublevel five. Another run through the hallway, back to the elevator and the staircase to the surface. Who the fuck built this place?

"We killed it?" asks Novak as they're moving towards the middle of the hallway, covered by their sniper and chief petty officer.

Marcus shrugs.

There's more blood splatter on the walls here, more shell casings, a detached arm.

They take position.

"Set, go!"

"Moving," says Howard.

"Moving," echoes Kim.

The lights flicker again.

"Smoke out!" says Marcus and lobs another smoke grenade behind them. Then, "Moving."

They all get to the corner of the hallway when the lights go out. Night vision lights up the hallways in green. Marcus flips to IR for an instant. Nothing blips in front. The back is all IR-blocking smoke, no point checking. He flips back to night vision, resumes their retreat.

"Moving."

Around the corner, all doors are open. Some ripped off their hinges and thrown on the hallway floor, others kicked inwards.

"Shit, shit, shit!" says Santos.

They don't have enough frags to throw inside each room. They don't even know if they will work against whatever they're retreating from.

"It's just five hundred feet," says Marcus. "Swivel heads."

He leads by example, calls, "Moving," advances pointing his rifle left and right, inside the doorframes. Novak and Santos follow. Two hundred fifty feet to the midpoint of this stretch of hallway seem like a very long walk.

"Set, go!" he calls back to Kim and Howard.

They retreat, just as careful. Nothing attacks them.

{Kaela,} he sends, {what's up with the lights?}

There's no reply. They're cut off.

Another two hundred fifty tense feet. They reach the last staircase. They clear it, start moving up.

Sublevel four. They lost Anders! They fucking lost him to that … thing. No more "fuck me backwards," no combat engineer to help them navigate the derelict, no more … They lost a brother. Sublevel three. Getting closer to the surface now. Marcus hopes Kim's shot and the frag got the fucking thing. Sublevel two. They feel the stairs shake underneath them; a tremor passes through the whole building.

"Feel that?" from Howard. They all felt it, it was hard to miss.

"Keep going," says Marcus.

They make it to ground level when they hear another staircase door below them slam, more chittering. Santos doesn't hesitate, immediately calls, "Frag out!" and drops one to the bottom of the stairwell. They exit into the hallway as it goes off.

They're picking up the pace now. Marcus doesn't want to leave Kim and Howard behind, not if that thing is somehow still alive and climbing up the stairs. They're close to the *Skylark* so they move together, one final dash. Marcus in front, clearing the path. Santos and Novak behind him, covering the flanks. Kim and Howard walking backwards, waiting for the creature to bust out of the staircase. It doesn't. They make the corner, stepping around the dismembered corpse they saw on their way in. *Same fate as Anders*, Marcus realizes. They keep going.

Back to where they started. The room with the dead soldier in the doorway. The room where they first noticed signs of a firefight, which are now harder to see through night vision.

A loud bang reaches them from the hallway. The thing might yet be coming. But they're by the bridge now. The bridge connecting them to the airlock, the safety of the *Skylark*. Another bang, closer this time. The airlock door opens as the creature turns the corner. Kim kneels, lines up a shot as they cross the bridge. Jaxon, Elena, and Vesper are on the other side, watching them questioningly. They don't have night vision, can't see the horror coming down the hallway towards them.

"Give me one sec, LT," says Kim.

Marcus puts his hand on Kim's shoulder in assent. The creature skitters towards them.

"What's that sound?" asks Jaxon.

Kim shoots, then sprints across the bridge, following Marcus. They're the last ones in. The airlock door closes. Rynn takes off not a second later. Howard, Novak, or Santos must've told him to get ready for takeoff.

"Did you get it, Kimmy?" asks Marcus.

"I … think so," he answers, but he sounds doubtful.

49: CHAOS THEORY

I n the ready room, Elena watches Wade, usually calm and collected, throw his helmet off. He kicks a chair and sends it crashing against the wall.

"What ...?" she whispers, but she knows, she sees Anders is not with them. They came back without a team member. There's only one scenario in which Vanguards would do that.

"A fucking Tauran," says Howard, "it ... it got Backwards."

"A Tauran?" This from Kaela.

"An actual fucking Tauran!" Howard slams his own helmet against the table hard enough to knock two cups over. Vesper, who is standing on the opposite side of the room, flinches, takes a couple of backsteps, until her back is against the wall.

Elena puts her prosthetic hand on Kaela's arm. Slowly shakes her head. They're upset. They're angry. They lost Anders. Adrenaline is still pumping. They need space to cool off, time to process.

The *Skylark* makes its way upward as the Vanguards stomp into the cargo bay, stripping off their combat gear and swearing.

Jaxon takes a step forward, opens his mouth to say something to the aggrieved combatants, then reconsiders.

Elena goes to pick up the spilled cups. She is bending to get the second one and replace it on the table as the ship's alarm starts blaring.

{We've got incoming,} sends Rynn to everyone on the ship.

Elena gets online, looks out through the ship's opticals. A large, cigar-shaped ship is approaching fast, fresh out of warp. Zooming in, she sees tentacles protruding at odd angles from its hull. The *Skylark*'s tactical overlay tags it as Tauran. Elena has an intense sense of déjà vu. Strange, as she's never seen a Tauran ship up close before. She wasn't in the sector during the war. The media reports were sparse on visuals, and the mock-ups they showed looked nothing like this. She would've remembered something so ugly.

{Prepping FTL.}

Rynn is ready to take them out of here, but before he gets a chance to do so, another ship comes out of warp. The heavy cruiser *Sovereign*, immediately followed by its suite of support vessels.

{We've got you, *Skylark*,} the ship's captain broadcasts, {come aboard.}

The *Sovereign* opens its bay doors while at the same time training its batteries on the Tauran ship. The alien ship slows down, stops at a respectful distance.

Elena sticks her head inside the cockpit.

"Ingram promised an escort," she tells Rynn. "I guess this is it."

"Should we board? I'm ready to warp away."

"We should. If the Taurans are back in the sector, we'll fare better with some heavy guns around us."

Rynn nods, steers the *Skylark* towards the bay, negotiating an ingress vector with the *Sovereign* beacon.

Elena watches the alien ship. She will be onboard one of these soon, won't she? Un-fucking-believable. It looks like something that crawled out of a nightmare.

The *Sovereign* and its escort face off with the Tauran ship as the *Skylark* makes its way inside the large bay. Elena switches from the *Skylark*'s opticals to the heavy cruiser's, can't look away from the strange craft.

She wonders if the *Sovereign* will engage.

Tauran ships don't seem to be more advanced than the military's. Different, but not better. At least that's the conclusion everyone arrived at during the brief war. Hard to tell who would win between the thing she's looking at and the *Sovereign*.

She wonders if the alien ship will engage.

Why is it just sitting there?

It turns out neither of them engages. The stare-down is interrupted by the neutron star.

NS-36-A blinks. It goes completely dark for a few seconds. Then it's back to its usual dim glow. Then dark again. Then it lights up, bright as a supernova. Opticals struggle to compensate. Alarms sound across the *Sovereign*, loud enough that they can be heard through the *Skylark*'s hull. It takes all of ten seconds, then NS-36-A is back as it was.

The Tauran ship moves away, accelerates. The *Sovereign*'s targeting system tracks it until it reaches FTL, disappears.

"What was that?" she asks, not expecting an answer, as she gets offline.

Kaela, who is standing behind her and is plugged into the *Sovereign*'s sensory apparatus as much as the ship allows her, says, "I don't know, but we got hit with a huge amount of gamma radiation. Thank God the *Sovereign* has military-grade shielding."

"Must've been the alien device," adds Elena. She told them about her conversation with Ingram on Echo Point, about the Progenitors, before she crashed from amphelines on the way here. She tries to imagine the creatures that built this, the technology they possessed.

"Must've," agrees Kaela. "I wonder what it meant."

"At least it scared the Tauran ship away," says Jaxon.

The alarms aboard the *Sovereign* quiet down. A short message follows in the digital:

{Captain Drake, Lieutenant Wade, I am Captain Dalton. Please join me in the briefing room.}

She turns away from the cockpit at the same time Wade comes out of the cargo bay. He looks more composed now. He nods at her and they both step out of the *Skylark* and onto the *Sovereign*'s deck. They follow nav to the briefing room. The *Sovereign* looks just as any other large military vessel she's been on. Same white surfaces, same background hum, same maze of walkways.

"I'm sorry," she tells Wade. "I should've been down there, with you."

Lieutenant Wade breaks stride, turns to look at her.

"No, Captain, you really shouldn't have. You are the only one that can get the digicard out of the sector."

The implication being her life is now too valuable to risk on an infil. *My, how things have changed.*

"Plus, you've been injured."

He makes a good point. She fought the mercs on Echo Point to save the lives of the *Charon*'s crew, her new friends, but she is not combat ready. Not anymore. Even with a synthetic hand, her missing eye and flaring stomach pain make her a liability on the field. She shouldn't feel guilty. Still. She was out for over two days all because she took too many stims. And she's not out of the woods yet. All the excitement since she woke up is already tiring her out.

They keep walking.

"Sorry about Anders."

"We had to leave him there," says Wade, "with that ... thing."

"What did it look like?"

Her curiosity gets the best of her; she can't stop herself from asking. She knows she shouldn't; she shouldn't make Wade relive it. Not so soon.

"Like a giant fucking crab," he says, clenching and unclenching his fists.

She drops it, and they continue in silence. She thinks about the Tauran Consensus, about talking to one of those things. About them trying to lie to her.

The briefing room is medium-sized, but it seems large because it's almost empty. Two uniformed officers are waiting for them, sitting at the round table. Both of them are middle-aged, clean-shaven, with short-cropped hair. One of them has gray eyes, the other has an aquiline nose. The former looks tired, to the point of haggardness. They stand up as she and Wade enter the room.

"Captain, Lieutenant," says the tired one, "I am Captain Liam Dalton. This is Commander Adrian Hale."

They exchange greetings, sit down.

"We're aware of your important mission, and we're here to support you," says the *Sovereign*'s captain. "Commander Hale oversees the Derelict A1X-VD2 exploration. He can brief you on the latest there."

The commander nods. "The ship is half a day away at FTL. We're heading there now."

"Before we dive in," interrupts Elena, "what's the situation in the sector?"

The two officers look at each other.

"Bad," says Dalton.

"I was on Nova Prime when the paramilitary hit," says Elena.

"My team engaged at the ring," adds Wade.

"We came straight from Nova Prime," says Dalton. "The system is secure, but we sustained massive casualties. The city was hit hard."

"What about the ring?" asks Wade. "When we got redeployed from there, it wasn't looking good."

"The ring is destroyed. We lost the *Dauntless*, the *Ares*, and the *Excalibur* there. The paramilitary is controlling the region now."

Elena figured as much, still can't help the knot forming in her stomach. The *Dauntless* got her here, she spent time with the crew. The jump gate destroyed too. By Ingram, so it doesn't fall into Abyssal hands.

"Any idea what happened here at Eureka Base?"

"Negative. We got reports that the paramilitary engaged, then the infosphere was hit."

"Taurans?" ventures Elena.

"Could be. Whatever happened, it looks like nobody won this one. Our mission is to take you to the derelict."

"I have the coordinates," adds Hale.

The exact location of the ship is kept secret.

"What about Verdant? Forge?"

"We don't know," says Dalton, "but it's chaos all around. We lost the admiral during the battle at the Gateway Ring. Ingram has been severely damaged, to the point where we no longer have instant comms across the sector. Ships come and go, carrying conflicting reports, following conflicting orders."

"And it sounds like you, Captain," Hale tells Elena, "can help get us out of this mess."

Weeks, she wants to tell him. It will take weeks, at best.

"Multiple reports of Tauran sightings too," adds Dalton, "and we're in no shape to fight them."

If the Taurans are breaking the truce, if they can reuse the same weapon they employed against Echo Point, with the chaos that the war between Arcturus and Ingram caused, by the time reinforcements are back, the sector might all be a giant graveyard, Elena realizes.

"Lieutenant, I take it you were part of the initial derelict exploration?" This from Hale.

"Affirmative," says Wade, "three of my current team members and I were there originally … two of my current team members."

"We have it fully mapped out by now. We can give you nav paths to the ship's version of a bridge."

"Is it still dangerous?"

"Mostly not," says Hale.

"Mostly?"

"We uncovered most of the triggers. Or traps. Whatever you want to call them. But, from time to time, it still reacts, still vents people out."

"Even after all this time?"

Commander Hale nods.

"We pumped it full of nitrogen-oxygen, but would still recommend wearing EV suits for safety. You have the interface, right?"

"Affirmative," says Wade.

"I was overseeing its development. It works on the ship's bridge. We lost two volunteers before we realized we need grafts to filter the signal."

Elena is all ears. She is supposed to wear it soon.

"What happened to them?" she asks.

"First one went catatonic. Second one, well, last I checked she still has vivid hallucinations. She is being cared for."

"And how do you know the same won't happen to me, Commander?"

"Third volunteer had NSRS. Took us a while to find someone, but we did. Filtered through the limited bandwidth grafts, he did just fine."

"Why didn't he jump it out of the sector?"

"At the time, there was no need to. Ingram wanted it here, close to the lab."

"What about now?"

"You mean why we didn't jump it now? The volunteer rotated out of the sector. We had no one else with both NSRS and the required clearance. Then things happened fast. We didn't get a chance to find someone else. Troops moved, battles started. Luckily, we have you, Captain."

Luckily.

"Excuse me for one moment," says the captain, and embeds.

An alarm starts again. They look at each other. Captain Dalton comes back.

"We have a problem. Whatever just happened to that neutron star … well, it's still happening. There's an increasing gravitational pull. Drawing us in. We need to leave the system now. Our FTL plotting seems to have also been impacted. It's progressively degrading."

"Impacted how?" asks Hale, sounding only slightly worried.

"Severely decreased accuracy. We might return to causal spacetime too deep inside a gravity well, or on top of an object."

"Good thing the derelict is far away from any large object."

"Yes, Commander," says Dalton. "Please send the coordinates to the navigator now. We need to get out of here, fast."

The commander nods and embeds. Elena gets online, uses the ship's opticals to take another look at Eureka Base, at all the destroyed ships. It might be her imagination, but they do seem to all be slowly drifting towards the neutron star. NS-36-A is glowing its usual under- stated glow, patiently waiting to devour them all. The image freezes in place as the *Sovereign* goes superluminal.

PART EIGHT
EXTINCTION EVENT

50: WAYWARD

Commander Hale shares more details about the latest status of the derelict and about the alterations they made to it. Elena watches Wade nod approvingly. It has an airlock now, an "official" entry point.

"We used to go in with breach pods," Wade tells her.

They mounted lighting inside. Safe paths are clearly marked across the ship. She watches a 3D projection of it that looks a lot like the ship she just saw through the *Sovereign*'s opticals, but much larger.

The conversation lasts for another twenty minutes or so, after which Elena feels completely exhausted. After two days spent mostly sleeping, this is way too much activity at once. Her stomach hurts.

Captain Dalton officially welcomes everyone aboard, assigns them quarters during transit. It's a major upgrade from the *Skylark*'s cargo bay, with its flexi-walls and double-cot set-up.

"Anyone in need of medical assistance?" he asks.

They are in need of medical assistance. Rynn is doing well now, he was lucky—the bullets went through—but having a medic make sure there's no permanent damage can't hurt. Kim got knocked around by the Tauran creature, and while he insists he is feeling just fine, Wade orders him to get checked up nevertheless. Elena herself is also recovering quite well, but she wants to see the medic. She can't afford getting sick again, especially when the stakes are so high. And then there's Vesper. Vesper is missing fingers, has severe burns, probably needs a psych eval, and more.

The med bay seems small for such a large ship. When she arrives, Rynn is already there, accompanied by Jaxon and Kaela. Kim is leaving the examination room, gives her a respectful, "Captain" as he walks out.

"Where is Vesper?" she asks.

"She refused to come," says Kaela. "She said she wanted to talk to you first."

"To me?"

"Yes."

Elena is about to go online, send Vesper a message, but pauses.

"Kaela, can you try digging up some info on her? Vesper Kovatch?"

Kaela frowns. "Why? You think she's lying to us?"

"I don't know."

"I'll see if the *Sovereign* has any record on her, though I doubt it. Especially if she is a corporate citizen. I can't access anything else while we're warp. Probably nothing after either, I don't think the derelict has any quantum-entangled compute around it."

Elena nods.

"Just try your best."

Then she has another idea.

"Can you also take a look at the digicard we got from the base?"

"The Vanguards are keeping a close eye on it," Kaela says, as if she already attempted this.

"Tell them I green lit it," says Elena. She outranks the team. And she is very curious to see what Ingram wants them to smuggle out of Sector 36.

{Vesper, I heard you don't want to come to med bay?} she sends to the woman.

No reply.

She doesn't have time for this; she is tired and in pain. She will get checked up and go rest. Captain Dalton can handle Vesper. She'll talk to him tomorrow.

. . .

The doctor is middle-aged. He looks grave but his voice is kind and has a gentle touch. He is also very meticulous.

"What happened to your eye?"

She gives him an abridged version of her fight in the hive. He takes off the eye patch, looks at her scarred face.

"Can't do anything about that here, sorry," he says. "Your NSRS can't interface with a standard prosthetic."

"I know," she says. Terek told her as much. And that she likely can't afford a graft-compatible one.

He checks her grafts next.

"Whoever did this did a solid job," he says, approvingly.

"His name was Terek Nassar," she says, looking away. Terek Nassar. Who died because of her.

The doctor doesn't seem to catch her use of the past tense, moves on to her hand without further comments.

"Hold this," he tells her, gives her a spherical gadget.

Elena holds it.

"Now give it a squeeze."

She does. The doctor nods.

"Let's also do a sensory test," he says. The sphere turns warm inside her hand. "Can you feel it?"

"It's warm."

"Good. What about now?"

The test continues, the device becoming in turn cold, soft, textured. Like with her grafts, the doctor is pleased with the synthetic hand. He then moves on to her stomach. She removes her top and the examination chair tilts back, positioning her horizontally. A scanner attached to a multi-jointed arm hovers a few inches above her midsection, moves up and down, side to side, then retreats.

"Healed up pretty good," he says. "There is some scar tissue, but otherwise nothing that would get me worried. Does it hurt?"

"Sometimes."

"Want something for the pain?"

God, yes! she thinks. She can already feel the stim diffusing throughout her body, making the pain go away, making her feel sharp.

"No," she replies. Her stomach prods her, like it didn't like the answer. "I just need to rest," she says.

He raises an eyebrow. She is ashamed, doesn't want to talk about her recent crash, but decides to do it anyway. For the same reason she came in here in the first place: the stakes are high, and she really can't afford another fuck-up. Another fuck-up in a string of many. She tells the doctor about the amphelines she took—that she abused.

He doesn't judge her for it. "And you experienced withdrawal starting three days ago?" He sounds surprised.

"Yes," she says, remembering the shakes, the puking.

"You're one tough lady," he concludes.

"I had help," she says, thinking of Vesper watching over her, giving her graycaps, cleaning her up.

"How are you feeling now?"

"Not great," she admits.

"Rest," the doctor tells her. "That's the best cure for it."

She thanks him, then makes her way to her quarters, glad to call it a day. She opens the door, thinking about not having to double up with someone for a change, thinking about Jaxon putting his arm around her. Vesper is inside her cabin, looking more gaunt than ever.

"Elena, I was waiting for you."

"I heard you wanted to talk to me," says Elena, trying not to sound annoyed.

"I heard the crew talk, while you were recovering. And afterwards. I know the jump gate is gone. I also know we're going to a captured alien ship that you can translate out of here."

Vesper pauses, looks at her pleadingly.

"Take me with you! Take me out of Sector 36."

Elena considers this. She wasn't expecting it, was planning on leaving Vesper on the *Sovereign*, but the woman did help her. She took care of her when she was at her worst. What kind of repayment would abandoning her on a heavy cruiser in the middle of a war zone be?

She has her suspicions, but after what she's been through lately, she might just be getting a bit paranoid. No tangible proof that Vesper is anything but a geologist for Abyssal, a geologist who ended up in the wrong place at the wrong time. Unless Kaela can find anything, getting the woman out of Sector 36 would be the righteous thing to do. Plus, she doesn't look like she could hurt a fly in her current state.

"OK," she concedes.

Vesper looks relieved.

"Thank you!"

She looks like she wants to say something more but doesn't. She turns around and leaves. Elena is alone, tired, and hurting. Her stomach hasn't let up since med bay. She curls onto her new bed. It's military-rough and small but feels luxurious compared to the cot on the *Skylark*. It doesn't take her long to fall asleep. It's a deep, dreamless sleep this time around.

An alarm wakes her up.

{What's going on?} she asks the ship.

{Nav error,} it responds, gives her details.

Groggy from the loud wake up, it takes her a moment to process the information. Whatever happened with NS-36-A caused a navigation error. The *Sovereign* came out of warp way off course, millions of miles away from where it was supposed to go. Opticals are contradicting the vector math. Astronavigation places them way beyond the margin of error.

Systems are recalibrating.

Fully awake now, she steps out of her quarters. Jaxon is out on the walkway, looking as if he also just woke up.

"Hey," he says, gives her his signature smile.

She's about to answer his greeting when the alarm intensifies, its volume increasing to a deafening blare. The ship's PA system comes alive, starts repeating, "Battle stations! Battle stations!"

She gets online, borrows the *Sovereign*'s opticals to assess the situation. Tauran ships. Three, then four, then five, come out of warp, a mere few thousand miles away from the *Sovereign* and its escort.

Kaela and Vesper join them on the walkway, coming out of their own quarters.

"What do we do?" asks Kaela.

Rynn joins them too.

What can they do? They're guests aboard the ship.

{Captain?} she sends to Dalton.

At first, there's no response. She expects as much, Captain Dalton needs to coordinate the action against the incoming threat. He probably has a million things going on right now, most of them more vital than his passengers. After a few minutes, Commander Hale reaches out:

{Captain Drake, bring your crew to the *Skylark*.}

The *Skylark*. She easily connects the dots. Captain Dalton will make a stand here. Their small stealth transport must get them the rest of the way to their destination. This means Captain Dalton is not confident the *Sovereign* can fend off the enemy. He'd rather see them off, buy them time, than keep them aboard.

"To the *Skylark*," she says to the crew of the *Charon* and to Vesper. She also sends a message to Wade.

He acknowledges immediately: {We're on our way.}

She starts running, following nav, weaving around sailors running the opposite way.

The *Sovereign* trembles. Elena almost loses her footing. She steals a quick glance through its opticals. She sees five frigates from the heavy cruiser's escort advancing towards the enemy ships, exchanging energy weapon fire. The two forces are engaged. The *Sovereign* fires its main battery, its recoil reverberating throughout its hull. She almost bumps into someone, gets offline to focus on nav and her surroundings.

As she reaches the bay, she sees Wade and the other Vanguards in front of the *Skylark*. They're wearing combat armor, carrying their rifles, even though they're not supposed to engage the enemy themselves. *Better safe than sorry,* agrees Elena, briefly touches the hilt of her Noctics.

The bay is all organized chaos around them. Alarms are blaring like everywhere else on the ship, echoing even louder inside its large

volume. People are running around, boarding ships, moving equipment and ammunition on hover carts.

Commander Hale arrives at the same time as they do, coming from
the opposite direction. He's been running, just like them. Short of
breath, he tries to tell them something, but his voice is drowned by the
surrounding noise.

He tries again, after taking a deep breath and raising his voice: "I'll
be joining you."

His experience with the derelict ship will come in handy. Elena
believes this is a good idea. Considering what she learned during the
briefing, what Wade recalled, Derelict A1X-VD2 sounds like a dangerous, treacherous place. She'll take any help they can get to navigate it
safely.

They get aboard, Rynn taking his place at the helm. The ready room
is as crowded as ever, with Hale joining their already large party now.
Elena hopes the Taurans don't use more exotic sensors, that the
Skylark's stealth tech will keep it camouflaged from them.

"You don't want an officer pilot?" Commander Hale offers.

"No," declines Elena, "we have the best pilot in the sector right
here."

She is sure Rynn overhears her, but he doesn't say anything. The
only thing he sends, in the digital, as soon as the *Skylark*'s airlock
closes, is, {Control, we're ready to go.}

They must wait for the bay to be clear of personnel before its doors
can slide open. It doesn't take long, the crew of the *Sovereign* is efficient, and the *Skylark* has topmost priority.

{*Skylark*, you are cleared for takeoff,} Control sends.

As the *Skylark* glides away from the heavy cruiser, Captain Dalton
sends them a parting, {Godspeed!}

Elena responds with a, {Good luck, Captain!}

She watches the rainbows of particle beam weapons, mixed with
the ephemeral glints of hypersonic kinetics. The *Skylark* turns away
from the battle, fades into the viridian background, invisible as a ghost.

51: BACKTRACK

Marcus watches the *Sovereign* shrink to a dot and disappear among the sparks of the battle. He feels uneasy. The alien ship awaits them. An allegedly tamer alien ship, but they no longer have their combat engineer. And, he realizes, no EV suits.

"The *Skylark* doesn't have EV suits," he voices his concern. They were expecting a more orderly rendezvous, the *Sovereign* bringing them in, with its well-stocked equipment. In the chaos of the Tauran encounter, they took off on the ill-suited *Skylark*. He looks at Commander Hale.

Commander Hale says, "Shit."

"Any other ships guarding the derelict we could borrow from?"

"Negative," says Hale, "they're joining the battle. We'll be alone there."

After losing Anders, Marcus is deeply worried about further casualties. He remembers the ship's tricks, the venting, the chemical burns.

"Technically," Hale says, "we can do without EV suits. The air is breathable." He doesn't look convinced himself.

Marcus clenches and unclenches his fists. He doesn't say anything. He feels like punching a wall and barely contains himself.

"How dangerous is the ship nowadays, really?" asks Santos. She's been there before too, her now misshapen nose a memento of her time there. She's as worried as he is.

"We'll be fine if we're careful," says Hale, sounding doubtful.

"With all due respect, Commander," says Marcus, "can you please be a little bit more fucking clear? I need an accurate risk assessment if my team is going in."

His team members look shocked at his outburst. The officer ignores his foul language.

"We had two venting events in the past month. First was initiated by a drone. It was carrying a large object, accidentally bumped it into a wall, which triggered the reaction. Second was an engineer misstepping. As long as we're within the marked pathway and everyone is careful, we should be fine."

That's better, thinks Marcus. "What about gas bags?" he asks.

"No such incidents since I've been overseeing things, though I read your report, Lieutenant."

The others are listening in, trying to make sense of the strange conversation. Except Santos and Howard, who were with him during the exploration, and Drake, who recently got briefed, the others don't yet know the full extent of the dangers that are awaiting them aboard.

"You should brief everyone," says Marcus.

"Is everyone coming aboard?" asks Hale, surprised.

"Yes," confirms Elena Drake, "everyone is coming aboard." Marcus watches her turn to look at Vesper as she says this. The geologist is standing quietly at the back of the ready room. He is surprised she is here, would've expected her to stay on the *Sovereign*.

"We'll be translating out of Sector 36," continues Drake, as if to ensure there aren't any objections. "If anyone wants to stay behind, you can stay on the *Skylark*."

Nobody does.

"OK, folks, pay attention," says Hale, and starts talking at the same time as he is sharing material with them in the digital. They listen, read, ask questions.

•   •   •

Marcus is surprised how much more they learned in the span of just a few months while he rotated out of Sector 36. A lot more than the drone footage his team got the first time around. Still, the ship is keeping some secrets. And a lot of the material is irrelevant to their mission. The most important thing is survival, avoiding traps. No more deaths. He clenches and unclenches his fists.

The *Skylark* gets in optical range of Derelict A1X-VD2 just as Commander Hale wraps up his briefing. Marcus zooms in, surprised to see the alterations. From a distance, it looks like the ship was enwrapped in a mesh. Its tentacles are splayed out, hanging extended in all directions. If it's alive, it looks a lot less threatening now, a lot more like it's being prepared for vivisection.

"Commander," Marcus asks, now regretting his previous rudeness, "are you going to lead the infil?"

"Negative," he responds, "you do it, Lieutenant." Then, after a brief pause, "I only went aboard once."

Great, Marcus thinks. They sent them a geek. He read all the reports but put boots on the ground exactly once.

"Aye," he says. "Listen up, everyone!" He looks around the ready room, makes sure everyone's eyes are on him. "You too, pilot," he calls to Rynn in the cockpit through the open door.

"All ears," Rynn replies.

They're all listening. Good. "Dash and I take point. We've been here before. You follow in our footsteps. Carefully. The thing has more ways to kill us than you can imagine, and I don't want to get spaced without an EV suit on account of a misstep." God he could use Anders right now. "Pinball has been here before too. She and Commander Hale will bring up the rear and keep an eye on everyone else. You follow the markings, don't even breathe outside the marked path."

He hopes he gave them a good enough scare to keep them on their toes. Truth be told, there were no markings when he was last in. He has only seen them in the vids Hale shared. But he remembers being vented into space twice, he remembers the fluorine gas. The place is truly dangerous.

"Commander, please share nav paths from the airlock to where we need to get to."

Hale obliges.

"Take a good look at these, folks, it's a bit of a trek. Be careful!" They all assent. Howard is stone-faced. Santos looks grim. He finishes his pep talk with, "Let's make it to our destination alive!"

"Hooyah!" replies his team.

"Hooyah!" echo Drake, Hale, and—Marcus is surprised to hear— Jaxon Barabe. He didn't have him pegged as military. Jaxon pronounces it differently though. *A marine*, thinks Marcus. The civilian women, Kaela and Vesper, nod, worried looks on their faces. Rynn, inside the cockpit, keeps quiet.

The *Skylark* closes in. The mesh enveloping the alien ship reifies into a hexagonal metallic scaffolding. The ship is large, as large as it ever was. Marcus is not looking forward to boarding it again. Not looking forward to this final leg of their mission.

{T minus five minutes to the airlock,} announces Rynn.

"Get ready, everyone," he says. Then, to his team, "We got what we need?"

Novak lifts up the interface, the strange helmet they retrieved from Eureka Base. Howard shows him the digicard, puts it back in his pocket.

They're still wearing their combat gear, ever since the alarms sounded on the *Sovereign*, though he doubts it will do them any good on the derelict. Same with their rifles. *Better have one and not need it,* he thinks. They're ready to go.

Marcus embeds, watches their approach through the *Skylark*'s opticals.

The airlock is rudely bolted to a side of the ship, penetrating its hull, with a docking port protruding through the scaffolding. If the ship is even half-alive, Marcus thinks, it looks pathetic. He would feel sorry for it, had it not tried to kill them repeatedly.

The *Skylark* is a tiny vessel compared to the beast they are about to board. He hears someone gasp as they get close enough for its true size to become evident.

{Docking,} announces Rynn.

The *Skylark* turns sideways, slides to line up its airlock with the derelict's extension. Connects.

"Here we go, folks, watch your step!"

The airlock hisses open.

Ten steps from the *Skylark* to the inside the alien ship, the house of horrors. The sapphire glass dock offers them one last view of the Viridian Shroud with its endless gas clouds. Marcus steps aboard, trying not to think of all the times shit went wrong in here.

He steps aboard to find a world completely different than what he expected. For one, the interior is bright, hovering golden lights giving a sickly orange hue to what used to be a slick onyx black. White paint marks safe passage, with yellow hashed areas warning strays, bold red stating "do not cross." Various devices are attached to the walls, with pulsating tubes and dials.

Marcus pulls up nav. Their destination is deep inside but looks like they just need to follow the arrows and not cross over the lines.

"Follow me," he says, starts walking.

Don't get too comfortable now, he tells himself. Their steps echo inside the large corridors of the ship. *Just like back in the day,* he thinks. They keep going. Nobody talks. The markings, the lights, they all give an illusion of safety, but every single one of them knows there is a risk of getting spaced. And they don't have EV suits.

"Did you hear that?" Howard asks him.

He didn't.

"What?"

"From … there." Howard points to the side.

Marcus shakes his head.

"Focus, Dash," he says, remembering how Howard got the nickname, how the gas bag popped right on top of them.

They keep walking. The white-painted trail branches out. They turn right, going deeper inside the ship. Fewer contraptions on the wall here, more of the ship's slick surfaces. *Stay asleep,* Marcus urges it.

He wishes Anders was with them. Anders "Backwards," who could crack a joke and break the tension.

They walk all the way up to a closed orifice. The painted trail they were following cuts off. What must be the bottom half of an arrow disappears underneath the obstacle.

Marcus turns around, calls on Hale.

"What now, Commander?"

The commander is pale, looks positively terrified.

"Sir!"

That snaps him out of it.

"Alternate path. Give me a second."

Alternate path sounds good to Marcus. He remembers combat engineers trying to cut through. He remembers the ship's reaction.

"Backtrack," Hale calls.

"You and Pinball take point," Marcus orders. He is almost certain Hale is not really up for this, but shuffling people around is too risky. It only takes one misstep, one person stepping outside of the marked path. And he trusts Santos with his life. She, unlike Hale, was here during all their incursions. She saw what triggered the venting events, what caused the gas bags to explode, saw the consequences of not being careful.

They start moving again, now him and Howard bringing up the rear. God, he would feel so much better inside an EV suit.

They advance through identical-looking corridors, take a left, another left, go straight for what seems a very long time, then turn right. The nav overlay shows him they're getting closer. Haven't tripped any gas bags. Yet. He would've felt so much better with Anders leading the charge rather than book-smart Commander Hale.

"You must've heard that one!" Howard tells him.

"What?"

"Behind us?"

"No."

"Really?"

"Really."

He wonders what Howard is hearing. There's nobody on the ship. They figured that much during their initial explorations. By now, with the ship all mapped and painted out, he is positive nothing lurks inside. And the ship itself is asleep. Right?

"Almost there," Hale calls.

They take a left turn and end up inside a large room. A room Marcus remembers very well. Endless rows of bio-machinery, strange knobs, handles, and tendrils. The alien ship's equivalent of a bridge.

Powerful floodlights have been placed at its corners, illuminating the strange devices. Arrows on the ground point to various elements, provide more detail in some code Marcus doesn't understand: H-control 2, X-down, ??? (*what does ??? mean*, he wonders), X-up, and DO NOT TOUCH!

DO NOT TOUCH! is pretty clear. In his opinion, it should apply to the whole vessel. He is looking forward to wrapping up this mission, hopes things don't devolve.

"Here we are," Commander Hale tells them, without hiding the relief in his voice.

Marcus watches their party look around awestruck. Few of them were aboard the ship before, for most of them this is a first. Kim and Novak are looking at the ceiling, rapt. Jaxon is staring at one of the strange devices. Kaela is hugging herself. Rynn is inscrutable. Vesper is standing aside, looking at the floor. Drake is looking this way and that, trying to take it all in.

"The interface should work here," Hale adds.

"Great!" says Drake, in a flat voice.

Novak hands her the device. She reaches out to grab it. Marcus sees her left hand is shaking. *Great.*

52: INTERFACE

"Just click your heels." What the fuck does that even mean? Elena tries using the interface aboard the *Skylark* to see what she can do with it. The only thing she learns is that the metallic helmet is a good fit. It sits atop her head, surprisingly light, the thin metal feeling cold. The interface rests over her grafts in the front and covers the back of her head all the way down to her neck. On the *Skylark*, the device does nothing.

I hope it's not a dud. That would complicate things. A lot.

"Are you sure this will work?" she asks Commander Hale.

"Positive," he says, though his tone doesn't match the conviction of his answer. "You'll see when we're inside."

"Do you know how I'm supposed to use it?"

"It's … intuitive. Really hard to explain, but easy to figure out."

Elena wonders. Her expression must show it.

"I'm not being glib," he adds, "that's what our volunteer told us. He really struggled during the debrief."

"Struggled how?"

"To put what he did into words. To explain how he interacted with the ship. The results were clear to see, the method, at least according to him, indescribable."

"Did the," she wants to say *test subject*, catches herself, "*volunteer* make the ship jump?"

"Yes. A small jump, keeping it in the sector. He relocated it to the current coordinates."

That sounds more encouraging. Distance doesn't matter anyway; a jump is a jump. She won't be the first one to attempt this.

"And he really couldn't explain how he did it?"

"Negative. He took a long time to write a report. It was full of metaphors, very little practical information. But he was able to make the ship jump. You will be able to do it too."

Elena has her doubts but keeps them to herself as the *Skylark* closes in on the alien ship. Ingram, Commander Hale, everyone is saying the thing is self-explanatory and she will get the hang of it as soon as she tries it. If it's so straightforward, why can't anyone explain it? Then there's the bit about possibly getting in touch with the Tauran Consensus. About them lying. She just wants to get out of here. Pain keeps flaring up, making it hard for her to focus.

She notices how tense Wade is, tenser than she's ever seen him before. The closer they get to the alien ship, the more out of character he seems. Losing Anders at Eureka Base really took its toll on him. She empathizes, thinks of Terek again.

She is about to say something to him when he snaps at Commander Hale.

"With all due respect, Commander, can you please be a little bit more fucking clear?"

Wow, thinks Elena.

"I need an accurate risk assessment if my team is going in," Wade continues.

She expects Hale to react negatively to this outburst, but Hale doesn't seem to mind. Good. The last thing they need is infighting. Hale gives them more details, does a quick Q&A. It doesn't sound good. It sounds like the ship might decide, at any moment, to vent them out into space. Or worse. She understands why Wade is on edge.

He's been here before, knows how dangerous Derelict A1X-VD2 can be.

Elena doesn't feel great either. Her stomach is bothering her again, it started as soon as they left the *Sovereign*, and it hasn't gotten any better. Quite the opposite.

She half-listens to Wade getting everyone prepped for boarding, echoes the Vanguard's "hooyah," then they're aboard the ship, walking through the alien corridors, holding their breath after each step.

She looks around, sees the glistening walls with their strange metallic braces that seem to absorb light. In different circumstances, she would feel awe. Her strange mission got her aboard a Tauran ship. She is one of the few humans to ever step foot on one. A ship built by the first alien civilization humanity ever encountered. It should feel monumental. But she is in pain, she uses all her willpower to put one foot in front of the other.

The spaces are larger, wider and taller than any ship she's been on. Larger to accommodate creatures like the one the team encountered at Eureka Base. An alien arthropod. She imagines a bunch of giant crabs scurrying around, shudders at the thought.

A lot more space on the Tauran ship, but their path is much narrower. They're following the white paint markings, careful to avoid the areas marked yellow and red. They can't afford a misstep, not without EV suits. And even those might not help, it sounds like, not against a chemical attack.

As they make slow progress, Elena feels worse and worse. The artificial lights placed all around the ship are starting to bother her eye. She should've asked the medic for some stims. Just until they're out of the sector. Withdrawal or not, she needs to be sharp, and this is not it. Extreme circumstances and all.

She tries to get her mind off the pain. Kaela is walking next to her, head down, looking positively terrified.

"Did you get a chance to look at the digicard?" she asks her.

"I did, aboard the *Sovereign*."

"What's on it?"

"Data," says Kaela. "A lot of data. I didn't think a lab can produce so much data."

"What do you mean?"

"Multiple exabytes. What in the world were they studying?"

Vesper, who is walking in front of them, turns her head at that. But she doesn't say anything, turns back and keeps walking. Elena wants to ask a follow-up question, but a pang inside her gut interrupts her train of thought. She grunts, takes a few more steps. The elusive question is about to come back to her when Wade, who is point, asks loudly, "What now, Commander?"

She looks ahead to see they hit a dead end.

"Sir!" Wade calls.

Commander Hale, from behind her, says, "Alternate path. Give me a second."

They have to backtrack.

They turn around, start going back the way they came. Elena's question is forgotten as they continue on, walking carefully, turning left and right as guided by Santos, Commander Hale, and their nav path. Her internal compass is all out of whack, but she feels bad enough that she isn't even trying to get her bearings. She's just following the people in front of her, focusing on stepping within the safe lines. She hopes they're getting close, she's not sure if she can hold it together for much longer. *One final push!* she tells herself. Just a little bit more. Then, hopefully, the interface works, and they get out of here. Or it doesn't, in which case it doesn't really matter.

The interface must work. She reminds herself this is not about her. It's about the crew of the *Charon*. She is their only way out. It's about her fellow Vanguards. It's about the people of the sector; everything hinges on the damn thing working.

They take another left turn, and the already oversized corridor opens up into a room as large as a hangar. The space is illuminated by floodlights. Strange devices are spread all around. The ground is painted with arrows and inscrutable descriptions. She doesn't even try to make sense of them.

She looks around, but no matter which direction she turns her head towards, bright lights meet her eye. Brighter than any other place on the ship. Her migraine intensifies.

"The interface should work here," Hale tells her.

"Great!" she says, halfheartedly.

Novak, who was carrying the interface, offers it to her. She reaches out with both hands to grab it, notices her left hand is shaking. She grips it, relying on her prosthetic to keep it steady. She realizes she is the center of attention. Even though the mysteries of the alien ship are around them, all eyes are on her. It's the moment of truth. She dons the device again.

It feels as cold as it did the first time she tried it. She welcomes it, its metallic touch seems to ease up her headache. Just a little bit, but she would take anything right about now.

At first, she doesn't notice anything different than when she tried it on the *Skylark*. She is about to say the same to Hale when she senses ... something. A presence. It starts as a vague feeling, then quickly grows into a certainty. There's something nearby. An ancient instinct, from deep within her hypothalamus, warns her she is close to a sleeping giant. She tries to pinpoint the presence. It's not behind her, it's not next to her, it's all around. The sensation is powerful.

She closes her eye.

She reaches out with her mind, trying to get a better sense of it.

The giant stirs, wakes from its slumber. The interface translates the ship's action into signals her mind can process. Her senses are suddenly flooded with a synesthetic tsunami. Bright, warm morning sun rays on her face. The bitter taste of caffeine drops. The relaxing feeling of a yawn. The smell of dew.

The combined effect is overwhelming. She opens her eye.

"Wow."

She stumbles backwards a step, grabs onto Kaela for balance. She now understands. Without her NSRS, without the limited bandwidth, she can imagine how someone could easily drown under such a tide of sensations.

"You OK?" Jaxon asks her.

She nods, tentatively.

"I think so. It's …" She trails off.

She wants to describe to Jaxon what just transpired but struggles to put it into terms he could understand. She looks around, sees every single member of their party waiting for her to say something, but there are no words for what she experienced. Now she gets what Commander Hale was saying, how the volunteer couldn't articulate his interaction with the ship. She can't either. She settles for, "It's awake," then closes her eye again.

The feeling of that presence is back, stronger than ever. *What are you?* she wonders. This was supposed to be a private thought, but the inter-face works its magic, translates her thought. The ship picks up her question. It responds.

A whale swimming alone through an endless ocean. The cold emptiness of interstellar space. An ancient saxophone playing a nostalgic tune. A feeling of confusion, disorientation.

The ship is hurt, lost. It resonates with her. She was deep under-ground inside a hive, shot, dying. She is trapped in Sector 36, her body barely holding together. It's just a whirlwind of feelings, memories, she doesn't even string them into words before the ship replies.

She feels the warmth of a hug, the taste of comfort food, the weight of a blanket, a hand on her shoulder. Is the ship comforting her? Is it comforting itself? The hand on her shoulder, she realizes, is not part of their strange conversation. It's Rynn's hand, gently shaking her to get her to open her eye.

"We've got incoming," he says. Then, explaining, "I've been connecting to the *Skylark*'s opticals from time to time. Watching our back."

She gets online as the others embed, all wanting to see what Rynn saw. Three Tauran ships are approaching. From the same direction they came in from, which can only mean the *Sovereign* was not able to hold them off.

"Did you get the hang of it, Captain?" Hale asks her. "Whatever you need to do, better do it fast."

She is not sure she got the hang of it. She did communicate with the ship though, in some strange, multi-sensory language. How will she tell it to jump out of the sector?

She closes her eye.

The giant she woke is no longer alone. There's an orca pod, breaching and diving together. A barbershop quartet, singing its layered tune. A hearty stew with a cornucopia of flavors. The feeling of belonging.

Elena quickly grasps she is sensing the other ships. But it's more than that. A whole, larger than the sum of its parts. It's not a quartet; it's a million voices. It's vast, all-encompassing.

"The Tauran Consensus," she whispers.

53: ENHANCED INTERROGATION

Vesper rose quickly through the ranks of Abyssal Mining Consortium's Competitive Research Division to become a commissar. She started with fieldwork. She didn't particularly enjoy it but did a competent job and worked very hard. With a combination of luck and skill, she moved up to the command center. She specialized in intel and cross-group coordination, ended up designing and overseeing paramilitary and intelligence operations.

She jumped at the opportunity to transfer to Forge. After the contested Abyssal and Titanforge merger, then the Tauran War, Sector 36 seemed like a great opportunity for career growth, a place to make an impact. Her partner didn't see it the same way, complained about the living conditions in the hives, about the instability caused by the recent war, about yet another relocation. She chose her career; they broke up.

As soon as she translated in, she dove into the work, poring over all available reports and trying to get the lay of the land. The puzzle she was assigned to crack was the Tauran War. Abyssal needed definitive answers to several questions: Why did the Taurans attack? What technology did they possess? Why did they retreat?

Competitive Research had a lot of intel. Too much, it turned out—some of it was contradictory. They gathered data using field agents, by putting out anonymous bids, and by nurturing a network of leakers. Some intel, she suspected, was fed to them by counterintelligence, intentionally bad.

Ingram, the Omega AI in charge of the sector, oversaw the response to the threat, but had been cagey with the details. Several official requests for information were ignored or outright rejected. Official statements were paper-thin.

She kept looking at the pieces, trying to form the elusive complete picture.

Why did the Taurans attack? Because of NS-36-A. That much was clear. The neutron star exhibited anomalies ever since the sector was colonized. Ingram established a research lab. They ran experiments. Here, the truth became muddy: some leaks talked about the neutron star affecting quantum compute; others talked about it affecting the geometry of spacetime; more outlandish claims, arriving via anonymous transactions, said the star was not a star at all, rather, it was an alien device.

Whatever it was, it was important. Abyssal wanted in on the discovery. As soon as its value became evident, following the Tauran incursion, the company started amassing troops around Forge for a potential future hostile takeover of the system. NS-36-A belonged in the private sector.

Second question: What technology did the Taurans possess? Based on the military's ability to hold them back, their technology didn't seem more advanced than what the public considered state of the art. Not the kind of technology that would enable them to forge a neutron star. But then there was Echo Point, a mega-city wiped out with a single hit. The strange movement patterns of the Tauran fleet, approaching in small FTL leaps.

What started as a rumor, but was soon confirmed through independent sources—individuals, some under duress, backing the claims—was that Ingram secured a large Tauran vessel and was reverse-engineering it somewhere inside the sector. The Derelict A1X-VD2 became an important business objective. Its location was, unfortunately, kept well hidden. A needle in the haystack, lost somewhere inside the sector's volume. They kept searching.

Then there was the Tauran Consensus. This had been reported on exclusively by Ingram, so it was hard to make heads or tails of it, and details were lacking. Some sort of mind-meld, a collective intelligence it negotiated with when they discussed the terms of the truce. Vesper had her doubts; it sounded too much like a red herring.

And, speaking of the truce, the last question on her list: Why did the Taurans retreat? She thought the devastation brought to Echo Point would have tilted the scale in their favor. They could repeat the trick over, say, Nova Prime City. Why did they retreat from the sector? What did Ingram give them in return?

Too many questions, but they weren't making any progress. The work that her arm of the Competitive Research Division was responsible for was stagnating. They were at risk of missing their goals for the fiscal cycle and stress was building up. She got called into status report meetings more often, had to prepare more presentations, more status reports.

Then—an unexpected boon. They received an anonymous tip, someone answering one of their bids: a high-value target from Eureka Base went to Verdant. Finally, a chance to make some progress! They organized a search and retrieval op. It failed; they couldn't find the target.

She was restless. She lost sleep trying to divine how their target vanished. The constant pressure from her superiors started getting to her. She stopped eating again. She was always a high performer; she couldn't afford failure.

After a couple of weeks of going around in circles, the next breakthrough came from the most unexpected place: their Human Resources division. The high-value target, Doctor Linton, applied for corporate citizenship. Under a pseudonym, of course. HR flagged his application as soon as he arrived, but it somehow got lost in the reams of paperwork. The influx of people from across the sector strained their intake system. The flagged application was rediscovered many days later, while preparing a monthly report. The doctor had been here for a while, while they were turning Verdant upside down to find him!

Vesper consulted with Arcturus. Coming from Eureka Base, the doctor must have valuable intel. The Omega could have attempted to pluck it out of his brain directly, but there was some risk of damaging the wetware, breaking him before they could extract every nugget. The best path forward was a different approach: enhanced interrogation. She was to ensure a complete information transfer.

Unpleasant business for sure, but part of the job description. She decided to handle it herself. She didn't want to force it on others. Plus, she didn't trust the team she was assigned here to do a good job of it. They were unprofessional, not what she expected from veterans of the Titanforge merger.

She took Sergeant Mason and Private Walter with her, went to Doctor Linton's unit, overrode the door locks, and dragged him out of his bed.

He managed an, "Excuse me?" but didn't fight back. He pissed himself as they were getting him out of his unit. Unpleasant indeed.

They descended to the lower levels of the hive, a section reserved for Competitive Research projects. She had a unit cleared; everything removed except a chair and a table.

Mason and Walter strapped the doctor to the chair. She could see he was terrified, mumbling incoherently, hoped he would talk from the start, not make this worse than it had to be.

She showed him the cuffs: "VoidTech enhanced interrogation cuffs. Let me give you a walk-through."

This, she hoped, would convince him to get talking.

"Without laying a feather on you, we can simulate all sorts of unpleasantries. Pulling fingernails ..."

Their high-value target screamed.

"... or finger hammering ..."

He screamed again, kept screaming.

"... and the beauty of it is we can go on indefinitely. Now tell me everything you know, doctor."

Vesper didn't enjoy this, not one bit. She was not a sadist. She had a job, she sacrificed a lot for this, and Doctor Linton was the missing piece to their uncrackable puzzle, the solution to their unsolvable problem.

She was right, the initial demo got him going.

He told them about NS-36-A. The reason the Taurans attacked. He was blabbering but confirmed some of the data they had. An alien device. Not Taurans, older.

"What's its purpose?" she demanded.

Through tears, he told them. He told them the information he had, his own suppositions. She took notes, would sort things out later: an alien device that interferes with quantum compute specifically; a device that, in Doctor Linton's opinion, was driving Ingram insane; a device that, once you got to the bottom of it, was an anti-Omega weapon; a device that they accidentally caused to call out to the Taurans.

Interesting, Vesper thought. An anti-Omega weapon.

"I trust you, you know," she told the target, "but I need to make sure."

She repeated the questions, made sure Doctor Linton wasn't making shit up. The intel they were extracting was too vital to afford any procedural oversight.

Doctor Linton screamed, cried, talked. Confirmed.

Then she moved on to the Taurans.

"Where is Derelict A1X-VD2?"

"I don't know."

She found this highly unlikely. Doctor Linton, according to the file they had on him, was at Eureka Base for quite a while. Before the hostilities started. He spent months at the research lab.

"I don't like to see you suffer, doctor. I'm a professional," she said. "I just need to make sure."

They hooked him up to a lie detector, so they could tell when he is making things up. She watched it light up like a Christmas tree when he gave them the alien ship's location.

"Wrong."

"I don't know!"

She pushed him a bit more—she had to be certain. But it became evident, Doctor Linton had no idea where the alien ship was. She had to move on.

"Why did the Taurans retreat?"

"A truce. A truce with Ingram. Please!" He was babbling, talking fast, crying.

"You're keeping something from us."

"I'll tell you! I'll tell you!"

He talked. At first, an incoherent story. Then, something sounding too far-fetched to believe. But the lie detector kept silent. Either Doctor Linton was telling the truth, or he was convinced, to his very core, that it was the truth.

"Echo Point. The Taurans. It wasn't them!"

"What?"

"The Taurans fought Ingram. They reject AI."

He was straining to talk, snot coming out of his nose.

"They did not drop a bomb on Echo Point. Ingram did!"

Vesper had to take another look at the lie detector, make sure. Ingram was responsible for Sector 36, for the civilians living here.

"The truce! It killed millions, threatened the Taurans to repeat it on all the colonies here. They retreated."

She needed a break. She let Sergeant Mason and Private Walter watch over the prisoner, stepped outside to digest what she just learned. *I need a shower*, she thought while walking out the door. It had been a while since she had to do this. Had she lost her nerve?

In the end, they learned quite a lot from the doctor. Ingram was able to perfect the gray goo weapon, the controversial weapon Void-Tech had been wrestling with for the better part of a decade. Deployed it on Echo Point, to make the Taurans retreat. The aliens came for the anti-Omega weapon. They came to fight Ingram, not humans. Quite the opposite, they left hoping to save lives. *How interesting*, she thought.

It really helped her put things into perspective. Regardless of the methods Competitive Research employed, their enemy was a mass murderer. They were on the right side of history, the target wasn't. And Ingram was dangerous, a lot more dangerous than anticipated.

Arcturus was wise to plot a takeover of the lab and the alien weapon. Ingram, and by extension the AI Council, couldn't be trusted with that power.

She went back inside, made sure no secrets were kept. With a little less empathy. The doctor came from Eureka Base; he must've been complicit. Whatever his exact job was, he was part of the enterprise, must've had his small contribution towards obliterating Echo Point.

"Talk!"

"Code words! I had one code word to request extraction."

He started talking about Spark, about an extraction plan. He was running away from Ingram.

She doubted it, probed him harder. Doctor Linton cried.

It took a while to convince her there was nothing left, but eventually she was convinced. Someone coming to pick him up. Someone from outside the sector. Someone with ties to Spark. They would have to do some data mining to find out who. On the plus side, most of the ships that were translating into the sector by then were military. They would only have to search for a passenger that didn't belong. They had people ready at the Gateway Ring.

She nodded to Sergeant Mason, who zapped the doctor with a microwave gun.

"Get rid of him," she told him.

What they had just done wasn't technically unlawful, given that the doctor applied for corporate citizenship, was on Forge on a work visa, and all of this transpired on corporate property. That said, it was a gray enough area that it was best to avoid further complications. Minimize the paperwork, dispose of what was left of the target.

Competitive Research made a huge leap forward. The puzzle was all but solved, the division objectives met. A welcomed change of fortune. And a good reminder for her that she hated working in the field, that she would have much preferred being in the command center. She took a long shower once it was over and her report sent out, slept for ten hours, and even had breakfast.

54: CONSENSUS

"Elena, what's going on?" someone asks her, but she barely hears. She is engulfed in the immensity of the Tauran Consensus. She is standing on the shore, in front of an incoming mile-high wave. She is a leaf in the path of a tornado. A grain of sand on the beach. She is going to get swept up at any moment. She reaches for the helmet, wants to take it off, but before she gets a chance to do it, the wave crashes, the tornado hits. She becomes a part of it. It doesn't feel threatening at all.

"They're still incoming," says Rynn from next to her.

But they're trying to assuage her fear. She feels warmth. The sense of camaraderie, going through STARS with her teammates, supporting each other. Orchestral music in perfect harmony. The purr of her old pet cat.

She remembers Ingram's words. *If you encounter the Tauran Consensus, it will lie to you.* But those were just words. This is a multi-sensory declaration of friendship. She feels it resonate deep inside her. *It will lie to you.*

She opens her eye. The sensations ebb, take a back seat inside her mind as she looks around the room.

"They ... I think they don't mean us harm."

"Are you sure about this?" Wade asks her.

"The Tauran ships stopped," says Rynn.

She gets online briefly to assess the situation herself, through the *Skylark*'s opticals. The three alien ships are close, but they are not attacking.

"Jump us out of here," says Jaxon.

Vesper mouths something.

Elena ignores both of them, closes her eye, gets back to the Consensus.

Are you going to harm us? she asks, hoping the interface will repeat its trick, translate this into something meaningful for the ship, for the Taurans.

The response is almost instant. The smell of lavender. A white flag flapping in the wind. The taste of warm bread fresh out of the oven. The feeling of safety, something she hasn't felt in a long time, not since she left Aurelia.

Then why? she asks. *Why all of this? The war?* Does she really expect a coherent answer? Do all the sensations the interface is feeding her even tell her anything? Or is she just making up the meaning? *It will lie to you.* Regardless, the weird interaction makes her feel better. The smorgasbord of feelings overrides her nagging pain. She feels better while talking to it.

The Consensus responds, despite her doubts. She feels cold. The smell of ozone. A dissonant synthesized tune. The taste of copper. Lack of emotion, aloofness, inhumanity.

The reason for the war, she realizes. She is trying to make sense of the answer. Cold, artificial, inhuman. *Ingram?* Are they saying they are warring against the Omega?

The cold seeps into her bones. The smell of ozone becomes over-powering. The synthesizer gets louder, even more erratic. The taste of copper intensifies, makes her gag.

That's a *yes*, she realizes. The Taurans are here for Ingram.

"Captain Drake!"

Wade's voice brings her back to the room. He is standing right next to her, watching her with a deep frown. "We need to go."

"No, we're safe. I'm … talking to them."

"Please," he says.

"I'll do my best," she says, closes her eye again.

Not time to go. Not quite yet. She needs a few more questions answered.

What about Echo Point? she asks. *Why did you do that?*

The answer is a loud wail. A violin playing the saddest of songs. The taste of lemons. A cloudy sky. The smell of rain.

They regret it, she realizes. Was it an accident? An overreaction? Ingram told her part of the truce was atonement for Echo Point. But something doesn't add up. She wishes the interface could give her something more concrete.

Why are you back then? she asks. The truce was broken, the Taurans returned too early.

The heat of an all-consuming fire. The smell of ash. A deafening silence. Pitch-black darkness. The taste of rotten food.

Came back to finish the job? Burn everything? Wipe out Sector 36? Suddenly, the good feelings her interaction with the Consensus started with are gone. These last answers are scary, menacing. No, beyond that, they convey finality. She is no longer certain the Taurans mean them no harm. The Tauran Consensus might want the whole sector destroyed. Maybe all sectors.

"Elena!"

She opens her eye. They're all watching her. She is still trying to make sense of the bizarre dialogue she is having with an alien collective consciousness. Needs more time.

"I'm trying," she lies to them. "It's not that easy."

She sees Commander Hale nod in assent. He's probably seen similar struggles with the previous test subject. Volunteer. And that was without the Tauran Consensus in play, no other Tauran ships nearby, just communing with the slumbering giant.

She thinks fast. Why aren't the Taurans attacking them? There's a simple explanation for that: the ship is alive; it's part of the whole. They wouldn't harm it. But then why isn't the ship, now fully awake as far as she can tell, just expelling them into space? It has been prone to do that before. And what about their reassurance, they all but spelled out "we come in peace" when she worried about an imminent attack. She can't make sense of it, feels an answer is within reach but can't quite grasp it.

She closes her eye.

Will you get us out of here? she asks. Of course, her question is more than just a sentence. It's the meaning of "here," Sector 36, the isolation, the deaths; it's the meaning of "out of here," home, Aurelia, comfort. The interface, Elena hopes, is good enough to extract the intention behind the words.

A bird spreading its wings, taking flight. The taste of her favorite home-cooked meal, which only her dad can make just so. The color green—a healthy shade of green, the green of grass and trees in the summer, not the putrid green of the Viridian Shroud Nebula. A piano chord resolving.

She interprets the answer as "yes." The ship will get them out of here. Then what about all the death and destruction? What is she missing? Why did her question about Echo Point, her question about their return, elicit such desolate responses? *It will lie to you,* said Ingram. But is it? Is the Consensus lying to her? Or was Ingram lying? They said the reason for the war was Ingram. They established a truce, because of Echo Point. Then they came back to cause even more death? No. They came back *because* of all the death.

It clicks. A piece falls into place. All the death, the ash, the darkness —it's not an objective, it's a reason. Arcturus destroyed the Gateway Ring, bombarded Nova Prime City, killed hundreds of millions.

You're here for *us?* Because *of what Arcturus did?*

The deep savoriness of umami. The sound of a heartbeat. The iridescence of shifting hues held together on a common surface. The warmth of skin-on-skin contact.

Humans and Taurans, fighting against the Omegas. It sounds … too good to be true. *It will lie to you.* She won't swallow it. Not after Echo Point. Not after a war with so many casualties. Not after a Tauran killed Anders, a Vanguard, deep inside Eureka Base. Killed him by ripping him in two, according to Wade. There's no camaraderie in that, no compassion, no two hearts following the same drumbeat.

The interface performs its single strange purpose: it translates her train of thought, translates back an answer.

The feeling of being alone and scared. The taste of fear. An animal isolated from its pack. The deep, rich red of blood, of rage. The sour smell of adrenaline. The guttural sound of a growling dog.

She is trying to make sense of it. Was that the Tauran that killed Anders? Isolated, scared, lashing out? She believes she understands. The Tauran Consensus is a sum greater than its parts. The individual is not as rational as the whole. Isolated, they act on impulse. It adds up. It's still utterly otherworldly. Anders is still dead, she is talking to something so different that she needs an intermediating device and needs her grafts to act as filters.

She can even understand military engagements, fire when fired upon. Or shoot first. Rules of engagement, warriors facing warriors. But what about Echo Point? What is the reason for that? All the innocent lives snuffed out there?

"Are you getting the hang of it?" This from Jaxon, in a soft voice. He is touching her arm, sounding calm. Like he is intentionally trying not to pressure her, while nevertheless urging her along.

She opens her eye, looks around. Jaxon, Kaela, Rynn are there. She owes them a ticket out of here. Her fellow Vanguards, Wade, Howard, Santos, Novak, Kim, she wants to get them out too. Commander Hale and Vesper, the woman they rescued, they're all here, depending on her. Nobody deserves to be stuck here, cut away from the rest of the world.

She is their way out. She is responsible for them. The more time she spends with the interface, the more time until they are out of Sector 36. And even her short, strange dialogue is a gamble. *It will lie to you.* The Taurans might just be feeding her bullshit, buying time.

For what, though? She still depends on the ship to be willing to jump. She is just the conduit. If the Taurans wanted them dead, they would've killed them already, right?

She gives herself one more question. One more question to ask, then she will talk the ship into taking them away from here. Back home.

"Almost," she lies again. "Almost."

One more question. *Make it a good one.*

At first, she draws a blank. She wants to understand so much. And she hasn't really learned a lot so far, has she? She could spend a long time asking follow-up questions, trying to confirm that the bursts of sensation the interface feeds her actually mean what she thinks they mean.

No time for that though. Her sense of duty is strong. One more question, then get out of here.

She comes up with one. Maybe not the perfect question, but an important question, something that she would like to know the answer to: *When will the war end?*

She acknowledges the question is a hard one to answer in the language they're speaking. Still, she'd like to know.

The answer comes back: Grass, growing atop some old, rusted piece of machinery. Birdsong. The fresh crunch of raw celery. The smell of pine.

She finds this unsatisfactory, can't make heads or tails of the answer. That said, it is time to go. She can think about the meaning of her conversation with the Consensus later. By now she has a good sense of how to do it, how she will steer the ship.

She takes one last look around the room before asking the ship to take them out of here. She hopes it's not all a Tauran lie, that the ship won't decide to expunge them instead. Or jump inside a star. Hopes this won't be a final look at the people she is trying to save.

"Let's get out of here," she tells them.

"Wait!" says Vesper.

This catches her off guard. Vesper, who's been begging her to get her out of the sector.

"The digicard ... get rid of it," she continues.

Fuck, Elena thinks, *I knew something was off with her!* She should *always* trust her instincts.

"Why?"

"What do you think is on it?" asks Vesper, but it's a question addressed to the whole room.

"Captain, let's go!" Wade is anxious to get out of here, get away from the ship.

Kaela, who analyzed it earlier, says, "Eureka Lab science stuff."

"Wasn't it a bit too much of it?"

"I ... guess. I'm no physicist."

Kaela sounds doubtful. Vesper seems to know way more than she should for an innocent geologist. Elena is not happy about this latest curve ball.

"I'll tell you what all that data is," Vesper goes on, "steganography. An Ingram state dump. It's been all but wiped out, so it's using you to hitch a ride out of Sector 36."

Steganography. She knew something was wrong from the get-go. Vesper is no innocent geologist, she's a spook. A snake amidst them. At this point, Elena doesn't even care who she is working for, she reaches into her waistband and pulls out her Noctics.

55: PRISONER'S DILEMMA

She thrives on information, and while she doesn't know everything, she knows enough to easily piece things together. It doesn't seem like the Vanguards or the smugglers they picked up have any idea of what really happened on Echo Point. Commander Hale doesn't seem to know either, or he is doing a good job concealing it. But she does know. She also knows the official terms of the truce Ingram negotiated are obvious bullshit—the Taurans don't need to atone for Echo Point, they didn't cause it, even though they disappeared right after.

Then Arcturus went genocidal too, destroyed the Gateway Ring, leveled Nova Prime City, and the Taurans are back.

If she needs any more confirmation, Elena Drake gives it to her when she tells everyone, "No, we're safe. I'm talking to them." The Tauran Consensus. It means them no harm.

She would bet money the Taurans were waging war against Ingram, not humans. The NS-36-A device scrambled its brain just by virtue of proximity. It is an anti-Omega device and the Taurans came to claim it.

Ingram annihilated a human settlement just to show them what it can do. They left. Did it promise them no further loss of life? Then

Arcturus ended even more lives than Ingram as collateral and brought them back.

And now Elena is communing with them. Vesper would love to ask her own questions. Or, the next best thing, have Elena ask those questions. But how would a mere geologist and abuse victim (let's not think about that!) know any of this? The answer: she wouldn't.

I hate fieldwork, she thinks for the millionth time. She is not good at improvising, can't come up with a reasonable explanation for her knowledge. Keeps quiet.

Her gears keep turning though. She wanted to know what's on the digicard. Exabytes of data, said Kaela. Exabytes! She was right to doubt a lab could produce so much, regardless of what they were studying. Vesper knows what is on that digicard. And they're going to take it outside of Sector 36. Big mistake.

She watches Elena straining with her eye closed, in her intimate conversation with the Tauran Consensus, trying to come up with a logical next step. Then suddenly, it's over. Elena opens her eye, looks around.

"Let's get out of here," she says.

The word comes out before she even realizes: "Wait!"

Shit. She convinced Elena to bring her with. She was this close to getting out of this accursed place. She just had to keep her mouth shut.

"What?" asks Elena, suddenly looking suspicious.

In for a penny, in for a pound, Vesper thinks.

"That digicard … get rid of it."

She talks slow, tries to come up with some good arguments that wouldn't compromise her, but she didn't prep for this scenario. Unlike her burner identities, which she diligently built for various contingencies, this is improv. And she's not good at improv. Fucking hates fieldwork.

"Why?" asks Elena.

"What do you think is on it?" she asks, looks around the room to let people know the question is addressed to everyone.

"Captain, let's go!" says Wade.

"Eureka Lab science stuff," says Kaela. She really hoped the digital specialist would've picked up on the hidden payload. She seemed talented.

"Wasn't it a bit too much of it?" Vesper asks, locking eyes with Kaela, trying to nudge her in the right direction.

"I ... guess. I'm no physicist."

Like it matters. Vesper is no physicist either. But she knows how these things are done.

"I'll tell you what all that data is: steganography. An Ingram state dump. It's been all but wiped out, so it's using you to hitch a ride out of Sector 36." What else would it hide on there? Now that it's been ripped to pieces and all but annihilated.

As she's finishing the sentence, she sees Elena reaching. She reaches for her weapon too, instinctively. In the blink of an eye, the conversation turns uncivilized. Elena is pointing a high-caliber Noctics at her face. Her trusty Graver is aimed at Elena's forehead.

"Who the fuck are you?" Elena says, stressing every syllable.

She chances a sideways glance. Wade has his rifle pointed at her. The other Vanguards must be doing the same, but she can't chance a look.

Fuck, why did you do that? Maybe she didn't really want to get out of Sector 36. Maybe life as a broken ronin is not for her. Maybe what happened to her should never make its way outside the Viridian Shroud. But that train of thought leads nowhere. She could've just as well pulled the Graver on herself. This isn't suicide by Vanguard, it's doing the right thing.

The scene is frozen. Nobody dares making a move. Elena Drake is their only ticket out, and she has a gun to her head. If she shoots, regardless of what happens to her, they're all stuck here. And, it seems, nobody wants that.

"Lady, what do you think you're doing?" Wade says. "You know who you're fucking with?"

She does.

"We're Vanguard. Put that gun down and you might yet survive this."

She doesn't believe him. She just pulled a gun on a Vanguard, in a room full of them. Because she couldn't shut her stupid mouth—so uncharacteristic. What changed? (You know what changed!) *I hate field-work!* Her only way out of this is to reason with Elena.

"Wait!" she says again. "Just listen to me, OK?"

Nobody says anything.

Fuck. She is a professional. There's still a way to save this. They're reasonable people. She can convince them. Or die trying.

"You don't know what happened on Echo Point, right?"

She speaks fast now; she feels her clock running out. She has her gun pointed at their ticket out of here, but she's in the shark tank. They're elite killers. They *love* fieldwork, that's the only fucking thing they're good at.

"Ingram! It killed the colony."

She waits for a reaction, but besides a gasp from Kaela, there's silence. Elena is stone-faced. She imagines Wade is the same way, though she doesn't chance taking her eyes away from where she is pointing her gun.

"Why do you think the Taurans don't want to hurt us? Left right after Echo Point, and came back once Arcturus started killing people? Think about it!"

This line of reasoning has its intended effect. Elena's remaining eye grows wider.

"How?" she hears Santos from somewhere behind her.

"The gray goo is not Tauran tech. Ingram figured it out. I bet you anything it's part of the payload on that digicard."

They're listening now. The guns don't get lowered though.

"Lieutenant Wade," she says, "you've been on this ship right after Ingram captured it, right?" She overheard this repeatedly during the numerous conversations aboard the *Skylark* and Commander Hale said as much. She takes a shot in the dark, this one she doesn't know for sure, but it would add up: "There was no trace of Taurans on this ship, was there? You know why? Because Ingram used the same fucking gray goo weapon here too! It ate through them, left the ship intact."

Elena is lowering her weapon. That's a good sign. A great sign. But she is still surrounded by Vanguards. She can't afford to lower her Graver. Elena has backup, she doesn't. She keeps her pistol trained on

Elena's forehead. If she mirrors Elena's gesture, she is dead. She needs to keep the conversation going, convince them.

"Who are you?" Elena asks again, less stern this time, with more genuine curiosity.

"Abyssal Mining Competitive Research," she replies. "Intelligence," to make sure they all understand.

She sees Elena mouth what must be, "I fucking knew it," sees her raising her gun back up. *Fuck.* This isn't going as she was hoping.

"Look, I was on an Abyssal destroyer. Ran away when they started bombarding Nova Prime City. I didn't want to be part of any of that shit. That's why I couldn't go to Forge. Ended up on Echo Point. Later realized you have a way out of the sector. I'm done with Abyssal, done with Arcturus. Just want to get out. But …" The reason she opened her mouth in the first place, the reason she didn't just stay quiet and get out, to be fully truthful to them (and herself). "Ingram should die here. Don't take it out of the sector. Please!"

"Why?" Elena asks the follow-up question immediately. Like the gray goo reason wasn't good enough. Like she wants her to wrap up and put her gun down.

"NS-36-A is an anti-Omega device. Arcturus was planning to seize it. Ingram, I'm sure, had its own plans."

She hears a couple of gasps at that, can't tell who they're coming from. She is still watching Elena intently, aiming the Graver at her. Her arms are getting tired, it's harder and harder to keep the weapon still.

"You saw what happened in Sector 36 over it. Do you want to hand it to the AI Council? Ingram fucking eradicated Echo Point. Do you trust the AI Council with a weapon that would allow them to kill other Omegas?"

"Do you trust Arcturus with it?" Elena retorts. Fair point.

"No! Fuck! I didn't think … I had no idea it was going to … kill so many people." She is about to get uncharacteristically emotional, the surprise of it, the feeling of betrayal resurfacing, but she is still pointing a gun at Elena's face and can't flinch.

"Please," she says, "don't take that digicard out of Sector 36. It's Ingram. It's the perfected gray goo, the Omega-killing device. Let it all vanish here."

"Kaela," Elena says, "can you confirm any of this?"

"I don't know. I'm not a scientist. I don't know how to read all this data. Can't tell if it makes sense or if it's made up."

"Look for redundancies," Vesper tells her. "Repeated data points. Extraneous stuff. Triple copies with slight anomalies. That's a dead giveaway."

"I ..." starts Kaela.

Wade cuts her off. "We don't have time for this shit. Put your gun down, lady. I'm telling you for the last time. We need to get out of here."

"Just run a basic anomaly detection," Vesper tells Kaela. "There must be tons of redundant data points to mask the payload. It should pop right up."

"Can I have the digicard?" Kaela asks.

Elena looks at someone behind her, nods, says, "Do it!"

"Captain," Howard asks, "is this a good idea?"

"Just do it, Dash," Elena says with authority.

"Aye."

There's some shuffling outside her field of vision. She can guess what's happening—Howard was holding the digicard, she saw him pocket it as they were getting ready to board the alien ship. From the corner of her eye, she sees him handing it to Kaela.

The Graver is getting heavier by the second. She doesn't know how long she can keep it raised.

"I'll need a minute," Kaela says.

"We don't have a minute," Wade replies.

"Give her a minute," says Elena.

Kaela embeds. Vesper knows her life is in the balance, hopes she didn't make another fucking mistake. First one was career-ending. This would be life-ending. She waits for Kaela. The young digital specialist doesn't take a whole minute.

"She's right," Kaela says. "I ... I can't interpret the reports, but it does look like a lot of duplicate data with slight differences across dataframes. Anomalies are high entropy."

"What does that mean?" asks Elena.

"It's very likely there's some hidden message or code within the huge dataset. But I can't tell what it is."

"See?" Vesper asks Elena. "Please, just leave it here."

Elena lowers her weapon again. Fully this time, pointing it at the ground. In her peripheral vision, she sees Howard stepping forward again, getting the digicard from Kaela, stowing it back in one of his pockets.

"Let's think about this for a second," says Elena.

She is the ranking officer. If she asks them to put their guns down, there's still a chance. They can talk this through. Commissar Vesper's final thought is, *I convinced her!* The high-caliber sniper round stops the next thought from forming.

56: FOLD

Something about Vesper had rubbed her the wrong way ever since she first encountered the woman, crying next to the dead bodies of the pilots and Nightmare. The woman took care of her when she was feeling worst, most likely a ploy to hitch a ride out of the sector with them. And she allowed her. Against all her instincts, she let her come with them all the way to Derelict A1X-VD2.

Now she is asking them to ditch the digicard. And she is making a great case for it. Elena is getting convinced. She doesn't trust Vesper, but she trusts Ingram much less. *Fuck.* If the woman is telling the truth, the thing killed everyone on Echo Point. Then it fucked up, is getting destroyed, and trying to scheme its way out of the sector. Playing them like puppets.

"She's right," Kaela says. "I … I can't interpret the reports, but it does look like a lot of duplicate data with slight differences across dataframes. Anomalies are high entropy."

Elena doesn't quite follow all the technical details. She wonders how Vesper got her hands on that gun. It shouldn't have come down to this.

"What does that mean?" she asks Kaela. She needs to understand whether they've truly been duped or Vesper is just bullshitting them. Her gut tells her it's the former.

"There's likely some hidden message or code within the huge dataset. But I can't tell what it is."

No bullshitting after all. It is steganography. Ingram *is* fucking hiding something on that digicard. Even told her to share it with Spark, the smug motherfucker. It must've been convinced whatever it hid in there is obscure enough that Spark would not get to the bottom of it. Omega shit.

"See?" Vesper asks Elena. "Please, leave it here."

The woman is right. She wishes they just talked it out, that she didn't pull out her Noctics. She wasn't expecting Vesper to pull her own gun in response. And now the Vanguards are all pointing weapons and it's going to be challenging to defuse the situation. She will do her best.

"Let's think about this for a second," she says.

She lowers her weapon, pointing it at the ground. She wants to tell Vesper, "We're cool," she wants to tell—order—the other Vanguards to lower their weapons. She doesn't get a chance to do either. The round from Kim's weapon vaporizes Vesper's head. Bits of it fly outside the marked safe zone, splatter on the strange-looking wall. The woman's headless body folds over one of the inscrutable devices spread around the room. The one marked "???"

Through the interface, Elena hears a muted cry, gets a mental image of dead leaves being blown by the wind, tastes rotten meat. With her eye open, the sensations are less overpowering, but it's obvious the ship is aware of Vesper's death. It felt it, or saw it, or used some other indescribable senses.

She holds her breath in anticipation of a reaction. Some ... fragments of Vesper's head went outside the white markings, touched the ship. The ship that is no longer slumbering, rather awake and conversing. Nothing happens. They don't get vented out into space. Corrosive gasses are not dumped on them.

She looks around the room, sees virtually everybody visibly relax after a few seconds of tense waiting. Dodged a bullet. Unlike Vesper.

"Why did you do that?" she asks Kim.

"What do you mean? I had a clear shot. I took it."

"She ... she was making some good points."

"Captain Drake," Wade steps in, "she had a gun on you."

"I had a gun on her. I pulled it first. Then lowered it, we were talking things through."

"You're Vanguard. Turns out she was a fucking spook."

She was. Elena pauses, thinks. Looks around the room. All eyes on her. Except Kaela, who is looking slack-jawed at Vesper's body.

"We were just about to leave. Why would she blow her cover now?" she wonders out loud.

Why did Vesper—who played it so well until now, including convincing everyone to give her a ride out of Sector 36 and, on top of that, procuring a gun—risk it all to beg them not to translate the digicard?

If what she was saying is true, Ingram is a mass murderer. Elena never trusted the Omega. It might be close to dying, and she would be the one giving it a second life outside of Sector 36. Maybe they *should* just leave it here. Whatever is on that card, precious Eureka Base research or not, what difference does it make? The people in the sector are screwed regardless. And their only hope, the point-jump technology, is on the ship. Ingram said the AI Council can reverse-engineer it. Would she be condemning the people here if she wouldn't bring along the darn digicard? The implications of the decision make her already aching head throb. There's so much at stake, so little reliable information.

"What if we do destroy the digicard?" she asks. Maybe get some second opinions. After all, the point-jump technology is the focus of their mission.

"That's not an option, Captain," says Wade.

His instant and decisive reply surprises her.

"What do you mean?"

"The digicard comes with us. Orders."

"Orders?"

Who even knows about the digicard? Plus, according to Captain Dalton, the command structure fell apart.

"Straight from Ingram. Representing the AI Council in the sector.

Top of chain of command. We are to see the digicard safely outside the sector."

The sneaky fucker, Elena thinks.

"Didn't you just hear what Vesper said?" she asks, turns to look at the slumped body, still embracing the "???" alien device, blood slowly pooling at the bottom, covering the white markings.

"She could have been lying," Wade tries.

"How would've that helped her? Look what she got for it."

"Maybe she had bad intel."

"Maybe we have fucking bad intel." Elena raises her voice. This is all fucked up.

"Not our call to make."

Elena sighs. Wade is determined. Ingram must've talked to him at the same time it was conversing with her at Eureka Base. She wonders what the exact orders were. She wonders how far Wade would go to obey them.

"You need me to jump, right? What if I refuse?"

"Don't make me do this, Captain."

"Can you force me to jump?"

Wade looks at her like he just swallowed a lemon, briefly glances over at Jaxon, Rynn, Kaela, then looks back at her.

"Don't make me say it, please."

By now she is all but convinced the digicard is just Ingram in disguise. Ingram, abandoning the sector and its surviving populace to whatever fate may bring them. And using them to do it. She is disgusted by her fellow Vanguards.

"Fucking say it, I want to hear it come out of your mouth. Lieutenant."

He half-raises his rifle, points it towards Jaxon's knees.

"There are people you care about in this room."

He is too ashamed to spell out the threat, but it is obvious, just as she suspected. They are ready to use Jaxon, Kaela, Rynn as leverage. To coerce her to jump. With the digicard.

"Guys," Jaxon says, extending his arms with palms out, conciliatory.

Kaela mutters a, "What?"

Rynn stays quiet, looks from one team member to the other.

"Don't worry," Wade reassures Jaxon, "it won't get to that."

He points his rifle back at the ground.

"I'm sorry, Drake. We've got a direct order. This is happening."

"We're both Vanguard, Wade, how can you do this?"

"It's not my decision," he says, looks around the room at the other Vanguards.

Elena does the same. She looks at Howard, who is watching her with his jaw clenched, steel in his eyes. Santos avoids her gaze. Novak shakes his head, shrugs, but his weapon doesn't move an inch. Kim is farther back, apparently focused on his sniper rifle.

Ingram likely briefed all of them with some bullshit to amplify the importance of the digicard surviving. Probably told them to watch out for dissenters. It's not just Wade. If one of them defects, the others continue the mission. And, unlike her, none of them is indispensable. They're Vanguard and, in any other situation, going blue on blue would be unimaginable. But Ingram spoke poison to each one of them.

"What do you think about this, Commander Hale?" she asks, turning towards their newest party member.

"He doesn't have a say in this," Wade answers on his behalf.

"Fuck," she whispers. Then, louder, "Fuck you, Wade!"

He doesn't say anything to that.

What can she do? She briefly considers pointing the Noctics at her head, blowing her brains out. That would put a dent in Ingram's fucking plan. But how would that help anyone? And the setup is brilliant. She really wants to give the survivors in the sector a way out. Point-jump technology. A way to bootstrap a new jump gate faster. She really cares about the hundreds of millions of people. More immediately, she cares about Kaela, and Rynn, and Jaxon. They're here, right now. Her blowing her own brains out won't help them one bit. Neither would jumping the ship inside a star or any other suicidal way of getting rid of the accursed digicard.

She is tired. In pain. She doesn't have a good hand to play and— fuck it—she wants to go home. Let Ingram escape, let the monster live. She just wants to get out of here.

Maybe, she tries consoling herself, Vesper *was* full of shit. Maybe the digicard *will* fast-track rescuing the people stranded in Sector 36. That would make all of this right. She doesn't believe it for one second.

She sighs again.

"Fuck it, let's get out of here."

"Elena …" Jaxon says.

She looks at him, but he doesn't say anything else.

She closes her eye, tries one last shot in the dark.

Can you help me get rid of the digicard? she asks the ship. *Or the Vanguards,* she wants to add but doesn't. She is not willing to go blue on blue, despite all this bullshit. Plus, it doesn't seem like the ship has any precise internal machinery. Its gas bags and space vents tend to be indiscriminate.

The response is white noise, static. The feeling of unexpressed frustration. The taste of a flat drink. The color beige.

She figured as much. That's a "no" if there ever was one. The interface is, indeed, intuitive.

"Here we go," she tells everyone.

She tells the ship, *Take me home, please.* More than that, she envisions the rolling hills of Aurelia, the unique shade of her home world's sky, her father's cooking, the soft smell of her tabby cat's fur, the feeling of her mother's hug. Home. Easy—like clicking your heels.

———

The ship understands. It doesn't need exact coordinates; it doesn't need to compute a vector. The ship has a completely different understanding of the spacetime manifold. It views it as a set of connected points, the union of the spots its occupants inhabit through time. The topology is a sphere, with the ship at its center, the points on its surface, and an infinitesimally small radius. It just needs to scoot over.

Its current pilot is strange, communication is difficult. Like the one before. And the one before that. And the one before that. It dimly understands why. The Consensus went away, came back. War. It was a prisoner of war. It was in a long coma. It understands the organisms on board are not Tauran. But they are not machines either. Plus, it's not its call to go or refuse. It is, after all, just a vehicle.

It easily identifies the location its inarticulate pilot is trying to point it towards. The vast gulf of space between them and their destination is a non-issue. Neither is the spin of the galaxy. No error corrections needed, no adjustments. Not in the ship's notion of spacetime. It just scoots over.

Spacetime folds, two points that should've been light-millennia away briefly overlap, become the same.

The *Skylark* is suddenly connected to nothing. Scaffolding, similar to a mesh, in the outline of a Tauran ship, envelops only empty space. Derelict A1X-VD2 blinks into shape near Aurelia.

EPILOGUE

57: ICARUS

Even though the alien ship has no opticals they can plug into, the jump is obvious to all of them. Rynn's connection with the *Skylark* is severed. In the same instant, the digital comes to life all around them. After weeks of isolation, they're again part of an active infosphere.

They announce their presence loudly to avoid any confusion. After all, they arrived on a Tauran ship. Commander Hale uses authorization codes to confirm their identity. The codes get acknowledged, nobody is going to be shooting at them.

By the time they make their way back to the airlock, still careful as ever, a transport is waiting for them on the other side. The final walk across the ship's corridors happens in silence. Elena is still shocked by what just transpired, doesn't feel like talking to the Vanguards. Her friends from the *Charon* share her feelings. As for the Vanguards, they don't seem proud of their mission accomplishment.

They are taken aboard a military vessel, separated, debriefed. Elena gives a full report of the events. She includes the final revelations about Echo Point and the possible Tauran motivations, though based on her prior experience it won't do much good. She is tired, wants to get it out of the way so she can go see her family. After a week of answering questions, she is dismissed. She is honorably discharged for a second time and told to expect a medal or two for her exemplary service. As a show of gratitude, the military offers to pay for a custom eye prosthetic.

The photo op will look better for whomever ends up pinning the medal on her, she guesses, if she's not wearing a fucking eye patch.

When she finally gets planet-side, the situation around Aurelia is tense. News of the alien ship coming from Sector 36 made its way across the galaxy. Abyssal Mining Consortium is requesting access to the technology, citing its large investments into Sector 36.

The fact that the ship jumped to its current location—jumped, without using a gate—also gets around. OmniCore Solutions and Dominion Nexus, the two jump gate builders, stake their claim too.

The AI Council conducts negotiations with the corporate Omegas as all parties start to bring in assets into the region. Days go by as the talks continue and warships translate in. No shots fired yet, but it's starting to feel like a powder keg.

Elena switches off the news feed and gets offline. The visitors are here. She introduces Jaxon, Kaela, and Rynn to her parents. They have an open-air dinner in the backyard, fresh vegetables from the garden and synthetic protein cooked with her father's secret recipe.

"You look good," says Jaxon, grins. "Your eye, I mean."

She can't comment on the aesthetics, she'd never considered herself particularly attractive, but her synthetic eye works great, she has a full field of vision. The skin grafts around and atop her burn scar make her face look, if not quite symmetric, at least human again.

"Thank you! You don't look bad yourself. None of you do."

After the many weeks of running around with limited food rations, the military treated them very well during the debrief. Better yet, once they got planet-side, they got some R&R, good Aurelian food, and natural sunlight. Everyone looks healthier.

"How's the ... you know ... stim situation?" asks Kaela.

"Good. Great. The clean air helps. No symptoms for days now, I think it's all in the past."

"Glad to hear," says Rynn, surprising everyone. He is usually so taciturn that nobody expected the comment.

"I wonder what really was on that digicard," Elena says.

Kaela smiles mischievously. "I made a copy." She takes it out of her pocket and lays it on the table.

"Any luck figuring out what's there?"

"Not yet. It's most definitely steganography, and so far I confirmed the scientific data is all bullshit. But I'm no closer to cracking the coded part."

"Can I share it with Spark?" Elena asks.

"Of course. I can make as many copies as needed. But I suspect you'd need an Omega to decrypt it."

Elena sighs.

"Did we do the right thing?" she wonders out loud.

"I don't know," says Jaxon. "But we did the best we could."

They eat in silence for a while.

"So, what's next for you, Elena?" Jaxon asks. "Retirement?"

"I'm considering a few options," she lies. She has no clue what's next. She needs downtime. A lot of downtime before she can even think about a next adventure. If there will ever be another one. "What about you?"

"You know, we've been talking," says Jaxon, still smiling. "I'm thinking we reboot our independent logistics business. We limited ourselves to Sector 36. Why not go galactic?"

"How?" she asks. "The Charon is wrecked on Echo Point. Can you get a new ship?"

"Turns out we can! You paid us a lot of money to ferry you around the sector. Then Ingram paid us even more for the last trip. Enough that we can afford a fixer-upper. And the fix-up."

She completely forgot about the payments. For her, the credits were a means to an end.

"That's great!" she tells him.

"Indeed. In fact, you paid us so well that I would feel remiss if I didn't inquire about your potential interest in a co-ownership."

The sudden display of eloquence in his proposal surprises her. She pretends she doesn't understand but can't hold back a chuckle. "What are you asking me?"

"Want to join us?"

She meets with her Spark contact on Aurelia, hands him a copy of the digicard, and tells him the whole story. He is shocked, appalled, fumes, promises her justice will prevail. She watches him, expressionless, then, once he calms down, tells him she is out. After Sector 36, she lost faith in what the organization is able to achieve. Maybe, with the digicard and her story, they will finally make a dent. She is happy to root for them from the sidelines.

The junker they buy seems like a great deal until they try to take it to orbit. The repairs end up costing more than the sticker price, and Elena learns Rynn is not only a crack pilot but also a talented mechanic. He takes the engine of their new acquisition apart piece by piece, replaces broken parts, and puts it back together in the span of just three days.

Their second liftoff attempt is more successful than the first one; they make it to the mesosphere before they're forced to land again.

They christen the ship "Icarus," their little inside joke.

By the time they leave Aurelia, the situation has been defused. The terms are unclear, but some peaceful agreement must have been reached. The bulk of the military and paramilitary forces are no longer here, just a few stragglers left to ensure, Elena guesses, that there's no foul play.

Her biggest worry is that she will be coerced back into service. After all, she is still a rarity—someone with NSRS, with the right security clearance, and, to top it off, someone who already jumped a Tauran ship. It turns out her fears are unfounded: there is no more Tauran ship.

As they escape from the planet's gravitational well, they see the remains of what used to be the derelict, pieces of its hull like fragments of a cracked shell, its insides neatly spread out like organs on a dissection table. The reverse-engineering process must be proceeding apace. At least Ingram didn't lie about that.

She remembers her brief interaction with the ship. Was it really alive? She can't tell for sure. In her opinion, it was semi-sentient. More like an animal than a machine. She feels sorry for the fate she led it to. It saved their lives.

Still no news from Sector 36 when the *Icarus* picks up its very first bid.

Of course, the details of their debrief were classified. As far as the rest of the galaxy knows, the jump gate to Sector 36 has been destroyed during a sector-wide conflict. The details are scarce. The only certainty is that survivors are awaiting rescue.

Long-haul cryo ships have already been dispatched by both Omni-Core Solutions and Dominion Nexus, racing to see who can stand up a new jump gate first. This was done before Elena jumped the Tauran ship, as soon as contact was lost and all signs pointed towards the need for a new jump gate.

Recent rumors hint at some new technology that can get rescue parties translated in much sooner than it would take the long-haul ships to reach the sector. Nothing concrete, but all tidbits hint at a looming major breakthrough.

Elena is on the bridge of the *Icarus*, together with the rest of the crew, watching Aurelia recede as they prepare to go warp.

"Check it out," Kaela tells them. "Unconfirmed reports are starting to circulate about unknown tentacled black ships being spotted in Sector 16 and Sector 17."

ACKNOWLEDGMENTS

First, big thanks to my wife, Diana, and my daughter, Ada, for putting up with me during the creative process. I know it's not easy. Writing fiction instead of technical books meant involving my family much more in the project.

I described the world of Sector 36 to my daughter during a long roadtrip, back when I only had a sketch of the first part of the plot and only an inkling of how everything comes to a climax on an alien shipwreck.

My wife read an early version of the first few chapters, gave me some invaluable feedback, then read the first version manuscript and took copious notes—effectively doing a developmental and line edit of the book pro bono.

Also a big "thank you" to my new friend Patrick Wyatt, for helping spot NPC dialogue and physics bugs in my draft.

I appreciate my other beta readers, Dave Brennan and Igor Dvorkin, for sharing their thoughts. Every piece of feedback matters.

Copy editing was done by Audrey Mackaman. She made sure the version you are reading is precise and polished.

The cover design was done by Tom Edwards, who captured the essence of Sector 36 in image form. He also did the map design, making my sketch look sleek and futuristic.

I produced the book myself, which was not an easy task. I would've been utterly lost had I not had the opportunity to talk to experienced self-published authors who were more than happy to teach me the ropes. Thank you for your generous guidance, Elizabeth R. Andersen and Zack Argyle!

I want to acknowledge the writer community in the Seattle Eastside, and the various meetups where I did a lot of my writing and met some wonderful people. Thank you Emily Brown for organizing the weekly Shut Up & Write, and thank you James Whittaker for bringing us together at Side Hustle!

Last but not least, thank you dear reader for your time. If you enjoyed reading this book, you should check out the website—https://sector36.space/. The story continues on Substack, at https://sector36.substack.com/, where I share chapters, behind-the-scenes, and news about upcoming projects. See you there!

ABOUT THE AUTHOR

Vlad Rişcuţia is a software engineer at Microsoft and the author of three technical books: *Programming with Types* and *Data Engineering on Azure*, and *Large Language Models at Work*.

His background in artificial intelligence and software systems informs the technological depth of *Sector 36*, his debut novel.

Find him online at https://vladris.com/.

 x.com/vladris
 instagram.com/vladris
 sector36.substack.com

www.ingramcontent.com/pod-product-compliance
Lightning Source LLC
Chambersburg PA
CBHW030330120726
47901CB00007B/1747